Love MISMATCHED

EMILIA REED

FOX DEN PRESS

For CS. ILU.

THERAPY SESSION NOTES

DR. LISA AMORETTI

Session Date: June 1, 20__
Participants: Lydia Richie (29) & Anton Richie (31)
Session Focus: Intake/Goal Setting for Treatment

Description:
Clients report they identify as a heterosexual, monogamous couple who reside in Denver, Colorado and have been married 7.5 years. Anton stated he works in finance; Lydia stated she owns several doggie daycares and a grooming shop.

Observations & History:
At start of session, couple were observed sitting on opposite ends of the couch, exhibiting stiff, uncomfortable body language. Tensions increased as Anton described reasons for pursuing sex therapy; primarily, his recent attempt to engage in an online sexual affair.

• Note: Anton stated this attempt was unsuccessful—intercepted when Lydia posed as another woman online and set up a "date" to confront him.

Lydia appeared reserved during Anton's description of events. When asked directly, she acknowledged the pain his actions caused, but reflected on her own discomfort with sex and intimacy as a contributing factor. On further questioning, Lydia described sexual barriers centered around feelings of shame/guilt related to upbringing, and discomfort with her body as an adult.

Emotional breakthrough occurred when Anton became tearful/regretful, and both expressed a shared desire to recommit to one another.

Assessment:
• Underlying feelings of rejection; damage to trust caused by attempted affair.
• History of emotional trauma contributing to sexual dysfunction.
• Couple exhibited positive outlook on their future and commitment to therapy.

Plan:
• Goals: improve trust and intimacy by addressing emotional challenges brought on by attempted infidelity and barriers impacting sexual health.
• Implement "sensate focus" treatment to improve couple's comfort level, sexual knowledge, and skills.
• Assign homework activities to practice sexual interactions at home.
• Frequency and expected duration of therapy: weekly sessions; 6 to 9 months.
• Communication will be <u>crucial</u> moving forward.

CHAPTER ONE

Mondays used to be my favorite.

This bleary notion reaches through a swirl of other thoughts at the sound of my grating alarm. But in the silence that follows, I can't remember—why aren't they anymore?

Sunlight spills across my pillow, and I retreat under the covers like a vampire, backing into something warm and hard.

Anton. My husband.

Before my brain comes online, in a moment made up entirely of old habit, my instinct is to flinch away from him. There are things to do. An important meeting, orders to place, payroll to—nope. I keep forgetting. That one's been taken off my plate.

Anton's hands snake lazily around my waist, pulling me against him, back into the present. And this time I overcome my thoughts and melt into his embrace. Press into his firm length. Feel it harden even more against my ass.

I look over my shoulder at his sleepy face. His still-closed eyes and smooth forehead tell me he's not fully awake, hasn't really thought about anything yet either. And I want to hang onto this moment—suspend us here, where nothing matters. I press a kiss to his stubbly chin, hoping to steal some of his calm.

He comes a little more alive in response; his arms tightening around me, lips grazing along my shoulder, up the side of my neck, behind my ear. Inhaling so deeply when he gets to my hair, it's like he's trying to breathe me in.

My thoughts invade again.

Make coffee, walk the dog. Run reports.

I close my eyes. It's a trick I've found sometimes works to shut down my brain and stay present—one our new therapist encourages me to employ. I focus on the heat of Anton's palms sliding down over my hips, past the hem of my cotton nightgown, dipping under the light fabric and up along my waist. Tentatively, his fingers work their way over my skin, leaving a trail of goosebumps as they cup the undersides of my breasts.

"Good morning, Mrs. Richie," he rumbles in my ear, sending ribbons of warmth through my core and along my limbs.

I arch my back in response, stretching the length of my body against him, thrusting my breasts into his palms. This is the part where I can't lose focus. Where I need to tune in to every movement and breath to kindle the heat inside me. This comes naturally to some people, but I'm not one of them. I understand this now.

"Good morning to you," I say in a low voice, fighting an urge to check the clock. I set an early alarm. There *is* time for this before the day starts. If we hurry.

And as Anton thrusts his leg between mine, lifting me and grinding against my center with his thigh, the slightest tingle forms within my core. I smile. Maybe I'm getting the hang of this.

His grip on my breasts softens, and his fingers find my

nipples. Well, the one cooperative one, and the other he coaxes. I reach back to stroke him as he works my body. He's clearly ready to go, but we're both in tune with the need to build my arousal. I have a "responsive" sex drive, as our therapist says. My mind might be on board, but the rest of me needs prompting. And the more we work my body, the greater my desire.

I rub my ass playfully against his naked form, and he groans. The sound unfurls something inside me, and I take it a step further—shifting my hips until his cock sits neatly between my bare ass cheeks, then slowly, sliding up and down the length of him, teasing his tip when it reaches my moistening center. I manage this twice before I'm seized and rolled onto my back.

"Where did you learn that?" Anton asks, his hazel eyes so dark they're almost black.

I take a second to catch my breath, staring up from my new position beneath him. When I try to move my arms, I find he's pinned them above my head, and my face floods with heat. Because I think I like it.

"I . . . I don't know . . . it just seemed like something to try," I say honestly. Nothing I ever do in bed is pre-planned. Usually everything is a reaction to him.

He's staring back at me with a carnal expression I've never seen, eyes drifting down like he's deciding where to start devouring me. And then it happens—for just a moment, my gaze drifts toward the bedside table, and I try to calculate the time. It's the tiniest flicker, but he clearly notices. And I freeze, caught beneath him.

"You're not supposed to do that," he chides.

"I—I didn't," I say. But I'm frowning because we both know it's a lie. "Okay, fine. But I stopped. Anyway, when she assigned our 'homework' I doubt she imagined us getting busy right before work."

He grunts. "Any time."

"What?"

"She said, *any time* we're making love, you're supposed to maintain focus."

"Okay, but Anton, I *can't*. Not if it'll make us both late."

He raises a brow, looking at me pointedly.

I open my mouth to ask if that's supposed to mean something, but then he says, "Maybe we just need to make you focus."

His voice is playful, but he's still holding my arms pinned above my head, and then his other hand wanders down, trailing along my waist.

"H-how?" I stutter.

He reaches my hip and rocks me toward him, onto my side, fingers scorching through my nightgown until they dip low enough to sneak beneath the hem.

"I have some thoughts," he says, laying his palm gently on the bare skin of my ass. He kneads my flesh in his firm grip, heating it under his fingers, then charting wide circles around the perimeter of my backside, bringing every inch of my skin to life. "But I think I like your suggestion best . . ."

I draw my brows together, unsure what he's talking about, though I'm having trouble thinking about anything other than the pattern he's tracing on my skin.

He brings his lips close, whispering low and salacious next to my ear, "You said you wanted to try spanking, remember?"

My eyelids flutter. Suddenly, I'm hyperaware of his hand on my backside, the reverent way he's kneading and caressing my flesh. And I want to put a stop to this—wrap the sheets around my body, shield myself from the very idea —*except*.

There's the faintest ache blooming between my legs.

Anton continues, hand circling warm and scorching against my ass, and I thrust back involuntarily, trying to imagine his palm coming down hard on the right side, or the left. What would it feel like—sound like? *God*. Would it sting?

A noise escapes my throat. Possibly a whimper. And with every circle of his palm, my core tightens until it's nearly throbbing.

"We could try it," he says, low and gravelly.

My face is so hot, I can't bring myself to look up at him. I shake my head. "It—it just seems—"

"Exciting?" he asks.

I bite my lip, unwilling to answer.

He whispers in my ear, "It's okay, Lydia. I won't make you call me *Daddy*."

I rear back to look at him, one hundred percent mortified, before I realize he's stifling a laugh.

He shakes his head, releasing my arms so he can trace his other finger over my nipple, leaving it hard beneath the fabric of my nightgown. "I told you the first time you brought it up, I'm not into that. I didn't think I'd like to spank you at all . . . until I did some reading."

I relax my arms, but his hands keep exploring. And while I can't ignore the way my body's coming alive, I wish we were talking about *anything* else.

"As it turns out," Anton continues, entering full Professor Google mode. "Spanking can relieve stress and anxiety, heighten intimacy, *and* provide pleasure." His one hand ministers to my nipples while the other continues fondling my backside. "When used as a consensual sexual act, it can cause the brain to release endorphins, oxytocin, and dopamine. And because it increases blood flow to the genitals, it can lead to heightened arousal."

"Did you actually memorize all that?"

"Just doing *my* homework," he says, and I wrinkle my brow until I remember our therapist saying Anton's job is to help me focus.

Well, I guess it's working. Because when I squeeze my legs

together, all I can think about is his touch and the tension in my thighs. My hands had gone still, but now I glide my fingers over his arms, tracing the outlines of muscle he works hard for at the gym, *needing* to touch him back.

"So, Mrs. Richie," he mutters, rounding my ass cheeks again with his palm. "It actually makes *sense* for you to want to be spanked. There's nothing to feel ashamed about."

His voice is hot and breathy against my ear, and I sink into the sound, unable to think of anything anymore except what it might feel like if he raised his palm and brought it down where it is right now—and how maddeningly I want him to. Then his hand *does* disappear from my flesh, and my core tightens. I squeeze my eyes shut.

But instead of coming down on my ass, his fingers trace purposefully between my thighs.

"Lydia." I open my eyes in the moment we both realize I am *very* wet. "You understood the assignment."

My face floods with heat. My breath hitches, but I don't shy away. "I—I think so."

His hand continues, exploring beneath my nightgown, gently parting my thighs. He locks eyes with me as his fingers stroke up my center, until his thumb makes contact with my clit and I gasp. But he doesn't pause there, dipping his fingers down again, then up, repeating the motion until I'm totally slick with my own juices.

"Seems we got you quite ready," he whispers. "What should we do next?"

Vaguely, I realize I no longer care what time it is as the ache between my legs resurges. I rise up, pushing my husband onto his back. Then I reach for the hem of my nightgown, pulling it up and over my head until I'm sitting on top of him, fully exposed. I don't look away when his eyes darken, taking me in—more homework I've been assigned. Instead, I hold his gaze and tune *in* to his arousal, letting it further awaken mine.

As the air heats between us, I reach back and find his cock stiff and ready. His thumb finds my center again, gliding over it in tight circles as his other hand reaches to tug lightly on my nipples. The ache inside me blossoms into a thrum. I pivot back with intention, running my slick folds over his shaft until I feel him harden to steel against me, and I guide him into my awaiting center.

"*Oh,*" we murmur together, pausing as my body adjusts to him.

And then I'm moving. Rocking my hips at first, heightening the way he fills me, then frogging my legs for better leverage up and down. He rocks lightly beneath me, letting me lead the rhythm—his thumb never leaving the sensitive nub just above where we're joined.

I arch backward, moving my breasts out of his reach but opening my legs wider to him, and another wave of heat surges through me as he focuses directly on my clit. I close my eyes, overcome by the sudden, intense sensation of his thick cock sliding in and out of me, pounding deep inside. His free hand finds my ass and squeezes, reminding me of the conversation that got us here—the spanking we very nearly tried. How he proved just getting me to *think* about something so profane could get me aroused.

And this is my undoing.

I come in a surge of forbidden pleasure, riding waves of hard-fought euphoria, squeezing Anton deeper inside me. As soon as I'm past my peak, he grabs my wrists and my eyes pop open as he drives upward into me, hard and relentless, bouncing me on his dick until I cry out as his release comes with a hard thrust.

"*Fuck.*"

We hold perfectly still in that moment. And the next. Then I collapse down on top of him, and he wraps me in his arms, pulling the tangle of covers over our naked bodies. Neither of us speaks for several minutes as we listen to the sounds of our breath returning to normal. Finally, Anton pushes my tousled hair off my cheek and kisses me.

"Looks like you aced another homework assignment, Mrs. Richie."

I smile, blinking back at him. "Who knew a former flunky could turn into such a good student?"

His eyes crinkle, and my heart swells—then stutters at an unexpected thought. *What if I had lost this?* We came so close. Just a few months ago, neither of us was happy, and I'd found his profile on a cheating app—Unmatched. He hadn't connected with any other women yet, so I created an account for myself, hoping to teach him a lesson. This resulted in a hookup that wound up devastating us *and* saving our marriage.

But if I'd rejected him, thrown him out . . .

If he'd connected with someone else and we never got this chance . . .

We would have lost so much, it hurts to think about.

"I love you," I say, spreading my fingers possessively against his chest.

"I love *you*." He lays a playful kiss on my nose. But then, as if sensing my thoughts, quietly repeats the words that ultimately led him back into my heart. "You are all I've ever wanted."

I smile, tangling my fingers in his hair, lingering another second. "Well, if you still want your job, you should probably get up and shower."

Anton grumbles, dragging himself out of bed, but his speed kicks up when he looks at his watch and registers the time.

I grab my phone off the bedside table and grimace. My schedule is actually more flexible than his, but . . . "We're both going to be very, very late."

He heads for the bathroom with confidence, looking like a

naked Olympian. "Morning sex is always an excuse for tardiness."

I snort. "*That* is one I haven't heard from my employees."

The shower comes on as I stand, and the trickle of fluid running down my legs makes me think to join him. However, our movements have stirred the seventy-five pound Akita mix who was previously sleeping soundly by the door. Heartthrob plants himself in front of me, wagging his tail and spinning in circles.

"Okay." I sigh. "Dog food. Coffee. Then shower."

I throw on my robe, vaguely registering the ring of Anton's phone behind the bathroom door.

"Hey, Sethie." I hear him greet his brother on my way to the kitchen. It's been nearly two months since their mom took a turn for the worse and we flew to Dallas. Since then, Seth has called regularly, if only just to say that nothing's changed.

But as I set Heartthrob's breakfast down for him, I'm startled by a crash from down the hall. I open my mouth to call out, but by the time sound comes, I'm already to the door.

"Anton!"

I find my husband sitting on the floor, wet and half-wrapped in a towel. His phone lays next to him on the tile. Behind him, our shower caddy and an array of shampoo bottles and body wash are scattered on the bottom of the tub under a spray of steam and running water.

He looks at the mess like he's not sure what happened and moves to get up.

"Wait. Are you all right? Did you hit your head?" I kneel and touch his shoulder. There's no blood. He doesn't appear injured, but he's super pale.

He shakes his head. "No, I—"

"Hello? Anton?" On the floor, Seth's voice echoes small and tinny, apparently still connected on speakerphone.

Anton retrieves it, turning it over to find the screen

completely shattered. He curses, but it comes out sounding hollow.

"Seth, what's going on?" I ask. "Did something happen with Sharon?"

"Lydia." My brother-in-law's voice comes through the speaker, low and somber. "She's gone."

CHAPTER TWO

Him

Seth and I follow our Aunt Betty and the last of the straggling neighbors outside, thanking them for coming and accepting hugs and well wishes. Or, my brother is doing those things while I stand stiff at his side.

"It was a beautiful service," Betty says, reaching up to cup Seth's square, clean-shaven jaw. "Sharon would have approved. She did such a nice job raising you boys."

"Thanks, Aunt Betty," my brother replies, letting her squeeze him into a hug, delivering the correct responses for both of us. "She would've been touched to hear that."

Betty turns to me like she might draw me into her arms too, but thinks better of it. "You take care of yourselves, you hear?" she says, getting into her car. "Anton, I told your lovely wife I want more than a Christmas card once a year."

I manage to raise my hand at that, but once she's gone, my legs give out, and I sink to the front steps of Mom's little ranch. "Thank God that's over," I say, loosening my tie.

My brother hands me a bottle of water from the garage, then settles onto the stoop beside me with a sigh. Behind us, Mom's orange tabby, Bruno, stretches up against the glass storm door, scratching his claws and wailing at us like some mythological beast.

"It was nice seeing so many people who really loved her," Seth says in a wistful tone.

I grunt. "Would be nicer if she were still here to love."

Neither of us speaks for a while. The sun is headed down, though it doesn't offer much of a break from the sticky Dallas heat. A kid rides by on a bike. Someone passes with a dog. A few cars come and go. The world goes on without our mother.

"Thanks for all your help this week," Seth says.

"I did shit," I say with a snort. "You had all the little details—the clothes she wanted to wear, the music she wanted at the church. You delivered the freaking eulogy."

I crack open my water, taking a long drink. It was torture, sitting in that pew, listening to his summary of our mother's too-short life. Except that he honored her beautifully. He even created a slideshow of pictures to play with the music, mostly from when our dad was still alive. That was the part that almost wrecked me.

"You helped with all the decisions," Seth says.

"Uh-huh. Because picking out flowers and choosing an urn makes up for how you spent the last five years."

My brother scowls. "We've been over this, Anton. I was already in Dallas. I'm not married. It made *sense* for me to take care of her. I got to finish college and live rent free while I did it."

"Best son ever," I say, raising my water in salute. And though I mean it, I'm pretty sure I sound like a dick. I don't know what's wrong with me. I mean, I *know*—this is grief. I miss our mom. But she's been slipping away for years. Her death ought to feel like a blessing, a relief. Only it doesn't. It just feels like a hole has opened up and something big is missing.

"I couldn't have been there for her without you," he says quietly.

"*Meow*," the cat wails behind us like a broken violin, announcing my wife's approach.

"There you are," Lydia says, peeking her head outside. "You two want to come in and get something to eat? There's still so much food. I don't think it will even fit in the fridge."

Seth hops up immediately, dusting off his suit. Mom would've fussed at us for sitting on the ground in our Sunday best, then forgiven him as soon as he flashed one of his dimpled grins. He's tall and muscular, like me, but he has her light hair, and her smile. And suddenly, I am so grateful for it.

"You coming?" he asks, hovering in front of me. But the blood is rushing in my ears and somehow it feels like all I can manage just to take my next breath.

Seth extends his hand. "C'mon. I haven't seen you eat all day."

I exhale, accepting the offer. And with enough strength for the both of us, he pulls me to my feet.

Lydia's gaze flits over me as we retreat inside, blue eyes flashing with concern. She exchanges a look with Seth, then bites her lip and hurries toward the kitchen. "You both must be exhausted. I'll get you a couple of plates."

Seth doesn't protest, and I slump onto the couch.

My wife returns with a strange assortment of fried chicken, dolmades, bean casserole, and tamales. I hold the food in my lap, but it seems like way too much effort to actually chew and swallow.

Seth takes his dish to the armchair across from me, and I find myself thinking about how we used to sit there with our dad reading books when we were little, and I wonder if he remembers that. Bruno winds between his legs, purring like an aircraft engine.

"So, Seth, what are your plans . . . now?" Lydia asks, settling on the couch beside me. "Or is it too soon to ask?"

"I don't know. There isn't much left for me here." I feel his gaze land on me. "I was kinda thinking of moving."

I raise my eyes from the cat, pulse throbbing under my skin.

"Oh yeah? Where to?" Lydia asks. Bruno spots her open lap and launches himself into it, curling up to shed orange and white cat hair all over her gray skirt. Vaguely, I think, *she never wears skirts*. And I wish I could appreciate this one.

My brother clears his throat. "Ah, Denver, actually."

Something stirs in my chest. It isn't earthshaking, but it's more than the numbness I feel like I'm drowning in. "Really?" I croak, like I haven't spoken for days.

"Yeah." Seth turns to me, looking uncertain. "I—I think I'd like to sell this place. If it's okay with you."

I release a long breath and set my untouched plate aside, letting my gaze wander around the room. Some of the things here stand out—the chair, a few knickknacks, some pictures. But the actual house? It hasn't felt like home for a while. Not since we had to move Mom out of it and into a care facility.

But the thought of Seth being in Denver—living so close? That does.

"Not my decision," I say quickly. "You've more than earned the right to do whatever you want with this place."

Seth shrugs. "It made sense to be here when I was needed . . . but I think I'm ready for a change."

"When were you thinking?" my wife asks.

"I have an appointment with a realtor this week," he says. "There are a couple things I'll need to fix, some painting to do, but I think it should be ready to list pretty quick."

Lydia studies the overflowing bookshelves, looking doubtful. "There's still a lot of stuff here. Do you want us to stay a little longer and give you a hand?"

I know for a fact Lydia has work piling up back at The Pooch Park and Ooh La Pooch. She hasn't said a word to me about it, but we've been in Dallas almost a week, and I've overheard her talking to her managers and her business partner, Henry. It's been a lot, asking her to step away from their businesses for so long, and at the last minute.

"We need to get home," I tell her. "Just have an estate sale, Seth. Get rid of everything you don't want to keep."

Seth and Lydia exchange another look.

"Uh, is there anything you're interested in?" he asks awkwardly. "I could bring furniture or whatever with me to Denver."

It's a practical question, but my lip curls at the idea of divvying up the remnants of our mother's life. I take another look around, deciding the reading chair is just a chair and not the memories made in it. But surely there's *something* here I'd like to keep? Stupidly, what comes to mind is the slow-close toilet seat Mom got all excited about after I left for college. I press my lips together. What I *really* want is to be able to talk to her. Give her a hug. Tell her I love her one last time and know she understands. But eventually my eyes land on a framed photo on the mantel. A family portrait. The last one taken of the four of us before our dad was killed in the car crash. I rise up and retrieve it, glancing down at the smiling family from the past.

I must've been nearly ten, and Seth was six or seven, missing his two front teeth. Mom is clearly restraining him in her lap, looking exactly the way I always picture her: poofy blonde hair, too-big glasses, and a huge smile. My dad has one arm around her and one resting on my shoulder, dark hair askew, like he just ran into the frame right before they took the shot.

"I'll take this." I hold up the picture to satisfy my wife and brother.

"Oh, I like that one. You look so much like your dad," Lydia says.

Surprised, I look down again. I was a scrawny kid in a Scouts uniform, and beside my dad's broad form, we hardly seemed alike then. But maybe I do resemble him now. Tall, with unruly brown hair, and the hazel eyes Seth and I both have. But there's something else about my dad that's different from me. I just can't put my finger on what it is.

Bruno suddenly scampers off Lydia's lap and up onto Seth's shoulder. "*Meow.*"

"Oh, excuse me. Did I forget your evening sardine?" My brother rises and heads for the kitchen, cat wrapped around his neck.

Lydia reaches out and gives my knee a squeeze. "Guess we should go pack."

I place a tentative hand over hers, and she smiles in my peripheral vision. I know she's trying to get my attention. Check in with me. Connect. And especially after the last two months, after we've worked hard to grow closer, it feels foreign not to just lean in and reach for her. Allow myself to take comfort in her hair, her skin, her scent. But for some reason I just . . . can't. I pull my hand away, trying to ignore the way the air cools between us as I head for my old bedroom.

"Sure, let's pack. It's an early flight."

CHAPTER THREE

I'm fully awake before my clock goes off. I've been watching it for an hour, going over at least three separate to-do lists for my first day back. But it feels like I need permission before untangling myself from Anton's embrace. When the alarm finally sounds, I quickly silence it, trying to take a moment to savor his warmth and comfort. This is actually the most we've touched since we left for Texas, and as his arms tighten around my waist, it occurs to me how much I've missed it. Except—something's different. I'm not sure what until I realize he isn't really *touching* so much as clutching me like a security blanket.

I turn to study his face. His eyes are open, focused out the window, but somehow much further away. I rest my head against his chest, breathing in his clean, earthy scent.

"Hey. How are you doing?" I ask gently.

At the sound of my voice, he tracks back. Into the room. Back to our bed. Or at least the vicinity. "I'm fine."

He's been telling both Seth and me he's *fine* for the past week. And I don't really think he's lying. I just don't think he truly knows. "Are you sure you want to go back to the office today?" I say quietly. "Carl said to take all the time you need."

Anton's body tenses, and he immediately shakes his head. "No. It'll be good to get back into routines. I was already feeling swamped before we left for Dallas."

He throws back the covers, and the next thing I know I'm in the center of the bed, alone. He slips into boxer briefs and is pulling on a shirt before I can think how to respond. For a moment, I wonder if I should try to regain his attention. Call him back to bed. Try just a little harder.

But the thing is, I'm also swamped. Henry and I put our Pooch II meeting off for a week, but he's anxious to go over the business plan and first-month reports. Our managers have done a decent job holding down the fort with me gone, but I need to make time to check in with each of them and get back up to speed. So as Anton's scent fades from the sheets next to me, I'm relieved he doesn't notice me checking my phone.

Or the face I make when I open my email and find out our newly hired groomer just bailed on us. My fingers fly all the way to the shower, copying and replying. Adding to our meeting agenda and scrambling for a plan to deal with her scheduled appointments.

I exit the bathroom ten minutes later, phone still in hand and a towel twisted in my hair. Anton stands in front of the closet mirror straightening his tie. He catches my eye in the reflection, gaze dipping to the damp towel gathered at my breasts with a faint smile—and maybe a flash of regret.

And just like that, I hate myself for *not* trying. He's struggling. Obviously needs my support, needs me to reach for him. But I didn't. I let myself fall into old patterns. Got sucked into work, and left him to fend for himself.

"See you for therapy at five thirty?" I ask quietly, hoping I can atone for my shortcomings there.

He pauses. "Right . . . it's Monday."

"We missed last week," I point out, not wanting to remind him why.

His gaze is far away, not looking at me anymore. "Maybe . . . could we rain check again?"

I raise my head in surprise.

"Sorry," he says quickly. "I think . . . I don't know. I'm just not . . . feeling it yet."

A lump forms in my throat. I probably understand *not feeling it* better than anyone. It's something I'm still working on—something we've been working on. But this seems like a strange time to put a hold on something that's been helping us both.

"Uh, sure. I'll let her know."

"Thanks."

For just a moment, I consider dropping the towel to the floor. Seeing if I can still make something happen. Remind him, no matter how he's feeling, that *we* are still good; we're getting better. But when I look back at his face, his eyes are somewhere else again. Unfocused. Far away. And I don't know, seduction seems like the last thing to try. He looks like he just needs a hug.

So I do—wrap him in my arms. Getting his suit damp with my towel, though he doesn't seem to care. "Take it easy today," I say, stroking my hand up and down his back.

He mimics my movements in return, but it's stiff, congenial. The way you might hug a relative you don't know well. And just then, his face looks so lost. Shattered. Like he truly needs something . . . But I have this weird feeling it isn't me.

He straightens and sighs. "I've got to go or I'll hit traffic."

CAPRICE

Are you guys back in town? How did the
service go?

Got in last night, hitting the ground running today.

I don't know. It was a funeral. Just glad it's over.

CAPRICE

I'm sorry. 🤍 You want to meet up this week?

LOVE to—I've missed your face.

How have things been? Have you gotten any more of those emails?

CAPRICE

Unfortunately.

Oh no. A bad one?

CAPRICE

Prefer to show you in person. Can we shoot for tomorrow?

I'll come over after work.

It's been three months since my journalist best friend published her article about Unmatched, the cheating app where she found my husband among a slew of high-profile philanderers. Caprice's investigation may have ultimately saved my marriage, but it set off a firestorm of hate mail from some less-appreciative people. Most of it has been rude or gross, but ignorable. Expletives and dick pics, according to Caprice, are sadly par for the course for female journalists. However, some of the messages have crossed the line into worrisome or even scary. Enough that I regularly track her phone and check in before work most days. I'm anxious to spend some time with her in person now that we're back. I have a feeling she's been downplaying the situation.

"Donuts!" My eighteen-year-old employee, Kai, spots the white bakery box balanced in my arms as soon as I step through the door of The Pooch Park II. They whisk it toward the brand-new break room, which Henry insists on calling our *conference room*. Relieved of one burden, I re-shuffle my armload of cleaning supplies and printer paper, finally managing to extend Heartthrob's leash to Francie, my manager at the front desk.

"Hey!" She brightens when she sees me, then notices the donuts and looks confused. "Is there a staff meeting today?"

"Nope. Henry and I are just going over the numbers. But I found myself in the Dunkin' drive-through on the way over." I wink at her. "Tell everybody to grab one."

She grins, then takes Heartthrob with her to the large dog playroom. I watch for a moment through the observation windows, still marveling that this place, which was a mess of brick and wires and dirt a few months ago, is now a cheery, brightly painted canine oasis.

Francie removes Heartthrob's leash and collar, then he bounds through the gate into the pack. For five seconds, he holds perfectly still, letting the other dogs get a good sniff, then he and a young Irish Setter go bounding away, chasing each other around the plastic obstacle course.

I let out a contented sigh. The last seven days have been sad and stressful, and I'm not thrilled about the way things went down this morning. But the tension in my spine eased as soon as I walked through the Pooch Park door. I know what to do here. I know just what's expected of me.

"Welcome back," Henry says, appearing from around the corner. He doesn't have much of an accent, but combined with his perfectly coiffed dark hair and aloof Mr. Darcy expressions, his voice is just British enough to make half my employees swoon. Once I glance at him, though, I snort.

"If Tom Ford only knew where you wore his suits." I grin, shaking my head. "Do you have a lunch date or something?"

Henry rolls his eyes. I spent our first couple weeks together trying to convince him he didn't need to dress to the nines at the Pooches (my nickname for all three businesses), but he has steadfastly ignored me. While he might be overly groomed, he quickly proved his business sense, so I mostly shut up about it. But since he *is* a handsome guy, his suits only add to the aesthetic. I've heard plenty of the staff whispering about their "hot boss" since he came on as my partner, and I know they're not talking about me in my messy bun and Old Navy leggings.

He straightens. "It's our first official meeting with a solid month of profit and loss. I didn't think it prudent to go on a full *retreat* just yet since we're still building clientele, but this is a major moment in our endeavor and I intend to treat it so."

I bite my lip at his stuffy tone.

"Well. I brought donuts!" I say, leading the way toward the *conference room*.

There are only four pastries left in the box when we get there, and I snag the last Bismarck, but Henry declines. We set up our laptops on the repurposed dining table I scored at a secondhand store, and he takes out his ever-present notebook. But as we sit down he looks at me and lowers his voice. "How is Anton doing? Did everything go all right in Dallas?"

I'm licking chocolate frosting off my fingers, grateful for the excuse to take my time answering. "The service was beautiful. Seth's eulogy especially." I pause, swallowing hard. I miss my kind, sweet mother-in-law, but I'm grateful her struggle is over. "Anton will be all right. He's taken it kind of hard, but I think he just needs some time."

Henry seems satisfied with that, and I'm thankful when we launch straight into spreadsheets, profit and loss statements, and cash flow projections for all three businesses. I'm not sure how long we spend there, but at some point the afternoon crew clocks in, and Francie brings us a couple of delivered sandwiches.

"So—not bad for one month in," I say, sitting back in my chair.

"Not at all," Henry agrees, looking surprisingly pleased with the numbers. "Considering we're averaging half capacity still, we should be doing quite well by end of year."

I nod. "So, what do you think about offering some kind of employee health plan down the road?"

Henry's gaze slides over to mine. "I've never heard you say that was a priority."

"The groomer we hired to start tomorrow? She left a message that she took a job at Pets 'N Co instead. A few of the daycare employees have told me their friends would love to work here, but they need something with insurance."

"I told you she was a weak candidate." Henry glares at me. "That guy who applied was a more solid hire."

"The *guy* had tangles in his bichon ears and had to be told what a lamb clip means on a standard poodle," I push back.

"Okay, but he had a bachelor's in—"

"A degree means nothing in grooming, Henry. What matters is how someone handles dogs, their knowledge and experience, and *skill*. That girl and Scarlet might not look amazing on paper, but they are talented in what they do."

"Don't get me started on Scarlet," he says, face reddening.

"Look, I know she's a hot mess personally." I roll my eyes. "But when she has it together, she can scissor and blend like a dog hair Da Vinci."

Henry exhales. "Look, if we call the guy back, there's at least a chance we'll have someone to groom the dogs booked for tomorrow. Otherwise, who else will do it?"

I bite my lip and scowl at him because he's making a familiar sour-faced expression, and I know he's trying to force me to say it.

"Fine. *I* will groom them—but I'm not just going to hire the first dog lover who walks in the door and can hold a brush. We need a stronger candidate. And we need to reward them for their skill. Which means we need something special to attract them."

Henry pinches the bridge of his nose. "Look, I think it's horrible that Americans have to pay for their healthcare, but the way the businesses are set up right now, we can't afford employee benefits."

I look at him completely straight-faced. "Do you know how expensive healthcare gets in this country?"

"Yes, of course—"

"Then you can agree it isn't just a competitive business decision. It's the right thing to do." I fold my arms over my chest.

He stares at his screen a long time, not looking at me, and for a second my stomach knots over this whole endeavor. If I hadn't sold half my company, there would be no discussion. I'd be doing things exactly the way I want.

"I will do some more research, but Lydia?" He turns his screen to face me and levels me with a stern gaze. "Ooh La Pooch causes more headaches and doesn't perform as well as the daycares. If you really want to pursue employee benefits, we need to close it, or at least consolidate."

I stare at him, open-mouthed. My eyes flicker back to his screen, though I don't actually need to see. I've known for a while the daycares were more profitable than the grooming. I was just trying not to think about how much.

"I'm not eliminating anyone's jobs," I finally say, eyes pricking.

Henry gives a stiff nod. "I thought you'd say that. Why don't you just think about it? We don't have to address this today. But if we intend to grow, *or* add benefits, some tough decisions need to be made."

Suddenly, all I want in the world is to run home to Anton, curl up on the couch enveloped in his arms, and hear him tell me everything's going to be fine. But then I remember the distance between us this morning, the faraway look in his eyes, and my stomach knots. How can I ask Anton to comfort me when I should be figuring out how to comfort him?

My phone starts vibrating on the table, and my sister Celia's contact photo—throwing a bouquet in her designer wedding dress—lights up the screen.

"I'm going to take this," I say brusquely. And it's officially a cold day in hell if I'm opting for my sister over anything. "I definitely need some time to process."

CHAPTER FOUR

Him

I'M FIFTEEN MINUTES LATE BY THE TIME I TALK MYSELF INTO getting out of the car. My head is a total fog. I probably should have stayed home like Lydia suggested. But I'm here now, and somehow even manage to put one foot in front of the other through the parking garage.

I hit the button for the elevator and run my hand over my face. I can't help feeling like I've made a mistake or forgotten something important. I go back over everything I can think of, but I don't know what it could be. Seth is selling Mom's house. I'm handling her taxes and the last of her bills. Lydia's been an amazing support to both of us. I know I haven't been super talkative this past week, but she has been endlessly patient and understanding.

Maybe I shouldn't have cancelled our appointment this afternoon. I just felt . . . weird going to sex therapy the day after my mother's funeral. At least Lydia didn't seem to mind. Physical intimacy is a lot of work for her, and she's got a bunch of other stuff going on. Maybe a break will be good for both of us.

"Anton! So nice to have you back," Riya says with some

surprise from the front desk as I exit the elevator. "I was so sorry to hear about your mom."

"Thanks," I say. It feels like I ought to add something. A detail for her benefit. But when my mind fails to produce any more words, I keep walking past reception, toward my office.

"They're in the conference room," she calls after me with some uncertainty. "Um, Carl thought maybe you weren't coming, so they got started."

I pause, trying to decide how I should feel about that. Everything that should be straightforward seems difficult today. "Thanks," I say again.

I drop my things at my desk and head straight into the meeting. As soon as I walk in, I note with irritation that a fairly new hire, Milo Briggs, is in my usual seat beside Carl. I take one of the open chairs closer to the door, trying not to attract too much attention. A couple people offer me sympathetic smiles. Carl is going over some items about account tracking. He catches my eye and nods. I pick up a pen, hovering it over a legal pad in front of me, but I'm the one who wrote the points he's going over, so it doesn't seem like I've missed too much.

Now that I'm physically in the conference room, all the energy I employed to make it here seems to evaporate. I glance at the clock on my phone, disappointed to see it's not even nine thirty. A text comes through, but it's just Seth replying to an earlier message, saying he'll call me later. My heart would have started pounding at that a short time ago, but now it feels depressingly non-urgent. I'm thinking vaguely about going to the gym after work, just *anything* that feels familiar and good, when Jin from client relations next to me nudges my elbow.

I glance up to find Carl—and most of the people around the table—looking right at me.

"Do you disagree, Anton?"

"Um . . ." I glance down, heat creeping into my face. I've

covered most of the pad in front of me with doodles. For a scrambling moment I think I can come up with something passable to say. Pull some numbers out of thin air. Relate them to . . . something. But I quickly realize I have no idea if we're discussing something account related, or like, whether to do a white elephant Christmas party. "Sorry, what was the question?"

Carl frowns, but doesn't miss a beat turning to Milo. "Mr. Briggs, why don't you take the lead on this?"

Damn. Not the Christmas party, I guess.

"Of course," Milo says, with the kind of just-out-of-college self-importance that makes me want to punch him in the teeth. I sink back into my chair. I should've stayed home.

When the meeting finally ends, I take advantage of my position near the exit and slink down the hall to my office, intending to close the door and work all the way through lunch. Even if it means answering every message in my inbox.

But as soon as I open my laptop, there's a knock on the door.

"Come in?" I say, trying to sound confident but landing on something more like confusion.

Carl enters the room, closes the door, and sits across from me before I can speak. He's a stately Black man in his fifties, and while he can be quite competitive in his role as CEO, he has gone to great lengths to take me under his wing. He's probably the closest thing I've had to a father figure as an adult.

"Anton. Good to have you back," he says. His voice is kind, but there's a note of benign disapproval.

I slump in my seat. "I'm sorry about what happened in there, sir. Maybe I'm not quite ready to be back in the office."

The second apology I've had to make to someone who matters to me before lunch. Awesome way to start my week.

"How was the service?" Carl asks calmly, poised in his seat. "My condolences again."

"Uh, it was nice," I say through my teeth. I know he isn't really looking for details, and I'm happier not rehashing the whole thing. "The flowers you and Eva sent were beautiful," I remember to add. "Thank you."

He waves his hand dismissively. "I know you and your mom were close. Actually, I was surprised to see you this morning. I just came in here to let you know I don't expect you back right away if you need more time, or even if you want to work remotely for a while."

I swallow hard. God, I must've fucked up in the meeting worse than I thought. Something deep in my brain shifts into panic mode. I'm tempted to take his enormous hint and walk out right now. But I take a breath and manage to pull a response together.

"Thanks, Carl. I actually think I'm better off digging back in. You know? Gives me something to focus on."

He nods steadily, considering my words. Then he clears his throat. "You remember Derek Norman from Colorado Springs? We've been talking seriously about a collaboration. Maybe opening up a branch office. I'd been planning to loop you in last week."

The fog in my brain finally dissipates and I pick up a pen. "Yes, of course I know Derek. And . . . that sounds like a fantastic opportunity."

"Agreed," he says, inclining his head. "But if we go through with this, Anton, I'll need my best people in place, doing their finest work."

I straighten. "You can count on me, sir."

A week ago, we would've shaken hands and that might've been the whole conversation. But I can tell something has shifted.

"I know that, Anton." Carl gives me a kind smile. "I just came in to say I'd like Milo to work in conjunction with you for a time. I think he could be an asset in this endeavor, and it'll be good experience for him."

My pen slips out of my hand and hits the desk. "With all due respect, sir, Milo's barely been here a year."

"You're correct," he says. "But I had him assist on your accounts while you were away, and he's shown a lot of potential. Even Myra Alvarez gave him a good report."

I swallow hard. He already put Milo with one of our biggest clients? It took me years to get to work with her. I swallow hard, unable to shake the feeling I've screwed up and now he's assigning me a babysitter.

As if he can hear my thoughts, Carl adds, "Anton, I'm bringing Milo in to help *support* you. I lost my mother as a young man too, and I know how hard that is."

He rises from the chair and I follow him to the door, shaking my head and wishing again that I'd just stayed home today. "I wasn't prepared this morning, Carl. I'm sorry. It—it won't happen again."

He turns to me, eyes softening. "Your mom's hardly been gone a week, son. Give your heart some room to heal before you ask a lot of your brain. Why don't you take the rest of today and clear your head? You can let me know where you're at in a day or two."

The door closes with a soft thud and I turn to look around my office. The desk, view, and art on the walls ought to feel familiar, comfortable. The way my mom's house should have. But just like back home, everything here feels like it belongs to someone else. Or I'm in the wrong room.

My laptop sits on the desk, containing files I might dig into this afternoon, but even though I meant what I said to Carl—I *want* him to know he can count on me—I have zero inclination to sit down and get started.

Out the window, my usually stunning view of the city and mountain backdrop is gradually being obscured by a weather system rolling in from up north. The sun being quietly blocked out behind a sky of clouds so dense I can't even see the peaks of the mountains. It would be a perfect day for a trail run. Maybe a bike ride. And now my feet are itching to take off somewhere and try to gather my scattered thoughts.

There's another knock on the door, and Milo pokes his head in. "Hey, Anton. Thought I'd check in and see if you need to be brought up to speed. Do you want to go over the Alvarez account?"

Deep inside, part of me is pissed to see him. But all I manage to do is turn away, glancing out the window again before I grab my phone and keys off the desk. Maybe Carl is right and I should at least take the afternoon.

I walk past him and mutter, "I'll be back."

I wind up taking my bike down the Cherry Creek Trail. All the way south to the reservoir where the path literally ends, or I might've kept going. There aren't a lot of people out on a Monday morning, and I ride fast both ways. Pushing my legs, and my lungs, to the limit. It feels like if I can just go fast enough, far enough, I could catch up to something. Except I don't know what. And every time I slow, my thoughts flood in, threatening to drag me down.

My mom is at the forefront, of course. It's like my mind was holding on to all these little details that somehow released upon her death. Things I haven't thought about in years. How she always sipped coffee from a yellow smiley face mug. The way she tried not to sound mad even when she was. How she came to *every* sporting event Seth and I competed in. And in less vivid color, there are memories of her and Dad. The two of them dancing quietly in the kitchen when they thought I was asleep. The way her eyes shone when she looked at him. The similar, wistful look she got when she smiled at Lydia and me.

The clouds that gathered and swirled over Denver earlier

have now moved east to wreak havoc over the plains, taking the barrier to the July heat with them. Just so no one in the city can forget it's the dead of summer. I'm dripping sweat by the time I roll my bike into the garage, so mentally and physically exhausted I just want to stand under a cold shower. Maybe toss a ball for Heartthrob. But as soon as I step through the door into our quiet kitchen, I remember he's with Lydia.

My heart sinks, footsteps echoing through the empty house until, blessedly, my phone rings.

"Seth," I say with a relieved sigh.

"Hey, man. I just finished with the realtor and wanted to touch base. Gonna move everything that's left here into storage, give it a coat of paint, then stage this place. Should have it on the market by end of the week."

"You can't use the furniture that's there?" I ask, with surprising irritation.

"Not unless I want buyers taking a mental trip down Millennial Lane. I got a big fat *no* from Chandra on the shabby chic living room." He pauses, and I can almost hear him smirking over the phone. "Although I did get several loud yeses out of her on the bedroom set."

I roll my eyes. Apparently feelings about our mom are not interfering with Seth's personal life.

"How soon did she think it would sell?"

"Eh, the market's not what it was. But we're pricing it right and it helps that I did those updates in the bathroom. Could be a few months, I guess."

I put the phone on speaker, letting his voice fill the kitchen while I dig through the pantry for lasagna noodles and tomato sauce. My brother has often been the bearer of bad news, but when I think of him being *here,* so close, it perks me up. "Just move as soon as it's listed. There's no reason to stay in Dallas."

He snorts. "Your couch is comfy, but I'm not going anywhere until Bruno and I both have a place to land."

"Fine. Come out to visit and we'll go apartment hunting. I know some pet-friendly places we could look at."

"What's the rush, Anton?" he needles. "It's almost like you miss me."

"Not really," I say. "I just promised Mom I'd keep an eye on your ass."

He chuckles again, but then his voice thickens. "You know, she told me to do the same thing."

We both get quiet.

"How you doing, big brother?" he finally asks in a different tone.

"Seth. Do me a favor and worry about the cat."

"I mean it," he says. "I was here dealing with every phase after her diagnosis, and I don't know, somehow that kept me sane. But you didn't get that process. Or the closure."

"That's . . . that's not it." I drop into a chair, the corners of my eyes burning. "Do you remember anything about when Dad died?"

He hesitates. "A little. Maybe the service and some people visiting."

I close my eyes, fighting the weird, empty burn in my chest as I try to verbalize my thoughts. "It's just, when he died, Mom was the one who held us together. She played both roles. Became our whole family. Filled all the gaps he left behind." I take a ragged breath. "There's no one left to do that this time."

"I think you're wrong—we need to do it ourselves." My brother's voice is so gentle I want to hit him. "Mom's gone, but *we're* still here. You, and me, and Lydia. We make our own family."

I let out an exhausted breath, wishing I could tell him that's not what I mean. But it feels too hard.

He waits a second, then tries to pivot the conversation, but he can't seem to pick a subject that isn't painful today. "How are you and Lydia doing?"

Seth knows everything that went down between my wife and me on Unmatched, the cheating app for married people where I was dumb enough to make an account. How she found my profile there and listed her own in response—and everything that happened as a result. He knows our marriage came to the brink. But he also knows things have been on the upswing recently. At least, until last week.

"We're good. Ah, just getting back into the rhythm."

"What, are you taking dance lessons?" he asks, but his tone is serious. "Anton, there's a reason Mom loved Lydia. She fits. She's good for you. Don't get so wrapped up in what's missing you lose sight of what's in front of you."

I twinge, remembering the way Lydia hugged me this morning. Something she's done hundreds of times. But for some reason, today, it felt like a hug at arm's length. Was that because of me?

"Just get your ass out here and let me worry about my marriage, Seth."

"I'm just saying, you two are lucky to have each other. All I've got is an old grouchy cat."

Sometimes, when things feel hard, I make my mom's lasagna. There's nothing really special about the recipe. It's so straight-forward I could probably make it in my sleep. But it tastes like the part of my childhood before my dad died when things felt whole. I'm on the second layer of noodles, letting myself zone out to a playlist of music without lyrics, when my phone pings next to the sink.

LYDIA

So . . . Celia just called. She's in town and wants to meet for dinner.

My brows shoot up. That's so unlike Lydia's sister, I have to read the message twice. She isn't one to show up without planning an itinerary two months in advance.

> Really? Where's Dr. Adam?

LYDIA

Medical conference at the Gaylord hotel. But
he has an event tonight.

Huh. That sounds like the kind of occasion where Celia would shine. She's a "life coach" and networked through half of her own wedding reception. I'm not sure why she'd miss an opportunity like that to drop in on the sister she barely speaks to. Unless she wants something.

> Do you want to see her? You could say
> you're busy?

The last time we saw Lydia's family, she got so scattered she rear-ended another car during the visit. Celia isn't half as critical as their mom, but neither of them bring out the best in my wife.

LYDIA

I don't know. She has the baby with her.
Maybe just wants to show him off.

I pause, looking down at the half-made lasagna in front of me. I know nothing about babies, and I'm no fan of Celia Cohen, but somehow after facing down end of life last weekend, meeting the newest member of the family doesn't seem like the worst idea.

I send Lydia a pic of the lasagna pan on the counter.

> I'm already making dinner. Let's meet our
> nephew.

CHAPTER FIVE

C ELIA INHALES DEEPLY AS I OPEN THE FRONT DOOR. "O OH , IT smells amazing!" She steps inside before I can open my mouth, handing me an enormous black diaper bag. "This was *such* a better idea than going out, Lydia. Thanks for the invite."

"Of course," I mutter, hefting her bag off to the side. As usual, my sister appears perfectly put together in slacks and a navy sweater set. Her blonde hair has been pulled into a chignon, and there's a signature string of pearls around her neck. She looks like she just finished giving a TED Talk. The only evidence that she gave birth three months ago looks at me wide-eyed from a car seat dangling on her arm.

"Is this Gabriel Edward?" Anton asks beside me, crouching down for a closer look. The round, rosy-cheeked child appraises him with a gaze not unlike his mother's, then cracks a broad, gummy smile and waves his arms. Anton smiles and waves back.

"Gabe," Celia corrects. "We *don't* use Edward."

Anton and I share a look. Neither of us is sure *why* Celia and Adam named him for our dad, especially if we're not even supposed to call him that, but before I can think too hard on it, my sister's face morphs into a mask of sympathy. She reaches out to squeeze my husband's arm. "Anton, I'm so sorry. My condolences about your mom."

"Thank you." He straightens, his voice becoming scripted the way it was through his mother's service. "We miss her very much."

Celia sets down the car seat, and Anton makes an excuse about checking the oven as she unbuckles the baby. She pulls him out wearing an outfit that matches her own, and smooths his wisp of dark hair, scanning our living room with him perched on her hip. "I thought you two were going to redecorate?"

I bristle. Here we go. The thing my mother and sister share most in common is an ability to pick out all of my short-comings.

"We were going to. But I opened my second business instead," I say, following as she takes the baby on a tour of our little bungalow like it's a quaint, walkable dollhouse. I only remember my sister visiting one other time, shortly after we purchased the house as a fixer-upper. She'd been on her way to Vail for a girls weekend, and I was eager to show off the home we'd foregone a honeymoon to buy. The most she'd said at the time was, *Well, it's not Turks and Caicos.*

Excited barking echoes from the backyard, and I step through the kitchen to let an eager-looking Heartthrob in from the yard. He rushes in to greet our company, tail wagging furiously.

"*Lydia,*" my sister shrieks. "Can you put the dog away?"

My view shifts from where Heartthrob stands politely trying to get a sniff of the new people standing in his home, to Celia holding her son high in the air like she's trying to save him from a pack of wolves.

"Oh. Uh—Heartthrob, go to your place."

My dog immediately, though reluctantly, obeys, retreating to his bed in the living room with a look like I'm denying him the chance to make friends. I appease him with a strip of dried sweet potato.

"Would you like to have a seat?" I ask my sister. "Can I get you anything?"

Celia eyes Heartthrob with a curled lip, like he might finish the chew and move on to her child. "Can't you put him somewhere?"

My eyes narrow. "Heartthrob is in his place, in his *home*, and won't bother us. He was just excited to say hello. Isn't Gabriel used to Pookie?"

"That's different," Celia mutters at the mention of her elderly Pekingese.

I roll my eyes. "How about I get you something to drink?"

"Water, please," she says wistfully. "You know. Breast-feeding."

"Oh. Yes, of course." I eye her boobs. According to my sister's social media, she's happiest holding a glass of wine, but it makes sense that she'd give that up in the name of sanctimony.

"Thank you," she says when I return with the water and a plate of bruschetta. "I'm so pleased Gabey could meet his auntie and uncle while Daddy works tonight."

I cringe, wondering if she realizes she's talking just like our mom.

"What *is* Dr. Adam up to these days?" Anton asks, stepping back into the room.

Celia raises her chin in her signature imperious style. This should be a doozy. "Well, he's on track to be offered a position at the Mayo Clinic this fall. Of course, someone spilled news of a competing offer from Cedars-Sinai, but he'll just have to make a decision if that's how it pans out. This conference is all about schmoozing with future employers."

"Wow," I say, shooting Anton another look. "He must be thrilled." We've only met Dr. Adam Cohen twice—the night before and the day of their wedding—but he made it clear in the space of twenty minutes that our lack of medical degrees made us unworthy of his time. I'm *still* trying to figure out how he and my sister happened in the first place. "Would that mean a potential move to California or Minnesota?"

"Well. California, hopefully," she says with a tolerant smile. "It'll be up to Adam. There's such a demand for plastic surgeons."

"What about your coaching, Celia?" I ask, because if there's *one* interesting thing about my sister, it's her self-built company. "Are you back yet, or are you still on maternity leave?"

"Adam's been asking about that too." Her face sours. "I've been doing some consulting here and there, but we're fortunate enough that I don't need to work. We might eventually pursue daycare, but right now I just want to savor my time with Gabey."

I blink. Obviously, I'm aware some women make the choice to stay home with children when they're little. I just never thought my sister, the junior version of Marion Stanton, our working mom extraordinaire, would be one of them.

"Don't your clients need you, though?"

She shrugs, staring down at the baby who waves a blue rattle back at her. "I know it's not for everyone, but I consider this time precious. Work can wait."

I just sit there with my jaw hanging open. She sounds like she means it.

"My mom did something similar," Anton says quietly over my shoulder. "Took time off to stay home with me, then with Seth. She said it was hard, but always insisted she'd do it again in a heartbeat."

"Exactly." Celia beams. "Selfishly, I don't want to miss any of his 'firsts,' but I also want to give him a good foundation. When I was pregnant, I spent a lot of time reading and thinking about the relationships we nurture. What we can give of ourselves that really lasts. If I stay home, I can be the one who's there for Gabe if he's hurt or sad, or if he needs anything. If I go back to work . . . someone else will do that. It just feels like a gift I can give him. One he'll have forever."

"Makes sense," Anton says in a faraway voice.

Celia gives my husband a gentle smile. "Maybe your mom felt the same way."

I open my mouth, sure there is something I need to say, even if I don't know what. But my nephew saves me, screwing up his precious, nurtured face and letting loose a shriek like a banshee. I watch my skilled, confident, life-coach sister as she rocks her infant gently, then moves to a more vigorous bounce before offering a pacifier he immediately spits out. Finally, she sniffs his diaper with a look of semi-desperation.

"He might be hungry," she says evenly, as if the sound isn't threatening to shatter the windows. "Is there somewhere I can—"

"Our room. Just down the hall," I say, jumping up to bustle her away. As soon as she's situated in the small armchair by our bed, I exit the room, my shoulders sagging in relief. I'm not sure if it's Celia or the wailing I need a break from, but the tension in my body eases as soon as I pull the door closed.

"Wow," I say, slinking into the kitchen. "Can you believe—"

"I know. She's such a natural," Anton says. "I never thought I'd say it, but motherhood seems to suit your sister."

That is *not* what I was going to say, but I shut my mouth, watching him pull the lasagna tray out of the oven. I only got home an hour ago, and we were so busy preparing for Celia's visit, I hadn't had a chance to really check in with him. I took it as a positive sign that he wanted company at all, but he looks completely different than he did this morning. His movements efficient and animated. Confident. Not distracted the way he's been the last few days.

I don't know what broke him out of his funk, but I don't want to waste the moment.

"Dinner smells wonderful," I say, wrapping my arms around his waist. And to my delight, he pulls me into his warmth. He smells like basil and oregano, and *Anton*. I breathe him in, letting go of everything we've been through this past week. Forgetting Dallas, my meeting with Henry. Not even letting myself dread getting through dinner with Celia.

"I came home early, so I had extra time to throw everything together."

I pull back, feeling stupid. Of course. He didn't prepare this whole meal after work. "Did something happen?"

He shrugs, slicing a few tomatoes to add to the salad. "You were right. I guess I need a little more time."

I frown, looking around the messy kitchen. Anton's lasagna recipe came from his mom. He always makes it when he's missing her. "I'm sorry. This was too much to ask of you."

He shakes his head, glancing down the hall leading to our room. "Actually, making dinner for you and your sister, meeting the baby . . . I don't know. It's refreshing. Nice to have something new to focus on."

A timer goes off on the stove. Anton moves to stir some kind of sauce and I withdraw to set the table. By the time my sister emerges—with a *sleeping* baby, thank God—we're just setting out the food.

"Do you want to lay him down somewhere?" Anton whispers, looking uncertain.

Celia raises her chin and shakes her head. "No. He should stay like this for at least an hour. I've gotten really good at eating with one hand."

Again, something about my sister's demeanor strikes me as so . . . different. I can't put my finger on it, but I am almost totally sure *our* mom would never have held either of us through a meal.

"Thank you," she says when I set a plate of lasagna and asparagus down in front of her. "Anton, this looks divine."

We go about eating in relative silence. Celia isn't quite the one-handed expert she professed to be, and I glance warily at the sleeping infant each time her fork clatters against the china, but he remains a peaceful little cherub. Actually, now that he isn't shrieking, I have to admit he looks pretty sweet.

"So, what's new, Ce? Um, besides the obvious." I gesture stupidly at the baby. "Is Mom at your house like, twenty-four seven? She makes it sound like she's Super Grandma."

My sister's jaw tightens, her eyes flashing ever so slightly. "Not sure I'd quite call it that."

"Really?" I niggle, sensing something I can rub a little salt in, for old time's sake. "I thought grandbabies were the new black."

To my surprise, Celia cracks a small smile. "Yeah, I thought so too. She did offer to come over and 'help' me once. But that consisted of taking a few selfies with Gabe to send to her friends and leaving when he started crying. So I guess, yeah, Super Grandma had super-important other things to do."

I nearly laugh out loud, only because this sounds exactly how I would expect our mom to *grandma*. But I'm also not sure what to say. If Marion Stanton could have made a list detailing what she wanted in a daughter, Celia checks all the boxes. Beautiful and popular, she launched a successful career, then married a handsome doctor and produced a handsome grandchild. But the real letdown in my sister's voice shifts something in my chest, and I actually feel kind of bad for her.

I am jarred out of my thoughts as Celia's fork tumbles to the floor, landing next to my shoe. She lets out a defeated sigh, looking from the sleeping baby in her arms to the plate where she's barely made a dent in her food.

Anton and I glance at each other. We're both mostly finished, and it occurs to me I need to *not* be like our mom. I should offer to take my nephew—hold him, so she can eat. But when my eyes drop to her snoozing bundle, my skin goes clammy and the words don't come. What I finally say is, "I'll get you another fork."

As soon as I step into the kitchen, I feel stupid. It's not like the baby is going to bite. But as I re-enter the dining room with a clean utensil, my pulse kicks right back up.

Anton watches, clearly waiting for me to do the right thing. But when too many seconds pass with me standing awkward, unable to speak, he clears his throat. "Uh, here. I'll take him, Celia."

She glances at him uncertainly, but then her eyes return to her plate and her shoulders drop in relief. "Actually, that would be great."

I watch wide-eyed as my husband comes around the table, kneeling next to my sister as she transfers her sleeping child into his arms.

"There." Celia exhales, adjusting a light-blue blanket under her son's head.

Anton stands and smiles. "Great. I've got him. Go ahead and eat."

For a second, she looks like she's not sure what to do with her free hands. Then she picks up her fork and knife, and digs into the meal like a starved woman. "Anton," she says between bites. "You could easily have a second career as a chef if finance doesn't work out."

He chuckles. "Lasagna is the one thing I really know how to cook." He sounds so wistful. I glance over, worried I'll find him a million miles away again. Instead, he's staring down into Gabriel's face with a surprisingly peaceful expression.

"Oh, Lydia!" Celia exclaims with familiar enthusiasm. "I

almost forgot. *How* are things going with the new partnership?"

"Great so far," I say automatically, mentally skirting my entire meeting with Henry this morning. "Having Henry on board gives me a lot more flexibility, and the new daycare is on track to be fully booked and profitable by the end of the year."

"Impressive," Celia says, though the way she arches her brow suggests skepticism. "Just think of what you could do if you ever truly level up."

Anton flinches and meets my gaze from where he stands by the windows. I blow out a hot burst of air. "Yeah, just think."

As soon as my sister sets her fork on her empty plate, I jump up to clear the table while my husband, sister, and nephew drift quietly into the living room. I make a lot of unnecessary noise banging pots and pans around in the sink, but definitely *not* trying to wake the baby for Celia to deal with.

Once the dishwasher is loaded and the counters completely wiped down, I gather myself and head for the living room, where low, downtempo music plays on the Bluetooth speaker. I find my sister perched on the couch and my husband pacing quietly by the fireplace in front of the family photo he brought back from Dallas. He's rocking Gabriel back and forth, and . . . I think cooing at him.

Celia watches with a melty expression, and I sink into a seat on the other end of the couch from her.

"Do you want to hold him, Lydia?" Anton asks suddenly.

"What?" My head snaps up. "Me?"

"Yeah." Celia smiles, shifting into her irritating mommy voice as she gets up to take the blue bundle from my husband's arms. "Auntie Lydie hasn't had a turn."

My head spins, my stomach twisting into a knot. I think I *should* want to hold my nephew . . .

Except I don't. At all.

"Um, he looks so peaceful. I don't want to disturb him."

"Nonsense," she says, sinking back onto the couch and scooting toward me. "It's easy with him asleep."

I retreat backward, sinking into the cushions and trying to figure out how to politely say *don't force your baby on me*, but before I can stop her, she places Gabriel in my arms.

I don't think I've held a human child since I babysat as a teenager, and actually, I'm not sure I ever took care of one this small. It isn't at all like holding a dog; he seems softer and more fragile. I am pretty sure I should feel some kind of warmth, adoration. This is my nephew—technically, my own flesh and blood. But I just desperately want her to take him back. The baby must've gotten jostled with all the transfers because he stirs, flexing his fingers and spitting out his pacifier. His eyes open, and when he looks up at me, my pulse spikes.

"I—I don't know what to do."

"You can give him the paci back," Celia says.

I scan the blanket, find the little plastic nub, and hold it to his lips. He opens readily when he sees it and almost immediately closes his eyes and settles back into slumber.

"There, perfect," my sister says quietly. "You will make a *great* mother, Lydia."

The knot in my stomach tightens.

And then I notice Anton watching by the window with this warm, contented look. He smiles at me, and the knot morphs into a sinking feeling. I thrust the baby back to Celia.

"No, I don't think so. Obviously, I'd make a terrible mother."

I get up from the couch, pausing a second before crossing to where Heartthrob snoozes in his bed. He raises his head as I curl up with him, then drops his muzzle into my hand, and I'm instantly more comfortable, stroking his chin and scratching the soft fuzz on his ears.

"Well. I guess I should probably be getting back to the hotel," Celia says, mercifully in her grownup voice.

Anton helps her gather up blankets and little plastic keys and things, and I drag myself off the floor away from my dog, if only to hasten her departure. "Guess we'll see you in another five years," I say, only half joking.

"Actually . . ." Celia turns to me with a strangely sanguine smile. "I was wondering if I could entice you and Anton to Ohio for Thanksgiving."

My mouth falls open. This is what I get for assuming having my sister over means the universe will leave me alone for a while. I look at Anton and scramble for an excuse. Celia might be extending the invitation, but Thanksgiving is always at our mom's house. And I just *can't*. Not this year.

"I thought Gabriel getting to spend his first Thanksgiving with all his family might be nice." She coos down at the car seat. "Especially if we're about to move."

Anton makes a sound I can't identify, and I turn to him, pleading with my eyes. Thanksgiving with my family is a particular hell we've weathered before.

"It's a nice thought for the little guy," he says.

I close my eyes, reaching over and squeezing his hand so hard it probably hurts.

"Yes, lovely," I say. "Will Mom be inviting Adam's parents too?"

Celia winces like she hadn't considered that specific toxic stew, but says, "Of course she will. Everyone will be invited. I'll even buy pumpkin pie."

"How domestic," I deadpan.

"Thanks for the invite," Anton says, finally coming to my aid. "We'll have to look at our schedules."

"But I *doubt* we'll make it," I add. "I'll have to talk to Henry, and then there's employee schedules to think about—it's a busy time of year."

"That's why I asked in July," Celia says with a laugh,

clearly not picking up on my distress. Or maybe she is. "Just think about it and let us know by like, September."

"Sure. Okay," I say. "We'll let you know."

Anton squeezes my hand, and in that moment I'm so grateful he understands my dysfunctional family and has my back. He lets go to help my sister with her diaper bag, and I wave, hoping it *is* the last time for years.

CHAPTER SIX

Him

"No way. In Hell. Am I spending Thanksgiving with them," Lydia says, then forces her mouth into some imitation of a smile. "I'd rather have forcible manicures every day for a week."

I shake my head, exhaling as I sink into the living room chair. "God, can you imagine? It'd be like her rehearsal dinner all over again."

"Oh, be more specific. Are you referring to when my mom started yelling at Adam's mom because the crystal on the table didn't match? Or Adam's dad lecturing us on there being no worthwhile universities west of the Mississippi?"

We both snort at the memory.

"You wearing your CU sweatshirt to breakfast the next day was a nice touch." Lydia chuckles, then looks at me curiously. "Though, for a second there, it almost seemed like you were going to tell Celia we'd come?"

"What?" I look up at her. "No, I was worried you were going to cave because she put you on the spot—probably on purpose. I was playing into her sentiment, but mostly trying to get her out the door before you agreed to something you didn't want."

"Oh." She considers this, then says, "Thanks."

In truth, Celia isn't terrible. Not like their mom. She can be judgy and aloof, but she isn't overtly hurtful. What's unbearable when she's around is the tension between her and Lydia. At least the baby broke some of that up tonight.

Heartthrob thrusts his head into my lap, wagging his tail, seemingly as relieved as we are that they're gone. But as I ruffle his fur with one hand and we settle into companionable silence, an uneasy stillness seems to creep back in. The house is suddenly too quiet again. Empty. Even with Lydia and Heartthrob here.

I push myself out of the chair. "I'll um . . . I'll go finish up the dishes."

"They're done," Lydia says, following behind me.

I get to the kitchen to find she's right. Everything's tidied up and the dishwasher's running. Even the counters are wiped down. It hardly looks like anyone cooked here tonight. "Oh. Thanks."

Lydia hovers next to me, and it seems like there's something else she wants to say. I just wish I could make this cold, vacant feeling go away. I grab Heartthrob's squeaky octopus toy off the floor and he lights up, racing ahead of me to the back door. "Seems like he could use a little fun after spending all night in detention."

"That's fair." She laughs, but as she moves to follow me outside, I sort of wish she wouldn't. Which immediately makes me feel worse. And apparently I broadcast the feeling, because she hesitates and holds back.

"I'm just going to catch up on a few things while you two play," she says.

Equal parts guilt and relief flood through me as I step into the yard alone. I should be pulling Lydia closer, not pushing her away. It was way worse earlier when I was home alone. But I need a second to try and make this feeling go away. This weird, empty stillness wrapping around me like a shroud.

The sun has mostly set, and the crickets start up their evening song, but the patio light illuminates our tiny yard. I launch the octopus into every corner for Heartthrob, sending him diving after it like a puppy while I try to figure out why I don't want to go back inside.

Things felt almost normal while Celia was here. More than they have since we left for Dallas. But all the awkwardness came flooding back after she left. Which is so odd—it should've been the other way around. Was it the distraction of entertaining? Will things be okay if I just make sure we have constant dinner guests?

I throw the octopus again. I felt this way at the office too. So that doesn't really track.

Eventually, Heartthrob slows his retrievals, and after a few more, finds a good-smelling spot in the grass where he can roll instead. I stand on the little patio watching him, and finally admit the emptiness inside me is just as bad out here by myself.

When I reenter the kitchen, Lydia has changed into her white cotton nightgown and presents me with a mug of tea. She's made one for each of us, which is surprisingly comforting. A flicker of memory, of my mom doing this for the two of us on lonely nights after my dad died, tries to push its way to the surface. But that seems like a bad direction for my thoughts, so I chase it away with words.

"How did the meeting go with Henry?" I ask, choosing the safest subject I can think of.

Lydia seems surprised when I bring this up, then scrunches her nose and looks away. "He suggested closing Ooh La Pooch or consolidating it within one of the daycares. I told him I'm not eliminating any jobs."

She leans against the counter, shoulders slumped, looking more defeated than I've seen her since before she opened for business six years ago. A pang of guilt twinges in my chest. Maybe I pushed her too hard to bring Henry on as a partner.

"Well, he only owns half of the business," I say, dropping into a chair. "You get just as much say about what happens."

She nods, sipping her tea, but seems distracted, like she's mulling something over. "It's fine. I just have to do some thinking."

Her phone lights up on the counter, and when she looks at it, she snickers and holds it up.

SETH

"Nothing is impossible. The word itself says:
'I'm possible!'"

"Did your brother just quote Audrey Hepburn?"

I roll my eyes. "Maybe you and Seth should get into motivational coaching."

She looks at the screen, thumbs clearly ready to fly with a comeback, but then she glances at me and sets it down again. "You never really said why you came home early today."

My stomach tightens, but I shrug. "I was just having a hard time focusing."

She considers this a minute, then sets her mug down and steps forward. And though I can see her second-guessing every move, she crosses the few feet to where I'm sitting at the kitchen table and lowers herself onto my lap.

"Maybe you just need the right thing to focus on."

I hesitate. She's trying to get something started. Something that, a couple of weeks ago, I would've pounced on without hesitation. I'm sure that version of me would be horrified that I haven't already reached up to touch her. Encourage her. She looks like a fucking cupcake in that nightgown. The swell of her pert breasts peeking out from the low neckline, her long legs parted across my lap. But absolutely nothing stirs inside me. Just a swirl of hollowness.

Ugh, I hate this. And I don't want her to think it's her fault. I *know* how hard she's trying. How much effort it takes for her to try at all.

"Maybe you're right." I set down my mug and bring my hands to her hips. She smiles, looking relieved.

Lydia leans in, laying kisses along my cheek and down my neck, and I close my eyes, trying to focus on the sensation. Just be present. It occurs to me this is actually a battle we've talked about *her* fighting, but it doesn't seem like the right time to mention that revelation. Because she's taking hold of my hands and guiding them along her thighs.

I open my eyes just as she touches my palms down on her warm, bare skin and begins to slide them up, until my fingers disappear beneath her cotton hem. Pretty much any straight man's dream—hands up the skirt of a beautiful blonde straddling him in a nightgown—but even as my hands move along her skin, it feels like something's chasing after them. Catching up to me.

Lydia thrusts her chest forward, recapturing my attention, and I bury my face in the space between her breasts, hoping to find my oblivion. Her skin is soft, her scent like warm French vanilla—but when I lay my lips on the swell of one breast, I'm as aroused as I would be kissing Aunt Betty.

Somewhat panicked, I refocus where my hands are, squeezing the supple skin of her legs, letting my fingers slide up the last few illicit inches. Lydia catches my eye at the exact moment I realize she isn't wearing panties. Which is, unfortunately, the same moment I'm forced to admit *nothing* is going to happen at all. And my hands fall back to my sides.

She freezes when she realizes I've withdrawn. "Anton?"

I cover my face with my hands. "I . . . I'm sorry."

Neither of us moves for endless seconds. But finally, she rises, dismounting me like a broken saddle. She disappears down the hall, then returns covered up in her bathrobe. I can't even bring myself to look her in the face.

I keep hoping she'll say something to make this not horrible. Give some kind of reassurance. Not that it will help. But when she doesn't, I hear my own voice breaking through the air. "It not your fault."

She sets the kettle back on the stove and pulls a chair up next to mine. Companionable. Friendly. Just a month ago I would have done anything to redirect that feeling. Take off her clothes, worship her body. Ensure we felt more like a married couple than friends. But right now, I am *so* grateful she's still here, next to me. That she didn't get upset and shut herself in our room, alone.

The way I used to.

"What do you think it is?" she asks. "I mean, obviously you're grieving. Maybe it's just too soon."

"I—I don't know." I sigh. "It doesn't seem to have anything to do with my mom, or even you. It's just . . . there."

"What is?"

I open my mouth to try and explain, but every way I can think to describe it just sounds dumb.

The kettle is heating up, and she rises to prepare more tea, not speaking again for a while.

"When did it start? Just last week?" she asks, dumping out the first mugs. "Is it there all the time, or does it ever go away?"

"I don't know." I chew on that for a second. "It definitely started last week, but we were doing all the funeral stuff. It seemed normal to feel bad."

She nods, re-pouring the water and adding a little sugar.

"Normally, exercise helps with any kind of stress," I continue. "But a twenty-mile bike ride did nothing for me today."

Lydia comes around the counter and reclaims the seat next to me, presenting me with a fresh mug of what smells like lemon tea.

"But . . ." I say, thinking out loud. "I did feel a bit better when I was talking to Seth about moving here."

"That's promising." She considers for a moment. "Has anything else felt like that?"

I'm about to say no, but I pause, realizing there was something else. "Um . . ." I say, reluctant to bring it up. "I don't know why, but I felt the best I have all day while Celia and the baby were here."

A line forms between Lydia's eyebrows. "Really?"

I shrug, raking my hand through my hair. "See? None of this makes any sense."

"Maybe it's just helpful having something different to focus on?" she guesses, holding her mug between her palms.

We sip our tea in silence, and I mull through the whole day again. My interactions with Lydia. Everything that happened at work. Talking to my brother. My sister-in-law and nephew.

"Seth was trying to tell me something." I scratch my head, wishing I could remember exactly what he'd said. "About us still being a family, or finding what's missing . . ."

"Well, he's right," Lydia says. "We *are* a family. And we'll probably feel even more like one after he gets to Denver."

"Yeah . . . I guess. I was mad at him and wasn't really listening," I admit. "Now I wish I had."

A quiet alert sounds on Lydia's phone. It's one that goes off every evening that I hardly ever register, reminding her to take a birth control pill. She gets up, walking automatically to the bathroom, as she often does. But tonight, for some reason, this action penetrates my mind. And stays there.

I jump out of my chair and follow. "Lydia, wait."

She turns in the bathroom doorway, brows furrowed. "Is something wrong?"

Suddenly, my mind is churning with my brother's message. With my own at-odds emptiness. And a new feeling I had just this evening, while holding Celia's newborn. An unexpected, contented . . . peace.

"What if—" I clear my throat. "What if *we* had a baby?"

She wrinkles her nose, then gives me the automatic answer we always give when people ask about this. "We will. Someday."

She continues into the bathroom, opening the medicine cabinet where she keeps the pink plastic compact and its ring of colored pills. But as I watch her take it from the shelf, I'm filled with the most foreign sense of dread.

"No," I say, circling behind her in the small bathroom so we're both staring into the mirror. I reach around her waist, gently tugging the belt of her robe until it falls open. I pull the two sides apart and run my hands up the front of her night-gown, snaking over every curve of her body until I reach her full, delicious breasts. I squeeze them together, grinding my fingertips over her nipples through the fabric until her head lolls back against my shoulder and she lets out a gasp. I'm not sure when it happened, but all at once I realize my dick is hard as fuck and I'm completely turned on. I press against her ass so it's clear she knows it too, and then I whisper in her ear. "I meant, what if we do it now?"

Her breath is ragged, still lost in the touch that *finally* brought us together, but she catches my eye in the mirror. "Do what?"

I pull her against me so her chest thrusts forward and we can both watch my hands work over her in the reflection. I tug her neckline down to reveal one nipple, then pin her to the sink, grinding against her with my hips, overcome with desire to push inside her. "Make a baby."

"*What?*" She stops moving, staring at me in the mirror, her forehead set with lines.

I slide the pill case out of her hand and place it on the counter, grazing my lips over her ear. "Let's grow our family. Now. Tonight."

She frowns, pulls her gown back up, and turns all the way around in my arms until we're facing one another. "That's not a good idea."

"It's a great idea. Why not?" I take in her flushed skin and mussed hair, breasts swelling, begging to be touched under her nightdress. And even though I have *always* found my wife physically beautiful, tonight I see her in a whole new way. She looks . . . ripe. Fertile. I press my erection against her stomach, aching to slide into her and—fuck—*consummate* seems like the only word for what I want to do.

But before I can reach down to lift the hem of her nightgown, reveal the naked pussy I know is waiting there for me, Lydia places her hand on my chest and shoves. Then, in the newly created space between us, she grabs the pill dispenser on the counter, punches a tablet through the foil, and swallows it.

"Because, Anton. *I don't want to.*"

CHAPTER SEVEN

I watch the lust fade from his eyes and wonder if I made a mistake.

For about half a second, before I remember what we're talking about. Making another entire human life—a person. Growing it inside *my* body. No, thank you. Not yet.

I pull my robe back together and tie the belt, watching my husband slump in defeat from the corner of my eye. Part of me wants to take him into my arms, tell him it'll be okay. But after what just happened, I doubt he'd find it comforting. And I need a little space.

"Look, I just . . ." I'm not even sure where to start. Obviously, he's been struggling in the week since his mom passed, which feels like both forever and no time at all. I never expected him to pull away from me, which has been upsetting considering all we've been through the last few months. But also not totally surprising, given the circumstances. "This doesn't seem like a good time to make that kind of decision."

He raises his head. "It seems like the perfect time."

I turn up my palms. "How?"

"You've got Henry at the Pooches now. The new location

is launched. You even said he wants to consolidate the grooming. That would make everything even easier."

I bristle. If that's what he took away from what I shared, he was *not* listening. But even that's beside the point.

"So, all you mentioned there was my job."

He hesitates. "Well, it's one of the biggest factors."

I force myself to breathe deep, trying not to sputter. "Did you ever think of asking if I'm *ready* to be a mother?"

His brows draw together. "But we've always—"

"We've talked about it. And made plans for 'someday,' and it has been fun to think about the possibilities. But daydreaming and doing—to my life, my body—are different things."

I'm not even fully aware of some of the things hitting my brakes until I hear them come out of my mouth, but they're true. My focus has been more on management than it used to be, but my work is still very physical. I am constantly lifting heavy dog food, heavy *dogs*, working with animals that aren't always predictable. I don't know how pregnancy would affect my body, but I can't imagine it would make any of that easier.

But if I'm honest, it's not the physical part I'm most stuck on. It isn't hard to picture myself with a giant basketball belly. But I draw a huge blank trying to imagine what happens after that. Even after spending the evening watching my sister dote over her son, I just can't even conceptualize myself as a *mom*.

To his credit, Anton thinks over my words a long time. "You're right. I can't do much to help with the physical part. Pregnancy happens to your body," he says carefully. "But I would support you, take on as much as I could for those nine months. And once the baby is born, you would never be on your own. That's the part that happens to both of us—it would be *our* life."

"Who's taking off work for maternity leave?"

"We both will," he says confidently. "Vesper has a generous leave policy."

"And when that runs out?"

He shrugs. "We'll figure out a balance. There are tons of working parents."

Everything he's saying ought to be acceptable, but somehow still falls flat for me.

"Look, Anton, I am not suggesting it's off the table. I just want a little more time before we jump in and start trying. We can still think about it down the—"

"When?"

I pause. "When what?"

His eyes bore into me. "*When* can we try?"

"I don't know . . . soon," I say, trying not to sound flustered. "Just not *tonight.*"

I am suddenly exhausted by this conversation. I turn away, moving into the bedroom, hoping we can leave it at that. But he's right on my heels.

"I'm going to need a real answer, Lydia. This—" He pauses, his voice growing solemn. "This is important to me."

"Of course it is." I soften, thinking of the look on his face while he was holding my sister's child. I don't want to deny him that. But my own reservations aside, I am also worried about him rushing into this right after losing his mom. "Why don't we revisit this when things have settled more. Maybe we can talk it through again in another six months-ish?"

He shakes his head. "We need to set a date."

I snort. "You want a deadline?"

"Sure. Because if we don't set one, we'll never do it. We'll just keep pushing it to the horizon . . . until it's too late."

Something twists uncomfortably inside me when he says this. I open one of my dresser drawers, staring at my favorite old, blue-striped pajamas next to a couple of lacy nightgowns. Ironically, part of me wishes I could just slip into the negligee and distract him. I may struggle with desire, but I'd be more than happy to initiate sex and chase down my arousal just to end this conversation.

Except I tried that earlier and he pulled away. He had zero interest in touching me until he decided he wanted to knock me up. What does that even mean?

I frown, grabbing the unsexy pajamas out of the drawer and turning to face him.

"I can't just set a date. I don't know when I'll be ready."

He looks at me, at the pajamas in my hands, fists tightening at his sides. "I thought this was something we both wanted."

I open my mouth to answer, but now I'm not even sure. *Is* a baby something I want? I think of my sister, who clearly loves little Gabriel, but she couldn't do a single thing, not even eat, without working around him. And then there's our mother. Who paradoxically loved and resented us throughout our childhoods, depending on the moment. A lot of that was probably the result of our dad leaving, but not all of it. What if, like her, I don't find out until *after* I have a kid that I didn't really want one? I couldn't bear for my own child to grow up feeling unwanted the way I did.

"To be honest . . . I'm not sure," I say in a shaking voice.

The look of utter surprise on my husband's face tells me we've been going about yet another aspect of life wrong.

"You're not sure you want a family?" His voice breaks.

I shake my head, avoiding his eyes. "And I don't know what could ever help me decide."

He flexes his jaw. "That might've been good to know before—"

He doesn't finish the sentence, but it still lands like a punch in the gut.

"Before what?" My voice shakes, blood rushing through my body. "Before we got married? Wasted all this time together? Were our last ten years a total sham? Maybe you wish you'd started with some hot mama willing to pump out a brood for you instead."

"Of course not," he snaps. "But . . ." His pause beats

between us like a failing heartbeat. "I don't know if I can *not* do kids, Lydia."

The room goes still. Maybe I didn't hear him right, but that sure felt like the slap of an ultimatum. And now all I can do is stare at the look on his face. The tight jaw and uncompromising gaze that tells me, no matter what I might be envisioning about the future, he's willing to consider a version without me in it. When I finally open my mouth, my voice comes out husky and raw. "Well. I guess this gives us both something to think about."

CHAPTER EIGHT

Him

MONEY MANAGEMENT IS A GREAT FIELD TO GET LOST IN. THE actual work is basically numbers and formulas and spreadsheets. No gray areas. No maybes. Just mind-numbingly neutral addition and subtraction. Money goes in, money goes out. Strategies work or they don't. It's pretty straightforward —interactions with clients aside. And lucky for me, I have an over-enthusiastic partner handling all of my client relations.

"Milo and I can take the new account," I say, jotting a couple notes in a Thursday meeting. I glance at my eager protégé, who straightens and nods with an air of self-importance.

I resist rolling my eyes because Carl gives us both a warm smile. "You two make an excellent team. Send me an update next week."

We leave the meeting, and I slip into autopilot. Breathing in, breathing out. Back to my desk and familiar routine. I wouldn't call this thriving, but I have managed to appear something like functional between nine a.m. and five p.m. the last few days. I go to work, perform, go to the gym, then home. Which is where the familiar leaves a bad taste in my mouth.

For the past three nights, I've slept on the living room couch. Withdrawn, the way I did months ago. Before the hotel, before Unmatched. Lydia's fallen into her own version of this pattern. Avoiding me, spending all her time at work. We barely exchange a few sentences or texts, and they're usually about takeout.

It feels painfully just like it did before. Only it isn't the same at all. I am still dying to touch her; she's still avoiding me. But our stalemate isn't about the sex anymore—it's what we want from it. And the two very different futures we seem to be imagining.

"Uh, Anton?"

I look up to find Milo blinking at me. It's like this tic he has, though I haven't noticed him doing it with anyone besides me.

"It's ah . . . it's after one o'clock."

I tip forward in my chair. "Are we late for a meeting or something?"

"No." Blink. "But you haven't gone to lunch yet." I'm so fixated on his blinking, I notice his gaze drift to my desk. To the wedding picture I've been staring at most of the last hour.

"Right. Lunch." I get up immediately, grabbing my gym bag from a drawer. Exercise is the only appetite I seem to have anymore. "Why don't you follow up with the Swansons. I'll be back in an hour."

After a forty-minute lifting session, my arms are jelly and I'm calmer than when I walked in. I didn't opt for a workout intending to do any thinking. But in the gym I'm always focused, careful attention on the weights and my form. I guess it's just enough structure to slow down my brain and allow me to focus on the thoughts I've been avoiding. And today, there were many.

But as I drape a towel around my neck and head for the locker room, I'm still at a loss for what to do.

I feel like I've been lied to. I know that's not really fair, but Lydia and I always talked about having kids like it was a guarantee. It was never a matter of *if*, but *when*. Starting a family didn't make sense when we first got married right out of college. We were both focused on getting started, buying a house, growing our careers. But it felt like the pieces were being woven together.

Until she pulled the rug out from under me.

Still, I've had several days to reflect on what happened Monday, and I'm aware I acted like an ass. I rushed her, pressured her. Let my desires take over, just the way I did with Unmatched. I know I need to apologize, and we need to discuss it all again from a calmer place. But I'm dreading the conversation.

"Anton, hey!"

I'm on my way past the cardio machines when I turn to see my friend and Lydia's business partner, Henry, sprinting on a treadmill, waving at me. He hits the screen in front of him, turning down the program until the belt slows and he steps off, catching his breath.

"Hey, man," he huffs. "How are you doing?"

My mouth quirks, wondering what might be so urgent it was worth ending his workout mid-run. But then he opens his mouth again.

"Just wanted to say I'm sorry about your mum."

My chest goes numb as guilt washes through me. I've been so preoccupied with Lydia, with wanting a family, I've hardly thought about my mother all day. My limbs are heavy. I hate that I let her slip so easily—I also hate that it feels like a tiny relief.

"Thanks, I appreciate it." I force a lump down my throat, then vaguely gesture around the gym, looking for a change of subject. "You here running from the dogs?"

Henry flashes a smile that's all teeth. "Had to. Your wife is running me ragged this week."

"Is she now," I say, my face a careful blank.

"Crunching numbers, meeting with contractors. She's making us look seriously at adding grooming to *both* Pooch Park locations." He pauses, wiping sweat from his forehead. "Think she's trying to prove a point."

"Yeah." The corner of my mouth twitches. "She . . . does that."

Henry arches a brow. "Yes, well. It's my own fault. I brought up closing Ooh La Pooch, and you'd have thought I suggested letting all the dogs out into traffic." He snorts. "But, based on projections for this new plan, she might actually be onto something."

"Really?" I ask, glancing at the clock, not really in the mood to talk about Lydia's business.

"I don't even think *she* realizes how beautifully it will set us up to franchise," he says, looking a little smug. "But so far, with some tweaking, the numbers should be there."

I hesitate. "Lydia wants to franchise?"

"Well . . . I haven't exactly brought it up yet." He taps the side of his nose. "But now that we're past the initial backlash, that's where I'd like to steer us. If we go that route, she could keep running some locations on her own if she wanted. But I could pretty much step back and let the Pooches run themselves. We'd both get what we wanted."

I study Henry more closely. Even in a sweaty T-shirt and shorts, just off a run, his posture is straight, his eyes sharp and exacting. The way he does business.

"You did a franchise before, right?"

"I bought one, yes," he says. "Ran it for a couple years before I sold it. Good experience, but I quickly learned the path to success is to be the *franchisor*, not the franchisee."

"And you really think it could go that way—with the Pooches, I mean?"

"I do. It will be demanding to go through development, but once the systems are launched—" He chuckles. "Well, first I have to convince her."

"Yeah, that's the hard part." I chew my lip. "Lydia can be reluctant to do anything she doesn't feel ready for."

"Oh, I've noticed." Henry chuckles. "But I think she'll get there."

"I—I think she could," I say, as much for him as for me.

"Thanks for the encouragement, mate. Let's hope." He glances at his phone and steps back onto the treadmill. "I certainly wouldn't complain if you put in a good word for me."

My mind is churning by the time I leave work for the day. Lydia is prone to overwhelm. We established that in therapy, though it's something we both already kind of knew. She tends to hit the brakes when *anything* starts to feel like too much. Not just sex.

Even her business partner gets it.

And I came at her demanding an insta-family, on her first day back at work, after a surprise visit from her sister, hot on the heels of my mother's memorial. I'm such a goddamn idiot.

I find myself driving by Ooh La Pooch and the two Pooch Park locations on my way home. Lydia's car isn't at any of them, but that isn't really a surprise. She often runs errands when things slow down in the afternoon. I should probably just go home and wait for her. She left Heartthrob behind this morning, and he's probably ready for a walk.

But I feel like I need to *do* something. Make some gesture. Not stupid flowers or chocolates, but something to communicate that it's okay if we wait. I miss my mom. I do want a family. And I still think in her heart, Lydia will too—when she's ready. But it doesn't have to be now, or even next year. She and Henry can focus on the franchise potential. I'll lean in on Carl's ideas for Vesper. But most of all, we'll refocus on each other. Pick up sex therapy again. Get more comfortable as a *couple* before we start creating new family members.

I'm struggling to think how to approach this when I recognize a brick and stucco building coming up on my right. Playful Pleasures, the *sensual superstore*. I pull in the parking lot on instinct, but once I'm there, I start to second guess. Sex is not the way to Lydia's heart and never has been.

But intimacy is. And more often recently, sex has been leading us to intimacy.

Another thing we've been learning about in therapy.

"Can I help you find anything?" A twenty-something white woman with dark hair and a septum nose ring asks from behind a counter as I walk through the front door. I really *wish* I knew exactly what I wanted. But since I don't, I cross the room so I can speak in a low voice.

"Uh, do you have any suggestions for like . . . an apology gift?"

The woman looks me up and down, making obvious note of my wedding ring, then crosses her arms. "That depends on what you did."

My face warms. I open my mouth, then close it again, reminding myself this is a sex store. Not confession. "I uh . . . I said the wrong things to my wife. I feel bad."

She smirks and I could almost swear the cat tattoo on her shoulder swishes its tail. "Never heard that before."

She curls a finger, then turns on her heel. I follow her on a meandering path through racks of lingerie, costumes, and suggestive gifts until finally, we reach a neat, colorful display of bottles and candles. The woman smiles at me.

"Have you ever given her a massage?"

"Um . . . no," I say, though I'm not opposed to the idea.

I've spent more time touching Lydia the last few months than I did the last few years, which has been so great it honestly hadn't occurred to me to move beyond the basics. Suddenly, I feel stupid for not thinking of it myself.

"Great!" She gestures to the shelf in front of us. "There are about a hundred ways to say you're sorry right here. You can go traditional, edible, or . . . you might even add some nice atmosphere with a massage candle."

"I'm not sure—wait, edible?"

She nods, snatching up several bottles and reading off the labels. "Let's see, we've got banana, watermelon, chocolate . . . ooh peppermint is always great for extra sensation."

I stare at the shelves. The colors blurring. The scents of each of those foods swirling through my nostrils.

She eyes me with a kind, albeit knowing gaze. "Want me to just tell you the most popular?"

"Please."

She plucks a relatively plain-looking clear bottle off the shelf and hands it to me. "Go with this one. It's got avocado, a hint of lavender, and best of all, a nice, silky feel. Also, it's vegan."

"Okay . . ." I say, turning the bottle over in my hand.

"You give her a good full-body rubdown with that," she says, walking me to the registers, "and as long as you're not a total douchebag, I'm pretty sure she'll forgive whatever you did."

"Thanks," I mutter, deciding it's safer not to plead my case. And anyway, now that she's summoned the image of Lydia's oiled, naked body in my mind, it's hard to think of anything else.

"Good luck with the missus," she says, handing me a black plastic bag.

I give a terse nod, but as I walk out to my truck, I'm feeling more optimistic than I have since Monday. I can walk this back. We don't need to make a baby—for now—we just need to reconnect.

I pull out my phone and shoot Lydia a text.

Will you go out with me tomorrow night?

CHAPTER NINE

"I DON'T KNOW, MAYBE THIS IS OVER THE TOP," CAPRICE mutters.

We're standing in an aisle at Great Buy, being surveyed by a wall of low-profile home security cameras. But my best friend is just sort of staring forward, not really looking at any of them. Her hair hangs loose and wavy, partially obscuring her light-brown face, and there are dark circles under her eyes. She keeps checking over her shoulder even though we're the only people on the aisle.

"If it would help you feel safer, or even just help you sleep, I don't see how it could hurt," I say gently.

"But it doesn't actually do anything to *solve* my problem." She sighs. "Maybe I just need to move."

I squeeze her arm. "You *love* your apartment. And your building. It's a safe place. And you don't know if this asshole even really knows where you live."

She grits her teeth. Whoever sent the email she received last night wants her to think they do. After Caprice published her initial article about Unmatched, she was contracted to write a series of follow-ups and related articles. I'd thought she was done with them, but apparently a new one came out yesterday. Within hours, she had a brand-new email. Which, in a single sentence, managed to feel much scarier than all the others so far.

Single girl—fifth floor—careful when you open the door.

"Hi there." A pasty white guy who looks about twenty years old approaches us. He's wearing a bright blue Great Buy shirt and ill-fitting khakis. "Can I help you ladies with the security cameras?"

Caprice gives me a look like this is the last conversation she wants to have with anyone, let alone some bro who hasn't even finished college, so I clear my throat and step forward. "Yes." I glance at his name tag. "*Brad*, can you tell us if any of these doorbell cameras can be installed in an apartment?"

"Hmm. Not many of them, depending on your building's restrictions. Most require drilling into a wall." He scratches his chin, then raises his eyebrows. "But actually, we have a new device that might be perfect. It replaces a peephole."

Caprice perks up a little. "How does that work?"

"You just unscrew the existing peephole and remove it," Brad says, picking up one of the boxes in front of us, indicating a diagram on the back. "Then this fits through the empty space and attaches on the back of the door. It's a good solution if you can't actually drill any holes."

"So, does it like, record anyone outside even if they don't necessarily knock?" she asks.

He nods. "Yep. You can adjust the settings to pick up as much or as little activity as you want, and control how long the videos are stored. You can even speak to visitors through your phone if you're not home."

I glance at Caprice. "Then you'd at least be able to screen everyone who comes by."

"Yeah." She exhales and takes the box. "Okay, that's something. I'll give it a try."

Looking pleased, Brad directs us toward the registers and we wander back to the front of the store.

"I think this is a smart move," I tell her. "Even if someone *does* find your apartment—which they won't—you won't have to interact. You'll be safe inside. But you'll have evidence if you need it."

"Yeah, I feel so much better," Caprice says in a flat voice.

I stop her before we enter the check-out. "Offer still stands —we have an air mattress and an extra room. You can stay with us if you need to."

She wrinkles her nose. "Thanks, but no thanks. Especially with you two doing the second honeymoon thing lately." She greets the person at the desk and taps her card "People get so pissed at me for 'ruining' their relationships. Why can't I get any credit for the one marriage I saved?"

And just like that, the pit in my stomach opens wide again. I swallow hard and glance away. Caprice grabs her receipt but takes a long look at my face as we head for the exit.

"Uh-oh . . . Did something happen?"

"I think the second honeymoon's over." I sigh. "Not sure there's going to be a third."

"He did *not* go back on that site," she snarls.

I shake my head, focusing on the heat rising from the pavement as we cross the parking lot. At least the sun is starting to go down. "No. He didn't."

"What, then?" she asks, clearly bewildered. "Did he catch you alone with your rabbit?"

I glare, offended by her insinuation, but she stares at me unapologetically. I stab my key fob to unlock my Toyota. "He wants a baby."

Caprice tilts her head like a clockwork doll as I duck into the car to start the AC, trying not to think about the cold look on Anton's face when he suggested kids were non-negotiable.

"Okay, catch me up," she says, sliding into the passenger

seat, directing the air vents toward her face. "I'm clearly missing some details."

So, I fill her in. On everything I can think of. How our relationship seemed to shift after my mother-in-law's death. How absent Anton's been, especially in bed. Until my sister came to visit with her baby—when boom, he suddenly couldn't keep his hands off me. As long as I agreed to conceive immediately.

"But how can he—" Caprice starts, then seems to reconsider. "Actually, let's back up. Weren't you guys going to do some kind of therapy?"

"Yes," I say, not meeting her eyes. Technically, we've been seeing a sex therapist. But I can't bring myself to discuss those details out loud. Even to Caprice.

My phone starts ringing and I glance down to see Seth's name lighting up the screen.

"Sorry. It's my brother-in-law. I should take this." I swipe to answer, putting him on speaker as I shift the car into gear to drive back to Caprice's apartment. "Hey Seth, everything okay?"

I ask the question out of habit, even now that Sharon's gone. But my stomach drops as it occurs to me—maybe he's spoken to Anton. We've been avoiding each other for days. Would he make some kind of decision about our relationship and use his brother to deliver the news?

"Just calling to see if you admit defeat," Seth says. "Since you never answered my last text."

I let out a low, relieved breath. I should've known. "I *have* a rebuttal," I say. "I happen to be driving or I'd one-up you right now."

"Sure," he answers breezily. "You take all the time you need. After all, *there are no shortcuts to any place worth going.*"

My eyes widen. "You did not just zing me live on the phone."

He chuckles. "Sorry, that wasn't fair. I had it memorized from my high school guidance counselor's office."

"I'm going to need to up my game before you get here." I laugh. Caprice gives me a questioning look, but I'm not sure how to explain our competitive motivational quotes, so I just shrug. "How's the house sale going?"

"Actually, just went under contract," Seth says.

"Are you serious?" I shriek. "Didn't you just list it? That's fantastic! When will you move?"

"The first people who saw it loved it, and even better, could afford it. I might be in Denver by next month if all goes well."

"Thank goodness," I breathe, realizing a moment too late that I have said this out loud. "Um, I know Anton will be excited to help you find a place here."

"Pretty sure he'd rather watch grass grow than go apartment hunting," Seth says, but then his tone turns more serious. "I haven't told him yet. I wanted to check in with you first to see how he's doing. It ah . . . seems like he's struggling with Mom's death more than I expected."

"Yeah, I agree." I glance at Caprice, who's listening intently, and for a moment I consider taking the phone off speaker. But my best friend has seen me through some ugly times in my marriage, and it seems silly to hide this when I really need her.

Seth exhales. "I tried to talk with him about it the other day, but . . . I don't know, it was like he couldn't hear me."

"He told me about that," I say, softening as I reflect on the conversation we had just *before* we came to blows over family planning. Things got intense so quickly, I'd almost forgotten he actually pulled away from me initially.

"He just sounded so . . . down. So alone," Seth says. "He was going on about all this stuff, talking about our dad dying and trying to hold the family together."

I furrow my brow. "He didn't tell me any of that. He just said talking with you about moving made him feel better."

"I'm glad something can." Seth's voice thickens. "I'm just worried about him."

My brother-in-law is possibly the most laid-back person I've ever met. He dealt with every blow of his mom's decline in stride. Never panicking or missing a beat, just getting her what she needed. I'm not sure how to handle this level of Seth concern.

"What do you think I should do?" I murmur, pulling into a parking space outside Caprice's building. I don't mention Anton's urgency to start a family, but part of me wonders if he already knows.

"I was going to wait till the house closed, but I might come out to look at apartments early, if you don't mind me crashing for a few days?"

I close my eyes, grateful for the umpteenth time Anton has the very best little brother. "I don't mind at all, Seth. I . . . I've been having a hard time reaching him, too."

"Maybe we just need to gang up on him," he says, sounding a little more like himself.

"Yeah." I manage a laugh. "Can't let him forget *we're* still his family."

But as soon as the thought leaves my mouth, I think of Anton's impassive face. Hear his words echoing back through my mind. *I don't know if I can* not *do kids, Lydia.*

What if Seth and I aren't enough? What if he needs more?

By the time we eat something and get the peephole camera installed, it's almost seven o'clock, but it works beautifully. We take turns coming down the hall from different directions and adjusting the settings, but Caprice has got the hang of it, and I can't help noticing the line that's been sitting between her eyebrows all afternoon has finally disappeared.

"Finally. Maybe I can get my brother off my back."

"You told Theo about the emails?" I ask, gathering up the remnants of sandwich wrappers from Snarf's.

"I sort of had to," she says. "I got a pretty bad one while he was here."

"And he hasn't descended on Denver with his SEAL team yet?"

She rolls her eyes. "He only knows about the *one.*"

I bite my lip, but don't say anything. Caprice's twin brother has always been super protective, but it got worse after everything that went down with her former fiancé.

"Have you been treadmill running again?" I ask when I see her hands have started shaking.

"Yes." She exhales. "I still don't feel super safe at the park by myself."

I frown. Like my husband, Caprice uses exercise as an outlet for anxiety and frustration. But nobody moves to Colorado just to run indoors.

"How about we go together Sunday morning?" I ask. "Actually, let's go every Sunday. It won't be too hot if we go early enough."

Caprice's eyes light up immediately, but she bites her lip. "Lydia, you hate jogging."

"I do." I give her an indulgent smile. "But I love you, and I know how much *you* hate running on a machine."

She straightens in her chair, clearly soothed by just the idea of channeling nervous energy outdoors. And now I wish I'd thought to suggest it earlier. "Well, maybe not *every* week," she says. "But it might be nice once in a while . . ."

"I did it with you before and I didn't die," I say with confidence. "I'm sure Anton would be quick to detail all the health benefits."

"Fine. Maybe a couple times," she says, and I love hearing some optimism seep back into her tone. "But if I agree to that, you have to stop avoiding talking to me about this baby thing," she says with a pointed look.

I toss our wrappers in the trash and sigh, moving across her little studio to curl on the corner of her couch. I've spent the last hour or so mulling over everything Seth said, but she's right, I have been avoiding talking about it.

"I don't know," I say dropping my face into my hands. "Half of it was the way he sprang it on me . . ." My cheeks warm as I recall the urgent way he pawed my body the other night. The way, I've had to admit to myself ever since, I've been hoping he would touch me again. "But Seth is right, Anton's hurting. He's lost nearly everyone he loves. So I just . . . I'm trying to give it some thought."

"Hold up." Caprice raises a hand. "I was there for that whole conversation. I did *not* hear Anton's brother tell you to heal him with a magic baby."

I twist my fingers in front of me. "You're right, he didn't."

He suggested *we* could be enough to fill the empty space. But Seth didn't see the way Anton looked with Celia's baby. What if starting a family is truly something Anton needs?

Caprice studies me with a frown. "Lydia, do *you* want a baby?"

"Ah, we've always talked about having kids someday . . ." I say, looking anywhere but at her.

"Talking about kids and wanting them are two very different things," she says with a sharp look. Caprice and her brother were the product of their mother's failed attempt to save her marriage. One of the reasons we became friends in college is because neither of us grew up with a dad.

"I do worry a little about balancing everything," I say, thinking of my sister trying to manage around her son. "I'm not sure Henry could handle things on his own if I had to step back. I don't want to do anything to disrupt the Pooches' growth."

"I wasn't really asking if you thought you could fit one in

around your business," she says more gently. "I was asking if you want to become a mother."

I bite my lip and look away. Caprice knows me well. She's met my mom and has a decent grasp on some of my most complicated feelings. But even I'm not sure how to describe the dread this particular question inspires.

"I wish I was one of those people who has always known they did or didn't want kids," I say in a weak voice. "I've never had a strong drive to start a family . . . But I worry I might regret *not* having one. I'm just scared. How do I know which is the right decision?"

"I can't tell you what to choose." She squeezes my arm. "But take your time and think about it. And for God's sake, *don't* have a baby if that isn't what you want."

I nod, because I understand what she's saying. Except Anton made it pretty clear the topic isn't up for discussion. We've fought so hard to be together. Could he *really* just walk away? Could I let him?

Aside from a brief, ragey time when I thought he was cheating on me, I've never imagined us apart. The future has *always* been Anton and me. But I take a moment, trying to picture us with separate lives. I come up with a vague, cloudy vision of him with some faceless wife and kids. It's hard to visualize, this nonexistent family of his.

What isn't hard to imagine? Anton happy as a dad.

But when I try to come up with a different, future version of me? I draw a blank. At best, I can see myself at work. But every time I try to conjure up some cloudy figure waiting for me at home, I only see Anton. Does that mean I'll be alone? Eating meals solo, walking the dog by myself. No one texting me to check in during the day or filling the house with the scents of baking lasagna?

I swallow. Close my eyes. I can still see the look he gave me the other night—the one where it was clear *I* was shutting us down. *I* was pushing him past some limit we might not come back from.

Again.

My chest aches.

We've been inseparable for ten years. Seeing each other through college, building our careers, supporting one another through family and personal struggles. Through good times and bad, as we said in our vows. So much between us just *works*, which is probably why we were able to weather Unmatched at all.

And here I am, thinking about bringing it to an end, when all he really wants—is a future together?

In the next heartbeat, I insert myself into that image with him. So it's a cloudy version of *us* with the faceless kids. It still seems murky, still somewhat terrifying if I'm honest, but somehow familiar enough *because* we're together. Maybe even . . . doable.

"Lydia? You're awfully quiet over there."

I take out my phone, only to have somewhere to look besides my best friend's penetrating eyes, which I'm not ready for just now. But when I do, I suck in a breath. There's a new text waiting from my husband.

ANTON

Will you go out with me tomorrow night?

I look at Caprice and bite my lip. Guess it's time to finish this conversation.

CHAPTER TEN

ONE DAY I'M GOING TO LEARN NOT TO ANSWER THE PHONE WHEN my mother calls.

"I *know*, you're busy and don't have time," she clucks before I can even say hello.

"Mom." I roll my eyes, but not without a hardy stab of guilt because that is exactly what I was about to say.

"How's the new daycare performing? You think it's going to make it?"

I grit my teeth, rethinking my guilt. "We're doing fine. It's been a lot of work, but we've already exceeded our own expectations."

"Really?" she says, with a clear measure of doubt. "Well, maybe that fancy partner of yours knows what he's doing."

"Or maybe I do," I mutter, pulling into our driveway. "I can't talk long. Anton and I have a date and I need to—"

"*How* is the poor dear doing?" she asks with affected sorrow. "Lydia, you give him a great big mom hug from me. I'm so glad you can at least make time for Anton around your career. You know, I've seen plenty of women lose husbands over—"

"Mom?" I cut the engine. "Is there a reason you called?"

"Oh. Yes, of course." She sniffs. "Celia said you got to meet Baby Gabey this week—isn't he the *most* precious—I'm only calling to see if you'd made a decision about Thanksgiving."

I blink, trying to let my brain catch up. "I told Celia I won't know until it gets closer."

"Yes, but can you find out?" my mom says, clearly unsatisfied with my answer. "I was considering going on a cruise, but then I had this marvelous idea to get all of us together. And you know, Celia and Adam are going to be moving. So this is our last chance for a real Thanksgiving at home."

"I thought it was Celia's idea . . ." I say absently, letting Heartthrob out of my car and heading for the porch. It looks like we beat Anton home. If I can get my mom off the phone, I should have time to shower and think about what to wear.

"It might've been. But you know, she's so scattered now. All she wants to talk about is breast milk and diapers." I almost laugh at the distaste in her voice. "Between you and me, she seems to need all the help she can get. I'm not sure motherhood is instinctive for her."

"Maybe it runs in the family," I mutter, but I can still hear my husband declaring Celia *a natural*. Which is a sharp reminder of the conversation ahead of me this evening; what's at stake.

"She dotes on him too much," my mom says, not listening. "Doesn't do anything that isn't about him. I've seen it happen, Lydia, she's going to lose herself if she's not careful."

My stomach has started twisting painfully as I imagine the future *I* could lose. With the person I love most.

"Maybe she needs one of those live-in nannies," I say without really thinking.

"Oh!" my mother exclaims. "An au pair—what a wonderful idea. I never had that sort of luxury with you girls, but Adam could certainly afford it."

I exhale, relatively sure that isn't what my sister wants,

but relieved to get my mom off my back. "Okay, glad I could help. Now I do have to go."

"Fine, but let me know about Thanksgiving. I'm going to call your sister." She sighs. "Lydia, you're so practical. Sometimes you really remind me of me."

I spend, admittedly, too much time getting ready. Partly because, working with dogs all day, I just *never* have a reason to really gussy myself up and look nice. But if I'm honest, I'm also nervous as hell, and experimenting with eyeliner is a great way to procrastinate. Because there's a lot more than just a date going on tonight. Each of us has drawn a line in the sand, and now one of us will have to budge—we can't just have a romantic dinner and pretend we haven't been avoiding each other the last three days.

Once I'm done blowing out and styling my hair, I put on a touch of lip gloss, a cute yellow sundress, and sandals with just a little heel. Anton made a reservation at D Bar, which makes this feel more like a special occasion than an armistice. It's one of my favorite date night spots in Denver—elegant, but casual, and Anton knows their specialty desserts are the part I like best.

"You look beautiful," he says as I meet him at the front door.

"So do you." When he frowns, I scrunch my nose. Because he *does*. He's dressed in jeans and a linen button-down, with a jacket folded over his arm. He's about a day out from a shave (my favorite), his wavy hair tousled, and when he looks at me there's even a glint of heat in his eyes.

We haven't said anything to each other yet about *why* we're going out, but there seems to be an unspoken understanding. We both know what this date is about.

When we get to the restaurant, we're seated in the middle of the room. Even with a reservation, it's a busy Friday night.

We take our time perusing the menu, and while our waiter is just the right amount of attentive, he mostly leaves us alone. But after we've made our selections and returned the menus, there's a moment when we look at each other and I'm not sure either of us knows what to say. Technically, tonight was Anton's idea, so it seems like I should give him the space to start the conversation. But after thinking everything over carefully the last twenty-four hours, I've made my decision and I'm anxious to move forward.

"I uh . . ." He clears his throat. "I owe you an apology," he says, straightening the knife and fork beside his plate.

"Anton—" I shake my head, but he holds up a hand.

"Please. Let me finish." He raises his chin, looking straight at me. "It wasn't fair of me to suggest our marriage was somehow contingent upon the decision to have, or not have, children. We've been together so long, and we've already done so much work on our relationship. You'd think that should've been obvious, but apparently I needed a kick in the teeth to realize it. Yet again."

I touch his hand on the table. He swallows and goes on.

"Some of this stuff with my mom has been hard. Harder than I expected. There are things I will always wish we could have shared with her. And while I try to make choices that will honor her memory, starting a family isn't just about what I want. It needs to be a decision we make together—even if that decision is to *not* have kids." He closes his fingers around mine and squeezes. "I just want you to know *you* are the most important thing to me, Lydia. Above everything."

My heart is in my throat. I wasn't expecting this at all, and for a few minutes I have to walk back through all my own soul searching the past few days. Second guessing the choice I've made. Should I rethink? Everything feels like it's changed.

But even with him sitting across from me, holding my hand, staring at me like I really am everything to him, the center of his universe . . . It's hard to forget the way he looked at me and said, *I don't know if I can* not *do kids*. And because I can't breathe when I think about the future—the one where I'm not enough, so he goes in search of more—I steady myself to stick with my plan.

Anton releases my hand and reaches into his jacket pocket. "I got you something."

He places a small bottle tied with a red ribbon on my bread plate. I pick it up to take a closer look before realizing what it is. The moment I do, every inch of my skin heats in a full-body blush.

The corner of his mouth pulls into a subtle smirk and his eyes flash. "I um, thought I could try to make it up to you after dinner."

My eyes dart around the room in a strange mix of panic and . . . heat? Oh God. I hold the bottle between both hands in an attempt to cover the label. Somehow sure that, situated as we are in the center of the room, everyone in the restaurant sees it. Knows what it is. Is imagining us using it.

I clench my thighs. Because as unnerved and scandalized as I am by this thought, I suddenly realize—I'm also kind of aroused.

And the heat in Anton's eyes tells me this is exactly what he was aiming for. "If you want, I can put it back in my pocket," he says in a gravelly voice.

I nod, handing the massage oil to him with immediate relief. But when his fingers brush mine, it's like a charge of electricity passes through us, and my breath catches.

My reaction must be completely transparent because he seems to dial in on it, leaning close, voice laced with hunger. "As much as I'd like to oil you up and eat you right here on this table, that part of the apology can wait."

My mouth drops open, my breathing ragged at his words. At the image they placed in my overstimulated head. Thankfully, as soon as the bottle is out of sight, my anxiety subsides. I take a breath, and my head starts to clear.

Which is good, because that's when our dinners arrive.

The waiter makes a fanfare about our choices, then the wine selection, and as soon as he leaves, I start eating so I have an excuse not to speak. But that doesn't stop me from stealing glances at my husband.

This man who has never before spoken . . . *dirty* . . . to me.

Reflexively, the cerebral, feminist part of my brain kicks in, trying to convince me not to call it that. It was a perfectly normal, playful conversation between a married man and woman.

That line of thinking lasts about thirty seconds before my ingrained prudishness regains control. It *was* dirty. And even more shocking . . . I enjoyed it.

God. I am going to give myself provocative whiplash.

But first things first.

"So, I have been doing some thinking of my own," I finally say, trying to ignore the heat still simmering in my core. "About all of this. And I think I'm ready."

"Ready for what?"

"Um . . ." I take a deep, stuttering breath. "To have a baby."

I can't quite read Anton's face. He's staring at me with a mix of confusion and skepticism. Maybe a little hope. "But you said you didn't want to . . ."

I purse my lips and nod. "I did."

His brows draw more deeply together. "Sorry, I'm having a hard time following."

I reach for his hand again, savoring the spark when my skin touches his. "We've *always* talked about starting a family. But like you said, we seem to keep pushing it out. I—I know most of that is on me. I can't deny that such a big decision really freaks me out, and would bring a lot of change. But when I think about *not* doing it . . . I don't know, it's hard to imagine a future with just the two of us."

It's the truth, on some level.

But what I've left unsaid only matters for a moment. Because Anton's face lights up at my words in a way I have *missed*. His eyes are warm and excited, and sparkling for the first time in weeks. And something blooms within me.

"Are you *sure* . . . ?" he asks.

Deep inside my head, a tiny voice says: *No.* Just as I hear myself say: "Yes."

Again, Anton's fingers tighten around mine. He reaches his other hand across the table so we're both holding on, looking straight at one another, and there's a slight sheen in his hazel eyes. "I—" He swallows. "I would love that. More than anything."

My throat tightens. And for a second it feels like I'm falling. I panic at first, afraid I've made the wrong choice. But when I meet his eyes again, I realize it's not just me. It's happening to both of us. We're sharing this, connecting, and this—*this* is what's been missing. Suddenly, the air is charged, like it was moments ago when he presented his gift and whispered those naughty things. Except now it isn't just lust crackling between us; it's more than that. Like I'm seeing him—our future—come back to life. I close my eyes, savoring the feeling, and I'm finally sure: this must be the right choice.

The air between us grows so thick with desire I can barely swallow. And as I imagine his hands on me, groping my thighs, my breasts, I think, *yes, this is it. We should do this.* Now.

Until I glance down at my lap and imagine a round, distended belly bulging under my dress.

I suck in a breath. And just like that, all my arousal, the connection between us, drains away.

Almost like he can read my thoughts, Anton clears his

throat and says in a husky voice, "You'll be so gorgeous, carrying our baby."

I dip my chin to hide my face. Because it doesn't land the way he intends. It makes *everything* worse. I think of my body, my curves—distorted and swollen like a balloon at first, then deflated and misshapen once it's served its biological purpose.

But when I look up, Anton is still glowing. Not just in his face, but deep within. Like he truly can't imagine anything more beautiful. So I grasp that and hold on with everything I've got—because maybe it *could* be the way he says?

"I guess . . . getting there could be fun," I say, trying to convince myself.

And then I giggle. I can't help it. Because, despite some improvement, we've been in therapy because I'm so bad at physical intimacy we almost lost our marriage. And it strikes me as hilarious, hearing myself suggesting *sex* as an incentive.

But Anton doesn't laugh. He arches a brow, stroking circles on the backs of my hands with his thumbs. "Seems like an excellent excuse to do homework."

My face warms, but I nod because he's right. We've probably already had more sex in the last three months than we did in the past three years. At least, until a couple of weeks ago. But I still have to concentrate on it a lot. It *has* started to feel like things are getting easier, more natural. But I know we've still got a ways to go.

He pauses his circles. "We could try some new things . . ."

"New things?"

"Yeah," he says with a perfectly straight face. "We did discuss spanking . . ."

I glance nervously around the crowded room, and hiss. "Stop. Not here."

His eyes darken and he leans close. "Then where do you want it?"

"*Anton.*"

I pull my hands away and cross my arms over my chest--only to realize when he starts chuckling that he's been messing with me. I scowl, leaning back in my chair. But as I glance down at the barely touched dinners going cold in front of us, I decide it's a game we both can play.

"You already owe me one apology, Mr. Richie. Are you looking to grovel?"

His grin fades, one hand drifting to the pocket where he stashed the massage oil. "I am. So sorry," he says in a low voice.

"You should be," I say, raising my hand to flag down the server. "You *know* how much I love the desserts here."

"Hi. Was everything all right?" our waiter asks, glancing cautiously at our uneaten food.

"Delicious," Anton says, his eyes fixed on me.

"That's great to hear . . . Can I interest either of you in dessert?"

"We'll take two boxes." I bite my lip. "We're having dessert at home."

CHAPTER ELEVEN

Him

It is truly a miracle we make it home. After we leave the restaurant, I press Lydia up against the door of my truck and kiss her so deeply, we both come up gasping for air. On the way to the house, we seem to hit every red light, and though my hand starts out politely enough on her knee, every time we come to a stop, my fingers creep a little farther up her dress. Until we pull in the driveway with my pinky dipping beneath the edge of her panties.

Once we get in the door, I lose control.

I feel like I've been starved, unable to decide where I want to touch her first. One hand slips the straps of her dress off her shoulders while the other picks up where it left off beneath her skirt. She's wrapped her arms around my neck and runs her tongue along my jaw, and we nearly fall over the dog trying to greet us as we play what feels like an improvised game of stand-up Twister—right hand ass, left hand tits. There are buttons down the front of her dress, but after fumbling at them a minute, I realize they don't actually do anything. So I spin her around to face the wall, making her laugh while I search for a zipper.

The most glorious thing is, nothing is getting in my way

this time. There's no bottomless, empty feeling, no wall of sadness blocking me from enjoyment. Just a strong, electric *connection* linking the two of us—like there's always been. But still, I pause and take her hand, tugging her gently down the hall.

"Can we—will you just do something for me?"

I lead her to the bathroom and open up the cabinet, carefully removing the round pink compact of birth control pills. Some have been punched out, but more are left than are gone. I extend it to her, meeting her eyes exactly where we stood four nights ago when she very clearly said no.

"Your choice," I say. "If you change your mind, I understand."

Lydia takes the plastic case and turns it over in her hands. Her breath is calm, but she's standing very straight and there's a tension to her movements. Finally, she looks up and seems to search my face. I'm not sure what she finds there, but as I watch, her eyes fill with warmth and her lips slip into a tentative smile. She takes a deep breath, and the next thing I know, she drops the compact with all the pills directly in the trashcan.

"Let's do this," she whispers, laying a soft kiss on my lips.

And that's all I need.

Forget zippers, I take her dress by the hem and pull it straight up over her head. She's left standing there in just a set of sheer white lingerie, and I take a minute to let myself marvel at her body. At her full, round breasts that seem to float above a narrow waist, which then blooms into soft, wide hips. The kind of hips that just *look* designed to bear children. The kind of full, voluptuous breasts that could feed an army of infants. God. Somewhere in the back of my mind, I remember a college biology class where we learned about nature picking and choosing, and I realize now I'm being sucked in by the results. That my wife's body is a con, a product designed to draw me in and get me to spread my seed. I know this, and I am fully fucking embracing it.

I slip my arms out of my jacket, pulling the massage oil from the pocket.

"Where should we—" Lydia's eyes flash to the bottle in my hand, and she wrinkles her nose. "Won't it make a mess?"

"Hopefully a big one," I say, but I grab a couple of towels and stalk her as she giggles into the bedroom, mesmerized by the sway of her ass and the peek of nipple I can see through her sheer bra.

I drape the towels over our bed, hoping that will appease her, though I'd be just as happy to buy a whole new set of sheets when we're through.

She glances at the bed, looking interested, if a bit wary. And for a moment I think she'll need me to help disrupt her thoughts. But then she comes at me, laying kisses all over my face as her fingers work down the buttons on my shirt.

"I feel underdressed," she says.

I growl. "I like you that way."

I let her get my shirt off, then kick out of my shoes and socks and help her remove my jeans, if only because my cock has been straining inside them since dinner. But then my attention is fully back on her. I sweep her long hair to one side and run my fingers along the edge of her bra, circling the darker points of her nipples showing through the material.

"I would like to drip oil right here and watch it drizzle through the fabric," I whisper. "But it's too fucking beautiful on you. I can't bring myself to ruin it."

Instead, I turn her around and undo the clasp, sliding the straps down her arms and reaching around to cup each full, perfect breast in my hands. Her left nipple stands at attention already, but the right side is shyer, and I spend a few moments working and teasing it the way she's shown me, convincing it to come out.

When it does, and Lydia lets out a light moan, I let my

hands travel down, gliding over her curves until I find the waist of her sheer panties. They're beautiful on her and I want to savor them longer, but I'm also dying a little of impatience, and they drop quickly to the floor.

I have no idea what time it is, except that it's late, and we're standing in the glow of a single bedside lamp, but it's light enough to let me take in every inch of her naked body. Instinctively, she moves her hands to cover herself, but I grab hold of her wrists and stop her.

"Please don't. You're so beautiful."

I bring her arms up until they're stretched together above her head, then I hold her wrists there and whisper in her ear.

"Turn for me. So I can look."

She hesitates for half a second, and then rotates, arms still in the air, breasts thrust forward, torso stretched long and gorgeous down to her round hips and naked sex.

"Fuck me," I mutter.

And we're not even to the best part.

"Lie on the bed," I say firmly.

This is something we've discovered in our few months of exploration and sex therapy. Lydia likes to be bossed around. Not in a demeaning or hurtful way. But maybe because she's so uncertain, she seems relieved when I take authority and tell her exactly what to do.

"Like this?" she asks, stretched out on her back like a banquet in front of me.

I grab a pillow and slide it gently under her head, then slip out of my boxer briefs and grab the oil off the nightstand. I lick my lips. "Just like that."

There are no instructions on the bottle, so I just shake it a couple times and break the seal. Lydia looks up at me, watching, her body pink and flushed in anticipation. And suddenly, I'm flooded with gratitude—that I get to do this with her, that we've been able to work through some major hurt in our marriage to have this moment together, despite our flaws.

"I love you," I murmur, then position myself over her with the bottle and watch oil drip and slide over her skin, running down between her breasts.

Lydia watches me do this with wide eyes, almost like she's surprised, pressing her breasts together to catch the oil as it runs over her body. I was already hard, but just the sight of this has me biting my lip, my cock turning to fucking steel.

I take her hand, and she glances up at my face as I drip oil across her palm and place it on my shaft. "Stroke me."

And she does.

Oh. My. God.

Her hand slides up and down, slick and wet, and for a minute it's all I can do to concentrate, stay under control. Not let loose and end our night before it's really begun.

Once I feel I can safely move, I go to work on her while she continues to work me. Pouring oil absolutely everywhere. Probably using up most of the bottle, but I don't care, because my wife looks like something out of a porn video, a fantasy, or at least a wet fucking dream. Every inch of her skin *glistens*. Slick and warm and so. Fucking. Hot.

Some part of my non-primal brain must still be working, because I remember this was supposed to be an actual "massage" and not just *Anton's X-Rated Fantasy Oil Play*, so I run my hands all over her, kneading her muscles, rubbing her skin, and pretending I have any idea what I'm doing while having the fucking time of my life.

Three or four months ago? No way anything like this would have ever happened. But here, tonight, Lydia is down with it. One hundred percent present and accounted for, closing her eyes and tipping her face toward the ceiling. Her hand has fallen away from my cock, but I'm so focused on her I don't even care, watching as gradually, her body seems to sink into the bed, visibly relaxed.

At some point my hand slips between her legs, and when it does her eyes flutter open, gazing at me through a haze of contentment as I slide one oil-slicked finger very intentionally up and down her folds, finding her clit.

She gasps in response, then narrows her eyes. "Is that a legit massage technique?"

"Mmm-hmm," I murmur. "If your masseuse is a sex-crazed lothario without a license."

She turns her head away and laughs. Until I slide farther down, dipping one finger inside her, and her laughter turns into a moan. Sensing I've landed at the elusive right time and place, I follow with a second finger and lean down to find her clit with my tongue.

I didn't buy a flavored massage oil, but it doesn't taste bad—and it is everywhere, so I lose myself a little, lapping up the taste of oil combined with Lydia, and getting lost in her velvety folds. My fingers keep a steady rhythm hooked inside her, and when her hips begin to thrust, I reach up her body until I locate her left nipple, standing out, waiting to be found. A few firm tugs there, several more thrusts of my tongue, and she comes apart, singing like a songbird, her pleasure echoing through our house.

When she comes back to earth, a big shy smile on her face, she looks over and grabs for me, starting to pump my shaft again, a little too fast and hard.

"Whoa, easy." I laugh, flinching away.

She looks up, shamefaced. "Sorry . . ."

I shake my head to reassure her, kissing her hand and shifting until I'm between her legs, staring down at her glistening pussy. Then I rub my cock up and down her slit, sliding easily through the mix of oil and her natural juices.

"Fuck. You're so slick." If I don't push inside her soon, this won't end according to our new plan, so I meet her gaze with intention and ask again. "You ready? Should we do this?"

She looks down at my cock poised outside her entrance, regarding it for a second like it's some kind of loaded weapon. And truly, I feel a bit like a cannon ready to go off inside her, so maybe we're on the same page.

She bites her lip, then looks back up at me, takes a deep breath, and nods. "Yes."

About a second later, I am buried *deep* in my wife, all the way to the fucking hilt. And God, I know we used some extra lube, but I can't remember her ever being so slick and warm and inviting. She has barely adjusted to my intrusion before I start thrusting, nearly losing all control. It's jarring. Obviously, I have been inside Lydia before, and lately sex has been so much better. But this time, with this new goal in mind—to *create* something, put a baby inside her—a strange, almost primal feeling takes over.

I watch my cock sliding in and out of her, watch her oil-slick tits bouncing with every thrust, and my thoughts are consumed by what will happen when I fill her with my seed. I am overtaken by abstract, carnal *need*, and with all of that churning through my mind, it doesn't take long for me to reach my peak—with a few great thrusts, I release inside her, and it is the most fucking fulfilling sensation I have ever had. I continue to rock into her, slowing, until I am completely spent. And then I gather her in my arms and pull her to me, overcome with joy, with gratitude, with emotions I can't describe.

"Thank you."

She strokes my hair, not saying a word, lying against my chest as we listen to each other breathe. I'm vaguely aware when she slides out of bed to go to the bathroom, but she soon returns, nuzzling back into my arms under the sheets.

"I love you, Mr. Richie," she whispers into my neck, and my heart is so full in this moment, with these words.

"I love you, Lydia. So much."

CHAPTER TWELVE

I CONSIDER PULLING MY PILLS OUT OF THE TRASH WHEN I SLIP away into the bathroom. Just sneaking the plastic case into the pocket of my robe and quietly taking them the rest of the month. Not really changing the plan so much as giving myself an extension. I mull it over while I pee, flushing away every drop of him I can squeeze out into the toilet. Anton checked in with me twice while we made love, asking if I was ready, and I said yes.

Because I am.

I thought it over all day before we went out. I thought about it through dinner. And again, before telling him to push inside me. Yes, I have a thousand reservations about pregnancy. About becoming a mother. I worry how it will change things—how it will change me. Not to mention our entire lives.

And though it was reassuring hearing Anton declare that we don't *need* to have a baby, I feel better going into this with intention. I can do this—for our future together. But also for him. Because he is clearly hurting for family, and who am I to deny something he wants so badly?

So, I leave the pills in the trash, and we stay in bed most of

Saturday and Sunday, relishing in our reconnection. Not making love the whole time, though we do more than once. But also talking, snuggling, and just being together. Gently erasing those four unpleasant days when we barely spoke while I tell myself hardly anyone gets pregnant on the first try.

Charlotte, my good friend, lawyer, and business mentor, invites me to lunch Monday, so I structure my morning around that, trying to push all thoughts of conception, pregnancy, and babies out of my mind. Ooh La Pooch isn't open Mondays, so this is my day to catch up, re-center, and refocus, and I am grateful Charlotte is willing to offer me her guidance. She helped facilitate the deal where Henry came on as my partner, and I'm anxious to check in with her about some of the ideas he's proposed for the Pooches.

Normally, Charlotte makes reservations for the two of us in stylish Cherry Creek North. Hillstone is a favorite of hers, or sometimes Cucina Colore. But today she is bringing along another of her mentees and asked if we could meet at Bread Bowls, a casual soup and sandwich spot. Which is actually fine. This way, I won't have to change clothes before I head to The Pooch Park.

After I place my order at the counter, Charlotte crosses the room and greets me in her standard suit and heels. She's a short, elegant Asian woman, with graying chin-length hair and a pink suit that matches her lipstick.

"Thanks for meeting us here, Lydia. I know it's not our usual fare, but I'm excited to introduce you and Marisol."

"Of course." I smile. I'll admit, I had been hoping for a more intimate conversation with Charlotte today, but she's so generous with her time and advice I'm not surprised she's in high demand.

She leads me toward a booth tucked away in the corner

where a petite Latina woman about my age is situating a pigtailed toddler in a high chair.

"Marisol, this is my friend, Lydia Richie, who owns the grooming shop and doggie daycares." Charlotte turns to me. "Marisol just—"

"*Mama!*" The little girl in the high chair shrieks.

Marisol turns to her immediately. "What's the matter, bebé?"

The baby looks up with wide brown eyes, reaching over the side of her chair toward a dropped toy on the floor.

"Uh-oh." Marisol retrieves the toy, then turns back to Charlotte and me with a tight smile. "Thanks for being flexible today. My ex was supposed to take Paloma, but canceled on me last minute."

I nod quickly, like I totally get it, but something tightens low in my stomach as I watch her lay a plastic placemat and a selection of cut up fruit in front of her daughter. Charlotte and I slide into the opposite side of the booth, and as Marisol unloads toys from a diaper bag, my hopes for a productive business conversation dwindle.

The little girl smiles shyly at me, and since I'm not sure what else to do, I give her a tentative wave. She grins and hides her face behind a toy, which even I have to admit is pretty cute.

"How old is she?" I ask, trying to make conversation. "She looks just like you."

"Thanks. She's almost eighteen months." Marisol scatters a rainbow of Goldfish crackers on the placemat.

I smile and nod, wondering what Charlotte thinks we have in common. "So, are you looking at starting a business, or—"

"*Sorry*, we were interrupted." Charlotte jumps in. "Marisol runs a subscription box company, Lydia. They have several concepts, but you've probably heard of WoofCrate?"

My mouth forms an *oh*, and I blush, deeply and immediately. "Yes. I absolutely have. Most of my clients rave about WoofCrate. You guys have some seriously cute toys and treats."

"Thanks." Marisol nods. "My company has a variety of subscription products, but the dog boxes have definitely been the most popular."

"Which is why I *had* to introduce you two," Charlotte says with a grin. "Marisol just relocated to Denver, and I'm trying to help introduce her to the business community while she settles in."

Marisol nods. "What's the name of your doggie daycare? I'd love somewhere to take our little Biscochito."

"Bizkit!" the little girl shrieks from the end of the table, startling me.

"That's right, 'Bizkit,'" Marisol says with a smile, handing her a sippy cup. "He's a little mutt I've had for years. Paloma is obsessed with him."

Our names echo over the loudspeaker, and Charlotte hops up. "You two keep chatting. I'll grab the food."

As Charlotte steps away, Paloma stares at me with wide brown eyes, then hands me a red crayon.

"Um . . . thank you," I say, reluctantly taking it from her sticky hand. "So, what brings you to Denver?" I ask, refocusing on her mother.

"My ex, unfortunately." Marisol sniffs, then rolls her eyes. "We split up shortly after I got here. But so far, the weather and lifestyle have been worth staying for."

"Oh." Her attitude reminds me a little of Caprice, though I can't imagine my best friend weighed down with a kid. "Yeah, it's great here. But I'm sorry about . . ."

She winks at me. "I'm not."

"Lydia, I was telling Marisol about your meteoric growth." Charlotte returns to the table distributing plates of food, then slides in next to me with her sandwich.

Marisol nods. "It sounds impressive. I wish I'd had an

investor waiting to swoop in and fund me before I expanded."

I raise my brows. "Did you go through something similar?"

She passes a few raisins off her salad to Paloma, who dutifully puts them in her mouth. "I'd been running absolutely everything myself, and I was exhausted. But I was also expecting this one." She nods to Paloma. "So I had to do something."

My gut feels like a stone as I try to imagine running all my businesses, trying to level them up, *and* prepare for a baby. It seems wrong, but every time I imagine what pregnancy might be like, I just envision a ticking time bomb.

"Obviously, it's a little different, since my model isn't directly client-facing," she goes on. "But I reached a point where I had to step up my production, which meant securing capital, bringing in more employees, and ceding a lot of control."

"Yeah." I glance at Charlotte. "The ah, control thing has been kind of a pain point for me."

Marisol smiles. "It's a major adjustment, taking that leap from relative stability into expansion. But it's imperative if you want to grow."

I clear my throat, humbled that my expectations about this meeting had been so very wrong. "My business partner, Henry, has suggested we consolidate our daycares and grooming shop for growth."

Charlotte's eyebrows shoot up, but then she gets a pensive look. "Actually, I can see why that probably makes sense."

"Hmm. Are you planning to continue growing organically, or are you considering a franchise?" Marisol asks.

"Oh, definitely—" I'm about to say *organic*, but I glance at Charlotte and knot my fingers. She'd brought up franchising some months ago, right before Henry bought into the Pooches.

"Lydia is primed for a franchise." Charlotte nudges my elbow. "I've been trying to tell her that for at least six months."

"Oh, I'm jealous." Marisol grins. "I'm not set up for it, but I wish I was. A franchise would be the dream, wouldn't it?" She chuckles. "Just set it and forget it, and watch the income roll in."

"I—I guess." I squirm a little. "I do enjoy running my Pooches, though."

Marisol straightens. "I would love to see your operation sometime."

I unknot my fingers, pulling out a business card that lists our locations, grateful for a more comfortable subject. "Sure. Bring Bizkit by The Pooch Park sometime and see if he likes it."

"Thanks." She takes the card with a smile and glances at her pigtailed toddler, who is now driving raisins like cars around her placemat. "I don't suppose you have any *child* daycare recommendations while we're at it?"

I laugh nervously. "Oh, my husband and I don't have kids . . ."

My pelvic muscles clench, my skin going clammy, wondering how true that statement really is. I suppose there might be a little cluster of cells dividing inside me right now. I push my plate away, appetite evaporating.

"Paloma definitely wasn't in my business plan." Marisol laughs softly, gazing at her daughter. "But somehow, once she got here, she became my *why*."

At these words, the baby starts kicking her legs, making a loud yodeling sound and rubbing her eyes with sticky fists. Marisol sighs, pushing her mostly finished lunch aside, packing up the snacks and placemat.

"That might be about all the meeting time I can ask of her. It's getting close to naptime."

I glance at my phone. We've barely been here half an hour.

"I can't believe how well you balance everything," Charlotte says, watching Marisol wipe Paloma's hands with practiced efficiency. "You make it look easy."

Marisol snorts, but as we rise from the booth to say goodbye, I'm dismayed the conversation has to end. It felt like we were just getting started.

"Guess I'll cave and get my dog that WoofCrate subscription he's been begging for," I say with a laugh. "Sorry I'm no help with childcare. But I'm serious—please come by The Pooch Park. I'd love to talk more."

Marisol lifts her daughter out of the high chair, sets her down, and gives me a warm smile. "Thanks, I'd like that too. Say goodbye, Paloma."

"Buh-BYE!" the little girl shrieks, waving a fisted napkin.

Charlotte moves across from me to finish her sandwich after they leave, and a Bread Bowls employee comes over to put the high chair away and sweep a huge amount of crumbs off the rug.

"Have you and Anton thought about having kids?" Charlotte asks suddenly.

I nearly choke on my baguette, my hackles immediately raised, just like when my mother asks. I glance at her, wondering if it's possible I *am* pregnant already and there's some way she can tell. But when I meet her eyes, there's no implication, just mild curiosity.

"Uh, I don't know. We've . . . talked about it."

She picks at her fruit salad. "I never found anyone I wanted to settle down with. Sometimes it feels like I might've missed out." She looks pointedly at the mess being swept up under Paloma's seat and shrugs. "Most of the time it doesn't."

I am going to hyperventilate trying to think of how to answer. Instead, I tiptoe to a safer subject. "Thanks for introducing me and Marisol. I'm excited to connect with her."

She preens. "I enjoy seeing my fellow businesswomen

succeed." We gather up our dishes, placing them in the designated bins as we head for the door. "But next time, we dine in Cherry Creek."

CHAPTER THIRTEEN

Him

"Looks more promising," Seth says as I pull my truck in front of the fourth apartment building on our list. So far, we've been striking out. The first place we saw turned out to be a dump. The second was great until we realized they wouldn't allow pets. And while the third seemed to check all the necessary boxes, the property manager couldn't explain its terrible, unidentifiable smell. Both of us are a bit frustrated at this point, but it's so nice just to have Seth *here*. If I have to spend the entire weekend house hunting with him to make that permanent, I will.

I open the door of my truck, hoping the fourth time's the charm. But when I look over, I notice my brother isn't actually eyeing the building we're here to see, but a high-rise across the street with a couple of cute girls standing outside.

"Hey, Casanova," I say, pointing the other way. "*This* is the place we're looking at."

Seth glances at the dated brick building behind me, sniffs, and turns back around. "What's wrong with that one?"

I snort, craning to look at the two brand-new, mirrored towers stretching at least thirty stories up. This is one of those neighborhoods dotted with a mix of small, older buildings and immense new luxury residences. As we stand there, a black Porsche Cayenne purrs up to the entrance and a guy in a three-piece suit steps out of the back seat, trailed by a woman taking selfies with a chihuahua dressed in a coordinating outfit.

"A little out of your league."

Seth raises one brow like I've presented him with a challenge, straightens the hem of his T-shirt over his jeans, and strides inside.

"I could see myself here," he says as I chase him through the automatic doors.

"Sure, great. Maybe as an extra for some influencer. Can we get back across the street so we don't miss the manager at the other place?"

He ignores me, so I follow helplessly as he enters a lobby that feels like a freaking luxury hotel—complete with plush furniture, pretentious artwork, an enormous fireplace, and a concierge desk.

"Hi there," Seth says, approaching a curly haired young white woman behind the counter. She does nothing to conceal the fact that she's scoping him out. "I'm interested in becoming a resident. Can you tell me if cats are allowed?"

"Oh, of course." Her face brightens. "Pets are always welcome at the Washington Park Towers. We actually have an in-house pet spa."

"You're kidding," I say, though I'm the last person who should be surprised. Lydia built her businesses on exactly this sort of demand.

"Are you familiar with our brand of living?" she asks. "Our residents expect the best, and that includes furry family members." She waves to someone over my shoulder, and I glance back to see a well-groomed lady entering the lobby with an equally well-coiffed poodle. "Do you have an appointment with our relocation specialist?"

Seth opens his mouth to answer, but I jump in. "We don't.

We'll have to make one and come back. Thanks for your time."

With that, I try to steer my brother out the doors. Seth's been working with some hot-shot real estate investors in Dallas, and while he's apparently done well flipping houses, there's no way he can afford this place.

"Whoa, hang on a sec." He places a hand on my chest and makes doe eyes at the girl. "Would it be possible to take a tour without an appointment? Actually, would *you* be available to take us on one?" He glances at the name tag on her blazer. "Eden?"

He gives her his best panty-melting smile, and when she giggles, my shoulders slump.

"Seth," I mutter. "I doubt this place is going to be in your price range."

He regards me with a patient smile. "Why don't you let me be the judge of that?"

I shoot Lydia a text to say we'll likely be late for dinner while Seth hands over his driver's license. The woman briefly disappears, and then we're off on an unofficial tour of the most ridiculously luxe living in Denver.

"As you can see, every resident of the Washington Park Towers can expect a level of luxury and service you won't find elsewhere," she says, leading us through the swank lobby toward the elevators. "The towers are joined up to the fifth floor pool deck and include a co-working space, lounge and game space, and a full-service bar." We exit the elevator onto what could only be the aforementioned pool deck. "In addition to our salt water pool and hot tub, we have a complete fitness center and offer an array of health and wellness services."

Seth strolls out onto the pool deck, hands clasped behind him like he's a man of leisure and isn't sleeping on my couch tonight after living in our mom's two-bedroom ranch the last five years. The pristine turquoise pool stretches between the two buildings with a row of loungers resting on a shallow shelf in the water, the entirety of its rectangle shape lined with cabanas and fire pits. There is an admittedly stunning view to the west—capturing the sweeping purple snow-capped mountains that bring to mind the lyrics of *America The Beautiful,* which is framed exquisitely between the two mirrored towers. Though I remind myself, everyone in Denver gets to enjoy that view without the price tag on this place.

The day has been hot, and Seth's gaze lingers on a young Black woman and a blonde stretched out in bikinis on the loungers. He turns to the concierge in her dress pants and blazer, looking her over like she's one of them. "So, do *you* ever get to come enjoy the pool yourself?"

She giggles again, twisting one finger through her curls. "Well, I haven't really had the chance to . . ."

I roll my eyes, stepping away to text Lydia.

> Seth is descending into hedonism. Send help.

LYDIA

LOL, where are you guys?

> This double tower place by Wash Park. It's ridiculous.

LYDIA

Oh, that's near Caprice's building! We went inside once. It's next level.

Is he really looking there?

I glance over my shoulder at my brother touring the deck like a Rockefeller, and while the whole scenario he's dragged me into is truly ridiculous, I can't help smiling. I've missed him. We've seen each other off and on the last several years, but almost all of our interactions have been limited to phone calls and visits related to our mom's decline. It feels good, having him here, doing something . . . well, maybe not normal, but one hundred percent *Seth*.

> He's having fun. But we'll prob need to look at some more reasonable places tomorrow.

LYDIA

> If you guys want to stay out later, go ahead. You know I can always find reasons to work late.

> I thought the goal was for you NOT to work so late.

LYDIA

> Yes. But I've been at Ooh La Pooch all day anyway, and Seth's only here for the weekend . . .

My brother leans casually against a wall, hovering over the concierge, who bats her eyelashes up at him.

> Seth might have other plans tonight.

> Do I need to come bend you over one of your grooming tables and remind you about work-life balance?

She doesn't reply right away, and I allow myself a wicked smile, taking a moment to imagine her face turning a deep shade of red at my text. Hopefully in front of a customer. I have to admit, I wasn't expecting Lydia to do a one-eighty on starting a family. But since I was already determined to reconnect no matter what, the fact that she *did* kind of opened a floodgate. I'd listened to a whole podcast on dirty talk before we went out the other night, and I have realized what a useful tool it is to help Lydia focus. It doesn't take much at all to make her squirm.

Finally, my phone buzzes again.

LYDIA

I'm not sure our therapist would agree with
your strategy.

But did I get you wet thinking about it?

Someone clears their throat behind me, and I glance back to find Seth holding the elevator, waiting for me.

"If you'd like to join us, there is a one-bedroom condo I can show you on the eighteenth floor," the concierge says beside him.

My brother gives me a look as we enter the elevator and rise through the floors, and for a second I'm certain he knows I've been sexting my wife.

Then I realize he'd probably approve.

Eden leads us down a plush hallway once we reach eighteen and opens up a door all the way at the end. "This unit has been freshly vacated, but it will give you an idea of what we have available."

Even my jaw drops when we walk into the residence. It's an open concept where the kitchen, living, and dining areas all flow into one another, giving it a spacious feel. The floors are gleaming polished concrete, and while all the fixtures and appliances are sleek and modern, the space still feels warm and inviting. Very much like a home. Seth wanders toward the wall of windows across the room, and I duck through a door leading to a bedroom and bath off to the left. Which, as I expect at this point, is just as expansive and fully appointed, with high-end brass fixtures, a free-standing tub, and separate rain shower. I turn to ask Seth a question when I realize he hasn't made it in here yet. I give Eden a polite nod as I walk back out to the living area, then join my brother standing by the wall of floor-to-ceiling windows.

"The view here isn't one of the best or most private since it directly faces the other tower," Eden says with a note of apology. "But you can still see the mountains if you look off to the southwest. And other units will be coming available."

"I like the view just fine," Seth mutters. He's staring fixedly across the way toward the windows of the matching building, and though I catch a flash of movement, I can't tell exactly what he's focused on.

"Are you done playing?" I whisper to him under my breath. "This has been fun, but . . . maybe tomorrow we can find a more reasonable spot?"

"Bruno would sure appreciate these windows." Seth works his jaw, gaze still focused on the opposite building. Finally, he straightens and turns to Eden. "I'll take it."

"You—wait, *what?*" I can't help myself. Pretending was one thing, but this is a step too far.

"Yeah. I'll take it." Seth pulls his gaze from the window, looking somewhat annoyed. But he doesn't speak to me. He just turns to the eager woman behind us. "I don't mind the view at all."

By the time my brother comes out of the real estate office, I have paced the entirety of the common floors, past the fitness center, in-house spa, multiple lounges and outdoor fire pits. But I still can't understand what Seth is up to or why. I know he's excited to get out of Dallas and start his life in Denver. Maybe this is a reaction to newfound freedom after essentially being a caregiver to our mom his entire adult life. I'm just worried about him getting in over his head, or at the very least, ruining his credit.

"All right. Should we grab Lydia and get dinner? I'm starved," Seth says when he finds me in the lobby.

"What the hell were you doing in there?" I ask, rising from one of the buttery soft leather couches.

"Credit application, deposit, all the normal stuff." He

shrugs. "Turns out cute little Eden has a boyfriend. Probably for the best."

"They let you put down a deposit? How? You don't have a job here yet. You've never even rented before. And even if Mom's house sells above asking price, it will never cover the price tag of even a studio here."

"I guess my account balance was enough for them. Can we eat?"

I follow him out the doors, my throat dry as a desert. "Okay, so I guess they have no issues taking advantage of people. Fine. But *I'm* here to look out for you, and Mom would totally flip if I let you—"

"Anton. I can afford it."

He's stopped on the sidewalk, looking me straight in the eye. My brother might be ninety percent showman, but we've never lied to one another.

"How?"

"Real estate's been good." He shoves his hands in his pockets. "I haven't had to pay rent living at Mom's the last four years, so I've been able to save up, and I made some smart investments. I've learned a lot. But this place isn't an investment; it's for *me*."

I close my eyes. "I just . . . I don't want you to do something you'll regret."

"I'll regret *not* living here," he says with a pointed look back up at the high-rise. "But you've got to trust me. The price tag isn't an issue."

We walk in silence back to my truck, and I try to wrap my head around all of this. I'm not sure what bothers me more. That my brother, who majored in *philosophy* at the University of Texas has apparently been killing it flipping houses. Or that I didn't know.

"Let's just pick something up," he says, glancing at the clock. "Lydia must be starving by now."

I glance at my texts and something curls in my gut. She never replied to my last one and I wonder if she thought it was hot, or if I pushed her too far. "Text her for me. Ask what she wants . . . and find out if she went home," I say, starting the car.

Seth chuckles, fingers tapping over his screen, then blithely asks, "How *are* things with you guys?"

My grip immediately tenses on the wheel. Apparently Seth knows more about the ups and downs of my marriage than I know about his whole life. But I quickly exhale, guiding the truck in the general direction of our house.

"Uh, it's been pretty good."

He waits patiently as I navigate through a busy intersection.

"I mean, guess I can't lie, things felt a bit dark right after Mom's service."

"Sucks being a couple of orphans." He nods.

"Yeah . . ." I hadn't thought of it that way. And for just a second that awful, vacant feeling starts creeping back into my chest, shortening my breaths. But then I look over at my brother and think about spending the evening with him. With Lydia. Once he moves here, we'll get to see each other all the time. And, I realize with sudden warmth, he'll be *such* a fun uncle to our kid. "I'm glad you're coming to Denver."

Seth grins. "I like it here. And I definitely need a change of scene."

His phone buzzes, and he snorts, fingers flying in response. "Lydia suggests we pick up from Little Anita's. She *also* says you took too long and she went home, but she'll consider a rain check."

I suck in a breath. At least that question's answered.

Seth's phone buzzes again, and this time he laughs out loud. "She says to tell you: *Love is not just something you feel, it's something you do.*" He looks at me sideways. "Did she just one-up me while flirting with you? I feel used."

I turn toward Little Anita's, my mood steadily improving.

My brother continues his back and forth with my wife, or so I assume, as he types wildly, pauses, then types some more. But when he doesn't share any more with me, a distinctly suspicious feeling creeps in. Which is validated when I pull into a parking space in front of the restaurant and Seth clears his throat. "Things are okay with you guys though, right?"

"You already asked that."

"Uh, I'm just being thorough," he says, fidgeting with my phone charger. "And um . . . *you* feel okay?"

"My wife just used you to insinuate she wants to have sex with me." I gesture toward his phone. "I'm fucking great, Seth."

"Can't argue with that." He laughs, but it sounds hollow. "I just—you've been through a lot this year with each other, and then Mom—"

"We're better than ever," I say quickly, and before I can think it through, "Actually, we're going to try for a kid."

The words hang in the air a surprising amount of time before Seth finally says, "Really?"

My shoulders tense at the surprise in his tone. "What? She didn't already tell you?" I snap, looking pointedly at his phone. Though part of me kind of wishes she had.

"Hey, don't get mad at Lydia." He holds up his hands. "I was the one who—"

"I know." I draw my hand over my face. "You two aren't exactly subtle. Whispering to each other, organizing this visit, comparing notes. I appreciate the concern, I really do, but Mom *just* died. It's going to take some time."

"I'm sorry, man." Seth exhales, then meets my gaze. "You're right. I need to back off. I just . . . want things to feel right again."

My pulse pounds in my temple. "Believe me. I do too."

"So . . . a baby, huh?" he says after a minute, in a forced tone. "You two sure you're ready for that?"

"You're the one who told me to *make our own family*."

He hesitates a long moment. "Not sure I meant—"

I open my door, forcing him out of the car. "Seth, let's get the food and get home. Celebrate Mom's house going under contract, and your cat's ridiculous new bachelor pad. But after that, you may remember my previously frigid wife is waiting to have sex with me, so . . . you can borrow my car keys. Or if you prefer, I have earplugs."

Seth follows me into the restaurant with a huff. "That's supposed to be my line."

CHAPTER FOURTEEN

WHEN I WALK INTO OOH LA POOCH JUST BEFORE SIX P.M. ON Tuesday, I'm surprised to find Henry, of all people, standing in one of his expensive suits in a pile of dog hair, speaking with my grooming manager, Scarlet. Judging by the looks on their faces, it's a heated conversation. When she sees me, she reddens and steps away from him, combing through the ears of the already immaculately groomed bichon frise on the table in front of her. Henry also takes a step back, bumping into one of the stand dryers.

"Lydia. I—uh, I thought you were at Pooch II today." He straightens, brushing at the sleeve of his jacket. "I was just . . . explaining the new POS system to Ms. Lawson."

I glance again at Scarlet, who looks like she's hoping the earth will swallow him. They're nowhere near the register.

"Yes, thanks for your *helpful* explanation, Mr. Hill," our employee says, sweeping the dog off the table and placing him in a kennel. With a flip of her purple ponytail, she starts stomping around, putting away her combs and brushes. Henry follows her closely with his eyes, but doesn't say anything.

Weird.

I head for the desk, glancing around the rest of the shop. Daniela and Alicia must have already gone home. There are only two other dogs awaiting pickup in the kennels against the wall.

"I just came in to run reports on the new system," I say. Which isn't really true. Scarlet texted me earlier that the tub drains were running slow. But I'm not in a hurry to bring that to Henry's attention.

"Right. Well." He shifts from one foot to the other. "I need to get going. Ah . . ." He glances back at Scarlet, hesitating a beat too long. "Good to see you, Ms. Lawson."

She meets his gaze, and for just a second it looks like she's going to say something. But then she presses her mouth into a line and turns away, and he's gone.

I bite my lip, not sure what to say. "Is um . . . is everything okay?"

Scarlet and I aren't close. She's a fantastic groomer, but an incredibly flaky employee, and kind of a mess personally, from what I know. Henry initially suggested we give her a raise and make her a manager to see if more responsibility would ground her, but I half expect her to just ghost us one day.

"Mmph," is all she says, slamming cage doors and snatching up a broom to start sweeping up dog hair.

The owner of a little schnauzer comes in at that moment, and I fumble through Henry's irritating point of sale system, but manage to check them out. Once the client is gone, I glance back at Scarlet and try a new subject. "So, did you and Trent do anything fun over the weekend?"

"*No,*" she hisses. "Why does everyone keep asking?"

Yikes. I set down the tablet and really look at her as she takes off her grooming apron and throws it into the laundry, her cropped T-shirt revealing a glittery belly button ring.

"Who else is asking?"

She freezes, eyes widening for a moment before she

exhales. "Never mind," she mutters, pulling the elastic out of her ponytail and shaking out her dyed curls.

I furrow my brow, still unsure of what I saw when I got here. "Scarlet, if there's anything you—"

"If you're going to be here, do you mind sending the rest of my dogs home? I just remembered I need to . . . be somewhere."

Before I have the chance to answer, she gathers up her things and sweeps out the door. For a fleeting second after she's gone, I consider calling Henry to ask what happened. If there's an issue between them, I should help sort it out.

Except . . . something tells me it might be better for me to mind my own business, at least for now. So I let it go and walk back to check on the drains in the bathing room.

I'm elbow deep in stagnant water when my text alert goes off in my pocket.

ANTON

Just leaving the gym. Do you want to eat out tonight? Or stay in?

Plumbing issues at Ooh La Pooch. Again. Not sure what time I'll get home.

Can you feed Heartthrob?

He doesn't answer immediately, so I run the trash to the dumpster and check out the bichon and a border collie when their owners show up. Then I really get to work on the tub drains, trying to figure out the source of the backup once it's clear they're indeed running slow.

I am standing in one of our two raised steel bathtubs, trying to get better leverage on the plunger over the drain because nothing else so far has worked, when Heartthrob runs in wagging his tail. The dog takes one look at me standing in the bathtub, cocks his head, and barks in total confusion.

"I could ask you the same thing," I say to him.

Anton comes in behind him with a plastic bag. "We brought you dinner."

My brows shoot up. "Oh, you're amazing. Thank you." I glance at the clock on the wall in the bathing room and grimace. It's later than I thought. I start to climb out, and Anton sets the bag aside to help me down.

"We thought you might need some sustenance. Your text sounded stressed," he says, guiding me to the floor with his hands at my waist.

"Really? You got all of that from two texts?"

"Yep. And your order for a Colorado Club from Mr. Lucky's."

I gasp, leaning in to kiss him. "Your interpretive skills are amazing, Mr. Richie."

He chuckles. "What's going on with the tub?"

My mood sours a little. "Both are draining slow, but nothing I do seems to help."

"And let me guess, you want to try and fix this without Henry lecturing you about the cost of a plumber?" He gestures to the drain.

I sigh. "You are *so* good."

Anton grins, then hands me the bag of sandwiches. "Why don't you let me work on it while you eat?"

I take the food without argument, having already tried everything I can think of to get the drains flowing. Heartthrob dances around me as I walk back to the front of the shop, dim the lights, and lock the front door. I dig into the stash of chews I keep in a desk drawer for him and he settles happily inside one of the empty kennels.

I have just finished a club sandwich that tastes like a turkey and avocado dream when Anton steps out of the back, shirtless, with a giant grin on his face. "Fixed it."

I stare at him. "No way. How?"

I hurry past the four empty grooming stations back to the bathing room, where I'm immediately hit with a familiar, putrid, wet smell.

"Oh." I cover my mouth and nose. "The hair trap. Why don't I ever remember that?"

Anton nods, closing the trap access in the floor. He runs a trashcan full of soaked, compacted dog hair to the dumpster and the smell immediately subsides. Even better, the tubs drain perfectly now.

"Thank you. I feel so stupid," I say, shaking my head when he returns. "I didn't even think to check that."

I trail off as Anton steps out of the bathroom drying his hands on a paper towel. Maybe it's my relief at having one problem solved. Or that we're here alone. Or just the fact that he looks like a god without his shirt on, but I find myself drinking him in. Something I know I don't do often enough.

"Have I ever told you how much I appreciate you getting your hands dirty to fix something yourself?" I say, stepping toward him.

"It's a strategy," he says, pulling me into his strong arms. "I don't mind being your handyman when you look at me like that."

I blush a little, eyes on the floor. "It's...um, super sexy."

Anton puffs up, flexing his biceps until I can't help giggling. And I adore the answering rumble of laughter that rolls from his chest. But it fades after a moment as he looks at me more seriously. "I've been meaning to ask . . . how are you feeling? Is anything . . . different?"

He holds me at arm's length, gaze traveling down my body like he's drinking me in. Until he centers on my middle, and I realize what he's asking.

"Oh." My cheeks warm. I shrug, looking away. "No, nothing so far . . ."

"When can we take a test?"

It strikes me as odd that he says *we*, but I blink and smile, sharing what I learned from a hasty internet search a couple days ago. "I'm supposed to wait till after a missed period. But we'll know soon enough. Mine is due this week."

His face seems to fall when I mention this, and I reach for him, drawing him close again, placing his hands back on my hips.

"I mean, maybe it won't come," I say, feeling weirdly reassured that I *don't* feel any different.

He raises his gaze to mine, eyes sparkling. He reaches for his discarded shirt, but I grab it out of his hands.

"Um, I—I like you better without it."

His lips tug into a smirk. "You're doing an excellent job on your homework."

I try not to blush. We saw the therapist yesterday, and my new assignment is to let Anton know when I find him attractive—something he has never struggled to do for me.

His eyes traverse my body. "Maybe you'd be better off without yours, too."

A burst of delight thrills inside my chest, and I take a moment to admit maybe the therapist has the right approach. I have always pulled away from this sort of back and forth. So uncomfortable in my own body, I never knew how to respond —how to nurture my own desire. I would simply avoid anything that might encourage my husband's touch.

But . . . I think I'm starting to crave it.

"Come on," I whisper. "Let's get home." I lead the way into the darkened front room of the grooming salon, but before I can stir Heartthrob out of his kennel, Anton's arm slips around my waist, pulling me back.

"You *should* have been home hours ago," he says into my ear.

I go still, a ribbon of guilt twisting through my middle. "I —I'm sorry. You're right. Things got away—"

"Didn't I warn you about working too much?" he growls, stubble tickling my cheek.

My eyes widen. I look around the darkened shop, at the shadows of four grooming stations lined up with four mirrors along the wall.

Do I need to come bend you over one of your grooming tables and remind you about work-life balance?

"I—" I gasp, a light tingle starting up between my legs. "You did."

He turns me in his arms, and I can see the arousal on his face in the dim porch light shining through the window. Feel it in the way he's gripping my ass.

I glance at the huge glass window at the front of the shop.

"Is the door locked?" he mutters in my ear, following my train of thought.

"Yes." My pulse spikes. "But . . . what if someone looks in?"

His mouth locks over mine, smothering my anxiety. "What if they do?"

And I realize from his tone he *likes* that idea. The risk of getting caught. Of being seen.

My chest pounds. I have to admit—it has never once occurred to me to have sex at work. It is possibly the least sexy place I can think of doing it. Not only that, it just seems . . . *wrong*. Not necessarily taboo, but like coloring outside the lines. Or crossing the street without a walk signal.

"Lydia," he says in an authoritative voice I recognize. It's one he's been cultivating to get me out of my own thoughts. "We are married. You own this place. We can fuck here if we want to."

Another flash of sensation zips through my core. I look up, and he walks me backward, holding my gaze, until I'm pinned against the grooming table in the shadows at the very back of the shop.

"And I can't lie," he growls, "I've *always* wanted to."

"I . . ." I gasp as his hand snakes under my shirt, pulling the cup of my bra aside to tweak my nipple. I bite back a groan. "It *is* pretty dark back here . . ."

"Yes," he whispers. "And your handyman just found a couple things that still need fixing."

He lifts me almost without effort, seating me on the grooming table, then reaches under my shirt and slips it over my head in one swift movement. One side of my bra is still pulled down, exposing my left breast, and he leans in to suck my nipple into his mouth while reaching around to unfasten the clasp.

"*Oh,*" I exclaim as he very gently bites down. And then he pulls away, leaning to one side to drape my bra on the little peg where we usually hang dog collars.

He steps back to look at me and narrows his eyes. "Don't move."

He disappears into the bathing room, and I startle at the reflection of my naked torso in the mirror on the back wall across from me. The one we typically use to see all angles of a dog's haircut. I cover myself with my arms, glancing over my shoulder toward the front door. Ooh La Pooch sits in a little strip of shops in an otherwise quiet neighborhood. There is a florist and a real estate office, but no restaurants or shops that would be open late. And while the porch light filters through the glass enough for us to see each other, the glare outside will keep anyone from seeing in unless they come right up to the window.

But still . . . I can't help thinking someone *will* come along and peer in.

"Eyes on me," Anton says, drawing my attention as he comes back from the bathing room holding a clean towel.

"Anton, maybe we should . . ." I trail off when I notice how he's looking at me. Like he's just walked in on something he's always wanted to see.

"The only thing hotter than you sitting here topless would be you on that table completely fucking naked." His eyes light up when I squirm at his words, but his voice quickly softens. "If you'd rather go home to our bed where you feel safer, I'll take you. As long as we can go right now."

I bite my lip. I am dying a little, knowing that he wants to do this *here,* on display. In a place I spend hours as a professional during the day. I glance at the front window through the mirror and shiver, feeling so exposed. But I know Anton wouldn't put me in a position where anything bad was likely to happen. We're in here with the lights off and the doors locked, after hours. And one glance at the bulge in his pants tells me he is *very* excited about that. Even if I'm struggling.

And when I think how different things were when we got home from Dallas—how sad he was, how he pulled away—I don't want to do *anything* to change how he's looking at me now.

Slowly, I slide off the grooming table until my feet touch the floor. Keeping my eyes locked on his, I kick my shoes off, slip my fingers under my waistband, and peel my leggings to the floor.

A few moments later, I'm standing in front of him, in the middle of Ooh La Pooch, in just a lacy purple thong.

"Fuck, Lydia," he mutters under his breath. "You don't know how many times I've imagined you here, just like this."

"You—You have?" I say, eyes locked on the floor.

He traces a finger up my side, sending a shiver through my skin. "Before Unmatched. Nights you were here working late and I was home—waiting, and waiting. I always fantasized about driving over and showing you just how much I missed you."

I raise my head, catching movement in the mirror—the shadow of someone walking a dog across the street. I suck in a breath, holding it until they move out of sight. But when they do, when nothing happens and it's still just the two of us, alone in the dark, I straighten. Emboldened.

"Show me," I whisper, stepping closer to him, allowing the tingle between my legs to course into a throb. "Show me what you would have done."

CHAPTER FIFTEEN

Him

I DON'T NEED TO BE INVITED TWICE. I CLOSE THE SPACE BETWEEN us, tip her head back, and kiss her deep, the bare skin of my chest hot against her naked flesh. My hand tangles in her hair, pulling her head back, exposing the column of her neck in the dim light. My grip is gentle, but firm as I run my lips along the edge of her throat, waiting until she emits the softest moan.

Then I release her, watching with a small smirk as she wavers on her feet, bewildered as to why I've let her go. I unfurl the fluffy towel I grabbed from the back, whipping it over the hard plastic grooming table like I'm a magician transforming the surface. I move to the far end and remove the curved metal grooming arm arcing over the top, setting it aside on the floor. Then I turn back to where she watches me.

"Bend over and hold the edge, Mrs. Richie."

I say it in a voice I've been developing just for her. One that's deep and authoritative, that seems to grab her attention, gets her mind to stop spinning. Focus. Follow directions.

And that's what she does. Stretching her arms out across the towel-covered table, gripping the far edge in her hands, presenting her bottom adorned in an uncharacteristic purple thong that is both a surprise and a delight.

"Like this?" she asks.

In response, I run my hands along her back, over her hips, down her legs. Tracing every major curve before me in the dim light, trying to memorize each one so I can revisit the way she looks right now in my mind forever. Slowly, I let my fingers drift back up along her skin until I reach her ass, where I let my fingers glide in worshipful circles over her cheeks. She tenses almost imperceptibly, and I draw out my movements, making sure she's *very* aware of how her backside is thrust out, presented to me.

"Lydia?" My voice comes out husky and deep, and I have to pull one hand back briefly to adjust my pants around my hard-on.

"Yes," she answers, barely above a whisper.

"Do you remember what I told you about spanking?"

I knead her flesh lightly, tracing the rim of her thong, giving her a moment with her thoughts.

"Yes," she finally says, slightly louder than before.

"And when I described the benefits I'd read about, did you like the sound of it?" I ask in a matching tone.

She takes less time to answer, muttering an almost impatient, "Yes."

"Good." I lean in, releasing a hot puff of breath against one of her beautiful, curved ass cheeks, following it with a reverent kiss.

And then I wait.

Her hips shift after several seconds, tilting her backside slightly toward me. When I don't make a move, she clears her throat. "Anton?"

"Yes, Mrs. Richie?"

"Are you going to, um . . . ?"

A smile tugs at my lips. I lay a second breathy kiss against her opposite cheek, teasing the inside edge of her thong with my finger.

"Is that a request?"

I don't have to see her face to know it must be burning. Not many seconds pass before I clearly see her nod in the shadows.

"Going to need verbal confirmation, Lydia," I say, stepping back, pulling my hand away from her heated flesh. I'm dying a little, looking at her without touching, but this is another thing we've been working on. It wasn't long ago I discovered, to my horror, that she sometimes went through the motions when she wasn't fully on board. "I won't do it if I'm not *sure* it's what you want."

Lydia exhales, but stays as I've positioned her, and there's just enough light that I see when her thighs squeeze together.

"Yes," she whispers, voice raw and urgent. "Do it. Please."

That's all I need.

My hand comes down on each side of her ass in quick succession, the smack of her flesh beneath my palm in the quiet shop delivering a surprising jolt to my dick.

"How's that?" I ask in a husky voice.

All I get back is a whimpered, "Again."

I lay two more slaps to her rounded cheeks. But then, instead of raising my hand a third time, I place both my palms against her heated skin, rubbing away the sting while I sense her body coming alive. Slowly, I drift one hand down the stretch of thin purple thong, sucking in a hallowed breath when I find the fabric already soaked.

"Oh, Mrs. Richie," I murmur. "This is what happens when you work too much."

I stroke my finger up and down over the outside of her panties, pressing them into her skin so she can feel how wet she's made them. And then I peel them away, sliding the lacy purple fabric down over her ass and letting it pool at her toes.

I take a fraction of a second to admire the peek of her glistening mound before I move in with my tongue.

"*Oh,*" she utters, with a slight startle. I've never come at her from behind like this. It's weird and backward and wonderful, running my tongue from her clit all the way up to dip inside her, spreading her taste up between her cheeks with my mouth.

My cock is full-on throbbing as the scene sinks in. Lydia, naked in the back of Ooh La Pooch, bent over a grooming table with my face between her legs. If there was a fantasy I could've unlocked all those desperate months ago, before we found our way back to each other, this was definitely it. I'm so fucking turned on, I have to yank myself to stand so I can get my pants off before I come.

"Guess we should've discussed your work habits sooner," I say, and I think I actually hear her mewl when I rub the tip of my cock in her juices, painting them all over the insides of her thighs. "Turn around, Lydia."

She takes a breath, then follows my instruction. I guide her back onto the table, positioning her right on the edge, and —fun fact—many dog grooming tables adjust higher and lower with the press of an electric switch. The one Lydia is spread over is already pretty high, so with a light hum, I lower her pussy so it's exactly level with my cock.

"We've got to get one of these for home," I mutter, and she covers her face and laughs.

I smirk at the sound, glad to lighten the mood for a moment, but I don't want to lose her, so I reach out and knead her ample breasts, coaxing and pulling at her nipples until she gasps.

"Are you ready?" I ask, positioning myself outside her entrance.

"Yes," she breathes, raising her gaze to stare up at me.

And I can't stand it a second longer. I ease into her in one barely restrained plunge.

"Fuck," I mutter as I get seated. Then it's only a moment before I start to move. At this perfect angle, we seem to fit like we were made for one another, and I quickly find a rhythm, grabbing her legs and holding them up on either side of me as I thrust.

When I open my eyes again, her head is turned toward the back wall, and I realize with a surge of lust she's watching us in the mirror. Her own body splayed out naked on the table-top, legs in the air, tits bouncing as I thrust.

I lean over her. "From now on, every time you come into this shop to work, I want you to look in that mirror and imagine yourself on this table, getting fucked."

Her body jolts at my words. Scandalized, embarrassed, but also a new, shiny thing—*clearly* turned on. I slide my hands between us, my thumb coming to rest against her clit, my other hand squeezing one taught nipple. She bucks in response, and I pound into her with new intensity, watching her writhe under me, clamping around me.

In that moment, I want nothing more than to pull out and shoot my load, empty myself all over her glorious, naked form. But the one thing in the world *better* than fucking Lydia in her workplace after hours is doing it with a purpose.

So when she comes, bucking her hips off the table with a shout, I let go deep inside her, sending my seed into her depths with a satisfied groan.

CHAPTER SIXTEEN

I GRIP MY RIGHT SIDE. "UGH. CAN WE SLOW DOWN?"

"Lydia, if we go any slower, that's called standing, not running."

"Sorry." I wipe sweat off my brow with my forearm. "Maybe it's the heat."

Caprice checks her watch as we ease to a walk. Again. "Yeah, seventy-six degrees Fahrenheit. Pretty sure that's considered torture in some countries."

I grimace. "I just have a stitch . . . I'll be good in a few minutes."

She tosses her sleek ponytail, giving me a pointed look. "Is that what you said to get out of your high school PE class?"

"Is it working?"

She ignores me, upping our pace to a power walk, forcing me to wheeze alongside her. "So, you never told me what you decided about the kid thing."

"Oh . . . yeah." I look away, wondering if we can navigate a whole conversation just trading topic changes. "Um, it might happen."

"What the hell does that mean?" she asks, narrowing her eyes.

I swallow, not really prepared to defend my current strategy of if-I-don't-think-about-it-too-hard-it-won't-really-happen. "Hey, I think I'm good! Let's try sprinting the rest of the way!"

Caprice falls in without protest, obviously relieved for the chance to lengthen her stride. Which lasts about fifty more feet before I cry out, crumpling into the grass on the side of the path.

"*Ow, sorry.* Stitch moved to my other side."

She sighs, glancing ahead of us. We're almost back to the parking lot where we started, thank God. "Look, Lyd, I appreciate you doing this for me. It's kept me from going crazy the past few weeks. But . . . maybe I'm good to resume running by myself."

I can't deny, part of me—my left side, seizing up with cramps currently—is ready to collapse with relief. If I had any aspirations left about my potential as an athlete, they've died a miserable death the last three Sundays, right here on this jogging path.

But the deeper, more rational part of me hesitates at her suggestion.

"Are you sure that's a good idea? What about the threats and creepy messages?"

"They've kind of . . . simmered down." Caprice shrugs. "Maybe those losers finally got bored. Or got a freaking life? I've had a few more shitty emails, but mostly the same kind of stuff I was getting before I wrote about Unmatched."

I peer at her. "That doesn't sound super encouraging."

"I told you, par for the course for women journalists." She rolls her eyes.

"What about the peephole camera? Has that shown anything weird?"

"Other than discovering my across-the-hall neighbor has a serious DoorDash problem? No. But it *has* made me feel a little safer at home."

I limp into the parking lot, slumping against the side of my 4Runner while Caprice works through a series of stretches. "Well, I mean, I *guess* if you feel comfortable. I don't want to hold you back . . ."

She smirks, despite a shadow briefly crossing her face. "How about I try it, but I'll let you know if things feel scary again?"

"Fine. Deal." I open my liftgate and grab the water I've been dying for the last half mile, pressing a hand over my cramping stomach. "Maybe I shouldn't have eaten that third donut before we left."

"*Three?*" Caprice says, biting back further commentary when a knot in my gut has me clenching my teeth. "Hey, you okay? Want me to drive you home?"

"No. I'll be fine," I say, straightening as the cramp subsides. My friend gazes down the path we just completed around the perimeter of Wash Park. "You want to go around again, don't you?"

She bites her lip, suppressing a smile. "Maybe. At something above sloth pace."

"As long as you feel safe enough to do it without me," I say, closing the back of my car. "I'm going home to take a long bath."

"Think I'll go for it." She shifts into an impatient boxer shuffle beside me. "Thanks for coming with me the past few weeks, though. It's meant a lot."

"I'll do it again if you change your mind . . . just give me a week to forget my agony." I survey the other people in the park as I open my car door. The paths are comfortably crowded, mostly with other fitness enthusiasts. It's not like she's by herself at night. I lean in, forcing her into an awkward, kinetic hug. "I'll still be tracking your location. You better text me when you get home."

"Will do," she says with a grateful, genuinely cheerful

smile. "I hope you feel better—maybe lay off the donuts for a week."

Anton's out somewhere when I drag myself through the front door, which is just as well. In the ten minutes it took me to drive home, my stomach went from somewhat unhappy, to mildly punishing, and is now shifting into time-to-pay mode. I make a beeline past Heartthrob and shut myself in the bathroom, turning on the hot water in the tub as I peel out of my sweaty clothes. I have yet to learn my lesson about breakfast pastries it seems, but a warm bath sometimes settles things down when I overindulge. And, thank goodness, it helps this time, too.

But after I've had my soak and finally climb out of the tub to pee, the whole world shifts when I see a bright slash of red on the toilet paper.

I didn't eat too many donuts. I was just getting my period.

At first, I'm so unprepared for the level of relief that washes over me, it's a good thing I'm sitting down. I mean, yay, my stomach is okay. But I don't think I even realized how *not* ready to be pregnant I was until this moment. I feel like I'm releasing a long-held breath.

Except as soon as I take in a new one, I realize what horrible news this is.

I failed. I agreed to do this, to ensure our future together. He wants a family so badly—*needs* this in order to heal after losing his mom. And now I have to tell him we're not having one.

I sit with that for a second, trying to figure out how I'm even going to approach this. What if he pulls away again, the way he did after we lost his mom? What if, somehow, he thinks I kept it from happening? A hot wave of guilt passes through me as I remember standing over the trashcan, ready to reach in and remove the pills. I *didn't*—though I definitely considered it.

But lots of women have trouble conceiving. This is only the first month—I've heard of it taking years. Some couples can't even have kids without medical intervention. And each and every one of them likely started here, where I am. Bleeding in a bathroom.

There is a pregnancy test under the sink next to my menstrual supplies. One Anton bought proactively in a surge of excitement. Another twinge of guilt shoots through me as I reach past it and unwrap a tampon. We didn't even get to use it. But it *will* still be there next month—or the month after.

I straighten up, helping myself to a couple of ibuprofen from the medicine cabinet now that I know the source of my cramps. Just as I put the bottle away, there's a soft knock on the door.

"Lydia? I'm home. Everything okay in there?"

In a weird flash of memory, I return to a similar moment, just months ago. When I was locked in another bathroom, processing information I had and he didn't. When I realized he was going to cheat—I was going to lose him—if I didn't make a bold move.

I shake the thought away. That already feels like another life. And neither of us has anything to hide this time. My entire waistline might be aching and swollen, but we'll chase away this disappointment together. The way we have been the last two weeks.

I pull on my robe and open the door. "Sorry. I'm okay, I was just taking a bath."

"A bath?" His eyes traverse me with concern. "Are you feeling all right?"

"I'm fine," I say quickly. Then I pause and soften my voice. "I got my period."

This has never been noteworthy information between us. For me, it's meant several days of discomfort once a month.

For Anton, it's only ever indicated a week of no sex. But I see the exact moment he registers what I'm telling him, and despite all my logic about the odds of conception, I still wish we'd beaten them.

"Oh," is all he says.

I bite my lip, watching his demeanor shift. His face flattens as if something inside him is retreating and I swallow a stab of panic.

"You know, hardly anyone gets pregnant on the first try. I wasn't even off the pill a full month." I look down to where I've folded my hands over my aching abdomen, then hastily add, "Anton, I—I'm sorry."

His gaze follows mine, and for a moment it almost looks like his eyes are shining. But he blinks, and when he looks up, his face is all concern. He takes my hand in his. "Why are you apologizing?"

"I just . . ." My voice comes out raw. "It's disappointing."

I don't say anything as he pulls me into his arms, wrapping me in the most comforting hug I think I've ever received. He rubs my back gently, laying a kiss in my hair.

"It's hard for both of us," he says.

I want to tell him it doesn't have to be. There's no need to be upset when we can pick up right where we left off; we can try again. But before I can say any of this, the cramping around my midsection intensifies, and I bite my lip hard, waiting for it to pass.

"Are you uncomfortable?" Anton says. "Let me help."

He goes in search of our heating pad, and though it's barely lunchtime, I change out of my robe into a cami and loose PJ shorts because real clothes sound awful. When I find him in the living room, he has the heating pad plugged in next to the sofa alongside my favorite blanket, with Netflix pulled up on the TV.

"We had some Ben & Jerry's in the freezer," he says, handing me the carton and a spoon.

I settle on the couch and he hovers around, tucking me in until I feel totally wrapped up and cared for. Which I love, but . . . feels a little weird. Anton has always been sympathetic in the past when I've complained about cramping, feeling tired, or an aching back during my cycle. But never this attentive.

"Well, what should we watch?" I ask, patting the empty space beside me.

He hesitates, not sitting. "I uh . . . actually, I might go to the gym."

"Oh," I say. My vision of us wrapped up, snuggling together as we see this unfortunate thing through dissolves, because of course. The gym is where he copes. "Yeah." I nod. "Sure."

He disappears to change his clothes, and I start a rom-com, trying hard to focus on fictional people falling in love. But as he passes quietly to the front door, I hit pause. "Anton, wait."

He leans in, cupping my cheek. "What can I do?"

For a moment, I can't tell if he's asking about period pain, or me not being pregnant. I lean into the warmth of his hand, my stomach bunching with dread. As if, somehow, he might leave and not come back.

"I just, um . . ." I know I shouldn't apologize, but how else can I assure *both* of us I didn't wish this chance away? That I'm still determined to make it happen?

"You just need to rest up and feel better," he says, letting go of me to head for the door.

Without his sturdy hand, I fall back into my cocoon on the couch. And even though I know he's right, I still hate watching him go.

"Mr. Richie?" I say quickly. "You know, this will be a great excuse to have a lot more hot sex."

He pauses at the door, and I thrill a little. That I managed to say *something* remotely right. Even though . . . I'm having a hard time feeling it. Despite the fun we've had the last couple of weeks, right now, if I'm honest, a few days *off* sex sounds nice.

My cheeks go hot and I look at my lap, hoping he didn't see it in my face. We've worked too hard to get where we are. Where we were.

But now I'm not even sure he heard me, because when he looks back, his face is achingly blank. "I'll be back in a little while. I . . . I just need to go clear my head."

He's out the door almost before he gets the words out.

Heartthrob raises his head to look at me from his bed, and when my eyes start to sting, he gets up and shoves his nose into my lap. I pat the empty space on the couch again, and he doesn't hesitate. He jumps up and curls close. I open my ice cream and hit play on the remote, snuggling my dog and watching made-up people get their happily ever afters.

CHAPTER SEVENTEEN

Him

My phone goes off as soon as I'm through the front door.

SETH

> Hey, bad news. Buyer financing fell through.
> Deal's off. House going back on the market.
> Looks like my move to Denver will be
> delayed.

My plan for the gym evaporates on the spot. I'm too agitated, too restless to get in the car. I need to move, propel myself, get my heart rate up—now. I'm already running by the time my feet hit the sidewalk.

At first, my direction feels aimless. My feet seem to carry me randomly through the streets. But as I settle into a regular pace in the midday heat, I realize where I'm headed. Into an adjacent neighborhood, past pockets of microscopic older homes mixed with oversized, unidentifiably modern scrapes, and through a major intersection. The houses shrink down on the other side, into modest bungalows and row houses, until a familiar greenscape spreads before me and I can see the mirrored towers of my brother's swanky new building reflecting the sky.

The building he should be moving into next month. Except now he isn't.

But I guess that's just the theme of the day.

I thought I might become a dad soon, But come to find out, I won't.

I power down the street, hanging a hard left in the opposite direction. Trying to keep the numbness in my chest from spreading to my arms and legs. Everything just feels so far away. Like all I wanted, all I needed, had just been right *there* on the horizon. And now I'm in a fog and I can't see anything. I break into a sprint, as if running fast enough could somehow help me find my way. Get me to what I need.

I'm almost all the way down the length of Washington Park when I slow for a woman and a little boy meandering down the path ahead of me. The kid is really small, maybe two or three years old, and he keeps picking up random leaves on the ground and running to her with them.

I'm not close enough to hear what she says, but I see her take each one, admiring it like it's a treasure, collecting them carefully in one hand. I blink, watching the scene in front of me, and suddenly it's my mom and me.

This one's perfect, Anton. Her whole face would light up when she smiled. *Let's bring these home, and I'll show you how to make a rubbing.*

I only realize I've slowed to a walk when the corners of my eyes start to burn. I look again at the woman on the path, with her blonde hair and rounded hips. From the back, she almost looks like Lydia. But the gut punch is when she takes the little boy's hand and turns to the side, revealing she's *very* pregnant with a second child. Suddenly, I get this urge—to reach for them? Embrace them?—this woman and kid I don't even know. It's so overwhelming, I turn and sprint back the other way.

And even though it's been years since we could have a real conversation, since she could recognize who I was, all I can think in that moment is how badly I want to call my mom.

It is somewhere over ninety degrees, and though it's a dry heat, my neck and shirt are drenched by the time I stagger up our street. I'm not sure how long I've been gone. Hours, maybe? Lydia's on the porch when I return, sitting in her pajama shorts on our swing, and my heart floods with something when I see her—relief? Need?

"I saw your car was still here. Did you go running in this heat?" Her face pinches when she takes in my sweaty appearance. But when our eyes meet, something shifts in her expression. "Anton? Are you okay?"

Sometimes, I'm not good at communicating—we both know this. It'll give our therapist fodder to work with for years. All I manage in this moment is a stiff shake of the head, but I guess it's enough. Lydia rises from the swing and pulls me into the house.

Heartthrob jumps up from where he's chewing on a soup bone when he sees me, and I steady myself with a hand on his head, but I only have eyes for Lydia. Hair pulled up, casually beautiful in her pajama shorts and camisole—a concession to the weather. She goes straight to the fridge and comes back with a large bottle of water. "Drink this."

I take it gratefully, guzzling for nourishment until she puts her hand over mine and tells me to slow down. I sink to the couch, and when she seats herself right next to me, I lie down, pressing my face into her lap, letting her stroke her fingers through my sweaty hair. And my God, it feels good. Comforting and consoling, and . . . a relief. Just to be here, safe, connected with her.

When my heart feels like it's slowed to a reasonable pace, and I'm relatively sure I'm not going to break something inside me if I speak, I roll to look up at her. Her face is smooth, calm, her eyes clear and present.

"I um . . ." my voice croaks when I open my mouth, but I

take another sip of water and continue. "Guess I'm having a hard time."

I doubt she needed me to state it, but she doesn't say I told you so, or look smug. She just nods and keeps her fingers in my hair.

"Seth texted. The house sale fell through."

Her fingers pause. She cups my cheek. "Oh, Anton. I'm sorry."

I close my eyes, savoring the warmth of her hand. Grateful when she doesn't try to make reassurances or give me a pep talk.

"Maybe this is the universe telling me to calm the fuck down."

"Or maybe," she says gently, "these things have nothing to do with each other."

I open my eyes, staring up at her. And for the umpteenth time since spring, I am so grateful. That I still have this woman in my life. That she didn't toss me to the curb when I somehow thought she *wasn't* everything I needed.

"You know," I say quietly, thinking of the woman at the park. "You're going to be a wonderful mom."

She stiffens a little, gaze shifting out the window. "I don't really have a stunning example to aspire to."

I reach for her hand and squeeze. "It's obvious, Lydia. You're just . . . warm and nurturing. Not at all like Marion. You'll be . . ." My voice trails off when I see her face, and immediately, I feel like an ass. "I'm sorry, this isn't the time—"

"*You* will make an excellent dad," she says quickly, earnestly.

And all the air leaves my lungs. My eyes drift across the room, to the family photo I brought back from Dallas. The image of my dad, long gone, now joined by my mom. I didn't get long enough with either of them. And for a bleak moment I let that thought weigh me down, wondering what the sense is in trying to create new life when everything is so impermanent. We're barely here long enough to love, and then we're gone.

But my eyes drift to my mother's steady smile, and I know she'd be first to dismiss that. *Every ending is a new beginning, Anton,* she'd say.

And maybe it isn't fair of me to contradict her.

"I think I'd like to try," I say quietly.

Neither of us speaks for a while. And I just lie there, sinking into Lydia's closeness. The soft warmth of her lap, her reassuring touch. But then her fingers begin to travel. Running up and down my side, moving slowly past my hip. Eventually, very clearly, making her way to the waistband of my shorts.

And for just a second, I want to let her. After everything that's gone down today, I'd love nothing more than to chase away all the doubts between us with each other's bodies.

But I recognize this touch. There's something in her approach. A layer of reluctance. Obligation. Like her focus is on what she thinks I need and not any desire of her own. I haven't sensed it in months, but as soon as it registers, my walls are up.

I move my hand down to cover hers, hold it still. Then readjust us on the couch so we're lying side by side and I can look into her eyes.

"What you said before, about trying to get pregnant being an excuse to have hot sex?" Her cheeks go pink, and I can't resist—I kiss them just to feel their warmth on my lips. "I'm all for the hot sex," I say.

She smiles, batting her lashes. But again, it feels forced.

I take a deep breath. "But maybe this is a good time to take a break."

Her lips part. Then, all at once, her eyes widen.

"I just mean from sex—trying to get pregnant." I squeeze her hands. "All of that. Not *us.*"

I touch my forehead to hers, listening as our breathing mingles and slows.

"Things have been good . . . getting better. Would you agree?"

She nods against me.

I raise one hand to stroke her hair. "I enjoy learning what turns you on. It's fucking hot."

She smiles. "Then why stop?"

"Because we've worked hard for this—for sex to be *fun*." I pull back to look into her eyes. "I don't want to lose track of that."

"A break . . ." she says. "For how long?"

"Until you're ready."

She furrows her brow. "And what makes you think I'm not ready now?"

"Lydia," I say flatly. "Look at me and tell me you're *dying* to have period sex."

Her face says it all. And even though I can think of a dozen ways for us to get off where blood wouldn't be a factor, I smile, pull her close, and wrap her tightly in my arms.

Several heartbeats go by. Then she whispers, "Should . . . should I go back on birth control?"

"*No*—why?" The words fly out of my mouth a little too quickly, and I feel myself flush. "I mean . . . Um, do you want to?"

"Do you still want a baby?" she asks softly.

"Yes. I do, very much." I let out a long breath, tangling my fingers in her hair. "I can't think of anything more wonderful than starting a family with you. But I don't want to obsess about making it happen when we should just . . . enjoy each other."

She nods, and something seems to ease in her eyes as she pulls the heating pad back over her stomach. "Okay."

I hold her close, resisting all my natural urges to stroke under her shirt. Breathe her in. Seek solace in her skin. It can wait until she's ready, till she comes looking for it. Instead, I snuggle her against my chest, keeping her close and safe. Our little family, such as it is.

We spend the afternoon that way, lazing in each other's arms. But that evening, after Lydia's taken another bath and gone to bed, I open my calendar and start doing math in my head.

CHAPTER EIGHTEEN

"So, as you can see, Pooch Park II is slightly bigger, but I managed to squeeze in elements I always wished we had at our first location. The dogs can be indoors or out based on the weather, and we have this fun outdoor turf space with misters, wading pools, and lots of shade when it's hot."

Marisol scans the outdoor area from where we stand behind a fence. "This is so adorable, so perfect," she says with a wide smile. "Hey, what kind of dog is that?"

I follow her gaze and grin, watching the one she's pointing to hop around, attacking a hose as one of my employees tries to refill a pool. "That's actually my Akita mix, Heartthrob."

"Heartthrob?" She chuckles. "How did he get that name?"

I smile at the memory. "When we first adopted him, he was so young, I got him this little pillow that made comforting heartbeat sounds. My husband used to tease that I was more in love with the puppy than with him, so I started calling him my little Heartthrob." I shrug. "It just stuck."

Marisol arches a brow at me, and it seems like she's about to ask another question, but then a bloodhound in the corner starts baying at two wrestling puppies, which sets a cattle dog barking for the sake of hearing his own voice, and the chorus of noise makes it impossible to have further conversation. I gesture toward the door back inside.

As we reenter reception, we peek back through the window into the little dog area to check on Marisol's terrier, Biscochito.

"Looks like he's found a friend in Carmelita," I say.

Marisol joins me at the window, watching her pup chase around with Henry's fawn French bulldog. Her smile is wide. "Thank you so much for inviting me today. I've *loved* seeing your Pooches. My hands have been full with Paloma since my separation, but I'm going to sign up for a weekly package. Poor Bizkit hasn't had enough exercise."

"Did you ever find a kid daycare you like?" I ask, mostly for conversation. She doesn't have her little girl with her today.

"We're on waitlists for a couple." She exhales. "She's with her dad today."

Her face is pinched, and I wish I had something to offer. I liked Marisol the first time we met, but after spending an afternoon together, I definitely feel like we could be friends. She knows hundreds of interesting little business hacks, and I appreciate her quick sense of humor. But I definitely don't know her well enough to comment on something so personal just yet.

Before I can think how to respond, Henry blusters in, making a beeline for the desk.

"Francie, may I have the tape roller? Thank you."

My green-haired employee ducks behind the desk, popping back up to hand it to him, twirling her curls in her other hand. Henry rolls the device over the lower parts of his dress pants in a practiced motion without noticing her heart eyes, then finally straightens, noticing us.

"Henry, this is Marisol Lopez," I say, making introductions. "She owns the subscription box company I told you about."

"Oh, yes." His eyes sharpen on her. "Good to meet you. Henry Hill."

"It's a pleasure," she says, shaking his hand. I tease Henry all the time for his three-piece suits, but Marisol's wearing a smart-looking wrap blouse and linen slacks, and it strikes me how professional they look. I have no real reason to feel insecure, but just for a second, it's like my mom is in the room. Eyeballing my *Life Goal: Pet All The Dogs* T-shirt and asking if I really wore it to work. I pull my gray hoodie off the back of the reception chair and zip it up, trying not to feel like a little kid watching the adults.

"Can't stay," Henry says, distracted by his phone. "Scarlet's bellyaching about the new point of sale system. Again."

I knit my brow. Normally, Scarlet channels all her complaints directly to me, at full volume. "Huh. Marisol and I were just there and she didn't say anything."

Henry shrugs, though he keeps smoothing his hair and inspecting his clothes. "I'll uh . . . I'll just run through it quickly with her again. Then I've got that meeting with the bank I was telling you about. Nice to meet you." He nods at Marisol, and then he's out the door.

"What I would give for a *man* to talk to the banks for me," she says, rolling her eyes.

I raise my brows in surprise. "Really? It doesn't seem like you need one." As soon as the words are out of my mouth, I wince, wondering if it sounded like a personal comment.

She shrugs. "You're in such a great position, Lydia. Your branding is on point, and The Pooch Park is very clearly meeting major demand. I see now why Henry couldn't resist dipping his toes in. I would've done the same in his position."

"Thanks. I don't know, sometimes I feel like such an accidental success."

"Sounds like a case of imposter syndrome," she says gently.

I frown. "Where do you see your business going next?" It's a polite question, but I'm genuinely curious. She follows me into Henry's *conference room* and I grab us each a water bottle from the fridge.

"I'm conducting market research for some new subscription concepts. In addition to WoofCrate, I also have a crafting box, a home brewing box, and an 'intimate pleasures' box." She glances at me and rolls her eyes. "That last one was my ex's idea. I hate giving him credit for it, but it's been a massive success."

"Oh." I wish my face didn't redden at the mere mention of sex. I might be getting more comfortable in my bedroom, but definitely not outside of it. "Were the two of you in business together?"

She barks a laugh. "Thankfully not. I just get to profit off his deviant ideas. But to answer your question, what I'd love more than anything is to grow my company to the point I can actually step back and have more time with my daughter."

I raise my eyebrows. "Really? It seems like you already balance everything so well."

"Thanks." An expression I can't quite identify crosses her face. "I'm glad that's what it looks like. Being a massive success will be part of my revenge plan post-divorce."

I twist the hem of my T-shirt. I don't want to pry. But I like Marisol a lot, and she doesn't seem shy about her personal life. "You said it was a recent breakup?"

"Yep. Just a few months ago. Erik—that's my ex—was outed in this article about married people cheating. It came out right after Paloma and I moved here to be with him."

A hot prickle travels up the back of my neck. "Really?"

"When I first found out, I was devastated. Embarrassed. Disappointed in myself for not seeing it." She sighs. "But now I'm just pissed."

I meet her eyes, my stomach somewhere on the floor. There is so much I could say—want to say. I know *exactly* what she went through because it also happened to me. I went through all the devastation, felt all the same things.

But I stop before any of this reaches my mouth when I realize . . . I actually didn't.

Unmatched brought her relationship to an end. But in the most backward way, it became a beginning for Anton and me.

Or at least, it felt that way until this week.

"That . . . that sounds like a lot to go through," I whisper.

She exhales. "Trust me, I wouldn't wish it on anyone. But when I'm feeling less sorry for myself, I know it's the best thing that could've happened. I don't think Erik's that into being a dad. If I'm careful, I think I can win sole custody."

She checks her phone again, this time straightening at whatever she sees. "Speak of the damn devil. Looks like he's already done with her today." She grits her teeth. "Guess I need to take off. Thanks, Lydia. Could we do this again, maybe get lunch or something sometime?"

"Of course. This was fun," I say, and I mean it.

Francie brings Biscochito back out to reception, and Marisol makes for the door, leash in hand, but before she gets there, a thought occurs to me and I clear my throat.

"Hey, I've been bouncing around some ideas for expansion and could really use an objective opinion. Could I shoot you an email?"

Marisol grins. "Only if I can hit you up with subscription box concepts."

I wave as she heads out the door. "It's a deal."

By the time I lock up Pooch Park II, everything outside is freshly soaked from an afternoon thunderstorm. We got super busy with deliveries after Marisol left, and it isn't until I'm climbing in my SUV with Heartthrob that I realize I haven't heard from Anton since lunch. I glance around the parking lot, half hoping to see his truck, thinking with a deep blush it wouldn't be the first time I worked late and he came looking for me.

But there's no sign of him.

I frown, checking my phone again, and that's when I notice a missed text about a Vesper work dinner. It's polite and matter-of-fact. Deferential. Gentlemanly. Exactly how he's been treating me all week.

And for a few days, it *was* nice. I didn't think at all about sex, or babies, or much of anything. I ate ice cream, wore my big, comfy underpants, and he just . . . gave me the space. But it's started to feel like ages since I got a suggestive text, or received more than a chaste kiss on the cheek. And I have to admit I'm a little restless.

The irony of this feeling is not lost on me. There was a time, very recently, when Anton keeping his distance would've filled me with relief. It used to be second nature for me, working late, avoiding him physically. But things have shifted.

And . . . I don't know. I get the sense he's waiting for me.

Going off birth control must have messed with my cycle because it felt like I bled forever. My period finally ended three days ago, and I have had plenty of chances to make a move, but . . . I just don't know how to start. I could ask Caprice for suggestions, though I can guess what she'd say. Which is how I find myself pulling into the parking lot of Playful Pleasures on my way home.

"I'll be ten minutes, tops," I say, cracking the windows for Heartthrob, grateful the rain cooled everything down. But as I force my feet toward the entrance of the *sensual superstore* for the second time in my life, checking over my shoulder for anyone who might recognize me, I can see why someone might subscribe to one of Marisol's intimate boxes. Sex and kinks delivered directly to your home—no embarrassing store purchase necessary.

The beep of the front door startles me when I walk inside, but not as much as the sudden tightness in my chest. So many things in my life were still uncertain the last time I was here. I force myself to take a breath.

"Hi! Welcome to Playful Pleasures," a woman calls from behind the counter. I recognize her Bettie Page hair and septum nose ring with a flood of relief and head straight to where she's putting sale stickers on what looks like a large quantity of alien-like dildos.

"Hi." I glance around the store, which is more crowded than the last time I was in here. "You um . . . I think you helped me before?"

She sets down her pricing gun. "I'm always happy to hear that. What can I do for you today?"

I glance at her name tag. *Daphne*, that's right.

"I think you'd . . . well, my husband and I were still kind of . . . learning the basics last time I was in." I swallow, too aware of my face turning red. "I guess now I'm looking for . . ." My voice trails off. *What?* What do I ask for? Something kinky? A flag that says *period complete*?

Daphne tilts her head, studying me. "Maybe you're ready to take things to the next level?"

"*Sure*," I blurt. I don't even know what she means, but I'm dying for someone else to take the lead.

She looks at me, tapping her deep mauve lip. "Is there anything specific you two are into? Or maybe a direction you're leaning? Role play? S&M?"

If my face gets any hotter, it's going to burst into flames. There's only one specific thing I can think of. One Anton mentioned on Unmatched when he thought I was someone else, but I'm not sure I can bring myself to say it out loud. Someone comes up beside me to check out at the next register, and I pivot away from them, ducking as close as I can get to Daphne across the counter.

"Um . . . I am pretty sure he wants to try butt play," I say, barely above a whisper.

"Fun!" Her brows shoot up initially, but then she gives me an assessing look. "Is that something *you're* interested in?"

My shoulders slump. I close my eyes, wondering if she asks everyone that question or if I am just that easy to read. "Not . . . really?"

"Okay, fair." She gives me a reassuring smile. "Don't get me wrong, there's tons of fun to be had there. But not if you aren't into it."

I let out a relieved breath and glance over at the next register, surprised to see a petite elderly lady paying for her purchases. She takes her black plastic bag and gives me a warm smile. "I never let my husband in the back way either, honey."

I look at Daphne, who waves and chuckles as the woman leaves. "Nice to see you, Arlene."

I am ready to bolt for the parking lot and call it a night, but Daphne comes around to my side of the counter, placing a gentle hand on my arm. "How about this? Just remind me what you bought last time you came in."

"Okay," I say, collecting myself. All I have to do is recite a list. "It was . . . a rabbit, some lube, and a blindfold."

"Excellent newlywed starter kit." She looks pleased with herself. I don't tell her we've been married almost eight years. "And since then you've had a chance to *use* all of those things?"

I hesitate. "Well, no. We haven't tried the blindfold."

She taps a finger to her lips, stares at the ceiling a moment, then looks back at me with a smile. "I have some ideas. Give me a moment."

After several minutes flitting around the store, she returns to the counter and presents me with a selection of different products.

"Okay, you can take or leave any of these based on your comfort level, of course. But you can definitely have some fun here without getting too intense." She picks up a set of long black satin ribbons first. "These can be used to play around tying each other up. They're a little gentler than like, rope or handcuffs. *And* you can try them with that blindfold you have."

I stop breathing when she hands the package to me, brain flooding with images of stern-looking men wearing leather and holding whips, standing over cowering, tied-up women.

"Bondage isn't necessarily about pain," Daphne says quickly, reading the look on my face. "It's just the 'B' in 'BDSM.' You don't have to do the whole master and slave thing. But even a little restraint, like your partner immobilizing your hands while they touch you, can heighten pleasurable sensations."

I give her a skeptical glance, but when I turn the package over, there's a picture of a woman with her hands wrapped in ribbons above her head while a man leans in worshipfully with his lips on her stomach. Their surroundings look perfectly tame, not unlike my own bedroom. And she doesn't look scared at all, she looks . . . like she's luxuriating in it. I keep the package in my hand and look at Daphne. "What else have you got?"

Her mouth quirks. "If you choose to go with the ribbons, they might pair nicely with these," she says, dropping a pair of red multi-sided dice into my palm. The sides say things like, *blow, nipple, lick,* and *thighs.* "Some people call them fore-play dice. They present lots of creative options, but obviously you and your partner can opt out of anything you're uncom-fortable with."

I look between the ribbons in one hand and the dice in the

other, connecting the two almost embarrassingly fast in my mind.

"What else?" I say, shifting my weight to unclench my thighs.

"Nipple suckers," she says with a playful twinkle, handing me a package containing two small, pink, rubbery lightbulb-shaped objects. "They're not for everyone, but they can be a fun way to spice things up."

I examine the package. "Do they um . . ."

"You squeeze them, and they suction onto your nipple," she explains, matter-of-fact. "It feels like a little pinch, but definitely tamer than some of the more hardcore clamps."

I glance at one of the nearby mannequins with metal accessories dangling from its chest, feeling the heat drain from my face. I slide the pink things back to her across the counter.

"Let's save those for next time," I say.

Daphne nods, understanding. "I do love a repeat customer."

As she rings up my purchases, the cat tattoo on her shoulder seems to swish its tail in my direction, and I stare at my brand-new bondage ribbons and sex dice, wondering if it might be a little overkill. I mean, I could just say: *Anton, let's go to bed.*

That just seems . . . hard.

"Thanks so much for your help. Again," I say, as Daphne hands over one of the store's black plastic bags.

"I like to keep my customers happy." She grins.

"I'll um . . . let you know what happens."

I turn for the door, but she stops me. "If you and your hub try these and still think you want more, come back and see me." She winks. "Actually, next time, you might try coming in together."

CHAPTER NINETEEN

Him

CARL WALLACE SITS BACK AFTER THE WAITER LEAVES, GENTLY swirling the wine in his glass, listening to Derek Norman recount his drive up from Colorado Springs. I have to admit, I had pinned my hopes on having dinner tonight with my wife and not my colleagues, but once I realized what this was about, the invite was clearly more expectation than request.

"Thank you both for joining us," Carl says, because I'm not the only one here.

"It's my pleasure, sir." Milo preens. "Thanks for the opportunity."

Carl chuckles, which makes me think he sees right through Milo's sycophantic fawning. I would find him more annoying if I wasn't so relieved to have him here. I have been in the Vesper office every day for the past several weeks, managing my accounts, meeting with clients, honestly trying my best. But there have been times I just haven't been fully present, my thoughts wandering in and out of the past, the present—some possible futures. I know my performance isn't going to fly long-term.

Lucky for me, Milo makes an excellent personal assistant. He's so hot to climb the corporate ladder, he makes most of my client calls, runs reports, and gets us both to all our meet-ings. Which has saved me so far. But I need to get my act together.

"So, Derek has come up to Denver this evening because we're getting ready to move forward with the branch office," Carl explains. "Obviously, he'll be holding down the fort, doing some hiring in the Springs, but we're going to need a couple people who can serve as go-betweens. Make sure there's consistency across both offices."

I sip my water. "Makes sense. We already have clients we work with long-distance in Pueblo and the Springs. It'll help us establish a stronger connection."

"While opening us up to a larger market," Milo adds.

"Exactly," Carl says, eyes sparkling.

Derek clears his throat. He's a big, burly business rancher type. The kind who wears a bolo instead of a tie and has clearly lived here all his life. "We're only just looking at spaces," he says. "Probably downtown, but there're some possibilities on the north end. The initial travel demands shouldn't be too intense, but once we open up, there might be a lot of back and forth."

Carl chimes in. "We're looking into corporate housing, or maybe even purchasing a company condo."

"Of course, whatever makes sense," Milo says without a thought.

I'm a bit slower to jump in. Not because I'm distracted— for the first time in weeks, my *full* attention is on Vesper Financial. But what Carl and Derek are actually envisioning is starting to hit me. Colorado Springs is about an hour drive from Denver when the traffic and weather are perfect. It's also possible to fly between the two cities. I travel down there periodically for the odd business trip, but this sounds more . . . involved.

"I know this is asking a lot as far as time commitment,"

Carl says. "Which is part of the reason we're approaching you two first, since neither of you has a family."

My chest shouldn't sting when he says that, but it does. "Well, uh, Lydia—"

"Oh, you've got to meet Anton's wife. She is something else," Carl says, grinning at Derek. "Multi-entrepreneur, expanding her business exponentially." He shakes his head. "I hope Vesper can achieve a shadow of her growth."

"She's really gone to the dogs," I mutter, knowing it'll elicit laughter from my boss. He and Derek start talking about their pets, and I sit back in my chair. Watching Milo track their every word and gesture, waiting for the right time to react or chime in. Just the way I did when I started working with Carl right out of college.

For some reason, I don't feel like I have the energy for it now.

I pull out my phone, schooling my face to look like I'm replying to client email. Then navigate to my texts with Lydia. According to the ovulation calculator I downloaded a few days ago, her next fertility window should start tomorrow. She hasn't indicated she's ready yet, which is fine. I don't want her stressing about this—I meant what I said about focusing on the fun. But if my instincts are right and our relationship has changed the way I think it has . . . it seems like it couldn't hurt to be strategic.

> So far tonight, Carl's talking more about dogs than finance.

LYDIA

🙁 Why wasn't I invited?

> The evening would be 1000% better with you here.

LYDIA

Where are you guys? Maybe Caprice and I should get a table and "bump into" you.

Elway's.

LYDIA

Oh, blah. More wines than desserts.

I chuckle. Sometimes Lydia can be delightfully predictable.

Go out with me tomorrow? I'll buy you dessert anywhere you want.

I mean, if you're feeling better?

LYDIA

Thought you'd never ask.

I am starting to feel like I've read every scientific fact and old wives' tale about conception on the internet. For example, I know Lydia's in her most fertile window the week right after her period. But one of the many sites that confirmed this also suggested eating fresh pineapple to hasten implantation, or yams if we want twins. Oysters were also recommended for a variety of reasons. There *is* some evidence to support her staying still for ten minutes after sex, to help the sperm find its way inside her uterus. And I read conflicting reports that if she orgasms right after I come, her cervix will suck up my semen. But I had to stop when I found an entire site devoted to ovulation and the lunar cycle. Even I'm not ready to go there quite yet.

Deep down, I know none of these things will really make a difference. But it's hard not to aim for some vague sense of control. So Lydia and I have been enjoying fresh pineapple every day with breakfast. Because why not.

But now that we're officially back in the "fertility window," I'll admit, I'm just excited for the chance to get naked with my wife. It wasn't hard to back off when she first got her period. I needed some time, and she wasn't feeling good. But then I decided to hold off a little longer, just keep my distance, see what would happen. I wanted it to be *her* choice to start again. But I also wondered if she'd miss it.

I guess she did. Because the second Lydia walks in the door from work, she's in my arms, and I'm kissing her. Her hands are in my hair and on my ass, and we both laugh when we nearly fall over onto the couch.

"Do you want to just stay in tonight?" she asks, coming up for air.

"No," I say against her lips. "I've been imagining you in a dress all day. I can't deny myself the real thing."

She giggles. "I could just put one on for you to take off right now?"

"Tempting as that is . . ." I run my tongue along her jaw until she shivers, then push her gently away. "We do have a reservation."

With a huff, she disappears down the hall to take the world's fastest shower before disappearing into our room. I feed Heartthrob while I wait, tossing his octopus toy outside until it's too hot for both of us and he goes in to flop down under the air conditioner.

Lydia emerges after about twenty minutes, and by then I'm pacing with anticipation. But as soon as I lay eyes on her, my throat nearly seizes up. She put on a simple blue and white sundress, exactly as I'd hoped. But oh. My God.

"Does this look okay?" she asks, fiddling with the straps. The dress itself isn't overtly sexy, but it clearly wasn't designed for someone with my wife's proportions. While it perfectly hugs her waist, the neckline plunges so wide and low, it edges on indecent. "It's a little snug. Maybe I should change?"

"Yes," I croak, reconsidering her offer to stay home. She looks so goddamn *fuckable*. I'm already hard. "I mean—*no*, don't take it off. *Yes*, it looks amazing—please don't change." My voice actually cracks.

She levels me with the most unexpectedly wicked gaze. Like she's considering unzipping my pants and taking me out right here. It's like a lightning bolt to my dick.

I look down, at my watch, just to get myself under control. "We should ah . . . go. If we're going to make it on time."

She picks up her purse and moves toward the door, and my eyes rake over her back. Her bare shoulders. The way the dress hugs her waist, then flares out over her hips. The hem is short, though not as scandalous as the neckline. But it would tease if she were to bend over.

"Wait, Lydia," I say in a husky voice.

She turns to look at me, and I lick my lips. Because I'm pretty sure what I say next will make her squirm. And I can't fucking wait.

"Before we go . . ." I swallow. "Take off your panties."

I see every thought march across her beautiful face. *What are you, nuts? Why would anyone do that? I'm not taking my*— Then I watch a slow blush make its way over her cheeks as she realizes what I'm asking. "You mean go to dinner without . . . ?"

She can't bring herself to actually say it. And just that has my pants so tight I'm not sure how I'm going to walk. "Yes. That's exactly what I mean."

She searches my face again, waiting to see if I'm joking. I make sure my expression says I most certainly am not. A minute goes by, and she's clearly weighing my request against her own comfort. If she says she doesn't want to, obviously I'm not going to make her. Six months ago, I would never have even made the suggestion. But so much has changed in our relationship. I have never felt bold enough to ask her this, but you can bet I've fantasized about it.

"We're short on time, Lydia . . ."

She presses her lips together. Then slowly sets down her purse and reaches behind her, lifting the skirt of her dress very purposely where I can't see. She looks right at me, and then with one slight movement, a pair of blue satin and lace panties fall to the floor around her ankles.

I am salivating. But I offer my hand as she steps out and I bend to retrieve them, tossing them to the little table where we leave our keys and other sundries. She looks at them almost wistfully, then opens the door and I follow her out to my truck. A neighbor two houses down waves from where they're mowing their lawn, and we both nod at a man walking his corgi down the sidewalk. But all I can think about is my wife's bare pussy under that dress.

I open the truck door and whisper in her ear, "This could be a short dinner."

CHAPTER TWENTY

I CAN'T BELIEVE HE CONVINCED ME TO DO THIS. I CROSS AND uncross my legs for what must be the tenth time since we sat down, glancing nervously around the restaurant, but it doesn't help. The couple across from us seems to look at me and laugh, a man near the door leers in my direction, and then there's our waiter, whose every question or comment seems somehow suggestive. *Oh yes, that dish is served with a delicate cream sauce.*

I am ninety-nine percent *sure* they all know I'm not wearing panties.

But the worst is my husband, who definitely does. He's seated himself next to me, where he can watch me writhe every time his hand manages to somehow brush my thigh. His eyes have been down the front of my dress since we left the house, and I'm more than a little concerned he's going to do something indecent. I almost want him to.

God, what is wrong with me?

I glance down, tugging at my neckline again. It plunges so low, it feels like my nipples will slip out if I breathe too deeply. I'd been planning to return the dress since I ordered it in the way wrong size, but I was feeling bold and excited as I got ready for our date. Only wearing the dress in public doesn't feel quite the same as it did in my bedroom.

And then Anton took my panties.

I clench my thighs.

"So, um—" I cross one arm in front of me in a futile attempt at modesty. "You never really said what the dinner with Carl was about?"

My husband's gaze rests unabashedly on my cleavage, but almost immediately, his posture changes. He looks away, taking a sip from his water glass. "Ah, he wants to open a branch office in Colorado Springs."

"Oh." I blink. That's not what I expected, but it makes sense when I churn it over in my business brain. "You guys have a lot of clients down there. That's probably smart."

His voice is flat. "It'll involve some extra travel."

"Well," I say brightly. "The experience will look good on your resumé."

He grunts, and then I register the tension in his shoulders. How he's straightened and folded his hands on the table. I could kick myself. I was hoping to distract with conversation, not kill the mood.

"Sorry. Maybe we shouldn't talk about work."

He softens, turning to look at me again. "Just don't really want to think about work when I'm dying to put my hand up that dress."

My cheeks flood with heat and I open my mouth to chastise him, but before I get the chance, our waiter appears.

"Here we are—the spaghetti and meatballs." He places a dish in front of Anton. "And oysters over angel hair." He puts a second plate in front of me.

I raise my brows at my husband. "This looks delicious. Glad I took your suggestion."

He returns my gaze with a gleam in his eye, and my heart skips.

Somehow, I manage not to spill oysters into my abundant

cleavage as we dig in. A song that played at our wedding comes on over the speaker above us. Anton's hand rests on my knee in a casual, affectionate way, and I can't help smiling over at him.

"This is really nice," I say, admiring how the light over our table accentuates the squareness of his jaw. "I um . . . it felt like we didn't get much time together last week."

He squeezes my knee, looking a little shamefaced. "I was trying to give you space. Maybe I gave you too much."

"You mean you weren't avoiding me?" I laugh when I say it, though it comes out a little sharp.

Our eyes meet, and his fingers stroke my knee. "Or maybe I was trying to make you miss me."

I sip my water, and it's barely noticeable, but his hand slides fractionally higher on my leg. My heart begins to pound. "Maybe it worked."

His eyes flash.

I look away, but I can't hide the blush blooming over my skin. "It's funny," I say, twirling angel hair on my fork. "Maybe it's the therapy, or I don't know, something. But things feel . . . different."

"Different how?" he asks, sounding genuinely curious.

I turn to face him, not sure how to put it into words. "Little things. Like . . . sometimes I find myself thinking about you when you're not around?"

His brows draw together. "Thinking about me?"

No, that's not right. I run my hands over my face.

"Uh, thinking about *us* . . ." I whisper, eyes glued to my plate. "Doing things."

I let my hair fall between us, watching his expression through the strands. He covers his mouth, and I can't tell if he's hiding a smile or a frown.

"Because normally you don't?" he asks, amusement clear in his voice.

"It's not that I *never* have," I say, sounding defensive. And for a second I panic, wondering if I shouldn't have shared this at all. "It's just . . . more on my mind now."

"That's interesting," he says, and now I'm *sure* I've offended him. But when I drag my gaze back up, the look in his eyes sends a jolt of heat straight to my core. "I've heard the body's most powerful sex organ is the brain."

"You're always so informed," I whisper.

His hand on my leg slides another fraction higher, dipping beneath the hem of my skirt. Vaguely, I'm aware of our dinners not being eaten, but my dress is suddenly so tight I can't imagine taking another bite.

"So, you didn't like the space I gave you last week," he says in a quiet tone.

I shake my head, distracted by the progression of his fingers.

"I have a proposal, then." This gets my attention. I stare up into his face, and he looks back at me, eyes hooded. "What if we try the opposite?"

I open my mouth, attempting to keep myself from panting, but one of his long, assertive fingers has parted my thighs and my heart is losing it. "Like—how?"

He leans close, nuzzling my hair. "Well, since we're supposed to be having fun, and you apparently can't stop thinking about me . . ." He smirks. "Why don't we see what happens if we fool around every day—or at least every other."

His hand goes still beneath my skirt. I glance nervously around, but the restaurant is crowded and loud, and no one's paying us any attention. He's just waiting for me, letting his hand sit there between my legs while I die a little.

"*Sure.* Let's try it."

I can't really think past what's happening beneath the table. What's going on inside me. But while this feels two hundred percent better than the distance we kept last week, we're also teetering on the edge of my comfort zone. And I'm pretty sure he knows it.

"Mr. Richie, my *most powerful sex organ* is going into overload," I warn.

To my relief, Anton chuckles and withdraws his hand. He reaches into his pocket and lays a generous amount of cash on the table. I stand immediately, ignoring the bare, wet feeling between my legs as he follows me out the door. "Guess we better get your brain into bed."

We don't quite make it there.

Anton parks in our tiny, detached garage, and we make out like a couple of teenagers in his car before stumbling through the backyard, groping each other much the way we did earlier today. The sun is almost fully set, but the two of us are illuminated in fading pinks and reds. An orchestra of crickets has already started up their evening song, but not so loud I don't hear Anton's sharp intake of breath as we lose our footing and tumble to the grass.

"Whoops," I giggle, landing on top of him, smothering his face under my chest.

He burrows his stubbly chin into my cleavage, igniting my skin, then reaches under my dress and grabs my ass, ready to hoist me back to my feet. But then he pauses.

"Actually . . . wait here."

He slides gently out from under me, ducks quickly into the garage, and emerges a moment later with the picnic blanket from the backseat of his truck.

"The stars are beautiful tonight," he says, looking at me and not the sky.

I shift out of the way, biting my lip as he spreads the blanket. Our backyard is tiny, with just enough room for a square of grass, some flowers, and a small patio crammed between our house and garage. But it's surrounded by a tall privacy fence, several bushy trees, and none of the surrounding bungalows has a window with a direct view in. Plus it *is* almost dark.

Still, my heart pounds as he stands in the middle of the blanket, inviting me to join him. "Is this another one of your focus exercises?" I ask.

The light and shadows in the yard make his expression intense. "Is it working?"

I approach slowly, reaching for him in the fading light. Running my hands over the rifts and valleys of his torso through his button-down shirt. Down his strong, muscular arms until, tentatively, they rise up and circle my waist. His breath releases, long and slow, as his hands explore up my back, to the zipper of my dress. He begins fiddling with it, then pulls away to look at my face, asking for permission. I glance around the yard again. It's darker now, only illuminated by the moon and a dim solar light on our garage. If anyone's going to see me, they'd have to peer over the top of our fence.

I turn back to Anton. The obvious desire in his eyes held back only by his need for me to process and decide. If I said I wanted to stop, go in, he wouldn't argue. We'd continue this in the privacy of our bedroom. I could get out the things I bought at Playful Pleasures, and I'm sure we'd have fun.

But something about staying, taking his lead, sends a flutter through my stomach. I'm uncomfortable, but I trust him. So, with some hesitance, I nod.

He draws the zipper down slowly, my core tightening with every inch. When the fabric hangs loose on my shoulders, I take in a deep breath for what feels like the first time in hours.

"Been dying to do this all evening," he says, reaching for the hem. And before I can overthink, he pulls the dress over my head, leaving me in just my blue satin bra.

His face is reverent as he leans in, trailing his lips over the remaining fabric, and I shiver as he slides each strap off my shoulders. Slowly, his fingers drift behind me once more, but he straightens before tugging on the hooks, always checking in.

God. Here goes everything.

I close my eyes and nod again, standing there astounded with myself as he releases the clasp, letting my breasts spring free in the warm evening air. And then I'm standing, heart pounding, completely nude in our backyard, in the middle of the city. He tosses the bra into the grass with my dress, then steps back, and it's the strangest sensation. I feel simultaneously exposed and . . . surprisingly exhilarated. I want to grab my clothes and run inside, but I don't. Because of the hungry look in Anton's eyes.

He stalks around me like a fox, gaze dark and heated. "You are so fucking beautiful," he mutters, circling behind me, setting my skin on fire as one hand cups and caresses my ass. I stand stiff and still, like a hunted animal. And the way my husband looks at me is not unlike a predator. But I swallow hard, because *this* is exactly what I longed for last week.

He leans in, his lips brushing mine, drifting down my jaw, neck, and collarbone, and over my heated chest. He gets to my left nipple and blows cool air across it, as if to draw more attention to the fact that it's out here for the world to see. And it responds dutifully, hardening and standing out under his attentions. He moves to the right, and manages to make that one tighten up too.

Anton looks up into my face, pinches one nipple in each hand, and gives them a firm tug. Something between a gasp and a moan escapes my mouth, and I clench my thighs as the sensation travels through me, settling in my core. His eyes light up like Christmas at my reaction.

I sink to the blanket, as primly as I can completely naked, and suddenly I'm reminded of a painting I studied in college depicting two Victorian couples having a picnic. The men were fully clothed, but the women were mostly nude. I knew it was a bold piece of art for its time, but it never really struck me as erotic until now. Because I feel like one of those women.

Like the painting, Anton keeps on his pants and shirt, but guides me to lie back, on full display for owls, and helicopters—but mostly for him. My limbs are stiff as he positions himself between my legs, my skin glowing in the moonlight. It's still early enough I hear people laughing and talking a few doors down, a neighborhood dog barking, and the sound of someone washing dishes through a nearby window. Close enough I'm afraid to make any sound of my own. But then Anton leans down, tracing his lips and tongue up the insides of my thighs, until the universe seems to shrink to just our yard, this blanket—his tongue and my flesh. My entire body warms before he even reaches my center. And when he does, I gasp.

I'm not sure how every time his lips touch down on my clit can feel like the first time, but this is surely the first time it's been done under the stars. And despite staying perfectly silent, muscles tight with the threat of being discovered, my hips buck and rock against his face and he moves easily in time. Reaching up with one hand to tweak my nipples until the want builds so much that my body seems to vibrate.

When I am near delirious with arousal, he pulls back, and my entire vulva throbs for his return. But the next thing I know, he's back between my legs, as nude as I am. All heated skin and muscle illuminated under the moon.

He hoists my legs into his lap, positioning his thick head against my entrance, and just the pressure is so delicious. I push forward, trying to get him to sink into me. But at that moment, a car drives slowly up the alley behind us and I tense. It comes to a stop nearby, and we hear people get out, talking to each other. I recognize our next-door neighbors' voices and try to scramble up, but Anton holds my legs in place, bringing a finger to his lips. His eyes ask me to trust him.

Doors slam, followed by more voices, and the entire time, Anton stares down at me, rubbing himself silently in my juices, maintaining friction against my clit while I listen, waiting for our neighbors, and apparently another couple, to move into their house.

And just when I hear them laughing and chatting about some restaurant, gathered literally on the other side of a few fence pickets from where I am laid out completely nude, Anton pushes his considerable length inside me and I respond with an audible gasp.

There's a hush in the night. My husband looks down at me with this expression like, *that's right, you just took me all in one go,* just as someone says, "Did you hear something?" And I lie there in torment, both because they might investigate, discover us, and I will never be able to show my face on our street again. But also because I'm full of my husband's throbbing cock, and so aroused I *need* him to start moving.

Behind the fence, someone mutters about raccoons, and then the whole group laughs and continues toward the house. Anton takes this as his cue and begins pumping slowly, and I seriously might die if I can't make a sound.

He smirks down at me and whispers, "Should I ask if they had a nice dinner?"

I lock my legs around his waist and arch my back, squeezing until he clenches his jaw, suppressing a groan, until *finally* the neighbors' door slams.

"God, you're so fucking wet," he grunts, picking up his pace immediately. "If I didn't know better, Lydia . . . I'd say this turns you on."

I claw at the blanket beneath my hips, scandalized that he suggested it; mortified he might be right.

But then I stop being able to think at all because his thumb has touched down on my soaking wet clit, and he drives into me until his intensity peaks with a whispered, *"Fuck,"* followed by several deep, hard thrusts. His thumb remains in place on my clit, and for the first time ever, I'm so tuned in, I actually *feel* him empty into me. He grinds just the right spot with one hand and clamps my nipple between his fingers with the other, and in a hot rush of *oh my God,* I lose control. I buck against his fingers, my walls clamping around him still inside me, and it is all I can do not to shriek so it echoes through the entire neighborhood.

Anton waits until the waves of heat subside, then gently pulls out, wrapping me in his arms and nuzzling my hair.

"Not a raccoon," he says. "Just a couple of fucking bunnies."

CHAPTER TWENTY-ONE

"Here's one of your favorites. Ask *her*," Henry breathes down my neck.

I shoot him a glare, turning back around to greet one of our regular Pooch Park clients. "Hi, Gail! Tomás will get Freckles for you," I say, nodding gratefully to my manager.

"Lydia, it feels like ages since I saw you!" Gail greets me with a big hug. "Wow, you look radiant, dear."

I laugh, shaking my head. Gail and her springer spaniel have been daycare clients since right after I opened five years ago, and she has always been one of my biggest supporters. "Thanks, I think it's just the heat today," I say, fanning my face.

"I wish it would do that to me," she says, cackling.

Tomás returns with Freckles, who wiggles and dances at the sight of his mom, but before I can even give the dog a treat, Henry clears his throat.

I sigh, annoyed by his persistence. "Oh, listen Gail. If you don't mind, could I ask a question? We're just doing a little informal market research."

"Sure, what's it about?" she asks, looking Henry and his business suit up and down.

"Since you use both our daycare *and* grooming," Henry says, jumping in. "We were curious if you would enjoy having the two services combined?"

Gail only thinks for a moment. "Oh, without a doubt."

"Really?" I say through my teeth.

"Actually, would I even be able to add extra baths between haircuts? I would definitely do that, especially if Freckles was already here." She beams at me. "Lydia, you're brilliant. It's no wonder you're such a success."

Henry smirks at me as she leaves. "So, that's six yeses, and let's see . . . not a single no from any client we've asked."

"It's an incredibly small sample," I mutter, not willing to grant him the satisfaction of knowing Marisol said the same thing. But I knew this would only be a matter of time once I saw his projections. I just need encouragement to get used to the idea.

"So, can I schedule the contractor to start the build-out?" he asks.

"Fine. But we'll only be able to move Alicia over here." I cross my arms. "It's too small a space for more than one groomer. And we'll need to see how *this* goes before we talk about renovating Pooch II."

"Yes ma'am," he says with a curt bow like I'm the queen.

I stomp outside to lick my wounds, and to make sure the dogs are being rotated since it's still pretty hot for late September. Even though we have misters and plenty of water for them to play in, I keep a close eye on our four-legged clients in the heat. When I stop to dump out and refill a wading pool, Heartthrob runs over to attack the hose, effectively soaking me in the process. But it's so hot I can't really complain. Once I've checked in with the afternoon employees, I slip away into my office.

Anton and I have another date tonight. Which is to say, we're actually dressing up and leaving the house rather than staying home and stripping our clothes off. It's been weeks since we began his new experiment—since that night in the yard. And even I have to admit it's gone better than expected. We haven't had sex every day, but three or four times a week, at least. And while we *do* seem to be getting better at the physical act, it also feels like we're growing closer. More in tune with each other's moods and emotions. Even our therapist got on board, admitting it was an interesting strategy.

I close my office door, pulling my still-damp top over my head and reaching for the box of new Pooch Park T-shirts Henry and I ordered for the staff. But as I glance at the mirror on the back of the door, I notice I'm kind of spilling out of my bra. That hasn't happened since I started shopping at Allure Lingerie and they fit me with a correct bra size. I take a moment to tuck myself back in, but my breasts are so sensitive they almost hurt, and I have to do it delicately. Now that I think about it, my waistline feels snug too.

Great. I'll probably get my period and it'll ruin the whole night Anton and I have planned. I open up the cycle tracking app on my phone to see if there's any chance we might squeeze in one more date before my flow begins, but when I study the screen to check the predicted start of my period, my mouth drops open.

I bring the phone closer to my face, scrolling up to the date of my last cycle, then back down to the predicted start for this month. Which was a week ago.

My skin is clammy. The app is not always super accurate, but I can't remember the estimate being off by more than a few days. I swipe back, hovering for a minute over the home screen, wondering if I should call Anton. Then I close my eyes and set it down, forcing several deep breaths in and out of my chest.

There is no need to freak out. This isn't an emergency. I didn't get pregnant last month, but everything was so stressful, I probably entered a date wrong and threw off the stupid algorithm. All I need to do is go home and take a test. Then I can laugh at myself for jumping to conclusions and we can still go out and have fun. I grab my purse and keys, mumbling something to Tomás about placing orders from home on my way out the door. The heat hits me like a wall as soon as I get outside, and I'm so focused on getting the air conditioning going in my car, I nearly pull out of my parking space before remembering I left Heartthrob and running back inside.

There has got to be some kind of margin of error with pregnancy tests. Like, how many kits can the manufacturer make that will really be accurate? I've taken two, but it seems like it might be worth going out to buy a third or fourth, to be on the safe side. Just to see if maybe that second line doesn't appear. There's got to be some chance of that.

I pick up the box again, re-reading the instructions, though there aren't many steps and I pretty much have them memorized. Then I Google *pregnancy test false positives*, glancing at the two plastic sticks on my bathroom sink.

And like an asshole, Google tells me home tests are ninety-nine percent accurate.

I lower myself to the toilet, placing my head between my legs.

I'm pregnant. I'm going to have a—

This can't be.

Except what did I think was going to happen after stopping birth control? Having near-constant sex for several weeks? Just a bunch of orgasms, apparently.

I feel altogether stupid, terrified, and if I am being honest, a little remorseful. Which, as soon as I think it, instantly makes me feel guilty. This is what Anton and I want—it's the next step for us as a couple, and as a family. I ought to be overjoyed. But when I raise myself to a sitting position again, staring down at my tender breasts and relatively flat stomach, I feel like I'm going to cry.

It isn't really the physical piece I'm dreading—well, okay, I *am* scared of what pregnancy will do to me. Of getting stretched out everywhere and never regaining the shape I have now. Of throwing up every morning. Of having to go through labor. But the prospect of being someone's . . . *mother*. Putting a baby first, before everything. Before the Pooches. Before Anton. Before me. I think of Celia, unable to even eat dinner without first appeasing Baby Gabriel. And for just an instant I get a flicker of resentment.

Followed by utter horror.

Because that is *just* like our mother.

I drop my face into my hands. I can't imagine bringing another human into this world and making them feel like a burden. Except apparently I already am.

The front door slams, and I hear Anton goofing around with Heartthrob, tossing his toy and wrestling. My stomach drops and I look at my phone. I didn't realize what time it was. After a minute or two, I hear him coming down the hall calling my name, and suddenly I'm not ready for this. I glance at the tests on the counter, wondering for a split second if I could hide them. Delay the moment a little longer. Before we stop being a couple and have to become . . . parents.

Anton appears in the open door with a grin. "This is a nice surprise—how come you're home so early?"

He takes in the scene—me, sitting on the toilet, looking just as horrible as I feel. And his face falls immediately.

"Lydia? What's wrong? Are you sick?"

I shake my head, though now I do feel like I might throw up. Had I felt nauseous before I took the tests? I can't remember. Or is that something that just kicks in once you confirm you're knocked up?

He steps into the bathroom, reaching for me, but then I see

his gaze flicker over the items scattered across the counter. The box of pregnancy tests he purchased last month. The carefully unfolded instructions, and the two plastic strips, lying side-by-side, with their matching not-even-a-little-faint pink lines.

He freezes, turning to look at me. Clearly registering exactly what I'm scared for him to know. "Is that . . ." He swallows. "Are you . . . ?"

The pure, lilting *joy* in his voice amplifies the knot of guilt in my stomach, unleashing my floodwall of tears. I cover my face with my hands, as if that might block any of this from being real. And then he's folding me into him, arms encircling me. Holding me, whispering excited reassurances in my ear while I utterly lose my shit.

"I don't think I'm ready for this, Anton!" I sob. "I don't want to get sick. I don't want my body to change. And *we're* finally doing so well. What if this ruins everything?"

"Shh," he says, stroking my hair. "It's going to be amazing, Lydia. *You're* going to be amazing. You don't need to worry about any of those things. I'm going to help you through it—we'll do this together."

He continues to rock me in quiet celebration in our cramped bungalow bathroom, while snot and ugly tears pour out of my face. "What, are you going to hold back my hair while I puke?"

"Yes," he says quickly, then chuckles. "If that's what you need. And I . . ." He hesitates, clearly searching for some other way to be useful as a will-never-be-pregnant male. "I'll clean the bathroom every day so it's a nice place to be sick."

This makes me snort, and though it's devoid of humor, it seems to set him at ease. I guess I should probably be charmed that he wants to take on some responsibility. But despite his reassurances and promises to be a team, I can't help feeling like I'm facing this by myself. When it comes down to it, he won't be the one dealing with nausea. His body will stay god-like while mine gets huge and misshapen. He won't have to think twice about anything. And though I'm sure he'll be there to cheer me through birth, *I'm* the only one who can take on that pain.

I raise my gaze to his, trying to think of some way to put these doubts into words. To make him see I'm the literal vessel and there's nothing he can really do but promise to change every single stupid diaper when this is over. Except when I look at him—*he* is actually glowing. Like, I've never really understood why people say that to expectant mothers, but that's the only way I can describe my husband's face right now. And because I hate myself for not sharing that feeling with him, my eyes refill with tears.

"I—I'm not sure I can do this," I sob.

"You'll do amazing, Lydia. How could you not?" Anton says, but I think he's still talking about pregnancy and I'm too scared to even say what I'm really afraid of. Because he clearly thinks I'm capable of being like his mother when *everything* points to me turning into mine.

"I didn't think it would happen so fast," I say, and this at least is the truth. Last month gave me a false sense of security. He'd wanted to get me pregnant, we'd *tried*, but when it didn't happen . . . I know people who have been trying to get pregnant for years. But for the life of me, no one seems to talk about it happening on the *second* try. "I'm just a little shocked."

"Me too." He wipes his hand over his face, and I turn at the quaver in his voice. Is he having doubts too? Is he as freaked out as me? But then he looks at me, beaming. "This might be the best thing to ever happen."

I narrow my eyes, unable to hide my skepticism. "I'll have to get back to you about that."

He laughs, and I gasp when he scoops me into his arms and carries me into our bedroom, cradling me like a treasure. The man works out like it's his lifeline, but I am not exactly petite, so I'm always amazed at how easily he can toss me around. And though I show no outward sign of my new "condition," my body already seems bigger. Heavier. More awkward.

"How are you feeling? Seriously?" he asks, laying me gently back against the pillows.

I press my lips together, not interested in ruining the moment for him, but I also want to tell the truth. So I focus on physical symptoms. "Not that different, really. A little tender. Maybe tired."

He clasps my hand in his. "How about we stay in tonight?"

I nod, my heart flooding with appreciation because he knows me so well. A few hours ago, I had been looking forward to going out, flirting and enticing each other through dinner. I was prepared to come home, receive *all* of his attention, and in turn, focus all of mine on him. And while it's been wonderful, learning new ways to please each other, feeling so connected these last few weeks. It has also been a lot of work. And I've learned enough about myself to know I won't get there at all tonight.

Anton slips off my shoes and tucks the covers up around me, somehow knowing just what I need. I close my eyes, thinking he's going to lie down with me, but instead, he rises from the bed. "How does stir fry sound—peanut chicken?"

I shake my head, surprising myself when I wrinkle my nose. That's one of my favorite dishes, but for some reason it doesn't sound at all appealing. "Maybe just a salad?"

"Anything you want," he says, backing toward the door. But then he hesitates, looking back at me with a strange expression. He comes back over, sinking next to me on the bed, and for a second I'm sure he's going to touch me and it's all I can do not to pull away. I mean, it's not like he can knock me up *again*. But the last thing I feel right now is sexy.

Instead of reaching for my body, tracing fingers across my

skin or searching under my clothes, he leans in and lays a gentle kiss on my stomach, just below my navel.

"I love you," he says softly. But for the first time in our relationship, I'm not sure it's directed at me.

I place my hand over the spot where his lips touched my belly, biting down on my lip. A cold sweat breaks over my skin, and I try to decide if I'm jealous or scared. Either way, I hope he can't tell.

"Stay here and relax," Anton says. "I'll bring you dinner."

My relief unwinds as he moves to leave, but when I see him in the door, phone in hand, I call him back.

"Anton?"

He stops, expression glowy again as he looks back at me.

"Maybe let's not tell anyone . . . just yet?"

His brows draw together, so I answer his question before he asks.

"I just thought um . . . I mean, I'm sure the tests are right. But we should probably get confirmation from a doctor. You know?"

He hesitates a second, then tucks his phone away and nods. "That's a good idea. Okay, we'll wait."

I let out a long breath. "Thanks for understanding."

"Of course," he says, smile returning. "For now, it'll be our private celebration. Just . . . the three of us."

CHAPTER TWENTY-TWO

Him

Six weeks of fucking. We've never done anything like it all the years we've been married. We never could have. Almost every single day, I either woke up hard and she rode me in the morning, or we were peeling off clothes the moment we walked in the door from work. The first week I was hesitant, wondering if she was going to pull back, lose interest. But she didn't. It's felt a bit like the honeymoon we never had. And it seems like my strategy fucking worked.

I glance at the clock. Our appointment with Lydia's doctor isn't for two more hours, but then we'll know for sure. I was actually surprised she was able to get in so quickly. It's only been six days since she took the home test. But when she said they had an opening, I promised I'd be there. I meant it when I told her we'd do this together.

I can tell she's a little freaked out, but every time I look at her—I can't even describe how it feels. Weird and fantastic. It sounds kind of primitive, but I just keep thinking there is a life growing inside her and *I* put it there. We did. Together. It certainly won't fill the space my mother left when she died, but it fills my heart in a strange way, knowing there's this new part of *us* on the way.

I get back to my office after a meeting just before four, and I'm about to gather my things and head out to our appointment, but I pause when Carl shows up at my door.

"Anton, I just wanted to say nice work this afternoon. We're in good shape with the Castro account, due in large part because of how thorough you are with your projections."

"Thanks, Carl. You know I like to cross my T's and dot my I's."

"Indeed," he says, clapping me on the shoulder. "While I have you, Derek and I have been discussing different space needs for the Springs office. I'd like you to drive down with me and look at some of the possibilities in the next week or so."

It isn't a question, so I just nod. "Of course. Should I coordinate schedules with Milo?"

"Let's make it the two of us this time." He gives me one of his broad smiles, then steps in and closes the door. "Anton, if you're willing to take this on, I think we could discuss making you a junior partner."

"That's . . ." I set my keys down and swallow. "Thank you, sir."

He grins. "I'm excited about this opportunity for you."

"I am too," I say, and I mean it. The last month or so has been a struggle, but I've been with Vesper since I got out of college and I've always tried to give Carl my best. "When do you think we might want to get off the ground?"

"Oh, it's going to take some time," he says. "Not before the new year. And Derek and I are still hashing out some organizational ideas, so realistically, we might be looking at spring."

"Well, I can't wait to hear more about it." We shake hands, and I thank him again. But my enthusiasm fades as he leaves my office and I pick up my keys again. There was a time when being offered a junior partnership would have been the most exciting news I could've received. But it looks like there will be a lot of big changes coming this spring.

The address Lydia gave me for her OB/GYN is right next to Rose Hospital. It looks much like any doctor's offices from the outside, but once I step through the door, the specialty is obvious. The waiting room is filled with women of all ages. Some aren't obviously pregnant, but many are, and the only other guy in the room sits with a lady who looks like she swallowed two watermelons.

A receptionist behind the desk gives me a skeptical look. "Are you here for an appointment, sir?"

"Umm . . ."

"We're here to see Dr. Sharma at four thirty—Lydia Richie?" my wife says, coming through the door behind me. I exhale, looking at her with a little thrill. Her presence gives me permission to be here, but also, I'm just plain excited.

While we wait for the receptionist to find Lydia's name in the system, I take her hand and squeeze. She looks fantastic. We both came from work, and it's still warm for September, so she's in shorts and a tank top. But I guess some of the things people say about pregnancy must be true because she looks more beautiful than usual. It has been so hard to resist putting my hands all over her since I saw those positive tests —especially after spending the last several weeks the way we have. But she's started complaining of nausea, and that she's tired all the time, and I've tried to respect that. I'm not even sure it's *okay* for us to have sex. I have a whole list of questions for her doctor.

"All right, we've got you all checked in. If you'll just provide a urine sample," the receptionist says, handing over a plastic specimen cup, "they'll call you back in a minute."

Lydia does as she's asked, but when she comes back, she

seems even quieter. After they bring us back to a room, take her weight and blood pressure, and ask the date of her last period, she still doesn't say much. When they ask her to undress, I'm starting to feel useless, so I take her clothes and shoes, folding and tucking them neatly aside while she situates herself on the exam table.

"Nervous?" I ask once she's settled in a gown with a paper sheet draped over her like a blanket.

"I guess," she murmurs.

"You . . . you look beautiful," I say, resisting the urge to tuck a loose tendril of hair behind her ear.

She glances at me, and it's hard to read her expression, but at that moment there's a knock on the door, and a woman with red glasses and deep brown skin enters the room.

"Lydia! Nice to see you!" She greets my wife with a warm smile, which Lydia returns, and I'm grateful to see her whole demeanor improve with her doctor in the room.

"Great to meet you," I say when Lydia introduces me.

"Well, your urine culture sure was positive, but we'll just do a quick ultrasound and get this all confirmed," the doctor says, approaching Lydia calmly and efficiently. "How are you feeling?"

"Fine, I guess. Mostly tired." Lydia lies back on the exam table while the doctor looks her over, pulling her gown aside at one point to examine her breasts. There is absolutely *nothing* sexual about anything she's doing. But all of this is so foreign to me, I'm afraid I'll be caught ogling, so I look away.

"All right, let's get down to business." Dr. Sharma adjusts the exam table and helps Lydia place her feet in a couple of metal stirrups that pop out of the end. Then she dims the lights and takes a seat on a stool in front of a small white machine. I expect her to pick up the sensor and place it on Lydia's midsection the way I've seen it done in movies, but my eyebrows shoot up as she opens a condom and slides it over a long white wand attached to the machine. "Transvaginal ultrasound," she says, apparently reading my face. "Best way to see everything in the early stage."

She squirts a lump of lube onto the tip of the condom, then turns to Lydia.

"There will be a little pressure. Let me know if anything is uncomfortable."

She reaches under the drape with the device, and I grab Lydia's hand. She looks at me and squeezes my fingers, and for a second, her eyes seem scared. But then the doctor flips a switch on the machine and our attention is drawn to a loud, rapid squishing sound filling the room.

"There we are," the doctor says, focused on a dark, bean-shaped image on a screen. She glances at us and smiles. "That's a nice strong heartbeat."

My mouth drops open. I refocus on the rapid rhythm, and my molasses brain finally catches up. "That's a baby?" I look at Lydia, but she doesn't return my gaze. She's staring wide-eyed at the screen. "That's *our* baby?"

"Congratulations!" The doctor types into the computer with one hand and adjusts the wand, appearing to take a few measurements. "My best guess . . . you're around seven or eight weeks."

"Wait. What?" Lydia tears her eyes from the image, staring at Dr. Sharma. "That can't be right. I just had my period in early August."

The doctor chuckles. "Technically, the first two weeks of pregnancy, you're not even pregnant. Those are the weeks your body gets ready to ovulate, preparing for fertilization. But they go into the total count." She pivots on her stool, taking a look at her laptop screen. "By the time you missed your period and took your test, you were already six weeks along."

Lydia clutches my hand, staring at the blob on the screen. "But I..." Her voice trails off.

I close my eyes, transfixed by the sound. The *life* that has joined us in the room.

"The good news is, your first trimester is already almost over. Once you get to twelve weeks, things tend to get smoother." Dr. Sharma presses a few buttons on the machine and it spits out two small squares of paper. Then she must withdraw the device from Lydia, because the image on the screen disappears and a hush falls over the room. As soon as it's gone, all I want is to hear it again.

The doctor cleans Lydia up, throws out the condom, and puts the machine away, handing us each a printout of the sonogram to take home. "Do either of you have questions?" she asks, looking at us pointedly over her glasses.

Lydia doesn't acknowledge her, just stares at the picture.

"When—" I croak, surprised by the emotion in my voice. "When will it—he—she? Be born?"

She flips the lights back on and references a calendar on the counter. "Let's shoot for . . . May sixteenth."

"Wait," Lydia says. Maybe it's the lights coming on, or mention of the due date, but she straightens, looking earnestly at Dr. Sharma. "What changes at twelve weeks that you were talking about?"

"Nothing, really." The doctor shrugs. "But it's roughly the end of the first trimester, which is when most women start to have more energy and feel better. Some people like to wait till twelve weeks to announce their pregnancies since there's a slightly higher chance of miscarriage in the first trimester."

Lydia's eyebrows shoot up. "You mean there's some chance it won't . . ."

I squeeze her hand. And the doctor is quick to shake her head. "I wouldn't worry about it. Some pregnancies do end early, and I could bore you with the statistics, but there's no reason to expect that. Just let us know if you have any bleeding or discomfort. Otherwise, I'll see you for your next check in four weeks."

She reaches for the door, and I glance at Lydia, who's staring at the ultrasound image in her hand, biting her lip. I can't tell what she's thinking. Whether she's excited or scared. Even I keep ricocheting back and forth between the two. I take her hand again and put myself right in front of her so she has to focus on me.

"Hey. Don't forget. We're doing this together." I lower my voice to a whisper. "Same way we got here."

She sucks in a breath when I say this, cheeks coloring, and for just a moment we look at each other, and every touch we shared over the last six weeks flashes between us.

"Dr. Sharma," I say hastily, stopping her on her way out the door. "Is it okay to um . . . well, can we . . ."

"Have sex?" the doctor asks, a smile tugging at her lips. My face goes hot. I had hoped I wasn't that obvious. "As long as everyone's feeling good, go ahead and have fun."

The door closes, and I turn back to Lydia with a stupid grin. But she's already off the table, half dressed, pulling up her shorts under the gown. I wait till she's wrangled back into her bra and tank top, and when she finally turns and picks up her purse, I open my arms.

"I can't believe this is real," I say, pulling her close.

She brings her arms up to return the hug, but stays quiet.

"Hey." I pull back to look at her. "Everything okay?"

"What? Oh, yeah." She smiles, but it doesn't reach her eyes. "Sorry, I was just thinking over what she said about twelve weeks."

My brows draw together. "She said not to worry about it."

"Yeah," she says, though her voice is uncertain. "I just think, like she said, maybe we should keep this to ourselves until then."

I stare down at her. "I'm not sure that was a suggestion."

She shrugs. But when she looks up at me, her eyes are pleading, like this is important to her.

"Okay." My shoulders drop. "It's only four more weeks."

She buries her face in my neck and lets out a deep sigh. And when she pulls back, she's smiling for real, glowing and beautiful. *Carrying our child.* And it's impossible to think about anything else.

CHAPTER TWENTY-THREE

ANTON WANTS TO GET DINNER ON THE WAY HOME FROM THE doctor's office to celebrate, but I claim nausea. Even though I haven't had much of that particular pregnancy symptom so far. Guess it would serve me right if it started for real now. I'm just not feeling very celebratory. More like bloated and uncomfortable. I've never had six-pack abs like my husband, but my stomach is still as flat as it ever was. But all my pants feel tight. Even my bras are fitting snug. And I'm so *tired*. What I want more than anything is to take a hot bath, put on my striped pajamas, and read a good book in bed.

But just as he climbs out of his truck in the driveway behind me, my phone rings.

"Oh God. It's my mom." I cover my face. I can't think of anyone in the world I want to talk to less at this moment.

Anton grimaces on my behalf. But, noting my paralysis, gently offers direction. "You don't have to tell her anything. We agreed—not till twelve weeks. But see what she wants or you know she won't stop calling."

He's right about that. I follow him up the front steps, swiping the screen and putting her on speakerphone as he unlocks the front door.

"Lydia, where have you been?" my mom harps through the receiver. "I called an hour ago and you didn't answer."

I open my mouth and almost say I was in a doctor's appointment, but catch myself before walking into that trap. "Sorry, set my phone down on silent. Must've missed it."

Heartthrob dances around us through the living room. I left him home today because of the appointment, and now he's insistent we make up for it, so Anton gets on the floor and pretends to steal his toy from him.

"Well, I'm calling because you have *got* to give me an answer about Thanksgiving. It isn't polite to leave the hostess hanging like this."

"Oh, sorry. I thought—"

"Celia insists we have to construct the whole meal around nap time." I can hear her eye-roll from four states away. "And when I asked her to make a pie, she said she'd *buy* one. Really, I'm trying to defer to her and Adam, being new parents and all. But you have to come balance out this nonsense."

My throat goes dry. New parents indeed.

I swipe to my calendar app with rising panic, counting the weeks until Thanksgiving. I'll be more than twelve weeks. Actually fourteen. I glance down at my stomach, trying to imagine what I'll look like by then. Could I still hide it? Or . . . maybe I won't need to. *Maybe it won't stick,* I think, with a hefty amount of guilt.

Movement catches my eye, and I glance across the room to see Anton gesturing at me, giving me a thumbs up sign. I narrow my eyes, trying to understand what he means.

"You need to hurry up and figure out flights," my mother goes on. "But *I* need to know so I can schedule manis for all of us." She pauses. "Do you think I need to include Sarah?"

I snort. "It might be rude to exclude Celia's mother-in-law, yes," I say, filling my water bottle at the fridge.

Anton has given up gesticulating and grabbed a paper and pen.

"I suppose," my mother says with obvious disdain. "Family holidays are so challenging."

I nearly choke on the water as I sip. "Yes, they are."

And then Anton steps in front of me, holding a paper with these words scrawled in black ink: *Let's do it.*

I look up at him, confused, mouthing, *do what?*

Anton flattens his mouth into a line and scribbles, *Thanksgiving in Ohio.*

I gape at him. He's lost his mind.

My mother prattles on, oblivious to our dispute. "You know, while you're here, we should have a family portrait taken. Our family *is* growing. Despite you and Anton."

I jab the mute button on the screen and hold it up between my husband and me. "You want to spend a holiday with her? Has this year not been bad enough?"

"You'd of course need to get your hair done, Lydia," Mom continues. "We can't have you looking the way you did at Celia's wedding."

Anton grits his teeth and glares at the phone, clearly aware of the terribleness of his suggestion. But when he meets my eyes again, they're oddly resolute. "You'll be fourteen weeks by then. It'll be the perfect way to announce."

"Nope." I shake my head. "I can do that without flying to Ohio."

"Of course," Mom goes on, "you and Anton may stay with me again, in your old bedroom. Since you and Celia have such a hard time getting along."

My husband and I stare at each other like she's in the room with us. I dig my nails into my palms.

"Think about it," Anton says in a whisper, despite the phone being muted. "We go out there, make the announcement, they fuss over you, then we come home. If you call her or post the news online, your mom will insist on seeing you and fly out *here*."

I press my lips together, groaning when I realize he's right. It will be bad telling her in person, but better than having her descend on us here. First, she'll gloat. Because she'll be getting something she wants. Then she'll parade me in front of all her friends, announcing it like she's the one giving birth. But Anton's right. After that, we could probably leave. There'd be nothing else for her to do but wait for the main event. I close my eyes, wondering if we could just lie to her about the whole thing until after the birth. I can't imagine going through labor with my mother anywhere nearby.

"Do I have to answer her now?"

Anton makes a face. "Do you want her to keep calling?"

I let out a deep sigh. "I hate when she feels like she's won."

He comes closer and takes my hand, laying the sonogram photos on the counter in front of us. "Look, she's not my favorite," he agrees. "But she *is* the only grandparent our baby will have . . ."

His voice drifts off as he says this, and for a moment I get scared this will trigger him somehow. Make him pull away, right when he's the one thing I desperately need.

Instead, he reaches for me, pulling me close to him. So comforting and reassuring with that one gesture, it's clear he meant what he said. We'll do this together.

"Lydia? Hello? Are you even listening?" My mother snipes through the air.

I fumble to un-mute. "Yes—sorry, Mom. You cut out for a minute. What were you saying?"

"I *said* it would be nice if you came out Tuesday instead of Wednesday. Then I could bring you and Celia to my book club."

Anton's grip around me tightens and he leans toward the phone. "We'd love to come for Thanksgiving, Marion. Thanks for the invite. Lydia and I both have commitments that Tuesday, but we'll fly out Wednesday. Oh, and we don't want to impose, so we'll be staying at a hotel."

My mother is silent for an entire five seconds. Much as she loves to railroad me, she's never successfully done it to my husband.

"Lovely to hear your voice, Anton. I'll let Celia know."

There's another pause, and I chime in. "We'll book the flights now. Can't wait to see you, Mom." Anton hangs up before she gets in another word, and I sink back into his arms. "Thank you. She just . . ." I don't finish my sentence, but I know I don't have to. My relationship with her is complicated, but Anton knows that better than anyone.

He nuzzles my hair. "How're you feeling?"

I wonder briefly if this is a question I'll just have to get used to. I've been asked multiple times today by every person who knows I'm pregnant. "Tired," I say, honestly.

His hands drift down below my belly button, lingering there protectively. But I'm surprised when I find myself wishing they'd wander elsewhere. Not because I'm aroused at all, actually. Sex has hardly crossed my mind since I took the test last week. What I miss is how much closer we felt with all that physical intimacy.

"Why don't you take a bath or something?" he says in a low voice. "Are you still not hungry?"

"I could eat a little something," I say truthfully.

He straightens, sliding around to face me. "Then I'll fix you a little something."

I look up, and his eyes are so warm, so *full*. My gaze flickers to the ultrasound images, and I bite my lip, glancing down at my stomach. "Oof. There's a picture and everything. I guess this is really happening."

His face seems to glow, and I home in on that, hoping some of it will transfer to me. *Not* being excited is starting to feel kind of . . . wrong. I'm worried he's going to notice.

"It just doesn't seem real yet," I confess. "Maybe it would actually help if I was throwing up."

He snorts. "Careful what you wish for."

I laugh, closing the space between us and laying my cheek against his chest, wishing we could stay like this forever. Just the *two* of us. Finally, however, one of the pregnancy symptoms that's become hard to ignore forces me to let go. "I really need to pee."

He squeezes my hand. "I'll make us a salad. Sound okay?"

I nod. But once I'm in the bathroom with the door closed, I stand there for a minute, studying myself in the mirror. I really don't look any different. Maybe my breasts are a little fuller. But I could just be retaining water from too many potato chips at lunch. Ugh, it's not like I *want* to look pregnant. The longer I can go without people asking me about it, the better. I'm not even looking forward to new clothes. I just want to fit into my old ones.

Staring at my midsection, it's impossible to even imagine something growing in there. Is this a message from the universe? Don't get too attached, because it isn't going to last? Or am I just unable to nurture, somehow? Not cut out for it. Like my own mother.

I close my eyes, desperate for something else to focus on, and my mind easily slips to the Pooches. Henry. I will have to tell him about this—but that can wait until I've dealt with my family. I frown, realizing I'll probably have to go along with all of his ideas now. He barely takes me seriously as a business partner as it is. I doubt that will improve after the birth, with a burp rag draped on my shoulder. This is what happens to women when they start families. Which is one reason I've been reluctant to do it.

But then I think of Marisol, efficiently conducting business with her toddler in tow. No one else calls the shots for her. She doesn't even really have a husband helping with her kid.

I pull out my phone, tempted to give her a call, beg her advice.

Only something makes me hesitate.

If I talk to her now, and anything happens in the next few weeks . . . that would be even more complicated. She'd be concerned, maybe upset. I don't want to burden her with that. This is why the doctor said people wait to share pregnancies until twelve weeks.

The one person I could, probably *should* confide in is Caprice. But when I think about calling her up with this news, her voice echoes through my head. *For God's sake,* don't *have a baby if that isn't what you want.*

I chew my lip. This *is* what I want—what Anton and I both want—a future together. And though he said we didn't have to start a family, it's clearly what he needs. I'm pretty sure Caprice still thinks I should have left Anton after Unmatched. But if I've learned anything about marriage over the last eight years, it's that it takes a lot of work, from both sides. I just wish I could think of a way to explain that so she won't be disappointed in me.

CHAPTER TWENTY-FOUR

"DID YOU DRINK ALL THE REST OF THE COFFEE?" I ASK, SETTING my mug down in front of our cold, empty Mr. Coffee. "I only got one cup."

"I didn't make a full pot," Anton says. He's not looking at me, unloading a couple of grocery bags on the table. At seven a.m. I blink at him, trying to comprehend his actions separately from his words, but it's like my wheels are spinning, stuck in my empty mug.

"Why?" I finally ask, unable to come up with a single reasonable explanation aside from a nationwide coffee shortage.

"I was doing some reading, and it's recommended that pregnant women limit themselves to one serving of caffeine per day." He reaches into one of the bags in front of him. "I thought we could try this?"

He's holding a small red package, and I make out the word *decaf* emblazoned across the front before my eyes cut back to his face. He seems to realize his timing is crappy, because he quickly adds, "I only allowed myself one cup too. Whatever restrictions you have, I'm also taking on."

I look from him to the coffee pot, biting back a remark

about his nobility. "What exactly are the health risks of *coffee* to pregnant women?"

"Caffeine is linked to miscarriage and low birth weight, among other things," he recites in that irritating Professor Google tone. He produces a piece of paper and sticks it to the fridge with a couple of magnets. "I printed out a list of pregnancy superfoods we can use as a yes-guide. It also gives a rundown of no-foods."

"No-foods," I repeat in a deadpan tone.

He pulls out a pack of bran muffins that truly look like rocks and presents them to me with a medley of berries and a cup of yogurt.

"Oh. Are you nauseated?" he asks when I don't reach for any of them.

"Yes," I lie, walking to the back door to let Heartthrob outside, suddenly anxious for a breath of fresh air. My bladder had me up at four a.m. contemplating my choices about this whole pregnancy thing. If he's trying to make me feel less happy about it, he's doing an excellent job.

When I turn back to the kitchen, he thrusts a package of ginger gummies at me and sets the kettle on the stove. "These are supposed to help. Do you want some mint tea?"

I grimace. For some reason, the thought of mint flavored tea actually does make me nauseous.

"I think I want a shower," I say, heading for the hall. The faster I leave for work, the faster I can ignore all of this *yes-no* nonsense. But Anton is still pulling goodies from his grocery bag.

"Your appetite might not improve until the second trimester. But it's important to take a prenatal vitamin every day, especially when you aren't hungry." He presents me with a large jar of gummy vitamins and stands there like Mary Poppins waiting for me to take my medicine.

"Will you be taking these too?" I snap.

"Huh?"

I grind my teeth. "Where did you say you got all this useful info?"

"Oh, I'll show you." He pulls up an app on his phone with a wide smile. "I made us a BabyBump account. It sends an email every week with tips and info, and lets us know how the baby is growing. See? It's already the size of a raspberry."

I glare pointedly at the untouched berries on my plate, but then he places the phone in my hand and I'm staring at an illustration that looks at first like a baby bird—until I notice the very human-looking head, arms, and legs. I scan down the email, eyes widening when I learn the creature growing inside me has apparently, at eight weeks, already formed all of its organs, and now has lips, a nose, and eyelids. I glance up to meet Anton's gaze, wondering if it will have hazel eyes that match his.

But then I scroll down to the *your body* section of the email, which details, in startling accuracy, many of the ways I currently feel. I still haven't thrown up, but I do feel nauseated. Exhausted. My breasts are so tender it hurts to just brush up against things. And I'm so freaking bloated and gassy I can't imagine trying to squeeze myself into a pair of jeans. It explains, in the same cheery tone my husband has taken on, that all of these unpleasant things are part of the miracle growing inside me. The miracle I get to meet in *only thirty-two more weeks!*

I hand the phone back to Anton, but it isn't until I see his expression that I register the tears running down my face.

"Lydia?" He stares, obviously caught off guard. There was nothing in that email that should've been read as anything but a total celebration.

Maybe that's my problem. We agreed to this. We worked toward this goal together. But now that we've achieved it, celebrating is the last thing I want to do—I feel like I need a support group. Instead of a bombardment of info on the *miracle* I'm creating, I could use tips on how to cope with second thoughts. Feeling like your body is no longer your own. Or coming to terms with the unsettling idea that you've made a huge, huge mistake.

I thrust my hand out, opting to pretend I'm not obviously upset. "Give me some of those vitamins."

He does as I ask, and I force myself to chew and swallow, glancing at the clock. It's so freaking early, and I'm still dying for another cup of coffee.

"Shower," is the only coherent word I form as I turn away from him, a wave of nausea trying to force the vitamins back up my throat as I fumble down the hall.

But the worst part is, while I'm officially miserable and feeling sorry for myself, I also feel *guilty*. For not having the reaction I know he expects. For not being happy and excited with him. A baby is literally the one thing he's wanted. The thing that could hold us together, act like a salve after his mother's death. And I am ruining it with my own selfish tears.

When I make it to our bedroom, I throw off my robe. Tossing it onto the unmade bed where it looks like a crumpled, huddled version of me. I yank off my blue-striped pajama top, then bottoms, throwing them toward the hamper and missing, then stomping over them on my way to the bathroom. To the shower where I doubt the water and steam will wake me up anything as well as caffeine.

But just as I reach the door of our bedroom, it fills with the tall, cut form of my husband. Anton stands there, drinking in my naked shape, his face impossible to read. My first inclination is to cover myself. My robe is across the room. But if he'd just *move*, I could duck into the bathroom and close the door. He doesn't. He just stands there, looking. Scrutinizing me so closely, I shy away from his gaze. I don't want him to see me like this. Bloated, unattractive, smeared with ugly tears.

I step back to grab the robe, but before I reach the bed he encircles me in his strong, steady arms. Holding me close against his body. Locking me to him in a warm but unyielding embrace. And it's there, held in place so I can't run from him, where I can't do anything to hide or deflect or pretend this isn't happening, that I fall to pieces in full-on sobs.

He must know—he *has* to. It's written all over me. I thought I'd be okay with this, but I'm not. If he hadn't already realized I'm not cut out to be a mother, it's obvious now. And how can he not hold that against me?

I wait for him to say something. Sigh maybe. Express regret that he chose the wrong woman—on so many levels, we know now. But instead, he sinks with me to the bed, pulling me awkwardly into his lap. And he holds me. Until my tears subside.

When my shoulders have stopped shaking, he pulls a tissue from somewhere and waits while I dry my face and blow my nose. It's cold in the room, and as I press closer to him for warmth, he shifts me onto the bed. Suddenly, I'm sure he's going to tuck me under the covers, give me a kiss, perhaps, and get the hell out of here. As any sane man would, faced with a hormonal, sobbing, snot-fest first thing in the morning.

But once my head is settled on my pillow, he straightens, looming over me. His gaze makes its way over my body, but doesn't rest on my stomach, like it has constantly the last week. There's something different about this. Something familiar and hungry. My face heats, and I cross my arms over my naked form as I realize what he wants. Not long ago, I used to dread the way he's looking at me. I was so uncomfortable in my own body, I couldn't grasp what it could do for me —for us. Recently, I've grown more confident, even come to look forward to this. But I'm not feeling it right now. I just feel swollen and kind of gross. But as I move to cover myself, my husband takes hold of my wrists, gently shaking his head as he raises them above me.

"Please. Don't hide from me."

I look past him, at the ceiling. "Anton, I'm not—"

He smothers my words with his lips. Then pulls back briefly, eyes flashing as he looks at me. And for the first time since those positive pregnancy tests upended our lives, I detect the barest tug of . . . something. Between my legs.

I try to lower my arms, intending to wrap them around his neck, pull him close, but he has them pinned to the sheets above my head. I squirm in his grip a little, but only manage to thrust my newly enlarged breasts toward his face. I'm not sure if it's hormones or just the temperature of the room, but both my nipples stand up bright pink and erect. Anton's pupils darken.

Still firmly holding me in place, he drifts down, running the flat of his tongue warm and delicious over each of my nipples.

I hiss. My breasts are so tender, I've avoided handling them much myself, but this is just the right amount of pressure and warmth, and so, so gentle. Each nipple obediently tightens in response, and before I realize what's happening, the subtle tug at my center blossoms into something more like an ache.

"Oh God," he whispers, voice laden with lust. "Just look at you, Mrs. Richie."

And then he releases my hands, trailing his fingers down through my hair, over my breasts, where I let out a sharp gasp. He skirts them carefully, letting his tongue slide down along my stomach while his hands trace over my waist and hips.

He glances up to meet my gaze when he reaches my thighs, then places a kiss at their apex before nudging them gently apart. My face floods with heat, my eyes slamming shut as his tongue lightly parts my folds. We had been exploring one another recently, for sure. But it's been a while since he gave me this specific kind of attention. And with pregnancy, like my breasts, I now realize my entire vulva seems extra sensitive and engorged.

He laps his tongue once up my center, bottom to top, and I gasp. Then he does it again. And again. The third time, my hips rise off the bed with his laps. Needing something to do with my hands, I weave my fingers into his hair, but as soon as I do it feels like I'm trying to hold his face between my legs and I let go, pressing them to the bed on either side of me instead. He makes no move to rise when I release him, rather parting my legs wider, swirling his tongue through my folds.

A sound escapes my lips, but it barely registers because with his breath against my skin, I've just become aware of the intense amount of moisture already between my legs. Anton seems to notice it too, drawing his fingers through it and spreading it over my thighs. I might be embarrassed if I wasn't so focused on his attentions. I clench my core muscles in anticipation, sure he'll rise at any moment and plunge his great length into me.

I *want* him to. I'm too slick for him not to.

But just when I think he's going to pull away and mount me, he sucks my clit into his mouth instead, sliding a long finger deep into my vagina in the same moment. My back arches off the bed, and he moves with me, mouth clamped in place as a light spasm teases through my core. Perhaps sensing this, he doubles down. Sucking and licking my clit with intensity, sliding his finger in and out.

The ache at my center intensifies, and he adds another finger, thrusting and sucking, and I am fully bucking my hips now. He moves with my rhythm, and vaguely, I'm aware of my sore, erect nipples bouncing, adding to the overall sensation. But then he does something, I'm not sure—it's subtly different. Maybe just a finger curling up against my inner wall. But just as he does, I have this moment where it's like I'm floating above myself, looking down at my naked form writhing across our bed, my handsome husband kneeling with his face between my legs. And then his lips create just the right amount of suction in just the right place, and all of these things collide in my head.

My whole body crescendos. My voice echoes off the walls with each wave, which I faintly register, are somehow more intense than ever. Until finally, I'm left trembling, eyes closed. Anton climbs onto the bed, and when I look at him, he's grinning at me. He reaches forward, beckoning me into his arms.

Which is when I double over in pain, gripping my midsection.

CHAPTER TWENTY-FIVE

Him

"Are you sure you're okay? Can I get you anything else?" I ask, clearing away the dinner dishes.

"I told you, I'm fine." Lydia smiles sweetly. "Just tired. Think I'll get ready for bed."

It isn't even eight o'clock and she only picked at her meal, but she went into the Pooches early this morning and she's barely holding her head up. "Go ahead. I'll finish in here."

She looks at me gratefully, sliding out of her chair, and I try not to leer at the cleavage peeking out of her V-neck, daydreaming about following, lifting her shirt over her head . . .

I force my eyes away. It's been nearly a week since I went down on her and made her climax, which triggered massive cramping in her uterus. We called the OB's office immediately and the nurse assured us it was totally normal after orgasm, especially in the first trimester. She said there was nothing to worry about as long as there wasn't any bleeding, and there hasn't been. But it was sobering for both of us. I've been afraid to touch her ever since.

I clear my throat. "Um, I was thinking I'd start clearing

out the second bedroom this weekend. Maybe get it ready for a coat of paint?"

She pauses in the door of the kitchen, glancing down the hall toward the room in question. "Isn't it a little soon? I'm still only nine weeks."

"I know, I just thought . . ." That I need an outlet, something to do with my hands if I can't put them on her. It's funny, you'd think I'd be okay backing off now. She's growing our baby; we reached the goal we set out to achieve. After talking with the nurse, we agreed to hold off on sex at least until the second trimester. But the more pregnant she gets, the more I just want to put my hands all over her, claim her as mine, again and again. "It's going to get cold this weekend. It seemed like a good time to start. Maybe we could go pick out colors together."

She gives me a strained smile. "But if it might not—if we don't even know what it is?"

I shrug. "I thought we could go with something neutral. The walls are pretty dark in there. I just want to brighten it up."

"And what about all the furniture and stuff? Where will I keep my laptop, and yours? The printer and our files? I've had a home office for five years, Anton. I'm not sure I can just work from wherever."

But you do all the time, I want to say. The kitchen, living room—our bed. She hardly ever sits in the other bedroom, at her actual desk. I bite my cheek. "Maybe, if we're going to be making space for a family, we should think about how to leave work at work."

At this, she bristles. "What is *that* supposed to mean?"

"Just . . . you have an office at the Pooches. I have one at Vesper—"

"That might work for your nine-to-five, Anton, but I own three businesses. I can't just not think about them when I'm not there."

I set my jaw. "Okay, that's fair. We'll . . . figure the space out. But there *are* going to be some changes, Lydia. We should start making a list of names. And have you thought about when you might step back to take some time off?"

She folds her arms over her chest, causing her already-snug shirt to pull down in front, and it is all I can do to focus on her face. Especially with her frowning at me like that.

"We're at nine weeks! According to the email you sent me this morning, this thing is barely the size of an olive. I just—I have decisions I need to make for next week. I can't think about what's going to happen in seven more months."

It's my turn to take offense. I've never actually called Lydia a workaholic, but her work-life balance, or lack thereof, was one of the factors that pushed me toward Unmatched last spring and made me feel like I had no other choice. She's become more conscious of it, and does her best to strike a balance, but sometimes I still get the vibe that she can't make time for me. Which makes me a little uneasy when I think about her making time for a family.

"Okay, when will you?" I ask as calmly as I can.

"Soon," she says, twisting her fingers in her hair.

I exhale, trying to take a gentler tone. "Look, I know you're already doing extra work—you're *making* our baby. But we need a plan because of your businesses. So you can step away and not have to work so much—"

"Are we really having this conversation again?"

I meet her eyes.

"I brought Henry on to help solve that problem—at your suggestion—and he's helped. I don't spend my weekends on payroll anymore. I hardly have to worry about any of the software systems or financial projections. But there will always be things that require me to be present—"

"Like your family."

She's quiet, and for a moment I'm afraid I was too harsh, that she might cry. Instead, she levels me with a cool gaze.

"Do you know what one of the weirdest things is about being pregnant? It isn't how tired I am, or how suddenly none of my clothes fit, or even that certain smells knock me over. It's that there is no way to *not* be present every second. I can never just set it aside and not think about it. Every bite I eat feeds our baby, every breath I take gives it oxygen, even which side I sleep on apparently matters. I am *present* for it. All. The. Time." Her shoulders slump and she turns back for the hall. "And right now, I'm exhausted."

Heartthrob follows her out of the room, but I stay still, leaning against the kitchen counter.

When I hear the shower come on, my feet unfreeze, and I head into the second bedroom—our office. There isn't a ton of stuff in here. A couple of desks, some bookshelves. A houseplant. Maybe Lydia's right and I'm being too pushy, wanting to change the space now. There *is* a lot going on for her that I don't have to deal with, much as I wish I could. But if all her energy is going into . . . gestation? I feel like I need to channel mine somewhere.

I step out to the garage, poking around until I've found a couple of empty cardboard boxes. When I come back in, I try to figure out where to start. The walls are the same dingy yellow color they were when we moved in. Lydia might be right that we don't need to turn the space into a full nursery just yet, but giving it a fresh coat of paint would be an improvement overall.

I've emptied the contents of the bookshelves into one of the boxes and am in the middle of unloading the second when my phone rings in my pocket.

"What's up?" I ask, seeing my brother's name on the screen. "Any news?"

"I generally like to start conversations with 'hello' or 'how are you?'" Seth says.

"Sorry." I grunt. "Stressful week."

"What's happening? Boss man still pushing extra travel?"

I clench my jaw. That's the part of it he knows. I don't love keeping the rest from him, but I'm trying to stick to what Lydia and I agreed on. "Not yet, but he's laying plans for spring." I clear my throat and change the subject. "So, is Chandra planning another open house for Sunday?"

"Actually, no, we're abandoning that plan," he says. "We won't need it because we went back under contract tonight."

I set down my armload of books. "No shit—that's fantastic!"

My brother's grin is practically audible. "I figured you and Lyd would want to know."

He's right. I abandon what I'm doing and trip down the hall, bursting into our bedroom to tell Lydia the news. Only I find her curled into her pillow, sound asleep, a book on top of the covers by her side. I approach the bed, ready to wake her up. But then I think about what she said earlier about being exhausted, and decide I don't want to disturb her.

I turn the light off and tiptoe quietly for the door. Heartthrob gets up to follow.

"When will you close?" I whisper to my brother.

"Next month. I might even be in Denver by Thanksgiving," Seth answers, matching my tone. "Why are we whispering?"

My stomach knots and I continue down the hall, through the kitchen, not stopping until I'm out in the backyard. Heartthrob runs out with me, excited to play, but I sink into one of the metal chairs, ignoring his urgent wagging.

"I—we won't—" I can't catch my breath. Why didn't I think of this? "Lydia and I are doing Thanksgiving in fucking Ohio."

"Okay . . ." he says, sounding confused. "I mean, that sucks for you guys. But no big deal."

Heartthrob drops a tennis ball in my lap, and I hurl it across the yard so it ricochets off the neighbor's fence. I can't believe I put Lydia's fucked-up family before my own brother our *first* holiday without Mom. I drop my head into my hand, wondering what I was thinking, how I could've let this happen.

But then I remember.

"We're going because—" I force myself to take a breath, knowing I should stop. I promised. Then I say it anyway. "We're having a baby."

"Whoa . . . Lydia's pregnant?"

"Yes." My chest swells with the confirmation, right before a trickle of guilt seeps in. "But—shit—you're not supposed to know. It's pretty early and she doesn't want to announce yet."

Seth chuckles, walking back his enthusiasm. "Okay, got it. Don't spill the beans and get you in trouble."

"Yeah, thanks, man." I exhale, sitting back in my chair. I wasn't really worried about Seth sharing the news. But I'm surprised by the relief I feel being able to talk with him about it. "I . . . we're excited."

"That is exciting—I should've given my congratulations first. I didn't realize you guys were so serious when you said you were going for it."

"Yeah, it . . . just worked out."

He clears his throat. "Well, sounds like you've got plenty to deal with next month. So let's not worry about Thanksgiving."

"No." I grunt. "Our family should be together."

"Anton, this sale could fall through like the last one," he says patiently. "If I do luck out and get to move that weekend, Bruno and I will share a turkey sandwich while we unpack."

I clench my jaw. It's not like we have a precedent of spending the holiday together. It never seemed right leaving Mom on her own, so Seth used to do a video call from her bedside, eating pumpkin pie off her hospital tray. "I just hate the idea of you spending it alone."

"I think I'm going to have a way better time than you. Unless you're thinking of having Lydia's mother declawed?"

I snort. "I'll take it under advisement."

"Good." His tone lightens. "So, when's the stork due to arrive?"

"May sixteenth, if all goes well."

"Okay." I hear him clap. "That gives me time to work on my fun-uncles vibes."

And actually, I can picture Seth being exactly that. Getting on the floor and playing with our kid. Taking them out for ice cream. Teaching them all manner of things from how to ride a bike to the best way to win at checkers.

For a moment, I wish I could call Mom and share the news with her, too. She would've been so excited, offering to knit something, or maybe to come help after the birth. But as soon as my heart starts to sink, I close my eyes and push it away. I can't stay sad about what I've lost when there are so many reasons to be happy about what's to come.

CHAPTER TWENTY-SIX

CAPRICE

Are you and Anton for sure spending
Thanksgiving in Ohio?

Unless the earth opens up and swallows me.

CAPRICE

Crossing fingers for seismic activity. 🤍

Can I ask a TINY favor?

Of course. What's up?

CAPRICE

Could you watch a video and tell me what
you see?

Sure . . . send it over.

My phone pings again as I exit the Dunkin' drive-through. I'm less than five minutes from The Pooch Park, so I pull it up once I'm in the parking lot. At first, I'm not sure what I'm looking at. There's a person walking toward the camera, they hover in front of it, then they walk away. The whole thing is only fifteen seconds long, and I'm wondering if she even sent me the right thing. But when I restart it, I recognize the hallway outside Caprice's apartment through the weird fish-eye lens of the peephole camera.

I sit up straighter and watch again.

It looks like a white guy carrying some kind of sack. He comes down the hall from the elevators, stands in front of her door, then turns around and heads back the way he came.

I turn up the volume and watch again. He doesn't say anything, and he's staring so hard at the ground I can't see his face, but there's a clear knock when he gets to her door.

I dial Caprice. "When was this? Did you get some kind of delivery?"

"It was Tuesday when I wasn't home," she says, voice wavering a little. "And no, I never have anything delivered."

I press my lips together. The guy could have just knocked on the wrong door. It happens all the time. Even my neighbors have received our Thai delivery before. But something about the video doesn't sit right with me.

"Did it seem like he was *trying* to hide his face?"

She huffs. "That's what my brother thinks."

"You showed it to Theo?"

"He wouldn't stop asking about the camera, wanting to know how often I checked it. So yesterday I gave him the passcode and told him to monitor my neighbor's DoorDash habit himself. Apparently he went through hours of footage. I had only glanced at it and assumed the guy was going across the hall."

I raise my eyebrows. "Was this the *only* weird thing Theo saw?"

She scoffs. "I mean, depending on how you define weird? But yeah, pretty much. The guy only came by once, and it was the only time anyone approached my door."

I tap my finger against my lips. "Well, my take—it definitely gives me a weird vibe. But since he didn't do anything besides knock, and it only happened once, I'm not sure what you can do."

"Yeah," she says, voice unsteady again. "That's sort of where I'm at too."

"What's Theo's opinion?"

She sucks her teeth. "He wants to organize a stakeout."

I chuckle briefly, but then I clear my throat. "Maybe you *should* check the videos more carefully. And it might not be a bad idea to run at the gym again, at least for a bit. Unless you want to resume our jogging buddy system?"

"If we make it a power walk," she says, amused. "That actually sounds nice. I feel like I haven't seen you in forever."

I bite my lip. It has been weeks—we've only met up for lunch once since I found out I was pregnant, but she asked a lot of questions about why I had no appetite. I haven't exactly been avoiding her since. More like keeping her sharp, journalist instincts an arm's length from my knocked-up hormones. But my nausea has started to settle and the weather has cooled. I might not be ready to tell her or anyone else our news. But I *miss* her. If I'm careful, she might not notice anything different about me.

"Let's do it. I'll see you Sunday morning."

I release Heartthrob as I push through the front door of The Pooch Park, donut boxes balanced precariously in my arms. Tomás looks up from the computer with raised brows. We don't have a staff meeting. I'm not even supposed to be at this location today, but I asked Henry for a face-to-face chat in *my* office, and the Dunkin' drive-through was between here and the house.

I set the boxes down on the counter, clutching the small,

hot cup of decaf I ordered with them, trying to pretend it's the real thing. Anton and I might disagree about what changes to make to our home, but I am grudgingly following his *yes-list*. I take prenatal vitamins every morning. I try to drink the sixty-four ounces of water I'm supposed to each day, even though it makes me pee nonstop. And I've been avoiding soft cheeses, undercooked anything, and alcohol. Not that I drink much anyway. But sweets aren't on any yes *or* no list—so they've become my vice.

I have to admit, though, it's a relief coming to work where no one questions what I eat, asks how I'm feeling, or otherwise has any clue about my *condition*.

"Dibs on the Boston cream," Tomás says, carrying the boxes to my office. "Actually, I'm glad you're here, Lydia. We're short-staffed and I could use some help unpacking the food delivery if you have a sec."

"Of course." I furrow my brow. "Who didn't show up?"

"Nadia is apparently having car trouble. But Jamal and Stella have got it, I think. We've just been tag-teaming."

I frown. We only hired Stella a week ago, and she doesn't have much experience. "Why don't you go back with them for a bit. I'll stay up front and unload the dog food. I'm just waiting on Henry."

Tomás disappears into the playroom in a chorus of barking, and I get started putting away a large pallet of dog food. It crosses my mind as I'm slinging forty-pound bags around that pregnant women aren't supposed to lift heavy things. But the food isn't going to put itself away, and I'm not about to make excuses to my own manager. There are only two more weeks left in the second trimester anyway, and despite my misgivings, everything's going ridiculously smoothly.

Ready or not, here a baby comes.

The door chimes as I'm stacking cases of canned food, and a high voice shrieks, "*BIG* doggie!"

I pop my head around the retail shelves to see Heartthrob nose to nose with a familiar toddler by the front door. She's looking at him with a face-splitting grin, and he's staring at her curiously with his tail arced over his back. Paloma reaches out and strokes his ears more softly than I would have expected, and in return, he slurps his tongue up the side of her face.

She squeals with delight. "Doggie kiss!"

Behind her, I spot Marisol holding Biscochito's leash. She catches my eye and waves, pointing to an earpiece on the left side of her head. "Right, Harold, but you told me the shipment would be here Friday and it hasn't even been sent out."

Oh. I recognize that sort of conversation. I take the leash out of her hand with a nod, then glance at Paloma, standing there in pigtails and an adorable white-corduroy dress. "Do you want to see where Bizkit plays?"

She claps her hands, and I wave at Tomás through one of the windows. He retrieves the terrier mix, but as soon as they disappear I realize the little girl can't see where he's gone. I glance back at Marisol, but she's facing the other way, deep in discussion.

"Um . . . is it okay if I pick you up?" I ask Paloma.

She raises her arms automatically. "Up! Up!"

Awkwardly, I reach under her arms. I handle four-legged creatures all day long, but other than Celia's infant, I can't remember the last time I held a tiny human. I'm surprised by how light she feels. And how easily she settles in my arms, fitting into the crook of my elbow and wrapping her little arm behind my neck. She smells faintly of strawberry yogurt.

As soon as she glimpses the playroom, her eyes go huge and she lunges forward, pressing her face against the glass. "Doggies!"

I smile, recognizing a fellow animal lover when I see one. My mother and Celia have always said I was nuts for dogs by this age. "Yes, look at them running around. Aren't they silly?"

Paloma watches, clapping, with a smile that lights up her whole face. I smile too, and out of nowhere, I'm flooded with an unfamiliar warmth. I realize, with some surprise, that I'm not in a hurry to put her down. It's . . . different than when I held my nephew. If I'm honest, Marisol's bright-eyed daughter is more interesting than a sleeping bundle. The expressions on her face and the way she pronounces words with so much care is undeniably cute. And she doesn't seem as fragile as an infant. When she turns in my arms and smiles right at me, that warm feeling intensifies. Vaguely, I realize it *must* be hormonally driven. But it causes something to ease in my mind.

Maybe I could do this? At least, if our little raspberry-olive is half as cute.

As I grapple to accept that I am now referring to the human-looking cluster of cells in my uterus as a fruit, Paloma turns her head and screeches. "Mama! Doggies!"

Marisol glances at us from where she stands by the front desk, still talking. She waves, and to Paloma's and my dismay, turns away.

Paloma juts her lip out and slaps the window. "Go doggies."

"Uh . . . what? You want to go in there?" I shake my head. "Sorry, we can't. It's only for dogs."

Paloma aims a surprising scowl right at me. "Go *doggies!*"

Pulse spiking, I glance back at Marisol, who's still pacing back and forth on her phone. Worried the little girl will start screaming during her business call, I set Paloma down and look her in the eye. "How about this . . . Um, do you like donuts?"

Paloma's eyes go huge and she claps, nodding. *"Pease!"*

Grateful for a distraction, I lead her into my office where the bakery boxes sit on the desk. I can't really remember anything Marisol fed her when we met at the restaurant, but the kid's enthusiasm convinces me she's had one before. I have Paloma climb onto the vinyl couch, then put a pink frosted donut with sprinkles on a paper napkin and place it in her lap.

"Fank you," she says adorably, smiling like the sweetest little cherub. And then I watch in horror as she proceeds to destroy the donut, only getting small amounts in her mouth as she squeezes until frosting oozes between her fingers, smearing the rest all over her face and clothes.

"*Oh*. Oh my—"

I reach toward her with both hands, but I have no idea what to do. Taking it from her seems like a bad idea. But do I just stand by and watch this pink frosting destruction until her mom finds us? Her outfit is done for. She's going to need a full-on bath. If we were at Ooh La Pooch, I could at least put her in one of the tubs.

At that moment, Marisol steps into the office and takes in the scene.

"I—I'm sorry," I say, wincing. "This did *not* go quite how I expected."

Marisol presses her lips together, raising her eyebrows at Paloma. "Did you get a dessert?"

She nods, beaming like she found a pot of gold, and holds out a fistful of goo. "*See?*"

Marisol glances at my face, then chuckles. Without missing a beat, she reaches into her purse, which I now realize is some sort of stylish diaper bag. "This is why baby wipes were invented. And why we *always* carry a change of clothes."

I stand by, twisting my fingers and feeling useless as she lets Paloma finish, then strips her down to a diaper and systematically wipes down every inch of her skin.

"I'm sorry," I mutter. "Her outfit was so cute."

"Her dad bought that," Marisol says, dismissively. "Honestly, who dresses a toddler in white?"

I look up, surprised by the humor in her tone. "Um . . . my mother did. And she got near hysterical if my sister or I dropped a single crumb."

"Oh goodness. If I freaked out over every mess, I'd lose my mind." She pulls a pink-striped shirt over Paloma's head and sinks to the couch, rummaging in her bag until she pulls out a tablet in a plastic case. "Here, P. How about some *Bluey*? Honestly, *I* could use a donut."

I blink. I'd expected her to swoop Paloma out the door, in a hurry to get far away from me and my wearable pastries. But since it doesn't look like she'll be unfriending me just yet, I hold open a box for her to select one herself.

She takes a bite of something chocolate frosted and sighs, sinking into the couch. "Oh, this is exactly what I needed."

I pick out a glazed ring for myself, stealing glances at Marisol while she closes her eyes and chews. She's dressed professionally, in slacks and cute chunky heels with her hair styled in trendy waves. Even with a toddler in tow, Marisol always seems so professional. So *together*.

But the exasperation currently on her face is something I can relate to.

"Supply chain got you down?" I ask, nodding at her phone.

Her lip curls. "Well, I shared your suggestion with my production team, and we did decide to go with a line of extra-tough dog toys. They're going to be part of their own specialized box. I'm really excited about it."

"That sounds perfect," I say, sensing there's more.

"Yeah. If my supplier ever gets his act together, it should be great." She sighs. "What's new with you? Any more thoughts about expansion?"

I snort. I might dread Caprice figuring out what I'm hiding, but for the briefest moment, I consider telling Marisol the truth. That I'm pregnant and overwhelmed. Afraid my business partner will exploit my maternity leave and inability to balance things to make changes I don't want. Part of me wonders if she's already guessed. I might not have a baby bump yet, but what if she can tell? Is there some second sense other mothers have? Maybe she could offer advice.

But she just waits for me to answer, so I force a breath in through my nose and out through my mouth, reminding myself there's no rush. Plenty could happen in the next few weeks, and there's no sense in sharing until after Thanksgiving when my mom's told the whole world anyway.

"Yes, I'm considering it. I'm still not big on a franchise, but Henry and I agreed to talk. There are some things I'd like to do, and . . ." I pause a moment, my mind spinning with too many logistics. "Well, it's worth having a discussion."

At that moment, the front door chimes, and I'm about to jump up to see if there's a customer when Henry blusters through the door.

"Hi, sorry—" He stops short when he sees Marisol and Paloma, then looks at me. "Ah . . . car trouble."

His hair is disheveled and his shirt un-tucked. Not only that, I know for a fact he just leased a brand-new Porsche. I glance at my watch, only just realizing he's nearly an hour late. "You look like you could use a donut too," I say, offering him the box.

Henry declines. So far, the man does not seem to have a sweet tooth in his body. That, or he hasn't created a spreadsheet for enjoying sugar.

"We've got to head out anyway," Marisol says, standing and gathering her things. "Don't want to miss story time at the library."

I wrinkle my nose, walking her out the door while Henry fixes himself some tea. "Sorry again about her outfit," I mutter.

"Are you kidding? Thanks for giving me five minutes to

talk on the phone uninterrupted. Juggling the business mom thing is no joke." She smiles. "But Paloma *never* cooperates for anyone but me. You're great with kids."

This catches me off guard. "I . . . I'm not. But I figured treats worked for Pavlov."

When I head back into the office, I close the door, ready to leave everything but the Pooches outside, at last. Henry has parked himself on the couch, texting intensely on his phone, and I watch with interest. He is apparently furious with whoever it is.

"Right," he says, tucking it away when he sees me. "Now, what was it you wanted to discuss. And why couldn't we do it properly in the conference room?"

I glance at him again. Like my husband, Henry keeps himself in superior shape, but he's a pretty tall man. He looks somewhat ridiculous folded up like origami trying to fit on my tiny IKEA couch. Back when I was only running a single Pooch Park and Ooh La Pooch by myself, this tiny office was my headquarters. Home base for everything. Some nights I even slept on that couch. I can see why Henry prefers his *conference room* at the new location, but I needed to be in my safe space for the conversation we're about to have.

"Well, I've been doing some thinking . . ." I take a deep breath. "What would you say to a Pooch Park III?"

Henry shifts his jaw, studying me. But as each second ticks by, I'm more sure this is the right move.

"I've been thinking over your suggestions," I go on. "And while adding bathing to the daycares is fine, I think we could do something really intentional with a new location. Make grooming part of the design from the get-go."

Henry shakes his head and chuckles. "You want another business? After . . . four months?"

"Go big or go home?" I say, avoiding his eyes, afraid he might laugh.

"Why?" he asks, sitting forward in what I have come to think of as his cutthroat CEO pose.

I purse my lips. "I thought all the reasons you needed came in tens and twenties."

He frowns, then leans back and sips his tea, looking like an out of place gentleman, crammed on my small sofa. "We could just keep running the three shops we have. They make money; they're plenty to keep you busy. Why make this the next move?"

I sit back in my desk chair, hand resting over my stomach—until I realize what I'm doing and pull it away. *That* isn't the reason. But it is a reason to put a plan in place. If we make these decisions now, there will be less room for him to second guess me later. Once he doesn't just see me as his business partner, but also a mother.

"Look, I know you want to franchise. You've wanted it since the first time you offered to buy the Pooches. And while we both know I have very different feelings, you probably understand better than me that a model like this would make that easier."

His eyebrows shoot up, but he doesn't say anything, so I continue.

"In the dog industry in particular, success only comes with the right ingredients. You suggested we close Ooh La Pooch—but I propose we open Pooch III and incorporate it there. We've already established there's demand. It would solve the overhead, reduce costs . . . maybe even get to a place we can offer employee benefits."

Henry straightens. "Ah . . . now I see."

I allow myself a small smile.

"So, your plan to avoid eliminating jobs is to create a whole new business model." He strokes his chin, then picks up the notebook he always carries and starts jotting things down. "Lydia, you're either crazy, or a very savvy busi-nesswoman."

I chuckle. "Maybe a bit of both." But as I watch him write, I realize how much I've missed this. With everything going on at home, and in my *womb*, I haven't been focused enough on the Pooches. I feel more energized sitting here hashing out this new vision for The Pooch Park than I have in weeks. But then my conversation with Anton flits through my head. How he wants me to step back, take time off. I frown.

Henry puts his pen down and shifts to his laptop. Crunching numbers, if I had to guess. My least favorite part of business planning. Which I guess is why this works. I supply the vision—he brings a talent for numbers and projections.

"We don't want to grow *too* fast," he mutters. "We'll need to do more market research. Scout locations. Maybe consider other areas of the city. And while I've still got some capital, I don't think we can really make a move on this at *least* until Pooch II's profits match Pooch I. But we are on track to get there, so maybe in the spring . . ." He pauses, squeezing the bridge of his nose. "You do know this will be a *lot* of work."

"I know," I say, and I can't help grinning.

He shakes his head. "I guess Anton was right about not giving up on you."

I furrow my brow. "What do you mean?"

"He told me you might come around about the franchise."

My mouth sours. That doesn't seem fair. "We might be laying the groundwork, but I'm not committing to that yet."

"Of course." Henry gives me a patient smile, then turns his laptop around so I can see a bar graph on the screen. "But if we do, in another five to ten years, our profits could be here."

My nostrils flare, studying the image. Truly, the Pooches have never been about the numbers for me. I have always been able to pay my bills. And as long as my clients and employees were happy, anything else they earned always felt like a bonus. But despite his ability to tolerate dog hair on

Armani, Henry's had dollar signs in his eyes since day one. And if he's been strategizing a franchise with Anton, maybe I'm the only one really invested in the Pooches.

I take a deep breath, thinking about Marisol keeping her cool while going through a divorce, dealing with inept shipping companies, *and* finding her daughter swimming in pink frosting. Then I reach for the bakery box on my desk.

"Well. I think this calls for a donut."

CHAPTER TWENTY-SEVEN

Him

"Hey, I was starting to worry." I peer out the door of our second bedroom when I hear Lydia come in with Heartthrob. "Everything okay with the Pooches?"

The dog rushes to greet me, spinning in circles a couple times, then leaning against me while I rub his favorite spot on his back. Lydia sets down her things and comes toward us down the hall, looking fatigued.

"Yeah, it's all good. I was just doing some more long-term planning with Henry."

"Really?" I quirk an eyebrow. "Did you . . . tell him?"

"Oh. No," she says quickly, one hand coming to her stomach. I've noticed she's started wearing more layers the past week or so, but the weather has also gotten cooler. "It wasn't about—it was other stuff."

I pause, waiting for her to elaborate. She's worked late more days than not recently. When she doesn't say more, I let go of Heartthrob and take her hand, pulling her with me into the room. "Come in here. Tell me what you think?"

Her mouth drops open as she rounds the corner.

There isn't really much to see yet, but it's already dramatically different. I pulled the desks away from the walls and moved some things out to the garage. Then I took the few pieces of art off the dingy yellow walls and gave the whole room a coat of primer.

"You've been busy," she says.

I grin. I waited a whole week after we first talked about it, but we're so close to the second trimester. It seemed like I could at *least* paint. I indicate a selection of samples stuck to the wall by the light switch. "This is just the base coat. We still need to pick colors. I was thinking maybe blues and grays, like these here. Unless you prefer a warmer palette?"

"Oh." She turns in a circle, like she's catching up to my vision. "Yeah, I guess we should probably decide . . ."

I indicate the three colors I've been leaning toward. "Charcoal Linen, White Dove, and Pike's Peak Gray make a pretty neutral color palette, but what do you think?"

Lydia follows where I'm pointing, scanning the colors for a couple seconds. "Uh . . . you pick what you like." She shrugs. "I'm good with anything."

My heart sinks. She steps toward the door like she's trying to retreat, but I place my hand on her arm. "Hey. I know I came on way too strong the last time we talked about this. It's . . . well, it's an adjustment for both of us. But I thought this might be fun to do together." I gesture around the room. "*Just* painting. We can hold off picking out furniture and . . ."

She fixes her eyes where my hand rests on her arm, and for a second I think she's going to lean in, share the moment, let me fold her into my arms. But she steps away. "Sorry, it's been a long day and I'm really tired. Maybe we could talk about it . . . later?"

I look around the room. Thirty minutes ago, it had been easy imagining a crib, changing table, maybe a rocking chair. Now I can't manage to see anything but unpainted walls. I follow her into our bedroom, unable to channel my feelings into anything other than irritation.

"Later? So like, maybe when the baby arrives?"

She slumps to the bed, falling back against the pillows, and my eyes inevitably land on her stomach, searching the contours of her oversized gray hoodie for any outward sign of what's to come. Does she look a little rounder, or is that just her clothes?

"Anton, it's still not even the second trimester. Do we need to talk about this now?"

"You're *eleven* weeks," I say stiffly.

"Which means there's twenty-nine more weeks to plan," she says, though it seems like her voice wavers on the number.

I close my eyes, letting out a slow breath. "It just seems like we should be able to find something we could focus on. *Celebrate.* Together."

"Sure," she says, sounding annoyed herself now. "We can do that. How about we celebrate . . . let's see, I think I got through my first whole day without feeling like I wanted to barf."

I frown, a low ache spreading in my chest as she sits up and unzips her hoodie. I knew Lydia and I were on different wavelengths when I first suggested having a baby, but I was sure, at some point, it would help bring us together.

She glances at my face and sighs as she pulls her arms free of her sleeves. "I'm sorry. I'm just tired, Anton. It's been a long week."

I sink to the bed beside her, recalling what she said the other day about not being able to escape pregnancy. Then I do my best to set paint colors and trimesters aside in my mind. "It's okay. How are you feeling?"

She winces slightly at my question, then trails her eyes over me with a strange expression. "I don't know, honestly. Different . . . weird."

"How so?"

She slips out of her shoes and socks. "I really *have* been

feeling better. Not as nauseous or gross. But there are other things . . . changes." Her eyes trace over me in an unfamiliar way, and I swear she runs her tongue over her lips. The air thickens between us.

Then she tears her gaze away and rises from the bed.

I furrow my brow, looking her over, searching for some clue about what she means. But then she starts tugging at her next layer of clothing.

"You know, I could really use a shower. That might help a lot."

I open my mouth to ask what she wants for dinner, not wanting to lose sight of the nutrition she needs, but the words die on my tongue as she pulls her shirt over her head.

The last week or so, I have been eyeing Lydia's midsection, watching for any sign of a bump. Something I could see and touch, that might make this all feel more real. For both of us. But her stomach has stayed maddeningly flat. And since she hasn't been feeling well, I've been trying to give her space. The last time I saw her fully undressed was two weeks ago, the night things went sideways after her orgasm. But suddenly, there *is* something noticeably different about her body.

"What?" she asks, noticing my stare.

"Uh, nothing." I swallow, shifting as my dick stirs in my jeans. "Did you um—did you get a new bra?"

She glances down and exhales. Then spends a minute trying to rearrange and tuck herself in. It doesn't work. The cups are clearly way over capacity.

"Here. Let me help you with that." My voice comes out husky and she pauses, eyes darkening as I approach. Which is . . . new. I slip my arms around her, fumbling for a stupid number of seconds with the tiny metal clasps. But all at once they come apart, and her breasts spring free like they were just bursting to be released, *both* nipples already fully erect.

"God, Lydia." I swallow hard. My wife has always had beautiful curves. Her breasts are, hands down, my favorite part of her body. But they must have grown at least two sizes since the last time I saw them, and with the rest of her unchanged, she looks . . . nearly pornographic.

She blushes beautifully under my gaze, and I sink to my knees, forgetting whatever else we were talking about. I'm a man worshipping at the temple of his wife's impossibly pregnant tits. Somewhere in the cerebral part of my mind, I knew this would happen eventually. Lots of things about her body will change. But my more primal brain was completely caught off guard. I reach out with both hands, dying to squeeze them, take them into my mouth, but I pause, glancing at her face.

"Can I . . . ?"

Her eyelids flutter, and she wraps her arms around herself, pressing the pale globes together until my mouth is bone dry. Her voice comes out needy. "I uh . . . I wish you would."

I look up in surprise. I've worked hard to cultivate my wife's sexual desire recently. It has never come easily, but once I learned it could be teased out, that she would come around and return my touch *after* she was aroused, things became more straightforward. However, I can't remember it ever happening on its own.

Almost like sex had been on her mind before this moment.

As we each draw our next breaths, I take her tits by the handful. Squeeze them lightly together, gauging with a near-painful shot to my dick, how much more they fill and spill out of my hands now. I run my tongue between them, then trace lightly over her skin, circling one very erect nipple.

She groans, pressing her thighs lightly together.

"Is this okay?" I ask, just to be sure. Because I want to trust what I see and feel, but because of our history, I'm also scared.

"Yes," she says, with a faint but undeniable hint of . . . lust.

I look at her face, considering. "Is this what you meant when you said you feel 'different'?"

"I—yes." She blushes deeper, her voice reedy. "It's actually been kind of distracting."

Oh. God.

"I want to know more." I blow gently across her nipple before pulling it into my mouth.

"*Oh*," she murmurs, and with that my cock is fully hard, pressing uncomfortably against the inside of my jeans. "I—all day, I've been feeling kind of—"

She breaks off, and I recognize the reluctance in her voice. The hushed, chaste tone she always uses when we talk about sex.

I pull back, releasing her taut nipple with a pop, staring up at her as she gasps. "Lydia?" I ask, desperate for verbal confirmation. To assure myself this is not just happening in my head. "Have you been at work all day . . . wanting to be fucked?"

Electricity bolts through me as her face turns a deep, dark red.

"*No*," she says primly. "That's not what I—"

I take her other nipple into my mouth, and she doesn't finish her sentence. "That's a long day," I say once I let go, running my fingers between her legs. She's in a thin pair of leggings, and when I brush along her crotch, I'm pretty sure both our eyes widen. "*Lydia*. You're so wet for me."

Her thighs clench hard in response, clamping down and trapping my hand. So I go with it, pressing my palm into the soaked fabric against her pussy. In seven years of marriage, I have never seen my wife actually . . . *horny*. She tears my shirt over my head, carnal urge flowing off her in waves, and it seems obvious there's only one thing to do.

Her thighs release, and I move to her waistband, sliding

her leggings down. When she's fully naked, standing before me flushed and wanting, I place a kiss below her navel.

But as I pull back, staring at the part of her body where *everything* is centered, I pause. And it's like someone dumps a bucket of cold water on my head.

"Fuck."

I pull back, stumbling away from her, running into the bed. Uncertainty seeps back into her posture, and she tries to cover herself with her arms.

"What's wrong?"

"I—we can't," I say, biting into my lip, my cock hard, my balls so tight, I have to breathe through the pain of doing nothing about it.

"But I *want* to," she says firmly, taking a step toward me, reaching up to squeeze her own tits like she needs it. And now I know what it's like to be the butt of a joke to the universe.

"Fuck, Lydia, I do too," I growl, eyes fixed on the floor. "I want nothing more than to toss you on the bed and fuck you senseless. But the nurse said—"

"She *said* it was fine," she says in a strained voice. "But 'if we wanted to be cautious,' we could wait till after twelve weeks."

"It's only one more week," I say through my teeth.

"It's *only* one more week," she parrots back to me. "Anton, look at me. I . . . I need you."

By some sheer force of will, I stumble to my feet and over to the back of the door. Her robe is hanging there, and I thrust it at her, pleading. "What happened last time—it was terrifying," I say, and the memory of her doubled over in pain is like an icy shroud to my dick. "Lydia, we're close. I promise, as soon as the doctor gives us the all clear . . ."

I risk a glance at her. She hasn't put the robe on, but she's holding it in front of her, thank God.

"As soon as she does, what?" she asks, voice stilted. And

then a look of utter devastation passes over her face. "Oh . . . God." Her lip trembles. She peeks down at her body before covering herself more. "Am I unattractive to you now?"

"*What?*" If there was anything I expected her to say, that wasn't it. I rip the robe out of her hands, the sight of her *gorgeous*, rounded body hardening my cock again instantly. I unfasten my jeans and take her hand, shoving it between my pants and underwear so she can feel for herself. "Lydia, you're so fucking attractive I wish it was possible to knock you up again. I am dying, I want you so badly."

Her mouth is open, and for a moment I let myself fantasize about those pretty lips wrapped around my throbbing cock. But then my memory floods with the sound of our baby's heartbeat. That regular, rushing surge that filled my ears—filled something else deep inside me.

She bites her lip, eyes dark. "Then, if you won't . . ." She looks down, blushing, then squeezes her hand around my dick. "Let me help *you.*"

It takes several moments for my brain to catch up with what she's suggesting. To emphasize her point, she steps back and lifts her heavy breasts in each hand like she's presenting them to me.

"You said you want to come on my . . . tits," she says. And fuck, just that word coming reluctantly out of her mouth is nearly enough to make me lose it in my pants. This topic came up between us on the Unmatched app, back when she catfished me into thinking she was another woman. And she's right. Fucking her tits till I come all over them is on my lust-list. Things I want—can't wait—to do to her. But we've been so focused on tuning in to her body, learning what she needs, we just haven't tried it yet.

I am nearly dizzy, watching her press those beautiful pale globes together, imagining my cock between them, and—

"Fuck," I say, shutting my eyes. "Yes . . . I do." Slowly, I reach out, tweaking each of her nipples until we both gasp. "But that wouldn't be fair."

I retrieve her robe from the floor, pressing a gentle kiss to her forehead when her face falls.

"Lydia. If I'm going to come on"—I swallow—"those glorious tits, it will only be after I make *you* come so hard you sing."

CHAPTER TWENTY-EIGHT

My first thought Sunday morning is sex. Like, literally, right after I open my eyes and blink at the ceiling. The instant I move, my body comes alive. My skin, my breasts, my core, all aching to be touched so badly I have to bury my face in my pillow.

Oh my God. *Why?*

Anton has already gotten up, but after last night it's not like I could turn to him and beg him to do something about it. Briefly, I run my own hands down over my body. Arching my breasts into my palms, toying with my *very* erect, aching nipples with a surprising sigh of relief. I keep one hand there, then let the other continue to explore, down between my thighs. Until I reach my already-moist center. I bite my lip, face flushing hot. This is . . . embarrassing. I have only ever felt this way after Anton has spent a *lot* of time getting me there. I don't know what to do with spontaneous arousal. I glance at my husband's pillow with chagrin, wondering if this is how he feels all the time.

Except he didn't last night. He was turned on, but had no trouble setting it aside when I couldn't.

Because he's a good parent.

The thought flits through my mind like a taunt.

But damn if my clit isn't nearly throbbing.

Softly, I close my eyes, slipping one finger between my folds. It doesn't feel like it would take much, just to move the right way, bring my body some relief.

Except.

What if something happened? What if Anton came back into our room to find me cramping like I was before, and I had to tell him what I did? What if, in seeking my own pleasure, I did something to hurt . . .

I swing my legs over the side of the bed, forcing my feet to the floor. Trying to shift my focus to a different, urgent need. My bladder.

I can hear Anton banging around in the kitchen after I pee, and I'm about to yell down the hall asking if he's already made our ration of coffee, when I hear my phone ring. It's Sunday, so not likely a business call, but I will take any excuse to not think about what's going on inside my body.

Until I see my sister's name on the screen.

"Hi," I say on a long exhale, wandering toward my closet in search of something that still fits.

"Hello," Celia singsongs through the receiver. "Just checking in to make sure nothing has changed for Thanksgiving. I know you still had a few loose ends—"

"How's Gabriel?" I ask, trying to collect myself in the full-length mirror while she prattles off his latest milestones. The pajama pants and T-shirt I slept in are already snug. If my mom doesn't guess I'm pregnant right away, she'll hound me about my weight before I even step foot in the house.

"Anyway, we're excited for you guys to come out! Gabey and I were just going over the menu, and—"

"Wait. Why are you doing the menu? Isn't Mom hosting?"

She clears her throat. "Well. Mom decided it was too much to ask her to baby proof her house now that Gabey's crawling. And since ours is already safe, it made sense . . . but she said if we're not eating off her china, she's not cooking the food. So . . . you guys haven't gone vegan or anything, have you?"

"No." I pause for a beat, trying to decide if this is better or worse. Or maybe just as bad, in a different setting. "We can't fly out until Thanksgiving morning. Sorry. But we'll eat whatever you guys want to make once we get there."

"Oh, I'm having it catered," Celia says. "*Way* too tired to cook with no help."

Something in her voice makes my shoulders drop, and for a second I wonder if she's actually dreading this as much as I am. But we've been adversaries so long, I can't help myself. "What, Dr. Adam isn't any good in the kitchen?"

She makes an impatient snort, and I can just imagine her pointing her nose in the air, getting ready to launch into some righteous speech about the demands of plastic surgery. But instead, she changes the subject. "Let me know if you two need a ride from the airport."

"I'm sure we can handle it." I don't know what else to add —*Can't wait to see you. It'll be great to catch up*—I've never been a wonderful liar. So I just say, "Let me know if there's anything we can bring."

"Will do," she says, and then actually adds, "I—I'm so glad you're coming."

I stare at my clothes long enough to decide nothing I own will fit comfortably, and I might have to either buy some larger sizes or break down and visit a maternity store. Only that thought is so unpleasant, I decide a shower is the best way to delay the decision longer.

But as soon as I shut myself in the bathroom, the doorbell rings and Heartthrob runs down the hall barking. For a second, still having had zero coffee, I can't focus enough to think who it could possibly be. Until I realize it's Sunday, and hurry to answer it.

"Morning, sleepyhead," Caprice says, standing on our front porch holding two cups of coffee from Pike's Perk a few blocks over. "Why aren't you answering my texts?"

"I—sorry, my sister called. What time is it?" I fumble for my phone, but I must've left it beside the bed.

"Almost ten. When you didn't show at the park, I figured you must've forgotten." She eyes the robe I covered up in with some suspicion. "Or . . . did I interrupt something?"

My stomach knots so fast, I nearly gasp. "Ah, no—I just got sidetracked. I'll get changed."

"The weather's not the greatest," she says, handing me a coffee and shoving the door closed with one hip. "We don't have to run."

Heartthrob realizes we have a visitor and rushes over to greet her, but she holds up a palm at his approach. "Back off, fuzzy wuzzy. Your hair does *not* go with my outfit." My dog looks at me, sneezes, then returns to his bed.

"Are you sure? We could still go," I say, looking doubtfully out the window. We're officially out of still-feels-like-summer-in-the-sunshine October and into the full cold bleak of November. The *last* thing I want to do this morning is go jogging.

"Nah, I'm not feeling it," she says, tossing her ponytail. "Let's just hang out and catch up."

For a second, I consider doing just that. Bringing Caprice into the kitchen and spilling everything. It's been one thing not telling my mother and employees about the pregnancy. About what's coming. Keeping it from my best friend has been one of the hardest things ever.

But on some level, I'm still dreading what she'll say. How she'll react. Technically, I hit twelve weeks a couple days ago. But since we don't have our next appointment until right before Thanksgiving, and Anton and I agreed to tell my family first, I tighten my robe and lead the way into the kitchen. "Sure. I've got bagels. Tell me what's new."

"Meh. Not a whole lot . . ." she says, settling into a chair at the table. Anton must've gone outside, or maybe he's back in the second bedroom.

I set my coffee aside and reach for the bagels, grateful to have something to do with my hands. Until my eyes rest on the list of pregnancy *yes-foods* and *no-foods* still stuck to the fridge. I snatch the paper off, shoving it on top of the appliance before she notices it. Then I remember the prenatal vitamins sitting on the counter, and block her view with my body as I shove the bottle inside a cabinet.

"Are you still working on that new story?" I ask, making a big show of loading the toaster and finding cream cheese. "The one about public art installations?"

"Yeah, that one's finished. It should run next week," she says in an uncertain tone. "I . . . I actually got a really nice nod from an editor over at *Denver Editorial*. She suggested I could level up if I follow this through."

I sputter, nearly dropping the cream cheese knife. Writing for *Denver Editorial* has always been one of Caprice's dreams. "Are you serious?"

She nods, and I grab her hand and start bouncing up and down.

"Caprice! Like, this is it! I mean, okay, it hasn't happened yet, but can we just take a sec to appreciate and enjoy this moment? You've worked hard, and your talent as a journalist is finally being recognized!"

She looks over and smiles at me, but it doesn't reach her eyes.

I rest my feet flat on the floor again. "Why am I the only one excited?"

"Because in order to do that, I'll have to do a deeper dive into cheating culture." She sighs, wrapping her arms around herself. "Revisit some of the stuff from the first article, then dig up even more, and I just—"

"Don't feel safe," I finish her sentence.

Her posture slumps. "I mean, it's an amazing opportunity. Any story they run could propel my career to the next level. But I'm just kind of over it, you know? I've written *stellar* articles on health trends, musical movements, fitness . . . Not one person ever sent me a death threat for analyzing weight training versus cardio."

"I read every one of them, and they were stellar." I frown. "But . . . *Denver Editorial.*"

"I know." She drops her face into her hands. "I should write an article about how women always have to give something up in order to gain."

I retrieve the bagels from the toaster with a nod of solidarity, spreading cream cheese and trying not to dwell on some of the trade-offs I've been making lately.

"Anyway, I've been dying to get that off my chest—to someone who gets it," Caprice says, straightening as I bring the food to the table. "Now tell me again, *why* did you decide to spend Thanksgiving with your mother?"

I sink into a chair and massage my temples, sipping the last delicious drops of my coffee. "Um, I don't remember anymore."

It's the wrong thing to say. Her eyes sharpen, raking over me carefully. "Is everything okay? Is something going on?"

"No, why would there be?" I ask, stuffing bagel into my mouth.

"Because when you came home from your sister's wedding last year, you swore you weren't going back to Ohio for at least a decade, barring some emergency."

I take my time chewing. I do remember saying that.

"Where's Anton, by the way?" she asks, glancing around.

"Uh . . . he has a project he's working on." I set my bagel

down. "Celia's going to be moving, so my mom made a big stink, wanting us all to have one more holiday at home. It seemed easier to just go than argue with her about it."

Despite there being some truth in that statement, Caprice raises a brow in a familiar, skeptical way. So, before she can really start peppering me with questions, I leap out of my chair. "Hey look, the sun sort of came out. We could still go for a run—let me just get changed."

In my room, I smoosh my swollen chest into a too-snug sports bra and bury my figure in one of my husband's old CU Boulder sweatshirts, debating whether it would seem suspicious if I beg her to power walk instead of run. But when I come back out with my sneakers on, I find Caprice leaning in the doorway of what's quickly looking like my *former* home office, watching my husband paint the walls.

"Anton says you're doing some redecorating."

My gaze immediately flies to where he's stirring paint across the room. He looks up, giving the tiniest shake of his head, letting me know he hasn't let the cat out of the bag. Though, by the way he raises his brows, he seems to think I should.

"Just refreshing a little," I say with a placid smile. "We haven't painted since we moved in."

"It's already a lot brighter in here," she says, peering closely at the swatches on the wall. "The colors are very . . . neutral."

"You know me." I turn up my palms. "Noncommittal."

Caprice snorts, but allows me to usher her to the front door. Which we open, only to find the sun long gone and buckets of sleet dumping down from the sky.

"Guess the forecast changed," I say, biting my lip.

"There's definitely some sort of front," she mutters. "Guess it's time to go home and make career decisions."

"I'll give you a ride," I say, grabbing my keys.

But when I let her out in front of her building and turn back toward home alone, my stomach crawls with guilty relief.

CHAPTER TWENTY-NINE

"Now that is an active little kiddo," Dr. Sharma says, coming into the room. "Look at you go, practically doing backflips."

Anton and I both have our eyes glued to the screen in the dim room. This is *very* different than the last time we were here. I've been hiding in a lot of oversized sweatshirts now that it's cold, but my stomach has just started to protrude, and the ultrasound tech is guiding the transducer through gooey jelly all over my midsection.

The air echoes with that loud, rhythmic whooshing sound again. The heartbeat.

And on the screen is the very clear outline of . . . a baby. Even I can make out the large, round head, and four limbs waving and kicking.

I suck in a breath. I can't remember the last one I took.

Anton is perched on a stool next to me, holding my hand, eyes glowing. His heart is so clearly full, it makes me smile. But as I look at him, I can't figure out how *I* feel.

I just—I guess I never thought we'd actually get here.

Thirteen weeks, almost fourteen. I never *wished* for something to happen; it just seemed like it would. The whole thing was too easy. Pregnant the second month of trying. No complications—unless you count the orgasm thing, which is supposedly normal. I've never even vomited. I was sure it couldn't be this straightforward.

But here we are. Second trimester, and I'm not any less pregnant—quite the contrary.

I try to swallow, but my throat is so dry, it takes a couple tries.

The tech has taken about a zillion measurements, but she seems to be finishing up now, typing a last few numbers into the machine while it hums with printouts. Then the whooshing goes silent, the image disappears, and it's only us in the room again.

But it feels just as crowded.

Dr. Sharma brightens the lights while the tech wipes my belly clean with a towel.

"I'll double check your bloodwork, but everything seems right as rain," the doctor says, studying the screen. "Any new complaints? Or new questions?"

"Um, can you tell if it's a boy or girl?" Anton asks, staring at the strip of black-and-white pictures the tech hands him.

Dr. Sharma smiles. "Not yet—too soon. That will have to wait until the anatomy scan at twenty weeks. We'll take a close look to see how everything's developing at that appointment, and if the baby cooperates, we can usually make a guess at gender if you want to know."

"I—" Anton looks suddenly to me. "I think we do?"

I nod immediately. "I don't like surprises."

He grins, relieved, leaning in to show me the printed sonograms. When he does, his clean, masculine scent breaks through all the sterile doctor's office smells, invading my over-sensitive nose as his arm brushes the side of my breast. And my hormones are still so totally out of whack, this alone sends a shot of pleasure through my nipples and down into my core. I breathe deep, fighting the urge to pull him to me, bring his lips down to mine right here in the ultrasound room. But I resist, turning my attention back to the doctor with the question I've been sitting on.

"So, now that it's officially the second trimester, um . . ." I hesitate, waiting as the tech exits the room. "I just wanted to ask—well, a couple weeks ago we called the office because I had some cramping after we—um—"

I can feel my face reddening steadily until Dr. Sharma clicks quickly through my file. "Ah, yes. You had some cramping after orgasm. Has it continued to be as intense? Does it usually last more than a few minutes?"

If I thought my face was going to ignite before, now it's on its way nuclear.

"We've been playing it safe," Anton says, saving me with his matter-of-fact tone.

"Oh, I see." The doctor gives us a warm smile. "Well, you have no risk factors or other concerns that I'd be worried about. So I'd say go ahead and resume normal activities—whatever feels good. But if you experience bleeding, sharp pain that doesn't subside, or any unusual dizziness, give us a call." She heads for the door and smiles. "Just stop at the desk and make sure you're scheduled again in about four weeks. Other than that, have a Happy Thanksgiving!"

Anton humors my sudden desire for burgers and milkshakes, picking up takeout from Park Burger on the way home, but we don't talk much. He's still wearing that gleam from the doctor's office, and I don't want to ruin it for him by verbalizing the fifty different anxieties circling the inside of my brain. First and foremost, admitting I should probably pack a suitcase since our flight to Ohio leaves at seven a.m.

Fortunately, my brother-in-law of all people saves me from my own spiral, standing on our front steps, waiting for us as we pull in the driveway. Anton barely throws the truck into park when he spots him, he leaps out so fast.

"What the hell, man?" He buries his brother in an extended hug, and they're almost like two handsome versions of each other, one with light hair, one dark. Anton pulls away awkwardly, clapping Seth on the back. "I thought you weren't getting here till Saturday?"

Seth gives him a roguish grin, and I can't help smiling too as I gather all our things and exit the car. "We wrapped up the closing quicker than I thought, so I packed Bruno up and hit the road early yesterday. Thought I'd drop in and say hello before you two skip town."

"I'm so glad you're here," I say, hugging him awkwardly, juggling my purse and takeout bag and milkshakes.

"Here, let me get some of that for you," he says, scooping things out of my arms and following Anton inside.

"We didn't get enough food—you should've told us you were coming!" I scold him. "And where's Bruno?"

He shrugs. "I'm good. He's asleep in the car, but I can't stay long anyway. We're meeting Eden with the keys to the new place in an hour." He sets our stuff down on the counter while Heartthrob runs in circles around us. He *loves* Uncle Seth.

But then, out of the corner of my eye, I notice a strip of paper fluttering to the floor. I forgot I'd been holding it in the car.

Seth bends to retrieve it before it even hits the ground.

"Don't be stupid. You eat my burger, I have some lasagna," Anton is saying, digging through the fridge. While Seth stretches out the paper, furrowing his brow.

I open my mouth.

"Oh—oh *hey!*" Seth holds up the strip of sonograms with a great big grin. "Is this the little bean?"

Anton has straightened, still standing in front of the

fridge. His eyes find mine, and when they do, they're filled with pride—and apology.

Seth looks from his brother, back to me, and it's hard to miss the moment he realizes he didn't follow his apparent directions.

I turn to my husband, voice thick. "What happened to sharing the news together? On Thanksgiving?"

"I—" He winces. "I'm sorry. We were talking the other day, and I was excited—"

"Who *else* knows?" My throat burns. "Did you announce it to your whole office? To Henry? Have I been bending over backward to keep this under wraps when everyone already knows?"

"Um, I wanna give congrats, but . . . I'm going to go check on my cat," Seth says, stepping out of the kitchen.

"*No one* else knows, and I am sorry I told him without you. I shouldn't have." Anton clears his throat. "But . . . does it matter at this point? We're flying out to tell your family tomorrow, Lydia."

I ball my hands into fists and step toward him, something hot and ragey boiling up inside me. Because after what we've been through—what I've been going through for him—how *could* he?

But when I open my mouth, nothing comes out. Because he's right. There's a baby growing inside me that's already developed for fourteen weeks. We're flying to Ohio, where we will tell my mom and my sister. Which is as good as telling the whole world. Seth already knows. Henry will know. Caprice.

My hands fall limp at my sides and I turn away, down the hall. "Taking a bath."

On the bed, my purple suitcase lays half-packed, surrounded by the slim number of viable outfits I've cobbled together after trying on nearly everything in our closet. Leggings are all still workable, but many of my shirts and T-shirts, and even my favorite gray sweatshirt, hide nothing anymore. This week's baby email—which informs me our fetus is now the size of a *peach*—described some women "popping" at the start of the second trimester. Like, one week you don't look pregnant at all, and the next it's a full-on baby bump.

Apparently my body got the memo. Every time I look in the mirror, I want to cry.

And my boobs. They make me look like one of those adults-only Hentai images. I've already sized up my bras, but I appear to have two inflated balloons on my chest, so out of proportion with the rest of me, they don't even look real. I frown. I've always hated the word, and I've only said it in the context of sex, but these are most definitely what Anton would call *tits*. Huge, and heavy, and obscene, and even worse—now they're tender in a way that makes me want him to grab them and pay attention to them.

I groan, pulling my robe over my bra and underwear and knotting the belt. All of this has to be one hundred percent hormones. Those sunshiney, weekly what-to-expect emails even said so. I mean, they didn't say *you will turn into Barbie and become indescribably randy,* but they did say my body would change, and sex drive might go up or down at the end of the first trimester.

Maybe there was no way for it to go down, so it had to go up.

"How's it going?" Anton asks, peeking in the door from the hall. I heard him and Seth chatting quietly while I was in the bath, but my brother-in-law eventually left, and now I feel terrible for how I acted. He deserved a proper welcome. I'll try to make up for it when we get back.

"Couldn't we just fly out tomorrow morning and come back after dinner?" I ask. "Do we have to stay the night?"

Anton chuckles, coming into the room with a white shopping bag. "Our flight leaves mid-afternoon Friday. But don't forget your mom scheduled family photos that morning."

I glare at him, sure that my nausea has returned. But the sensation in my chest simmers into something more like heartburn. "Have you checked the weather? Are there any snowstorms coming? Maybe our flight will get canceled and we won't have to go."

He gives me a sympathetic smile. "All forecasts across the country say it's the clearest, sunniest Thanksgiving anyone can remember."

I slump onto the bed.

Anton sweeps my hair away from my face, tucking it behind my ear. "I bought you something."

He hands me the shopping bag, and I reach inside to find several basic T-shirts, and what looks like one fluttery gray top. My jaw drops as I realize the tags are from a maternity shop in Cherry Creek. He must've known how I was feeling, and actually went shopping for me. I look up at him, a lump forming in my throat. On some level, I know this reaction, too, is over the top, but I don't care. I'm just grateful for my husband.

"I thought you might like something new, that actually fits," Anton says. "The gray one even coordinates with Marion's specifications for the photo shoot."

"Anton—" I look at his face, at the soft light in his eyes. "Thank you."

"Try it on," he says gently.

I turn away. In part, because I'm self-conscious about how I look. But also because lately my nipples seem to have a mind of their own in front of him. I had no idea it was possible to feel ridiculous and horny at the same time, but here I am. Before I can get distracted, I drop the robe and slip the new top over my head.

I step in front of the mirror on the back of our closet door and suck in a breath. It's a pretty V-neck, gathered in a twist below the bust. I'm not sure if it's the empire cut, or just the way the fabric drapes in front, but it's actually really flattering and draws attention away from my inflated boobs. Unfortunately, it seems to do this by *accentuating* my growing belly.

Anton's eyes dance over my shape, and I have to look away. He is clearly thrilled about the changes. "Wow," he says. "You look really . . . preggers."

I turn, leveling him with a dead-eyed stare. "Please don't *ever* use that word to describe me again."

He gives me a sheepish smile and scratches the back of his head. "Noted."

"I—I can't wear this," I say, turning back to the mirror. "I mean, it's beautiful, thank you." I blush. "But . . ."

"But what?" he says, snaking his arms around my waist. For a hot second, I get excited, thinking he's going to touch me—*really* touch me. My nipples are so hard, they're showing through the fabric. Instead, he tenderly embraces my belly in the reflection. "You look beautiful. You *are* beautiful. You're going to be a wonderful mother."

Bile rises in my throat. Or maybe it's just heartburn. I bite my lip and look away. I had been thinking I couldn't wear the top because it makes me look too pregnant. I keep forgetting that's the whole point of this trip.

"It was really thoughtful, thank you." I lean up to kiss his cheek, hoping to encourage his hands to wander elsewhere. I lean my head against his shoulder. "If only we were going on vacation. And not to see my family."

"Don't forget I booked us a hotel," he whispers in my ear.

"Now *there's* something to give thanks for," I say with genuine relief.

Anton grins in the mirror, and now I'm sure he's going to turn me in his arms, smother all my doubts with his lips. I feel like a fire that needs to be put out; just the pressure of his hands feels amazing. I want them to drift from my belly to my new, enormous *tits*. Pull my top off and suck the ache out of each nipple. Help me settle the throb that's been humming between my legs. I've never wanted Anton so badly. Not without him waking my body up first. I'm still a little embarrassed about it, honestly. I should just reach for him, that's what our therapist would say to do. Just touch him myself, help get things started. But as I stare at his hands on my rounded body in the reflection, his scent filling my senses, I just need him to reach for me first. Show me he wants me . . . like this.

Our eyes meet in the mirror, and for a moment his gaze darkens, his grip tightens, and I *know* he does. I glance at the bed behind us, waiting for him to toss the suitcase and everything else to the floor because we are both feeling this. It's what we both need.

But then he withdraws his hands from my body and lays a chaste kiss in my hair.

"We'd better finish packing and get some sleep," he says. "We need to be at the airport by five."

CHAPTER THIRTY

Him

"WHAT DO YOU MEAN THE HOTEL IS OVERBOOKED?" I GLARE AT the white, balding man behind the front desk of the Westin Cincinnati.

"I'm terribly sorry, sir. This happens sometimes on extremely busy weekends. The system is supposed to leave room for cancellations, but . . ." He swallows. "It appears everyone has actually checked in."

I glance at Lydia beside me, bundled in my old CU sweatshirt, looking exhausted and overwhelmed. It was more of an ordeal than we expected getting through the Denver airport early this morning, making it onto the flight, and actually finding our rental car once we arrived in Cincinnati. She looks like she's ready to head out the door and walk back to Denver.

"Look, surely there's got to be something? A tiny, cheap room no one wants? An overpriced presidential suite? Or can you call an affiliate hotel and find us something?"

The man adjusts his glasses and turns to his computer. "It's Thanksgiving Day with the Bengals playing, sir. But I can check around."

Lydia's phone lights up with a call from her sister and we

exchange a look. We were supposed to be at Celia's half an hour ago.

I squeeze her hand. "Don't worry. We'll find something."

She gives me a pleading look, then steps away to take the call. As soon as her mother gets wind of the situation, she'll insist we stay with her. Which will be so much worse than if we'd just agreed to that in the first place. Marion loves nothing more than being put in a position of influence. She'll spend the next two days invading Lydia's space and making her feel like she should thank her for the lodging.

And once she realizes Lydia's pregnant, the narcissism will crank up to a thousand.

I wipe my hand over my face. This is not how I saw the holiday going at all. Before we left Denver, it felt like we held all the cards. We were traveling, staying, and announcing the pregnancy on *our* terms, the way I'd promised Lydia we would. Now it feels like all that control is slipping through my fingers.

The concierge hangs up his phone with a pained expression. "I'm sorry, Mr. Richie. Our affiliates are all in a similar position." He adjusts his glasses with a cough. "I'm not supposed to say this, but ah . . . you could try your luck with Airbnb?"

I glare at the guy. Though I realize he didn't personally overbook the rooms, that doesn't make me any less pissed off. But in my head I'm already moving on to the bigger problem, which will be shielding my wife from my mother-in-law.

"I'll expect a full refund for the stay," I snarl.

I find Lydia on a bench outside the lobby restrooms. She sits up, looking hopeful as I approach, but her face falls when I shake my head.

"It's a total shit-show." I slump down next to her. "I'm sorry. This was all my idea. I never meant to do this to you."

"You couldn't have known. It was a decent plan." Lydia

exhales, then says in a small voice, "Celia invited us to stay with her."

I sit up, studying her face carefully. Between the hotel and spilling the baby beans to my brother, I feel like I've already fucked up so much. I don't want to read her wrong and make it worse. "Is that—do you think you could handle it?"

Lydia and Celia don't have the smoothest relationship. And Celia's husband Adam is his own piece of work. But neither of us has to say aloud that staying with them would be a major upgrade over rooming with her mom.

"I don't want to be here at all," she says, still pale, her mouth set in a tense line. But her expression is less panicked. More resigned. "You were right, though. It'll just be worse if we don't get it over with."

I take her hand and squeeze. "It's just one night. We'll be out of here in twenty-four hours. And I'll be by your side the entire time."

"Sure." Lydia grits her teeth. "I mean, it's just Thanksgiving dinner with my mom."

"You two made it just in time!" Celia says, spatula in hand when she answers the door. The house is one of those massive, gentrified scrapes with an indeterminate design, but is clearly the nicest one on the block. Inside, it's like a vast, minimalist museum, scattered with more baby toys than furniture. It's so sparsely furnished, I'm about to make a joke about them having it staged when Dr. Adam himself thrusts his hand into mine.

"Anton," he says, gripping my fingers like a vice.

"Adam." I nod, eyeing the blue scrubs he's wearing with his gray cashmere sweater. "I see duty calls, even on holidays?"

"What can I say? It's part of the job." He chuckles like he's said this exact line many times. "Can I get you a beer? How about you, Lydia? Champagne? Glass of wine?"

She looks at him and grimaces. "Ah, just water for me. Got a little airsick on the flight."

I catch her eye, feeling encouraged when she smiles. We haven't really discussed how she wants to handle the announcement, but I'm leaving the timing up to her.

"Since when do you get airsick?" Marion appears from around a corner holding a champagne flute, looking like a dressed turkey. Her sweater glitters with so many sequins she resembles an Olympic ice skater.

"Marion, how nice to see you! You look . . . radiant." I insert myself between her and Lydia, intercepting the hug, and more importantly, the assessing gaze she has zeroed in on my wife. Luckily, if there's anything my mother-in-law likes better than nitpicking her daughter, it's getting attention herself.

"Anton, you flatterer. I see you're just as strapping as ever." She squeezes my bicep as I release her. "I was so sorry to hear about your mother. It must've been painful, watching her slowly slip away like that."

Her expression is like a kid waiting for a firework to go off. Which is why we keep her at a healthy distance of a thousand miles. For a moment, that familiar darkness rises up inside me. There have been so many *good* things to focus on, I'd managed to bury my grief to the point I could almost forget about it. But Lydia grips my hand at my side and squeezes. And finally, I'm able to force myself to swallow. "I uh . . . thanks. It was."

"Lydia, it's been too long. You look . . . *healthy*," Marion says, wasting no time scanning her up and down.

"Thanks, Mom." Lydia slips her coat off and drapes it over her arm, navigating a hug with it between them, effectively blocking her mother from her stomach.

"Aren't you hot in that sweatshirt?" Marion asks, lip curled. "It's awfully casual."

"Nope. I'm fine," Lydia says, keeping her responses clipped. She turns to her sister. "Celia, where's Pookie?"

Dogs will always be Lydia's comfort zone, and I'm not surprised to see her searching the room for her sister's elderly Pekingese.

"Oh. Um . . ." Celia's mouth tightens.

"It wasn't hygienic, having a dog walking around on the same floors Gabriel's learning to crawl on," Dr. Adam interjects without pause.

Lydia gapes, obviously horrified. "So you—?"

"He's living with my friend Bethany," Celia says, quickly turning away. "I . . . I need to check on the green bean casserole. Adam, will you show them the room?"

"Let the boys take care of that." Marion inserts herself between Lydia and her suitcase. "I never get to see my baby girl."

Lydia gives me a dreadful look, and I scramble for something to say to stay by her side, like I promised. So far, Lydia's done more to support *me* since we walked in than the other way around. But before I can open my mouth, Dr. Adam grabs the suitcase out of my hand.

"Guest room is this way," he says, leading the way up a set of floating stairs. "Too bad about your hotel."

When I look back, my wife is disappearing into the belly of the beast with her sister and mother.

I grab her suitcase and hustle after my brother-in-law, aiming to complete the task and return downstairs as quickly as possible.

"So, how's the finance world?" Adam asks, sounding more obliged than interested.

"It's fine. Are your parents not here yet?" I ask, realizing they hadn't made an appearance downstairs. And if I change the subject, I can avoid getting sucked into a work conversation.

"No." He scoffs, leading me through a hall past what seems like countless doors and bedrooms. "My little sister graduated Princeton this year, and they promised her a cruise in the Seychelles."

"Oh." I raise an eyebrow. "They don't mind missing Gabriel's first Thanksgiving?"

He glances at a closed door, then breezes into the bedroom next to it. "He's seven months old. It's not like he'll remember it."

I follow him into another sparsely furnished room, where he sets down the bag. While my wife and her sister aren't close, I've known Celia long enough that I'm surprised by the decor. She and Adam have only been married about a year, but her last apartment was decorated more country farm-house than minimalist angles.

I stand in the door, straining to hear what's going on down in the kitchen, but if Marion's getting out of hand, it's happening in hushed tones. Which is all the more worrisome.

"Well, here it is," Adam says, smoothing his hair in a mirror, despite already resembling a Ken doll. "There's a bathroom across the hall. Gabe's room is next door. Hopefully you won't need earplugs."

I chuckle, though I can't tell if he's joking. "Fatherhood treating you well?" I ask, genuinely curious.

He shrugs, glancing at his phone. "Yeah, it's great."

"Where is the little guy?" I ask, realizing I haven't seen him since we got here.

"Napping."

As if on cue, a cry sounds from the other side of the wall. Adam immediately slips past me, and I figure he's going to see to his son. But once he's out in the hall, he heads for the stairs, not the next-door bedroom.

"Celia, he's up!" he calls, descending to the living room.

Lydia's sister rushes up the stairs past me, wearing a splattered red apron as Adam drops lazily into a chair across from a bright-white sofa.

"Help yourself to a beer, Anton," he says, looking at his phone.

"Sure," I mutter, grateful for an excuse to leave the room. "I'll go do that."

I wander down a short hall, past a beautifully laid formal dining room, and through another door leading into a large open kitchen and second living area. This one is slightly warmer and softer, albeit still sparsely furnished. Lydia is seated at the breakfast bar, hugging the counter like a shield. Marion leans casually by the sink, still balancing her champagne flute in one hand.

"Smells delicious in here," I say.

Marion smiles, her eyes narrowing. "Yes, we were just talking about that."

Lydia glances at me, her expression already resembling a cornered animal. I move closer, wishing I hadn't let myself get pulled away.

"Anything I can do to help?" I ask.

Marion gives a derisive chuckle. "Not when everything's heat and serve."

I look around the room again, noting several foil pans laid out on the counter.

"I'm sorry you two flew all this way for . . . Whole Foods." She sniffs. "If I'd known—"

"I'm sure it'll be fine," I say. "Seems like Celia's got her hands full."

"Yes." My mother-in-law clucks, draining her glass.

Lydia remains uncommonly quiet, and I notice she's folding a pile of linen napkins in front of her, shaping them into fans and fastening them with silver napkin rings.

"Anyway, the photographer will be here tomorrow at ten o'clock sharp," Marion says, as if she hadn't already sent us a calendar invite. She sniffs. "I hope you brought something appropriate to wear, Lydia."

"Of course." Lydia hasn't looked up from the napkins, and I realize she's actually folding and smoothing the same one over and over.

I settle onto the stool next to her and place a hand on her thigh, wishing her mother would find something to do so I can check in with my wife. "We'll stay until noon, Marion, but then we'll have to leave to catch our flight."

Marion opens her mouth, no doubt to make some other tedious demand, but before she gets the words out, Celia blusters back into the kitchen with a chubby, bright-eyed baby on her hip.

"Okay! Sorry, quick diaper change and I guess there'll be one more joining us for dinner." She smiles at her son and bounces him. He grins back at her, and something squeezes in my chest. I try to catch Lydia's eye, but she hasn't looked up from the napkins.

"Wow, he's gotten so big," I say.

Celia looks my way, pride beaming on her face.

"My goodness, Celia, don't hold my grandson so close to the oven." Marion crosses the room, extending her arms. "Oh Gabey, let Nana rescue you from Mommy."

Celia untangles his little fingers from the pearls around her neck and hands him over, looking reluctant, but relieved to have a free hand.

I feel useless just sitting here watching her do everything, so I slide off my stool, taking Lydia by the hand. "Lydia and I can help put things on the table if you're ready to serve."

"Perfect. Thanks." Celia rushes around the kitchen, taking multiple pans out of the ovens, and I grab a couple of potholders, taking them from her and placing them at random on the table in the next room. Lydia follows wordlessly with serving spoons and forks for each one. As we finish, Celia pulls a banana out of the fruit bowl in the kitchen and slices it into long fingers. "Adam! Dinner's ready!"

I follow Marion into the dining room where baby Gabriel has started fussing and squirming in her arms. I'm not a parent yet, but it's obvious he isn't happy about something. Finally, he lets out a wail, and Lydia startles, looking pale.

Marion bounces him, frowning at Celia, who's dragging a fancy wooden high chair to one end of the room. "I don't know what's wrong. He must be teething."

Celia also frowns, looking at her son. Then a look of understanding dawns on her face and she reaches for him. "Mom, your sweater—the sequins are digging into his skin."

"Oh, don't be—"

Celia snatches the baby away, and sure enough, angry red marks are pressed into his bare, chubby thighs. "Why don't you check everyone's drinks?" Celia barks at Adam, who wanders in, staring at his phone as she rushes the crying baby out of the room.

Marion presses her lips together as we watch Adam open up a bottle of wine. "Celia seems to be struggling with motherhood," she says dismissively, removing the foil lids from the dishes on the table. "Perhaps we should start without her."

The room fills with the scents of turkey, mashed potatoes, and stuffing, and Lydia abruptly covers her nose.

"Zinfandel?" Adam asks, reaching the bottle out between us.

Lydia puts a hand over her glass and I shake my head, sticking to my support plan. "Uh, maybe later, thanks. We'll stick with water."

Celia comes back into the room with a happier-looking Gabriel wearing a different outfit. She straps him into his high chair and presents him with the banana slices, which he quickly squishes in his fists.

"Please start, everyone," she says, taking a seat still wearing her apron.

Silence settles over the room, broken only by a few burbles from Gabe, as plates are passed around and we each take various helpings. Despite her criticism of the food, everything looks delicious, and I can't help noticing my mother-in-law piles her plate high. Lydia barely takes a spoonful of everything.

"So, Richies, what's new in Denver?" Adam asks, setting his phone aside.

I turn to my wife, sliding my fingers through hers under the table. This has got to be as good an opening as any to share the news.

"Uh, well . . ." She clears her throat, then flushes pink. "We had a great first quarter with the second Pooch Park."

"Oh, awesome news!" Celia says, sounding enthusiastic for the first time since we got here.

I curl my fingers tighter in Lydia's, wondering what she's doing, but she won't meet my eyes. She's focused on her sister. "Thanks. It's exciting. We still have so much room for growth."

"I'm glad to hear the new partnership is going smoothly," Celia says.

"Is your business still on hold, Celia?" Marion asks. "Any firm dates on returning to the office?"

Adam and Celia share a frosty glance.

"We've been discussing an au pair," he says.

"*One* of us has," Celia volleys back. "I'm not in a rush."

Marion makes a face that reminds me of a cat's butt. "It will be good for you to get back to work, sweetie. Honestly, I can't imagine what I would have done if I'd been stuck at home with you girls. Of course I loved you, but going to work every day saved me." Her lip curls. "One can only take so much hide-and-seek and *Sesame Street*."

Next to me, Lydia has stopped eating. She stares at their mother with wide eyes.

"I don't see it that way." Celia shakes her head. "Maybe

I'll feel differently when he's older, but since I have the privilege and we have plenty of money, I can't imagine not spending every day with Gabe while he's little."

"Until you've been out so long you're obsolete to the workforce," Adam says.

"Because obviously child-rearing women hold zero value," Celia hisses.

Marion turns to Lydia, studying her with narrowed eyes before breaking into a simpering smile. "What's your opinion, Lydia? Will you be staying home with Gabey's little cousin?"

Lydia had been pushing mashed potatoes around on her plate, but she freezes, fork in hand. I glare at her mother.

"Wait. What?" Celia says, looking at her sister.

Marion's eyes light up with satisfaction. "I don't know why you're being coy. Did you think your own mother wouldn't notice? You can't stand food smells, you're not drinking. And sweetheart, that sweatshirt of your husband's isn't hiding anything. You're looking pretty round."

Celia brings her hand to her mouth, staring at her sister. "You're pregnant?"

Adam's phone starts ringing at that moment and he wastes no time stepping out of the room.

"I . . ." Lydia looks at me like she's about to cry. I try squeezing her hand, but she pulls out of my grip and hugs herself like she's trying to disappear.

"Yes." I gather myself up, putting a protective arm around my wife, refusing to let her mother ruin our moment. "We were about to make the announcement ourselves. Lydia and I are expecting in the spring."

CHAPTER THIRTY-ONE

I AM GOING TO THROW UP. ANTON'S ARM RESTS LIKE A WEIGHT on my shoulder. He produces the sonogram, which gets passed around the table, and I hear the rumble of his voice, but can't make out what he's saying above the roar in my ears. All I see is my mother sitting across from me, leaning back in her chair with a satisfied smirk.

" . . . know what you're having?"

"How far along . . . ?"

" . . . are you feeling?"

It's like a choppy ocean of words, tossing me around. But I can't break the surface.

Until I realize everyone's waiting for me to speak. Celia's eyes are a blend of sympathy and excitement. I look up at Anton, searching for his comfort, his concern. But when he looks down into my face, he's beaming. The way I've always imagined a proud father might. It's similar to the look that used to shine in his mother's eyes. Something in my chest squeezes—*this*, this is what I've wanted for him.

But then I meet my own mother's gaze across the table. See the way her mouth curls up on one side, her eyes gleaming—not with warmth or maternal anticipation, but mirth. And I realize she knows. She sees me.

"We—we're excited," I manage to say. But the words come out sounding only half true.

"Oh Lydia, *you'll* be a great mommy," our mom says, giving my sister a sideways glance. "I mean, how could you not? You're so much like me."

I need air. I need to leave. But the room tilts when I try to get my feet under me, and I grip the table, afraid I might fall out of my chair.

My mother claps her hands at the baby in the high chair. "Both my girls are going to be mommies! Baby Gabey's going to have a baby cousin!" she shrieks.

At this, Gabe's little brow furrows with uncertainty. He looks at Celia, who tries to distract him with a small piece of bread. He throws it on the floor, looks back at his grand-mother, and starts to wail. Honestly, I wish I could too.

I watch my sister jump into action, trying to wipe bananas off her son and unbuckle him as fast as she can while his screeching grows in intensity. She looks harried and exhausted. And all I can think is—that's going to be me. When the little *peach* inside me emerges, I will be at its mercy too. If it demands I jump, I'll have no choice but to guess how high. Except Celia does it all with a glow, a satisfaction I don't have inside me.

Because our mother never had it either.

Anton's out of his chair now, setting aside the thrill of our announcement to stand awkwardly by my sister like he wants to help but isn't sure how. All the while, our mother just sits watching, not lifting a finger. Like she did her time as a mom and is now enjoying seeing her daughter slave away the same way she did.

"I—I need the restroom." I rise from the table, shoving my chair back.

But before I can escape the dining room, Dr. Adam comes

back, holding a tube of something. He hands it to Anton. "Here. For the stretch marks. This really helps."

My legs propel me from the room.

I don't know where I'm headed, but my mother's laser gaze, assessing my body, my stomach, keeps me going as far away as I can get. Out into the living room and up the modern, floating staircase barricaded by plastic gates. There are baby obstacles everywhere. A mat on the floor with arches covered in dangling things, an expensive-looking swing, some other contraption with a seatbelt that must do something. There are little soft toys everywhere, and suddenly I wish I could bury my face in Heartthrob's fur. *How* could my sister ever, ever give up her dog?

When I reach the second floor, I'm not sure where to turn. There's a hall with a bunch of doors, and I know one of them is designated ours, but I guess I just have to try them.

The first room looks like it hasn't been touched since they moved in. Celia's desk sits in the middle of the room. There's an empty bookshelf in a corner. Some art prints and her framed diplomas rest on the floor against the wall, but the desk is piled with unopened boxes and it looks like no one's been in here for months.

The next door is a bathroom, but when I open the one after that, I lean heavily against the doorframe. It's the only room in the house that clearly has my sister's touch. The crib, dresser, and changing table are all a traditional style, white and bright. The window hangings, rug, and rocking chair are plush. Soft and welcoming. There's a little shelf filled with picture books. Tasteful photos of friendly farm animals on the walls. And the name *Gabriel* written out in bold letters hanging above the crib. It looks like a photoshoot from some catalog, not a room that a baby actually uses. It doesn't even smell like diapers.

"Hey. Just thought I'd see if you need anything?"

I turn around to find my sister. Sans infant, thank God.

Though I can't help wondering whose care she left him in, of all the people to choose from downstairs.

"I um . . ." I don't even realize I'm crying until I hear the tremor in my voice. I gesture to her son's room for a distraction. "This looks nice."

"Thank you," she says, more warmly than I can remember her speaking to me my entire life. She scoots past me toward the dresser, grabs a tissue, and I'm grateful to take it from her. "I'm so sorry Mom spoiled your news."

I look at her face, take in the sincerity in her eyes, and I nearly break into full sobs. Not because I'm sad about the botched announcement. Not for any reason my sister would guess.

"For what it's worth, you look beautiful. And I'm excited for you," Celia says.

My head spins. I can't remember the last time my sister offered me a real compliment. Or one that wasn't at least partly backhanded.

"Thanks. Um . . . I'm still getting used to the idea."

Her eyebrows rise in some sort of understanding. "*Oh*— yes. Well, I wasn't expecting Gabe either. Initially, the idea of him was quite a shock."

I press my lips together, not bothering to correct her as I turn her words over in my head. "I thought you guys planned—"

"It doesn't matter," she says quickly. "The important thing is, after all my initial doubts and worry, he has turned out to be the single most *special* thing in the world."

And this is where I get off, I think. Because I finally understand—my issue isn't really about the baby. It's about me.

"You seem pretty great at being a mom," I say quietly. Since apparently we now say nice things to each other.

She sits in the rocking chair by the window, leaning back like it's a place she spends a lot of time. "I think you have to want to." She glances toward the hall, down the stairs. "I'm not sure Marion ever did."

My stomach, already near my feet, works its way into the floorboards.

A happy-sounding burble draws our attention to the door as Anton appears at the top of the stairs, carrying a very smiley baby Gabriel.

Of course. She chose him.

"There she is. I told you we'd find her," he says in a placid voice I have never heard.

My sister rises from her chair with wide arms and an open smile. All signs of her being tired or exhausted have gone. She looks nothing if not restored.

"Hello!" she says as her son reaches for her from my husband's arms. "Were you looking for Mommy?"

Once he's in her arms, he visibly relaxes, nestling into her chest. She closes her eyes, stroking his hair. Anton looks on next to me with a tranquil smile. I step back toward the door.

"Um, we'll leave you if you're going to—" I gesture around, trying to indicate things I'd rather not think of. Breastfeeding, diapers.

"You look tired, Lydia. You should go lie down." I'm actually grateful to hear my sister's more-familiar patronizing voice. It's almost soothing. At least I know how to respond to it.

"I'll do that," I say, grateful for the excuse to hide from our mom. "Don't wait up for me for dessert. I'll have pie for breakfast."

Celia's eyes fall on my husband as she settles back in the rocking chair and starts pulling at her shirt. "Thanks again for your help, Uncle Anton."

He nods. "Guess I'm going to need the practice."

I'm in the next room, what must be our bedroom judging from the suitcases, before he finishes the sentence. The furnishings aren't nearly as welcoming as the nursery, but the sleek, modern bed has a fluffy duvet which I climb under, trying to bury myself.

Anton closes the door and comes to settle beside me. And I guess this ought to feel comforting, but I'm surprised to find myself wishing he'd leave. I just want to close my eyes and make *everything* go away. I want to be back in Denver, with my dog and my job, with no more big announcements or major life events coming at me. I just wish things could be normal again.

"That didn't really go the way I thought it would," Anton says after a while.

"Yes it did," I say into the pillow. "It was always going to go like that."

He doesn't seem to know what to say to this. Instead, he climbs under the covers with me, and we lie there a long time, until the last of the daylight fades and the room has gone dark.

Eventually, I sneak out to go to the bathroom, because pregnancy. I'm not sure what time it is, but I'm surprised to find the whole house quiet and dark. I'm actually starving now that the worst of the drama is over, but not enough to risk running into my mother downstairs. There's every chance she's lingering with a glass of wine somewhere.

Instead, I slip back into our room, removing my sweatshirt, leggings, and bra because I am now a furnace. Quietly, I slide back under the covers in my T-shirt and underwear, trying not to disturb Anton. But as I curl up next to him, seeking the reassurance of his steady breathing, his hand drifts lazily over, gently caressing my thigh.

I close my eyes. Wishing we were back in our own house, in our bed. Anton shifts closer, continuing to explore the way I wished he had yesterday. Sliding his hand over my hip and along my arm. Brushing my T-shirt lightly where my nipples stand out against the fabric. And as he does, the heat inside me reignites. My already-warm skin grows hotter, liquid arousal shooting through my core, bringing back that strong, insistent ache between my legs. My thighs clench together, and I know I'm ready for him. I don't even need to check. I am slick and hot and yearning, no other foreplay necessary.

The problem is, this is not *me*. This isn't who I am. I've always had to work at intimacy—with Anton's help. Touching, exploring, warming me up. It's become part of our process, something we've learned how to do. If we get my body started, then my brain will get on board. And I can tell that's what he's trying to do. But something has short-circuited. He's hardly touched me, barely looked at me, and here I am, nearly ready to come.

I pull away, roll into the covers on the far side of the bed. As if, somehow, I could escape myself. Get away from this new, strange body that feels and acts nothing like my own. Once I am fully cocooned, wrapped up in the sheets like a mummy, not baring an inch of skin, I register the distinct lack of other movement. The silence in the room.

And I realize too late what I've done. Anton reached for me. I've been dying for him to touch me for weeks, and he finally did, but I pulled away. Shut him down. Rejected him exactly the way I always used to.

I open my mouth in the dark, trying to find words, to help him understand.

Except I can't. I don't even know myself.

CHAPTER THIRTY-TWO

DENVER WELCOMES US HOME WITH COLD AND ICE. THE MILD weather, so perfect for giving thanks and feeling grateful, was chased away by plunging temperatures and a frost advisory, coating the roads and the air on Black Friday with a bitter layer of ice.

Our flight didn't make it in until eleven thirty, and by the time Anton and I navigate the holiday crowds in the concourse, take the underground train to the terminal, and trudge all the way out to the farthest walkable parking lot, it's nearly midnight.

The sound of my suitcase wheels grinding across the pavement might be permanently ingrained in my ears, but at least it means there are a thousand miles between my family and me.

"Go ahead and start the car. I'll load the suitcases," Anton says, opening up the back of my Toyota. I think that's more words than he's said since we left Ohio.

He had gone for a run before I got up for breakfast, but returned in time to shower for my mother's photo shoot. She came over early to rearrange my sister's furniture, then determined she needed to be at the center of every portrait, as the family "matriarch." Celia had to change Gabriel's outfit twice to meet her specifications, but Mom didn't say a word about my fluttery gray maternity top. Just eyed me up and down with a smug smile that seemed to say *now it's your turn.*

Dr. Adam got an emergency call just as the photographer got started, so we wound up with a bunch of awkward photos of Celia and Gabe flanking our mom on one side, and Anton and me on the other. All of us little farther from each other than looked natural. For about half the session, the photographer joked about us pretending to like each other in an effort to move us closer together, but I think he eventually gave up.

There were a lot of teeth, and no smiles. Except from the baby. When he wasn't screaming.

The whole car shudders as Anton slams the liftgate and climbs in the passenger seat. I can still see my breath under the dome light, but he got the ice scraper out and cleared the windshield, and the defroster is doing its job.

"Are you too tired? Do you want me to drive?" he asks.

I shake my head, pulling out of the parking space, honestly invigorated now that the Ohio trip is behind us. The Pooches are closed for the holiday weekend, so I'll take a couple days to recover, but Henry and I have an expansion meeting Monday morning, and I plan to hit the ground running.

"Well, I wouldn't say we made it out unscathed, but at least we're home," Anton says, echoing my thoughts. "How are you feeling?"

I exhale, stopping at a booth to pay for parking. Things have been awkward since last night. I appreciate the effort he's making. "I think this one earned a place in my Top Ten."

"Ouch." We have informally ranked events with my family since college. The Top Ten is *not* a place of honor. "Even above Celia's rehearsal dinner?"

"*Yes.*"

He chuckles, leaning back in his seat, and it doesn't even sound forced. "Now we can share the news with everyone, at least. *That's* a relief."

My hands tense on the wheel, navigating the maze of roads from the Denver airport back to the highway. I have to admit, when I was planning out my Monday meeting on the plane, I hadn't thought to put that on the agenda.

"Yeah . . . guess we'll have to."

Out of the corner of my eye, I see him flinch. Then he reaches over, placing a hand on my stomach as I drive. "Hard to believe we're going to be parents. It's starting to feel real."

I swallow hard, squinting down the dark road. I'm not sure how to respond.

"Well . . ." he says, and now he does sound forced. "Who are you going to tell first?"

"I—" I take too long to answer. "I don't know."

Anton sort of snorts. I look over at him. "Or do you just not want to tell anyone ever?"

"What? Of course I do." The words come out of my mouth with sincerity, but my tone is defensive.

He shifts in his seat, turning to face me. "I'm just trying to understand," he says in a voice that doesn't feel at all understanding. "Most people get excited when they're expecting. You aren't. You don't want to design a nursery. You won't discuss names. You won't buy maternity clothes. You won't even tell your best friend this is happening."

"I *am* going to tell Caprice," I say, reluctance thick in my voice.

He shakes his head, a line cutting deep between his brows. "Sure. Eventually, you'll have to. I'm just trying to figure out why you haven't yet. What it means."

"It doesn't mean anything, Anton. As I've said before, it's still early and I have a *lot* of other stuff that matters to me—"

"Just like your mom."

I grip the steering wheel so hard, my knuckles turn white. "Excuse me?"

"Isn't that what you've always said your mom did? Never had time to come to performances or sporting events because she was too busy doing her own things?"

I blow out a hot breath. "Pregnancy isn't exactly a dance recital."

"I just need to know right now, Lydia." His voice dips low and sad. "Do you—do you not want the baby?"

And suddenly we're back in our bathroom, arguing about birth control last July, and I'm trying to tell him I'm not sure about having kids. And he's giving me that stony look and saying. *That might've been good to know.*

For a second, tears prick my eyes and the car drifts over the white line on the shoulder, but I quickly correct the wheel. I didn't even realize I'd been dreading this question—having to answer it for myself.

Because when I think about it, I don't want any of the things that are happening to my body. I don't want the changes to our home. Or Anton's affection. I don't want our lives upended with diapers and crying. I don't want our schedules turned upside down.

Do you not want the baby?

Or do I not want to be a mother?

Is that a different question, or does it mean the same thing?

Suddenly, I notice Anton's posture changing next to me. He straightens, facing forward, and the air between us shifts like darkness descending on the car. We come to a red light, and though my 4Runner's tires slide a bit on the icy pavement, we do come to a stop. And as the late-night traffic crosses in front of us, I turn to look at my husband's face, but I'm not prepared for what I see. His expression, blank and removed. Like he's interpreted my silence as my answer.

I open my mouth. "Anton—"

But as I speak, a light catches my attention in the rearview mirror. No, it's two. A pair of headlights approaching in the dark. I pump the brake to get their attention, because they're coming so fast, and I know there's ice, and—

My hand flies to my midsection.

"They're not going to stop."

CHAPTER THIRTY-THREE

Him

"*Please.*" I clench my fists, begging the police officer in front of me. "I just need to get back to my wife."

"I'm trying to make sure I understand what happened—"

"Sir, can I take a look at that cut on your face?"

I turn my attention from the police officer and her endless questions to a paramedic approaching with a look of sympathy. "How is she?" I ask. "Is she okay?"

He glances over his shoulder at the ambulance where Lydia was taken forever ago. She was up and walking when they got here, said somehow she didn't feel hurt—thank God —but she was scared. They closed the doors to give her privacy at some point, but the longer she's in there, the harder my heart pounds.

"My partner's with her, don't worry. She seems remarkably well, all things considered." He glances at the two wrecked cars in the intersection, then reaches out and swabs my forehead with something that fucking stings.

At that moment, the back of the ambulance opens up and the female paramedic sticks her head out, waving us over. When we get there, they mutter back and forth to each other, but my eyes are glued to Lydia, lying on a gurney looking pale and no less afraid.

"Anton," she says when she sees me, a tear spilling down her cheek. I scan her again, looking for any new sign of pain or injury. Apart from looking disheveled, she somehow has fewer scrapes than me, but she's clutching her hands to her stomach and the look on her face—

"Hey. D-does something hurt?" I want to climb inside to be with her, but the other paramedic is moving around now, grabbing supplies, and I realize she's prepping her arm to put in an IV. My eyes widen, but I'm afraid of getting in the way, so I grab my wife's foot at the end of the gurney and squeeze.

"I—I don't know," Lydia says, still scared and confused. "They want to take me to the hospital."

The paramedic next to me nods, sticking something to my forehead. When he's satisfied with that, he starts packing up to leave. "She has some mild vaginal bleeding," he says in a low voice. "*Not* a lot, and she says there's no pain, which is good. But we want to take her to Denver Health to get checked out."

"Bleeding." I let out a breath. More like a gasp. "Is the baby—"

"They'll be able to tell a lot more about what's going on at the hospital," he says, managing to sound both rushed and incredibly reassuring. "She doesn't seem otherwise hurt, so it might be nothing."

I nod stiffly. My shoulders won't release. "Can I—I'll go with her?"

The police officer comes over, clearing her throat. "Sir, I'm going to need your insurance info for when the tow truck gets here. And if you don't mind, I do have a few more questions before I can complete my report."

The paramedic gives me a compassionate nod. "I know this is stressful, but do you have another ride? We'd like to get her there as soon as possible."

I glare at the officer, but Lydia's pale, dazed expression makes me shut up and put on a brave face. "My brother's on his way." I keep my tone as even and confident as I can, but as I watch them place an oxygen mask over my wife's face, it feels like my chest is coming apart. "Don't worry, Lydia. I— I'll meet you at the hospital."

And then they're closing the doors between us, and the ambulance turns its lights on, and they're driving away, siren blaring through the night.

The police officer turns to me and opens her mouth.

"Excuse me." I pull out my phone and turn away. Dial a number I've had forever and never called. She picks up on the fifth ring, sounding groggy.

"Hello?"

"Caprice." My voice breaks. "Lydia—look, there was an accident, she—"

"*What?*" she says, instantly awake. "Is she okay? What did you—where is she?"

My voice is shaking now. "They took her to Denver Health. Can you—I'm still here with the police—"

Through the receiver, I hear a clatter, then some swearing, but she comes back and says, "I'll be there in twenty minutes." Then hangs up without another word. I don't even care, I'm just grateful Lydia won't be alone.

"Okay, so I was able to get a statement from the other driver," the officer says, going down her checklist when I finish. "Now I just need—"

"Anton! Fuck, I got here as soon as I could." My brother hollers from his car on the side of the road as I pocket the phone. "Is Lydia okay?"

"I don't fucking know," I say as he puts his arms around me, and that's when my chest finally fissures. "They—they took her to the hospital."

He's still for a moment, bearing the weight of what I've said, holding me up. But when the police officer comes over and starts talking about her report again, he lets me sink gently to the ground to talk to her, going over to Lydia's car to get our insurance information.

I follow him with my gaze, taking in the entire wreck for the first time—the other car, some kind of pickup truck, looks one hundred times worse than Lydia's 4Runner, its front end crumpled beyond recognition. The driver hit us so hard, the force sent both vehicles across the entire intersection. We're all lucky no one happened to be coming the other direction at that moment. The woman who was driving got out and was walking around, thanks to her airbag. But she was covered in glass and blood, and ultimately went to the hospital. Which is good, because if she was still here I'd be losing my shit in her face. But it's just me, my brother, and the police in the glow of red and blue lights. The air thick with grief and uncertainty.

I let my head drop to my knees, trying to slow my hammering pulse, get my breathing under control. Because I've been here before. A different crash, in a different time, on a different road. We weren't with my dad when it happened, but we'd driven past the accident, not knowing it was him. I remember looking out the window into the darkness and flashing lights, realizing the twisted metal used to be a car. Not long after we got home, the police showed up at our door. Then my mother quietly asked an officer to sit with Seth and me as she stepped out onto the front steps and broke down.

And now I'm here again, alone with my brother, with the police and flashing lights, still raw because we *just* lost our mom. And if anything happens to Lydia now, or to—

I think of her hands clutched over her middle and my heart seizes. God, this is *my* fault, all of it. It was my idea to go to Ohio. *I* got her pregnant. *I* wanted to start a family.

If I hadn't—we never would have been here.

And I sink even further as it hits me for the second time

tonight—Lydia didn't want this. She tried to tell me, *so* many ways, but I was only focused on myself. I didn't hear.

So she went through with it—*for me*. Because that's what she does.

The sex. The nausea. The fucking vitamins and food restrictions. The invasions on her body.

And then I made her go to Ohio to parade around for her mom because I thought any family was good family. Because I *still* couldn't see.

I already had what was most important.

I rake one hand through my hair. If it wasn't for me, we would've spent Thanksgiving at home with my brother, maybe Caprice. We would've eaten turkey sandwiches, Stove Top stuffing, and if I was feeling adventurous, I might've baked a pie. Today, we would have done some online shopping and taken Heartthrob to the park. Lydia could've used the time to relax, away from work. We could've worked on some of the homework from our sex therapist.

Instead of finding ourselves at this icy intersection, halfway between the airport and our home. With everything hanging in the balance.

If I had just listened.

"Hey, man," Seth says, approaching quietly. And somehow, I am positive he knows. He must've heard all my thoughts. "I think they've got what they need here if you're ready to go."

I look up. I ought to leap—race for his car. But it's like there's a weight inside me, anchoring me to this curb.

He tries again, with a new edge of concern. "Come on, Anton. Let's go catch up to Lydia, make sure she's good."

I shake my head, eyes burning.

Because either way, she won't be.

"She—we don't know if the baby's okay."

His fist tightens at his side, but he speaks in an even tone. "They'll be able to tell at the hospital, right? So let's go."

I drop my head into my hands, making no effort to move. "I—I can't."

"Why not?" he asks.

I shake my head. "Because . . . I did this to her."

His brow furrows. "I thought Lydia was driving."

"*No*—I knocked her up."

Seth drops to his knees in front of me. "Anton, we're talking about your wife possibly losing your fucking baby. Which, I'm pretty sure, also puts *her* life at risk. You have to go to her."

My limbs feel like lead. My lungs. I can't breathe.

"I want to!" I gasp for air. "But I don't think she'll want me there."

"What? Why the fuck not?"

"Because she didn't want the baby!" I roar, my whole face stinging. "She only went along with it because it's what *I* wanted." I choke. "And because I made her feel like she wasn't enough."

Seth sits back on his heels and stares at me, his face so haggard it crosses my mind he might be as worried as I am. "Look, Anton, I've known Lydia a long time. Since I was a sixteen-year-old kid. And I'm sorry, I know you love her, but sometimes you are so fucking wrong."

"You don't understand—"

"Just shut up and listen." He grips my knees. "You two went about this whole thing the stupidest way possible, as usual. I don't doubt Lydia had reservations, or that she was scared. But I know her—she's been a sister *and* a mother to me. And there is no way she would've gone along with this if she didn't want a baby at all."

I meet his eyes, and they're hard and earnest. Because Seth only ever says what he truly believes. But there's something else shining in his eyes—something I recognize immediately.

Fear.

He's afraid for Lydia. For me. And for himself, because he

loves her too. Because even though he spent the last five years caring for our mom, weathering her decline and dealing with her death like a fucking soldier, we still lost her.

And if we've learned anything over the course of our lives, it's that there's always more to lose.

CHAPTER THIRTY-FOUR

THE RIDE IN THE AMBULANCE FEELS BOTH HOURS LONG AND ONLY like a minute. The paramedics are kind, keeping me talking the whole time, distracting me from the mental loop my brain is stuck in, playing the accident over and over. The look of despair on Anton's face at the traffic light. The black sky. Headlights gleaming on the ice.

Everything gets chaotic again once we reach the emergency room. My reassuring paramedics hand me off to hurried doctors and nurses. Another ambulance arrives at the same time with a man who is screaming and covered in blood, and by comparison I am *clearly* fine—aren't I? But they wheel me into a room where a lone nurse starts asking me questions while the other guy is rushed down the hall by a crowd.

"I hope he's okay," I murmur as she tags me with a plastic bracelet and takes my blood pressure.

She looks at me like she's not sure who I'm talking about, and I realize I'm not sure either. "Welcome to Black Friday in the ER," she says with a shrug.

I answer many of the same million questions I've already answered. Giving my medical history, details of my pregnancy, describing what happened. I saw the blood; there was only a little. The nurse gives me more fluids, someone comes and takes labs, a doctor ducks in to shine a light in my eyes and ask if I'm having any cramping, which I'm not. I feel remarkably okay, considering what our cars looked like when the ambulance drove off. My neck is a little stiff, and I'm sure I'll be sore in places tomorrow, but I don't seem to have any injuries.

So why am I filled with a sinking sense of dread?

They want me to go to the bathroom, which is great because I haven't gone since Ohio. The nurse unhooks me from several cords and monitors, and guides me across the hall. But as soon as I pull down my underwear, I start shaking. The paramedics had me put on a pad to see if I was going to bleed more, and it's soaked in a bright smear of new blood.

I close my eyes, tears spilling down my cheeks. I need Anton here; I need to hold his hand. Look into his eyes. Hear him say it will be all right. But then his question, his face before the crash, comes flying into my head like an accusation.

Do you not want the baby?

I sink to the floor, curling into a ball. All I can think about is the little peach-sized life tucked inside me.

The life I'm supposed to keep warm and safe. Protected. Because I'm its mother.

I *want* to be its mother.

I'm staring at the wall, waiting on an ultrasound when Caprice storms in. She's not who I was expecting to see at whatever hour this is past midnight, but when her eyes find mine, the relief on her face mirrors my own. She crosses the room and folds me directly into a hug.

"Anton said you were in an accident—"

"You talked to him?" My lip trembles. "What did he say?"

"He'll be here. Thank God you're okay," she breathes into my hair. But after a moment, she pulls back, taking in the IV, the hospital gown, the monitors beeping in the corner. "*Are you okay?*"

I look at her, my lip trembling, so comforted to see her, to have someone by my side that I love. And so fraught with guilt about what I have to explain.

I shake my head. "I'm—" I bite my lip, tears spilling down my face. "Caprice, I'm pregnant."

She takes both my hands in hers, sinking to a chair next to the hospital bed.

"I've known since September. I don't know what I was thinking. I should've told you." I stare down at the thin white sheet, trying to swallow past the lump in my throat. "I just didn't think—I was sure something would happen—" My voice breaks. "Well, I guess now it has."

She squeezes my hands and doesn't let go. "What did they say? What's going on?"

My voice is unsteady. "The accident was horrible. But we both seemed fine. Anton has some scratches, but I couldn't find anywhere that even hurt, except . . . I'm bleeding a little." My nose burns. A knot tightens in my chest. "They've ordered an ultrasound, bloodwork, and a million other things. But no one's sure of anything yet." I pull my hands out of her grip, placing them over the tiny mound of my belly.

"Hey." Caprice moves her fingers gently over mine. "Whatever happens, you're in the right place."

I nod, another tear rolling down my cheek.

Some monitor starts beeping behind me, and after a minute the nurse comes in holding a new IV bag. "Hey, good news. Radiology's almost ready for you. We'll head down in just a few minutes."

"Great," I say. Because I can't think what else to say.

She finishes changing the IV, resets the machine, and leaves again.

"I'm sorry I didn't tell you," I say in a low voice.

Caprice's mouth tightens. A hundred different thoughts pass over her face, but she shakes her head gently. "I guessed two weeks ago, Lydia. I figured you'd tell me when you were ready."

I draw my knees up under the sheet, feeling even more awful, if that's possible. "I've just been so scared. Not of the baby—well, I thought that was it for a long time. I just finally realized . . . I'm not sure I should be someone's mother."

Her face softens. "Why do you say that? I think you'll make an excellent mom."

My brows shoot up in surprise. "Have you met Marion Stanton?"

"Well, yeah." Her lip curls in sympathy. "But girl, you're *not* your mom."

I shake my head. "If anything, I'm worse. Caprice, we were sitting at Thanksgiving dinner, and she was talking about how much she cherished being at work and not having to be home with us when we were little, and I just realized—I'm going to feel the same way." A sharp stab of heartburn rises in my throat. "I haven't been looking forward to diaper changes or singing the ABCs. All I could think was how I would just *lose* myself, staying home with nothing else to focus on."

Caprice just looks at me. "Lydia, I'm not a parent. But that doesn't seem unreasonable."

"Yes, it does." I stare at my knees. "You should see my sister. She's set her entire business aside for her son and dotes on him like he's her new reason for being. I can't even bring myself to discuss nursery paint colors with Anton, but you can tell Celia thought about every detail of Gabriel's room, down to the fabric of his curtains. I just can't get excited at all —and what if I feel the same way *after* the baby's born? Every time Celia asked me to hold Gabriel, I couldn't wait to give him back."

"Maybe you just don't like other people's kids." She scoots her chair closer, squeezing my arm. "You know my mom had Theo and me for all the wrong reasons. Her whole life, her career would've been different if she'd realized our dad wasn't worth it. But she loves us."

"That's *your* mom, though."

"I think that's a lot of moms." Caprice sits back in her chair, eyes on my hands, which have drifted back to my stomach. "You are a warm, nurturing person, Lydia. In ways Mama Marion could never be. I know it's always been hard for you to balance things, and obviously, you've got some misgivings about motherhood. But I'm getting the sense you *want* this baby . . . and I don't think you have to choose one or the other."

"I—I do want it."

I close my eyes, stomach knotting over all the times I wondered if the pregnancy would *stick.* Thinking all my problems would've been solved if it hadn't.

"God. I actually thought I might be a better mom than I had, but I failed before I even got started," I say, unable to hold back the tears any longer. I gesture at the hospital bed, the machines, the whole ER outside the curtain. "I couldn't even keep the baby safe long enough to be born."

My somber mood is interrupted by a commotion coming from the hall. At first I think another trauma case must be coming in, but then I hear shouts and arguing over the other medical chaos. And a moment later, a familiar voice yells, "Let me see my fucking wife!"

Then the curtain whips aside, and Anton's standing framed in the door, looking worried, and injured, and wild-eyed. His gaze meets mine as soon as they register me, then dips down to where my hands rest over the sheet—taking inventory of our whole family.

"Sir!" A breathless security guard crowds into the doorway and gestures around. "We can only allow one family member at a time."

Anton and I look at each other, then Caprice clears her throat. "Um, I might've said I was your wife so they'd let me in." She rises from her chair and kisses my cheek with a half-smile. "I'll give you some time with your husband now." I watch her exit, nodding at Seth hanging back in the hall. The security guard follows. And then there's just Anton and me.

"Are you okay? I—I just need you to be all right." His voice comes out broken.

My lip trembles. "I think *I* am, but . . ."

We stare at each other for a breath, both of us trying to express so much with just our eyes. And then he's reaching around all the cords and IV tubes, pulling me to him, clutching me to his chest. A machine comes unplugged and starts beeping, but I don't care. He smells so good—musky and earthy, and like *home*, and I just want to close my eyes and pretend that's exactly where we are.

CHAPTER THIRTY-FIVE

Him

"Mr. Richie?"

I turn on my heel just outside Lydia's door. After the ultrasound, the doctors couldn't give us a straight answer about what might be happening, so they admitted her to the hospital "for observation." It's at least quieter on this floor, but they've been observing for like five hours and nothing has happened.

"Hi, I'm Dr. Sloane. We met downstairs." She holds out her hand, and I shake it, though her face blends with the dozens of others I've seen since we got here. "How's she feeling?"

I shrug, sipping bad coffee from a machine down the hall. "She's sleeping, finally. Things seem about the same."

She nods. "I just wanted to follow up before my shift ends. I checked in with the nurses and they've reported she's had less bleeding over the last couple of hours. I also consulted with my colleagues about her ultrasound, and while our primary concern is still placental abruption, we agree, if the bleeding stops and she still doesn't experience any pain in the next forty-eight hours, her risk should be low."

I run my hand over my face. "Translate that for me? Sorry, it's been a long night."

She gives me a gentle smile. "That means that unless something changes, there's a good chance your wife will be fine and her pregnancy will progress normally."

I blink at her. "Like, we could just go home and forget this happened?"

"You would need to follow up with her OB to monitor her for a while. But yes, it's still early enough in her pregnancy that this trauma could be negligible."

I let out a long exhale, because this is exactly what I needed to hear. But then another question occurs to me. "If for some reason . . . If something went wrong and she—we lost it. Would *Lydia* still be okay?"

She presses her lips together. "If that were to happen, it would be like a miscarriage. Since she has no other injuries from the accident, her risk would still be low." She reaches out to touch my arm. "Lydia *and* the baby are doing well at this point. There's no reason to think either of them won't be just fine."

"Okay. I just need her to be—" I stop, remembering to breathe in again. "Thank you."

"You're welcome." She bobs her head, then visibly brightens. "I don't expect to see you when I come back on Monday, so I just want to say good luck."

I creep into Lydia's still-dark room, making my way to the chair I spent the night in by the light of the monitors still beeping away in the corner. She's curled up on her side, but when I lean over to pull her blankets a little higher, I hear a quiet sniffle.

"Lydia?" I whisper.

She raises her head, reaching for a tissue on the tray table, and my stomach drops. *Unless something changes*, I think, immediately echoing the doctor's words in my head.

"Hey, are you okay?" I ask, opening the blinds to let in

some of the gloomy morning light. "Has something started to hurt?"

She winces, turning away from the window, but shakes her head, her body continuing to vibrate with sobs. This goes on for a minute and she still doesn't speak. I'm not sure what else to do, and she won't look at me, so I set the coffee aside and nudge her. "Scoot over, make room."

She complies, somewhat surprised when I squeeze into the bed amid her wires and cords, wrapping my arms around her and tucking her head against my chest.

"Tell me what's wrong," I say in a low rumble.

At first, she presses her face harder against me, like maybe she could just sink in so far she won't have to speak. But after a while, after my shirt is damp from her tears, she says in a shaky voice, "I—I don't want to lose the baby."

My body stills. A thick lump makes its way into my throat, but I just whisper, "Me neither."

We lie there, holding each other a few more minutes, each of us with a protective hand over her belly, listening to the steady rhythm of her heart monitor.

"Did something . . . change?" I hate asking, but I can't stop thinking of our conversation in the car before the crash.

She lets out a long, slow breath. "Anton, I've always wanted a family with you. I just realized I was scared. Of things being different, of becoming a mom." She shakes her head, then takes my hand and squeezes. "And . . . I was scared you wouldn't wait for me to be ready."

If I thought there wasn't anything left to break inside me after last night, I was wrong. I open my mouth, trying to choke out words. "You thought I wouldn't—?"

She presses her face into my damp shirt and nods as it dawns on me—of course. This is what I've shown her. That I can't wait for her. That I'll look for someone else. I tore both our hearts to pieces doing exactly that on Unmatched.

And now I've done it again.

I close my eyes, trying to figure out what to say, how to *exist*—if the woman I love, who's already given me more chances than I deserve, thinks this of me. Finally, I pull back, holding her face so I can look into her eyes.

"*You* are my wife, Lydia. *You* are the only woman I ever want to mother my children. When I imagine our babies, they're in *your* arms—with your eyes and your hair," I say, curling her blonde strands around my fingers. I take a deep breath. "But when I've envisioned a future where I'm *not* a father, it's always with you, too. If the last few months—the last ten *years* have made me sure of anything, it's that. Whatever happens to us, whatever choices we make, I will be beside you."

She stares at me, searching deep, like there's something she's trying to find. Some reason to question or doubt. Something that maybe used to be there. But after a few moments, she bites her lip and her expressions clears. There are still tears in her eyes, but her cheeks are pink, and she looks at me with the most beautiful smile.

"I love you, Mr. Richie." She takes my hands and clasps them together with hers over her stomach, lowering her voice. "And no matter what happens, I hope this little peach knows that's what they're made of."

We are bustled around by nurses all Saturday morning. They're in and out with the occasional doctor, including Lydia's OB, and there's more bloodwork and ultrasounds. Lydia is still bleeding that evening, but it's so much less, and the baby continues to look so strong, that Sunday morning, we're finally told she can go home.

"I'd like you to stay on bed rest for a week as a precaution," Dr. Sharma says before we're discharged. "That doesn't literally mean stay in bed, but really try to limit your activity. No heavy lifting, don't even go for walks. And no sex. Things inside you may still be healing, and we want to give them the best chance we can. Come see me for a follow-up in a week and we'll go from there." She squeezes Lydia's hand and looks back and forth at the two of us. "I'm *so* glad you're both okay."

While we wait on discharge paperwork, Lydia asks me to log into our BabyBump account. I'm a little hesitant. It seems overconfident, seeking out things to get excited about just yet, but I don't want to crush her enthusiasm, so I pull it up on my phone.

"Let's see, it says the baby is the size of a navel orange at fourteen weeks," I say from the chair next to her bed. She's changed into fresh clothes I grabbed her from home, including another of my old CU sweatshirts.

"Peach was cuter," she says with a shrug. "What else is new this week?"

I scan the page, raising a brow. "Apparently our little fruit might already be growing hair. *And* can make facial expressions."

Something about this makes Lydia laugh. "I wonder if they'll make your broody, hangry face."

"What? I don't make a—"

I stop when I look up and realize her laughter has died, and she's clutching her arms around herself, looking lost. I get up and pull her into my arms.

"I—I hope we get to find out," she whispers.

I kiss the top of her hair. "Me, too."

There's a knock on the door, and our nurse bustles in. "Okay! You guys are all discharged." She enters trailing an over-the-top enormous bundle of brightly colored balloons. There must be more than thirty of them, taking up so much room Lydia and I can hardly see each other. "Also, these were just delivered. Good thing you didn't miss them!"

"Um, thanks," Lydia says, ducking to try to look at them. "Do you know who they're from?"

I back up to the windows, where I'm finally far enough away to see that all the balloons say *Congratulations!*

"Oh yeah, there's a card. It says: *Our thoughts are with you. Love, Mom.*"

The nurse makes a confused chuckle as Lydia peers at me through the helium forest. Lydia lost her phone in the wreck, but I told Celia what happened when she called me yesterday to check in. Word must have finally reached Marion.

Grudgingly, I have to admit my mother-in-law's conflicting sentiments—congrats and sympathy—are spot-on.

But when I see the new layer of stress on Lydia's face looking at the balloons, I clear my throat and turn to the nurse. "Um . . . is there a chance these would brighten the day of anyone else in the hospital?"

She glances at me, and for a second I expect an argument about the gift. But then she nods in a way that tells me she's seen plenty of complex family dynamics. "Sure. I'll send them down to the mom and baby unit. I'm sure they could find a way to use them."

Lydia looks at me, eyes grateful, and I squeeze her hand. "Thank you."

CHAPTER THIRTY-SIX

BED REST TURNS OUT TO BE THE LITERAL HARDEST THING BEFORE I'm even forty-eight hours into it. Anton has me set up on the couch in our living room within arm's reach of the TV remote, five books from my nightstand, several of my favorite snacks, and my laptop. But I feel like I'm coming out of my skin by noon on Tuesday. My phone did not survive the accident, and while Anton's promised me a replacement, I'm pretty sure he's dragging his feet in an attempt to help me "rest."

I reach for my phone to text Tomás, then remember *again* and yank open my laptop. I didn't even realize how much I move around and communicate during the day until I couldn't do either.

I only had some light spotting this morning, which comes as a huge relief, even though I'm starting to seriously question whether I'm going to make it through the week on this couch. I'm dying to at least take Heartthrob for a walk, though he seems content to just curl up nearby and keep an eye on me.

A knock on the front door lifts me out of my funk. I'll take any reason to get off my butt, even if it's just an Amazon delivery. But after I look out the window, I fling the door open with more enthusiasm than I've had all day.

"Henry!"

He looks me over carefully, standing on my porch holding a pink box of Voodoo Doughnuts. "Thank God," he says in his faint British lilt. "I couldn't discern from Anton's message if we were talking bumps and bruises, or you were in a coma in the ICU."

"I might be less bored in a coma. But I'm mostly in one piece." I open the door for him to come in, eyeing the box in his hands. "Henry, did you bring *meeting* donuts? Is this official business?"

"Actually, I was given pretty explicit instructions not to come over here and talk business." He clears his throat, looking over my shoulder presumably for Anton, who's not here. "So no, these are definitely *not* meeting donuts." He hands me the box with a wink.

I grin at him, open it immediately, and bite into a chocolate and sprinkle dream. "I always knew partnering with you was a great idea. You want one?"

Henry shakes his head and chuckles, taking a tentative seat in the armchair across from me while Heartthrob sniffs his tailored suit pants.

"So, how's Carmelita? And Scarlet? Tomás? Actually— everyone?" I ask, settling back into my nest on the couch. "If you can't tell, this is killing me."

He leans forward, resting his elbows on his knees, looking more serious than I expect. "Actually, I'd really like to know how *you* are first."

I meet his eyes, and flinch. That's only fair. We told him about the accident and said I wouldn't be able to work this week. But maybe it's obvious there's more to the story. I shouldn't make him guess. "Well, aside from having barely survived both a holiday with my mother and an accident that totaled my car . . ." I bite my cheek. "I'm nearly four months pregnant. Anton and I are expecting in May."

Henry's brows shoot up. Maybe that wasn't one of the guesses he'd made. "Oh, wow." He wipes a hand over his face, then straightens. "Congratulations."

"Thanks," I say quietly, skirting his gaze.

"I knew something else must be going on. Really, I'm relieved it's . . ." He hesitates a moment. "Are you planning to —I mean, will you be able—"

"I will keep running the Pooches," I cut in, instantly rankling at the suggestion that this will impact our business relationship. "My doctor put me on bed rest for this week, but just as a precaution after the accident. Once I replace my car, I should be back in full swing."

He sits on this a minute, looking relieved. But then his brows draw back together. "Well, obviously we need to at least push back the expansion."

"What? *Why?*" I ask, a little too sharply.

"Lydia, our tentative plan was to move on Pooch III in the spring. Now, I know you're excited to consolidate and move forward with our franchise model." He looks at me pointedly. "But surely you're going to take a little time off to—"

"*Henry.* You don't need to worry about me stepping away or slowing down," I say through my teeth. "I've already launched a grooming salon and two daycares at this point. I think I know what I'm doing on the business end. And even if I do need to be out for a little while, don't give yourself the impression this changes our plan and you can just run things the way you want."

He frowns. I've never spoken to him this way. But I don't like him suggesting how I ought to balance the Pooches with my life.

He sits back, clenching his jaw the way he does when he's irritated, and folds his hands in his lap. "All right. You asked how everyone at the Pooches are doing? I'll tell you. My phone has been blowing up with questions I can't answer. Tomás wants to know about dog food orders. Francie has employee scheduling requests. And *Scarlet* . . ." He looks away, clearing his throat. "Every one of them is already asking when you'll be back, and you haven't even been out two days."

I straighten, noticing for the first time since he got here that everything about him is slightly askew. There's dog hair on his sleeve. His socks don't match. And when he unfolds his hands, they seem a little unsteady. I glance up at his face, and it finally clicks. Henry's nervous?

"Look, I've no doubt you'll find a way to juggle everything once you've . . ." He gestures at my midsection. "But I need a plan for any time you'll need to be away." He looks at me dead on. "To be clear, Lydia . . . I'm not trying to run anything without you. I *can't* do this at all by myself."

I straighten. Blink. Part of the reason Henry and I work well together is because we balance each other out. He is amazing with spreadsheets and numbers, timesheets, and payroll, and taxes. But when it comes to employees and dogs, and day-to-day operations . . . he's right. That's really my wheelhouse.

I clear my throat, biting back a furtive smile. "Okay, you're right. We need a new plan if I'm going to take some leave."

His shoulders fall, his whole body visibly calming.

"I do intend to be gone as little as possible. But I hear what you're saying. We can push the Pooch III plan out a little, just so I'm not trying to launch that and give birth in the same month."

He pulls out his ever-present notebook and starts jotting things down, and for a second I try to envision what things *will* look like in another five or six months. In my head, it's easy to romanticize coming home from the hospital with a sleeping little bundle. Taking it back and forth to the Pooches with me, managing supply orders and meetings while negotiating feedings and changing diapers. But then I think of little Paloma in my office, covering herself in pink frosting while her mom was on the phone, and I blanch. I remember Marisol saying how much she prepared, knowing she was expecting her daughter. I make a mental note to invite her over.

"I—I don't want to lose our momentum for the expansion though," I say, trying to refocus. "Let's do monthly check-ins and continue laying the groundwork on paper, at the very least. So when we're ready to pull the trigger, everything's good to go."

Henry nods, then sets his notebook aside. "All right, that sounds good long-term. But in the meantime . . ." He reaches into his pocket with a somewhat calculated smile. "Anton said he's been scrambling between work and insurance figuring out your car situation. So I thought I could at least help with one thing." He produces a sleek new smartphone from his suit pocket and holds it out to me. "Obviously, you'll have to sync it with your own settings, but it's been activated with your number, so you're all ready to take calls and texts."

The phone lights up and vibrates as he hands it to me, and a message pops up on the screen.

UNKNOWN SENDER

"To the world, you are a mother, but to your family, you are the world."

I snort. I don't need to sync my contacts to know that's my brother-in-law. I scroll through what turns out to be a backlog of messages from the last several days, trying to discern the business ones from the personal.

UNKNOWN SENDER

Anton told me you're on bed rest, but if you don't call me by this evening, I'm coming over.

That would be Caprice.

UNKNOWN SENDER

Heyyy, I know you're out sick, but can I have
next Friday off?

UNKNOWN SENDER

Lydia, my BABY. Call me immediately so I
know you and my new grandbaby are all
right. Have you started thinking of names?

UNKNOWN SENDER

Heard about the accident, glad you're okay.
Can we order more oatmeal shampoo this
week?

"Guess I'm all reconnected now," I say, rolling my eyes, but I'm also smiling. Gripping the phone gives me a sense of calm and control I've been longing for the past few days. "Thanks, Henry."

He chuckles. "I admit, it's a somewhat selfish gift, but I thought you'd appreciate it. I'll write it off as a business expense."

"I never thought I'd be so eager to manage employees and place shampoo orders."

With that, Henry rises abruptly. "Well, I have been threatened with bodily harm if I stay and stress you for too long, so I'll be off. Got to try and hold down the dog fort for a few more days." He grimaces, but then looks at me, softening. "Things do seem to be healing up well, though?"

I give a tentative nod. "Looking good so far."

"I'm truly glad."

After he leaves and I've synced up my contacts, I start making lists. I want to talk to Marisol about how she navigated Paloma's birth around her business. But I also consider asking my sister if she can spare a few minutes of coaching, if she's still capable of that. And when Anton gets home, we should probably discuss childcare. Suddenly, five more months doesn't seem like very much time to prepare.

I pause a moment, swiping back over to my messages where I pull up my husband's name. After thinking a moment, I send him a GIF of a dog taking a phone call.

ANTON

I see Henry delivered you from the Dark Ages.

Not a moment too soon. How's your day going?

ANTON

Work is dull. But I finally heard from that woman's insurance company and it sounds like we get to go car shopping.

Yay?

ANTON

How do you feel about minivans?

Don't they have like eight seats?

ANTON

Room for five more?

Is that a suggestion, Mr. Richie?

ANTON

To proceed knocking you up with quints?

I am ashamed to admit how immediately hot that gets me.

Too late. Already knocked up. You'll have to wait.

He sends me a peach emoji next to a hand, and at first I smile, thinking of our growing baby. Until I remember the most recent BabyBump email said it was now the size of a navel orange. I stare at the message, confused. Until I Google *peach hand emoji meaning* and my face burns right off.

> The doctor said NO sex.

ANTON

She didn't say no sexting . . .

> Let's talk cars again. How about another Toyota?

He sends an eggplant next to a peach, which I *don't* have to look up.

> Anton, I'm SERIOUS.

ANTON

Sorry . . . terribly attracted to my pregnant wife who I can't touch. Does it bother you?

I let out a slow breath, resisting the urge to rub my hardening nipples.

> It bothers me that you can't touch me either.

> But if you don't stop, I won't be able to follow doctor's orders.

He doesn't reply for a minute, and I can just picture the satisfied look on his face. It would serve him right if his boss caught him with inappropriate food emojis. I help myself to another of Henry's donuts, trying to bring my body back under control, until finally, the phone chimes again.

ANTON

Toyota is fine. Maybe Honda. How do you feel about EVs?

CHAPTER THIRTY-SEVEN

Him

"Hey, Anton." Milo pops his head in my office door. "Are you headed to the two o'clock meeting?"

I glance at my watch, eyes widening. "Uh, yeah. Just give me a sec."

I close my laptop and sweep it off the desk with a legal pad and a pen, trying not to look as flustered as I feel. I've been sitting here, trying to work myself up to tell Carl that Lydia and I are expecting in the spring, which might affect my availability for getting the branch office off the ground. I really should have done it before this meeting.

We enter the conference room and take our usual seats. Me, beside Carl on the end, and Milo right next to me. Before we're even seated, he's got his notebook and pen poised and ready. Can't knock the guy for making himself look good.

Derek Norman is on Carl's other side, which isn't a surprise given the nature of this meeting. There isn't an empty seat in the room. Even the receptionist, Riya, comes in at the last minute and leans against the wall. She is *very* pregnant, and when I realize there's nowhere for her to sit, I leap up and give her my chair.

"Thanks, Anton," she says, looking awkward, but grateful. "That's really sweet of you."

I nod, trying to imagine Lydia making it so far along. It still feels hard to envision. She hasn't had any more bleeding the last five days, and the baby's heartbeat was strong when we saw Dr. Sharma on Friday, so she was given the all clear to return to work. But I'm having a hard time believing we're fully out of the woods.

"Thanks for joining us, everyone," Carl says, wasting no time getting started. I grab my notepad and pen, getting comfortable against the wall. "As I think you all know, Derek and I have been exploring a partnership to broaden Vesper's services and make ourselves more available to our clientele in Colorado Springs."

There are murmurs of confirmation and a few enthusiastic claps before Carl goes on.

"I'm thrilled to announce we've found a space and are working on developing a team to sync the two offices as cohesively as possible. Spearheading that goal will be Anton Richie, who's moving into a junior partner role."

The murmurs turn to shouts of enthusiasm and a chorus of congratulations. I straighten against the wall, making what feels like appropriate gestures and facial expressions, acknowledging the sentiments. But I feel like I'm underwater. I knew Carl was going to make the new branch official today, but I had no idea he was going to do it like this.

He continues, listing other people who will play a part in the new company structure. I see Milo puffing up his chest while trying to look humble before Derek makes a few comments, but I don't hear any of it. All I can focus on is the creeping sense of dread sinking into my stomach.

In my pocket, my phone vibrates and I take it out just for somewhere to direct my attention.

LYDIA

Got a couple more daycare tours scheduled.
Hopefully we'll like these ones better!

How did it go with Carl?

I swallow. The first daycare we saw was *not* inspiring. It was in an old, converted house, and while everything looked clean and the place had a good reputation, it seemed very disorganized and the people working there gave us the impression they were short-tempered and stressed.

Anything has got to be better than that place.

No chance to meet with him yet.

I flinch as I hit send, wondering if she'll know it's not the truth. But before I can ruminate on it further, I realize Carl is clearing his throat, preparing to make another announcement.

"One last celebratory note, albeit a bittersweet one, this Friday will be Riya's last day with us. She's decided to stay home with her baby girl." Carl gives Riya a warm smile. "We're going to miss you around here—make sure you bring that kiddo by sometime so we can meet her."

"I will," Riya says, dabbing at her eyes. "Everyone's been so great. I'm going to miss you all. But I can't wait to spend some time at home being my little girl's mom."

By the time I leave the office at five o'clock, I'm mulling over an idea, but I'm not sure it's one I'm comfortable with. After checking in with Lydia, who *promises* she absolutely will leave work by six, I decide to swing by and see my brother.

I still can't get over the ridiculously luxe building he lives in. There are lines of Teslas, BMWs, and Mercedes parked outside. And every person I pass is dressed in head-to-toe designer clothing. Turns out I have to check in with the concierge just to get access to the elevator.

I've hardly stepped foot here since Seth moved in two weeks ago, which I feel bad about. It just felt like I should spend every moment I could with Lydia while she was on bed rest. But that part *is* better, and it seems like I should at least make sure my brother isn't sleeping on a mattress on the floor.

When the elevator opens on the eighteenth floor, I hear faint music coming down the hall to my right. It gets louder the closer I get to Seth's door, until I recognize one of Mom's favorite Sinatra songs. Doubtful, I ring the bell. When nothing happens, I go ahead and pound on the door with my fist.

"Anton! You made it up here fast!" Seth yells when he finally answers. He's in jeans and a T-shirt that shows off muscle I don't remember him having, his hair is tousled, and he's in need of a shave. But his expression is brighter, happier than I can remember it being for a while. Behind him, Bruno is strutting around, crooning out of tune with Ol' Blue Eyes.

"They are going to throw you out of here before you even unpack," I say as he turns down the volume on a surprisingly compact Bluetooth speaker.

"As it turns out, the lady across the hall is hard of hearing." He chuckles. "And the couple on the other side of me are on an extended tour of Rome. Anyway, you're my first visitor!"

"Seth, I've been here before."

"Yeah, but I've never buzzed you up." He grins, looking like a little kid. But then peers more carefully at my expression and closes the door. "What's up? Everything okay with Lydia?"

"Yeah," I say quickly. "She's fine. Went back to work this week." I step fully inside, expecting to wade through a sea of unpacked boxes, until I realize the whole apartment is fully furnished and unpacked. Not with any of Mom's shabby garage sale finds, but like, real furniture. There's a retro-looking couch and coffee table, a cushy orange chair that looks like somewhere you'd smoke a pipe in a bathrobe, and even a little glass bar cart to one side. It looks like Don Draper should live here. "Wow, um . . . I love what you've done with the place?"

Seth chuckles, scooping up the cat, who yowls in response. "I didn't keep much from Dallas. Bruno and I are kinda starting from scratch."

"It . . . it looks nice," I say, deciding the details of my brother's existence are none of my business. I just hope I don't ever have to help him through a bankruptcy. He sets down the cat and gestures me toward the couch. Bruno struts over to look out the floor-to-ceiling windows. "He seems to like the view."

Seth smirks a little, perching in the orange chair. "Yeah, we do a lot of people-watching."

"I uh . . . I came over to . . ." Now that I'm here, relaxing—or trying to, in my brother's swank mod bachelor pad, that feeling of underwater dread creeps back in.

"Hey man, are you all right? You just went really pale."

I shake my head. Then nod. Then just sit there, confused.

"Do you want a drink? Maybe a water?"

"Water's good," I croak. Once he's brought me a chilled bottle from the fridge, I'm able to swallow. And then I just feel kind of stupid. "Sorry, uh, long day at work. Do you ah . . . want to come over for dinner?"

"Sure. As long as you're not making lasagna again." He laughs when I shoot him a glare. "I mean, you're a great cook, but Mom made it *every* week. I don't know how you eat it all the time."

"We can pick something up on the way," I mutter, checking the time on my phone.

"Cool. I'll buy, since I'm the one being picky." He hesitates a moment, watching Bruno weave around my ankles. "Anything else going on?"

My shoulders slump. I pick up the cat and set him on my lap, where he immediately curls up and starts purring, the way he's done since I was in high school. It's surprisingly comforting. "Do you remember Mom staying home with us when we were little?"

A line forms between Seth's brows. "Uh, I guess so? I mean, she went back to work when I started preschool, but sure, I have a few memories of like, finger-painting with her and stuff."

I press my lips together. That's not really where my thoughts were.

"Is Lydia thinking of staying home?" he asks, clearly confused.

I shake my head, straightening, resting my fists in my lap. "No." I sigh. "But do you think it would be weird if . . . I did?"

He pauses a moment, catching up in his head. Finally, he looks at me and grins. "Naw, man. You'd probably be freaking great at that."

I look at his face, trying to gauge if he's just humoring me, but if he is, he's doing a hell of a job.

"Seriously, remember when we were kids and you spent a whole week helping me learn to tie my shoes? You never got impatient, just kept telling me to try again. You already like to cook. You're organized. And you'll look adorable pushing a stroller with all the mommies at the park."

I glare at him and he laughs. But when I look down, stroking Bruno's ears, I can't really argue about any of those things. Well, except the stroller part. "I don't know, it's just something I'm considering. Things have been changing at work, and I haven't loved the idea of leaving the baby in daycare."

"If screening childcare is even half as bad as trying to find good cat-sitters, I don't blame you." He pauses. "And I'm assuming you of all people know if you can afford it?"

"I actually haven't gotten that far. I only started considering it today." I shrug. "I just needed to talk about it before bringing it up to Lydia. In case it sounded crazy."

He looks at me thoughtfully. "Honestly, maybe it's exactly what you need, Anton."

I sit, ruminating on that while Bruno purrs loudly my lap.

Seth stands, pocketing his phone. "C'mon, let's grab food. I just finished unpacking today and I'm starving."

I rise from the couch, gently transferring the still sleeping cat onto the cushion next to me before following Seth to the door. He looks back at me, grabbing his keys.

"Just to be clear though, you *don't* want me spilling the beans on this over dinner?"

I roll my eyes. "That would be correct."

CHAPTER THIRTY-EIGHT

"Thanks so much, everything looks great. We'll be in touch," Anton says as we duck out the door of Orchard School For Early Childhood, the facility where Paloma now attends daycare.

"Marisol's instincts continue to impress. That was the best one yet," I say, clutching a few brochures on our way down the sidewalk. This was the fourth tour of the fourth daycare facility on our list, and while most of them have seemed like perfectly adequate childcare facilities to my untrained eye, this one left me with a slightly shinier overall impression. "The last one was okay. The staff were friendlier, at least. But this one had a nice atmosphere, and the whole place felt like a well-oiled machine."

"Mmm hmm." Anton nods, holding my hand firmly in his as we walk back to my new Honda through the slushy parking lot. I turn to study him. He asked a lot of questions on some of the previous tours, but I realize now he's been mostly silent the last hour.

"I guess the waitlist is sort of an issue." I run my free hand over my almost five-month bump. "If it's really more than a year, we'd have to figure that out. Or I guess look into hiring a nanny in between . . ."

Anton doesn't say anything, just climbs into the driver's seat and starts the car.

"Everything okay?" I ask, fastening my seatbelt carefully under my stomach. I still get a little wigged out every time we have to travel in a car.

He turns to look at me thoughtfully. "Can I talk you into a milkshake?"

We wind up at a little burger place I read about near Wash Park that spins peanut butter cookie shakes you have to eat with a spoon, they're so loaded with big pieces of cookie and peanut butter cups. Anton says it's not a shake if you can't drink it, but he's obviously wrong.

Christmas music plays overhead and everything is decorated for the holidays, just as it was at the school. The last four weeks feel like they've flown by.

As we wait for our food, I set the school brochures aside and pull up the app where I've been tracking all the stuff like childcare options, baby names, and must-have baby supplies. I'm making a few notes on the Orchard School, when Anton clears his throat.

"Do you remember me telling you Carl was interesting in opening up a branch office in Colorado Springs?"

I set my phone aside, giving him my full attention. "Oh, yeah. Wasn't that ages ago? Is it still happening?"

"He first brought it up last summer. I don't think we've talked about it since. Anyway, things are starting to happen with it. Carl is partnering with a colleague down there, but he wants someone to travel between the two offices for continuity."

I raise my brows. "And that would be you, I presume? It sounds like a cool opportunity."

Everything about Anton's posture says the opposite, but he nods. "Yeah, it is. We'd get to improve the customer experience, expand what we offer . . ." He pauses as our milk-shakes arrive and I reach for my spoon. "Anyway, if I'm on board, Carl will make me a junior partner."

I suck in a breath and clap my hands together. "Anton! That's amazing!"

He stirs his shake with his useless straw.

"It could be," he says. "But it would mean I'd be gone a lot. Like, upwards of twenty-five percent of my time could be spent in the Springs. And there might be stretches of time I'd need to just stay down there. Like, so much Carl is looking at buying a company condo."

I sit back in my seat as his point finally sinks in. "Oh. I see."

He glances up at me.

"I mean . . . if we figure out childcare, it would be work-able. But it does change things . . ." I stir my shake, trying to wrap my brain around this shift in our future. It sounds like I'd be on my own some of the time, getting the baby to and from daycare. And some overnights. And if anything went wrong, there's a chance I'd be dealing with that solo, too . . .

"When would all of this begin?" I ask.

He exhales, pushing his shake aside. "They think the new branch could be off the ground by May."

"Wow, okay." I rest my spoon on my napkin. I'm due May sixteenth. "Um, maybe a nanny would be a better option for us, then. There would be fewer logistics. Maybe I could even get help in the evenings—"

"I don't want that, Lydia." Anton's voice is sharp, though he looks like he's going to be sick. "I don't want you to have to *hire* someone to fill in for me—I want to be there. If you're up in the middle of the night taking care of our child, I want to be able to help." He picks up the school brochures, then sets them down with a curled lip. "I don't love the idea of our kid being with strangers during the day, but if we're not even there to be parents at night . . . ?"

I frown, shaking my head. "I know, but I don't see any other way."

He shifts uncomfortably, wiping up a drip of ice cream with his napkin. "There are different ways people approach this. Celia, for example . . ."

My eyes widen, my pulse hammering suddenly in my forehead. Is he really going to pull this on me now? "No. We discussed this. I'm sorry, I just can't—"

"Not you, Lydia." He takes my hand in both of his, looking right into my eyes. "What if *I* stay home?"

My lips part. "You?"

"I—I've been thinking about it a while. I know it's not the norm for dads, but fuck that. The more I think about it, the more it makes sense. Our finances will be tighter, but they would be anyway, paying for childcare. And I could probably do some consulting on the side for extra cash."

I blink at him, trying to jump my brain out of its lag. First he was going to be junior partner, now he wants to quit his job?

"It wouldn't have to be forever. We could still put ourselves on a waitlist for this place and see how it goes." He gestures to the brochure. "But I *want* to be home with our baby, Lydia. I want to be around to be their dad the way my mom was around for me."

At the mention of his mother, the corners of my eyes prick with tears. It's been five months since she passed away, and this first holiday season already feels heavy with her truly gone. I squeeze his hands and lean toward him.

"I couldn't do it—stay home," I say truthfully. "But if this is really what you want . . ."

He nods without hesitation. "We had a meeting about it the other day, and it was all I could think about. I just can't put my whole heart into a job if it means not being there for you, and never getting to see our family."

I glance at the brochure and blow out a breath. "Well,

maybe I can stop worrying about tuition. And I still haven't touched that money from Henry, so we would have that cushion."

"I spent the past week going over our budget," he says, shifting into his no-nonsense finance tone. "Healthcare will be one of our biggest costs, but we can make it work. And Lydia, you should be *so* proud—the Pooches are already doing well enough to keep us afloat and comfortable. Anything extra I bring in on the side will just make things easier."

I smile, raising a brow. "Maybe I'll push Henry harder on employee health insurance."

He chuckles. "We won't be surviving on ramen noodles. But if things start to feel hard, I can always go back to work. Even if it's to a different firm."

I study him more closely, my heart warming when I register the true joy in his face. He wants this—maybe he needs this. Briefly, I imagine Anton at home, cuddling our little infant. Changing their diapers, feeding them, taking them out in a stroller. And of course, that very domestic modern male image somehow lights a fire inside me, sending out waves of arousal into my nipples and between my legs. Because this is what my hormones do to me now. I've gone from having to concentrate so hard to even *have* sex, to it taking all my focus just to avoid thinking about it.

"Well." I let out a breath and look down, resting my hands on my still-small bump to divert my attention. "I was okay with daycare because it would allow me to keep doing the things I want. But if being home with our baby is what *you* want, and it makes sense, then I really can't argue."

Anton's eyes glitter, and the way he smiles really does remind me of his mother. He picks up his milkshake glass and holds it out until I pick up mine to clink against it.

"To the best thing for all *three* of us."

CHAPTER THIRTY-NINE

Him

"All right, Mr. and Mrs. Richie . . ." an older white man says, glancing at the screen as he comes into the room. "I'm Dr. Francis. I hear you had a bit of trauma a month or so ago, but it sounds like things have been going well since?"

Lydia and I look at each other and nod. Dr. Sharma sent us to a high-risk specialist for the baby's anatomy scan in order to "take a closer look and be sure everything is still good." Which all sounded fine until we got here. On the surface, it looks like any other doctor's office, but as soon as we walked in, the mood was clearly different. The waiting room was more somber, the office staff gentler, the informational posters on the walls more concerning. I haven't said anything to Lydia, but I can't help wondering if Dr. Sharma's concerns are bigger than we thought.

Lydia grips my hand a little tighter. Maybe she's feeling it too.

"Okay, let's take a look and see how things are going," the doctor says, sitting on a stool by the ultrasound machine, which seems bigger and fancier than the one at our usual clinic.

Before the doctor came in, the ultrasound tech was already

hard at work taking countless measurements of the baby at what seemed like every possible angle. She's been pleasant, but we've been waiting impatiently for real answers. The one comfort has been watching the little form on the extra-large screen across the room, waving its arms and legs to the rhythm of what sounds like a strong, steady heartbeat. I've been quietly mesmerized the entire time.

The doctor applies more jelly to Lydia's rounding belly and mutters back and forth with the tech in a medical jargon I don't follow. From what I can tell, he is going back and double-checking every measurement she already took. I swallow dryly, adjusting my seat on the stool.

"Well, looks like you've got yourselves an active little kicker," he says to Lydia with a chuckle. "Are you feeling any of this yet?"

She shakes her head, staring at the screen. "No . . . but watching this, it sure seems like I should."

"You will. Any time now." He smiles. "And it looks like everything is growing just the way it ought to be." He proceeds to go through, showing us various angles of the head and body, rattling off information I can't hold onto about size, proportions, and statistics. But he never stops to express concern. "Okay, finally, I want to show you this right here." He zooms in on an area I can't make heads or tails of, and from Lydia's expression, neither can she. "This is the placenta. Appropriately sized, good placement . . ." He pauses, moving the transducer more carefully over her abdomen, back and forth over the same spot while we hold our breath. "Yep," he says, sitting up confidently. "I see zero indicators of an abruption, or any other concern."

We both look at the doctor, and slowly, I exhale.

Lydia bites her lip. "So, everything's okay? We don't need to worry?"

He gives us a kind smile. "No. You should go home and

enjoy your holiday. This is the most uncomplicated pregnancy I've seen all day."

It feels like the entire room relaxes, even the little figure on the screen.

The doctor turns back to the tech and they resume their exchange of jargon and measurements. But then the tech turns to us and smiles. "Do you want to know the gender?"

Lydia and I look at each other, then she gives my hand a firm squeeze.

"*Yes*," we say together.

"Good, because we're being given a show right now." She chuckles, gesturing at the screen. She repositions the transducer until we're very clearly looking between two kicking legs. Then she freezes the frame and draws a circle in the middle. "See these three parallel lines? Kind of looks like a little hamburger?"

"Yes," Lydia whispers, but this time I'm the one gripping her hand.

"Looks like you're having a little girl—congratulations!"

Suddenly, I am grateful to be sitting down. It feels like gravity just re-entered the room, shoving me down on my stool. A daughter—we're going to have a little girl just as beautiful as Lydia. My eyes are burning, but I don't look away until the tech shuts off the machine and starts wiping Lydia with a towel. The doctor turns on the lights, and then he's in front of me, shaking my hand.

"We'll send the imaging back over to Dr. Sharma for you," Dr. Francis says, heading for the door. "I love delivering good news. Even better before the holidays." He smiles warmly. "Good luck to you both, and Merry Christmas!"

We celebrate with chicken parmigiana from our favorite Italian restaurant in front of the Christmas tree at home. December can be kind of a brown month in Denver, but the weather has decided to keep things magical for us, blanketing the city in a soft, powdery snow for the holiday weekend. Christmas is Monday, the Pooches are closed tomorrow, and we have nothing to do and nowhere to be but with each other.

I put on some low holiday music and clink my sparkling water glass against Lydia's. "To our healthy little . . . I believe it's a mango this week."

She smiles, reclining on the couch, and I pause a moment, looking at her. Even just in leggings and a maternity top, she strikes me as so beautiful. Her hair falls lush and loose around her shoulders, her skin glows, and her bump is now big enough it's almost in proportion with her outstanding tits. *Almost.* I shift, trying to ignore the growing erection in my pants. God, I had no idea how sexy pregnancy would look on my wife.

"To our little *girl*," she says, eyeing me with a warm smile.

Something swells in my chest. "Guess we just eliminated half the names on our list."

"There are a couple that work both ways." She shrugs, taking a bite of pasta. "But I didn't like most of the boy names anyway."

I laugh. "Maybe you knew. Mother's intuition?"

She stares out the window at the falling snow, looking thoughtful. "Maybe . . ."

I sit up straighter, setting my dish aside on the coffee table. "I didn't want to bring it up before the appointment, but . . . I spoke with Carl today."

Her eyes widen, and she sets her food down next to mine. "How did it go?"

"He wasn't thrilled, for sure." I sigh. "Actually, he was kind of angry at first. And that's probably my fault for letting him think I was on board for too long. But we talked it through, and eventually I think he understood, on some level. He is also a dad."

Carl Wallace's daughter, Annabelle, is in her twenties. Somehow, I doubt he was ever home with her much as an infant. But every time I've seen them together, it's been clear how much he loves her.

"So, what are the next steps?" Lydia asks. "You don't need to resign yet."

I shake my head. "I'm going to stay on until the baby comes and see if I can help them find someone to take my place."

"Didn't you say Milo was pretty eager?"

"He is, but he's young and Carl wants him working under someone so he can learn." I recall the rest of our conversation and chuckle. "Carl also made clear I'm welcome to stay at Vesper and just not travel."

Lydia's eyebrows rise. "I mean, you could . . ."

"No," I say firmly. "We need childcare, and I really *want* to stay home. To be the one caring for and nurturing our daughter." Something tightens in the back of my throat. "I think my mom would've loved knowing I'm doing that."

Lydia smiles softly, reaching up to tangle her fingers in my hair, placing a kiss on my cheek. "You're right. She would have."

We sit there a while, finished with our dinners, just listening to Christmas music and watching the snow fall outside the window, and it's one of the best evenings I can remember having since we've been married. I pull Lydia back against me, wrapping her securely in my arms, and place my hands protectively over her bump. She's warm and soft, and it relaxes me just breathing in the scent of her hair pooling against my chest.

"I called Dr. Sharma," Lydia says, so quietly I almost don't hear her. "She um . . . she said we should be safe to . . ."

I pause, then smile big into her hair as I realize what she's trying to say. Amused, because it's always so hard for her to even *talk* about sex. But it tells me plenty that she called specifically to ask.

"Is that so?" I say, shifting my hands from their polite position on her stomach to the much *less* polite region I've been struggling to avoid for weeks. I give each of her breasts a gentle squeeze and she rocks her hips back against me, pressing her ass against my already-hard dick.

"Yes," she breathes.

Her nipples harden under her top almost immediately, and I run my fingers over them through the fabric, watching her close her eyes, sinking into the sensation.

"God, it's been . . . how many weeks since I've touched you?" I whisper.

"*Ten,*" she says almost immediately.

I can't help chuckling. "Fuck, Lydia. That's a long time." I bring my lips to her ear. "I've taken so many showers, fantasizing about these beautiful tits to get my release."

Her eyes snap open and she pulls back with an offended look. "At least you've *had* a release."

"You're right," I say, at once chastened and so fucking aroused, thinking of her simmering in want for weeks and weeks. "Oh, Mrs. Richie. Let's take care of that, shall we?"

In one fluid motion, I grab the hem of her shirt and pull it up over her head. As soon as I do, my jaw drops at the sight of the bra she's wearing. It's red and green and sheer, and I can see her swollen nipples straight through the fabric, both of them hard and clearly aching to be touched. I run my hands reverently over the cups, circling the centers, my cock turning to fucking steel in my pants.

"You went shopping," I say in a hoarse voice. And then I trace my fingers down to the waistband of her leggings. "Did you buy a matching set?"

"Guess you'll have to find out," she whispers.

I don't waste any time. Her leggings and socks are off and

across the room, in Heartthrob's bed before I can take my next breath. The dog turns his head as if to say, *this again?*

"You look like a Christmas present," I say, taking in the sheer red and green thong below the beautiful swell of her belly. She reclines and gazes at me through her lashes like some kind of festive fertility nymph.

"Will I be on the naughty list for letting you unwrap one of your presents early?" she asks, circling her fingers around one of her nipples through the fabric.

My mouth goes dry. I run my hands up and down her smooth legs. "I doubt Santa will be pleased. He might send one of his elves to spank you . . ."

She presses her thighs together, her blue eyes darkening until they're almost black.

"But I have a gift I want to give you too," I say.

She bites her lip. "We shouldn't open everything. It'll ruin Christmas morning."

I rise to my feet, flashing her a wicked grin. "Oh, I'm pretty sure it'll only enhance it."

My erection is so stiff, I can barely walk down the hall to the office-nursery. I finished painting a couple weeks ago, and recently it's just been accumulating boxes of things needing to be set up and assembled. The perfect place to hide an awkwardly large gift.

I pull off the blanket I stowed it under, stick on a large red bow I've been saving, and carry it back down the hall.

"What . . . is that?" Lydia asks, uncertainly.

I place the long gray fabric object on the floor in front of the Christmas tree and stand back. It's S-shaped, with one end arching up higher than the other, separated by a dip in the middle. "It's a chaise."

Her brows draw together, studying the curving lines of the new furniture. "Like a chaise lounge?"

"Uh huh," I say, extending my hand to help her off the couch. "Try it out."

I hold her hand as she approaches it, my mouth salivating at the sight of her bare ass cheeks framed in red and green when she turns around. She steps over the lounger, then finally settles into the dip, laying her head back against the larger curve and draping her legs over the smaller one.

"It's comfortable," she says, running her hand over the velvety fabric. "But where will it—"

"In our bedroom. Or out here. I guess we could even try it in the yard . . ." Our eyes meet as I pull off my shirt and sink to the curve where her legs rest. "It's a sex chaise."

Her lovely lips part, and I shudder, imagining sliding my cock between them. Ten weeks *is* a long time. Lydia studies the furniture again, like she's viewing it for the first time, looking at the way it cradles her body. "So how—"

"Like this," I say, grabbing her ankles and giving her a firm tug, sliding her further down into the scoop of the S until her hips are propped up on the lower curve. "And . . . a lot of other ways. But this is the one I want to try first."

I home in on the Christmassy green thong with its decorative red bows, sliding my fingers under the edges, forcing myself to go slow even while I'm dying to tear it off.

"This . . ." I sigh, running one finger along her already-damp center. "I want you to wear this for me again Christmas Day."

Hooking my fingers under the lace at her hips, I slide the colorful fabric down her legs, exposing her glistening pussy, all trimmed, turned up, and waiting for me on the curve of the lounger.

"*Oh*," Lydia says, suddenly understanding as I sink my face easily between her legs. Her entire sex is upturned and accessible to me from this position. I slide my tongue between her labia, spreading her copious juices everywhere, lapping up the taste of her like it's already Christmas morning.

"Fuck, you taste even better now," I mutter, sliding one finger inside her slick canal and darting my tongue over her hardening clit, then clamping my lips over it and sucking quick and firm.

"Ah!" She arches up off the fabric curve. "Anton, I—I need—"

"I know what you need, Mrs. Richie." I straighten up, kneeling in front of her, but keeping my finger pulsing slowly in and out of her. I watch her eyes close, then curl my finger inside her, pressing and sliding the tip firmly up against her inner wall until she moans. "You need something a little bigger inside you, don't you?"

She nods vigorously, eyes still closed while I continue to slide my finger in and out of her soaking pussy. With my other hand, I reach out and pinch one nipple still trapped under the fabric of the holiday bra. She gasps, then I move my hand over and tweak the other. "And *I* need to finish unwrapping my present."

I repeat this a few times, still stroking my finger inside her, until she is utterly whimpering. Then I withdraw gently. I help her readjust until she's sitting up, then I hold my glistening finger in front of her mouth. "I want you to taste how much you want me."

Her eyes flicker to mine for a moment like she's not sure, but maybe she sees the desire in my eyes because she looks at the finger in front of her again, and takes it into her mouth just like it's my fucking cock. I groan.

"*Fuck.* That's right. Don't miss a single drop—it's the most delicious taste in the world."

By the time she finishes cleaning my hand, I'm regulating my breaths to stay under control. I pull my pants off quickly, then straddle the chaise naked and throbbing in front of her. She reaches behind her, thrusting her chest forward as she releases the clasp of her bra, and I pull it off as soon as it loosens, her swollen tits springing free in front of me like a fucking dream.

"Goddamn," I whisper, taking a moment to caress and lift

them, squeezing and sucking them into my mouth, circling each nipple until it's hard as my cock.

I slide closer to her, gripping my shaft and rubbing my crown through her juices until it's well and fully slick. "How bad do you want this, Mrs. Richie?"

She makes a frustrated, needy sound that I've *never* heard, but would pay to hear again. Then arches her back, cupping her tits and rocking her hips toward me.

"That bad?" I slap her slippery pussy gently with my cock. "Guess we better do something about it."

She raises her head to watch as I position my head at her entrance, her mouth open, nearly panting. I can tell she wants me to drive it in hard, but I'm having too much fun and I *am* trying to be a little careful, so I slide into her slowly, inch by inch until I'm fully inside her.

Now she is panting, flailing her arms around, gripping my thighs.

"Everything feel okay?" I ask cautiously.

"Yes," she says, wild-eyed. "But Anton, start moving, *please*."

I suppress a grin. "Whatever you want, Mrs. Richie." I go for a disinterested shrug. "Happy wife, happy life."

She screeches as I pull out and thrust back in, both because I'm pretty sure it feels phenomenal, but also she *hates* that phrase and can't fucking argue right now.

"Who's needed to be fucked for ten *long* weeks?" I ask, keeping up my rhythm, pumping in and out. But when she doesn't answer, I stop moving entirely. Her eyes pop open, and I ask again. "Who needs fucking?"

"Oh God." She looks down to where we're joined with distress, then covers her face with her hands. "I do. I—I need it."

I resume my pace immediately. "That's right, pretty mama."

She moans again, closing her eyes, and I increase my pace,

sensing it's what she needs. My balls are slapping in her juices, her tits bouncing to the same rhythm, and her face is the most beautiful thing of all, eyes closed, lips parted, right on the cusp . . .

I reach out, grasp and pinch both her nipples with another thrust, and a sound releases from her throat like a song. I maintain my thrusting, letting her ride out her pleasure on my cock until it's clear she is well and truly spent—and there's going to be no repeat of the cramping. Then I pull out of her, grab my shaft in my hand, and pump myself empty. All over her stomach, her face, and those gorgeous, round tits like I've been dying to for months.

With a grunt, and the last of my effort, I push her breasts together, admiring the way they look decorated in my seed before rubbing it lightly into her skin. Then I look down to find her smiling, contented up at me, and whisper, "Told you I was going to make you sing."

CHAPTER FORTY

FACING THE MIRROR, I DECIDE I LOOK LIKE A GIANT SERVING OF cotton candy. The light-pink sweater dress clings to and enhances my thirty-week bump, putting it out there for all to see with zero subtlety. When I turn to the side, it's not much better. Celia picked this dress because I'm having a girl and because it's "spring." Obviously, she's never spent spring in Denver. It is currently sleeting and should be dumping snow by evening.

"Maybe we should cancel," I say. "The roads will be bad later, and I don't want anyone risking their lives for this."

Anton comes up behind me, placing his hands on my hips, then slowly running them over *all* of my abundant curves. "I'm in favor of that plan." His lips trace along the side of my neck. "You look delicious—now take the dress off so I can eat you."

I clench my thighs, shuddering under his touch. We already fucked first thing this morning—yes, I'm calling it that. I was bent over gripping the kitchen counter and actually came *twice*. If the two of us remember how to do anything besides sex after the baby is born, it will be a miracle. On some level, I know the situation has a lot to do with hormones, but considering where we started, I will never truly understand how this is my life.

Anton has my dress hiked halfway up my trembling thighs when we're interrupted by a firm knock on our bedroom door. "Are you decent? Let me see!" my sister calls.

"Fuck," Anton whispers in my ear. I let out an exasperated sigh.

"Almost ready!" I yell, smoothing my clothes back into place.

My husband gives Celia a polite nod as she enters, muttering to himself about checking the hors d'oeuvres.

She literally squeals when she sees me. "Oh my gosh, you look so cute!"

"That's kind," I say, curling my lip at the mirror. "I'm not sure how I'm supposed to keep getting bigger for ten more weeks. It doesn't seem like my body can physically stretch much further."

Celia titters a knowing, if slightly evil laugh. "Oh, it can, and it will."

"That's what they said in our birth class." I sigh, then notice her arms are empty. "Where's Gabriel?"

"With Grandma in the living room," she says through her teeth. "I am trusting her to keep him alive for a few minutes, though I'm sure I'll be paying for his therapy too, someday."

"His too?" I try to catch her gaze in the mirror. "You doing okay?"

She examines my sleeve so closely she could probably count the fibers in the threads. "It's nothing. Just the move has been hard, and Adam—"

"Is Adam?" I say before I can stop myself.

She looks at me so sharply, I wince. But then she lets out a soft exhale. "Yeah."

"Um . . . I'm sorry." I have no idea what else to say. I may have a hard time breathing the same air as Dr. Adam, but she must love him. And I know too well how complicated marriage can get. "We've done therapy. Maybe it'll help you guys."

She snorts. "Oh, he won't go. It's just for me. But thanks. It *is* helping. And so is being here this weekend, actually."

I laugh. "Well, I guess I should say thanks? If you hadn't insisted on throwing me a baby shower, I probably wasn't going to make time for one."

"Nonsense. Every new mom should be celebrated." She fusses with my hair, and for a moment, I fight a twinge of guilt. I skipped out on her baby shower before she had Gabriel. At the time, attending any event centered on my sister was easily the last thing I wanted to do. But I'm beginning to sense a shift between us, and now I sort of wish I'd been there for her. "By the way," she adds, lowering her voice. "Please don't mention anything I said about Adam to Mom."

I catch her eye in the mirror, and I'm surprised to find her gazing back, steady and serious. "Sure. I—I won't."

I don't need to ask why. But the look on her face makes me pause. My ever-confident, always-knows-how-to-proceed sister almost looks uncertain. Before I can decide whether to ask her about it, we're interrupted by a distressed cry from down the hall. Celia disappears so fast, it's all I can do to waddle after her, but once I finally make it to the living room, I can't tell what's going on. Celia is across the room, holding Gabriel protectively to her chest. Our mother is by the front window, arms folded over her *World's Greatest Grandma* T-shirt. My husband is glaring at her, standing in front of Heartthrob, who just looks confused.

"I'm telling you, that beast *bit* my grandson. Get it out of this house now," my mother says, pointing at my dog.

"*What?*" I rush toward Heartthrob, then pivot halfway there, looking at Celia, who's inspecting her son limb by limb.

"He did nothing of the sort. I saw the whole thing," Anton says firmly, though he shoots a worried glance at my sister and nephew.

I stand paralyzed between them. Heartthrob has never shown any sign of aggression toward children. He's usually remarkably sweet and tolerant of them. But he's a big, powerful dog. If something happened, if he was provoked, he *could* seriously hurt Gabriel and the consequences would be devastating.

Celia looks up from the eleven-month-old clinging to her chest, her face a mask of relief. "I don't see a mark on him. Are you sure that's what you saw, Mom?"

"Of course I am. That dog growled at my grandson," our mother snarls.

"I thought you said he bit him?" Anton says.

Gabriel turns in Celia's arms, looking at all the flustered adults around the room. When his eyes light on Heartthrob, he reaches out with both arms and a giant grin. "Woof!"

Heartthrob wags his tail.

Anton and I look at each other and exhale.

He turns back to my mom. "So, he didn't bite the baby, and you're just not going to mention the part where Gabriel pulled himself up on the coffee table and was grabbing for your water glass before Heartthrob distracted him?" he asks. "Or did you not see any of that because you were too busy staring at your phone?"

She huffs, turning to me. "Lydia, you have to be careful. Men never truly know what's going on."

Anton snorts. "Maybe Heartthrob was growling at *you*."

She curls her lip, but as she starts to reply, there's a knock at the front door. Anton goes to answer it, clearly glad for the distraction, while Celia leans over to show Gabriel how to pet Heartthrob gently. I sigh and start the baby shower playlist she sent me last night. She actually compiled 200 songs with the word "baby" in the title.

"Hello! Congratulations!" Marisol says, stepping inside with Paloma, who rushes over to give me a hug.

I lean down to squeeze her back and she touches my belly with wide eyes. "Whoa. *Big* baby!"

I laugh. "Almost as big as you."

Heartthrob strolls over and licks her cheek, making her giggle. My mom grunts and heads for the kitchen.

From there, we greet a procession of guests. Tomás comes with his husband Julian, each of them bearing pink gift bags. They're followed by Seth, carrying a gorgeous basket of pink flowers. Then Charlotte, who hands me a card with a wistful smile. Scarlet shows up with Alicia and a handful of the Pooches crew, followed by Henry, a couple of my favorite long-time clients, and finally Caprice, who hands a wrapped gift to Anton, then greets me with a giant hug.

"Hey there, beautiful mama," she says in my ear.

"Thanks for being here," I say.

"Are you kidding? It's the first party for Lydia Junior!" She winks. "But also, your mom, sister, and husband all in the same space? I wouldn't miss this for the world."

I glance toward the kitchen. "You have no idea."

Once everyone's arrived, things become sort of a blur. But Celia runs everything so efficiently, I don't stress about it. Anton and my mom form a truce long enough to set out food buffet-style in the dining room. We play some *very* stupid, but lighthearted games. And because this is Colorado where weather forecasts are an inside joke, the sun eventually peeks out, allowing people to spill out of our cramped bungalow into the backyard. Celia even convinces our mom to make herself useful recording the gifts and who they're from as I open packages. Which keeps her so busy, she doesn't have time to offer commentary.

Finally, after all the blankets and toys and little outfits are unwrapped, I sit up and smile at all the people gathered to help us celebrate the start of our little family.

"Thank you all so much for coming," I say, drawing everyone's attention. "It means so much to us. We're excited for all of you to meet our little girl."

I get a swift kick to the upper right side of my belly, as if she's trying to punctuate her presence.

"Do you two have any names picked out?" Charlotte asks, looking curious.

"I still like Eileen," my mom says, which is her own middle name. I can feel Anton roll his eyes.

"Sorry, Mom, not on the short list. We're still debating."

We actually settled on a name yesterday, but decided to keep it between us until she's born.

"How long until we can put her to work with the dogs?" Henry asks, and everyone laughs, but there's a subtle anxiety to his tone. He has asked me almost daily if we should hire someone to help out while I'm gone.

"I do expect her to be a regular around the Pooches," I say, looking up at my husband and raising my brows. He gives my hand a light squeeze and nods. "But actually, Anton's decided to try out being a stay-at-home dad for a while."

There is an audible gasp from my mother, but if she makes any proclamations, I don't hear them over the chorus of encouragement and congratulations, the loudest of which comes from Caprice.

"Way to go, Mr. Mom!"

Anton actually blushes a little, but when Seth claps him on the back, his smile lights up the room.

Henry comes over, telling us several times what a great idea he thinks it is, and what a cool dad Anton will be, until I finally have to make excuses to slip away to the bathroom. But as I reenter the hall after washing my hands, I hear Caprice's voice coming from our almost-finished nursery.

"Hey, girl. How're you doing?"

"Oh, pretty good, all things considered." I recognize

Marisol's reply, though she sounds a little stiff. "Didn't expect to see you here."

"That makes two of us." Caprice chuckles. "Listen, I just want to thank you again. I know things haven't been easy since—"

"I don't regret it."

I bite my lip. It was not my intent to eavesdrop, so I decide to just walk by before hearing anything else. But as I do, Paloma spots me from her seat on the floor, surrounded by a pile of board books.

"Cake time?" she asks in her high, hopeful, two-year-old voice.

I pause at the door and smile. "How did you know?"

Marisol snickers. "She thinks she gets dessert every time she sees you."

"Sounds like a perfect friendship to me." I wink at Paloma.

Caprice makes a hasty move for the door, giving my shoulder a squeeze. "Love what you guys have done in here, Lyd. I'm going to grab some food." She clears her throat. "Nice to meet you, Marisol."

Marisol nods but doesn't say anything, and I stand there after Caprice leaves, trying to decide if I should say something. I've wanted to approach Marisol about Unmatched ever since she told me her ex-husband was outed in Caprice's article. I didn't realize they'd actually worked together.

But then Paloma starts begging for cake, and Marisol scoops the books off the floor, asking her to put them away. "I hope you don't mind Paloma helping herself to your library. She's obsessed with *Moo, Baa, La La La!*"

"Not at all." I shake my head. "No one else is here to read them yet."

She looks around the gray and white room with a warm glow. "Your nursery looks amazing. I'm so happy for you, Lydia."

"Thanks, me too," I say, though my stomach gives a nervous flip at the thought of the space being occupied soon. "The decor was mostly Anton, but I'm responsible for the dog accents," I say, gesturing to a silhouette print of an Akita on the wall.

"Of course." She chuckles. "Your husband is adorable. I love that he's excited to stay home."

"I am too," I say, letting out a long breath. "I don't think I could do it. I still don't know how I'm going to balance every-thing *with* his help."

"I won't sugarcoat. It's a lot." She looks at Paloma, who is studiously shoving books in the crib, on the changing table, and the chair. "But your little girl will be worth it."

Paloma turns to us empty-handed and claps. "All done!"

"Good job helping!" Marisol says, collecting the books again and putting them back on the shelf where they go. "*You* earned some cake."

In the dining room, I find Anton in a white apron, serving up pieces of pink polka-dot chocolate cake, looking like a sexy domestic god. When he sees me, he smiles and acciden-tally smears filling on his cheek. I can't resist. I close in on him, laying a kiss directly on the chocolate, subtly swiping it off with my tongue.

"Can a pregnant lady get some dessert?" I ask.

"Are you suggesting I didn't serve you enough this morn-ing?" Anton whispers, slipping one hand down to squeeze my ass.

My face immediately heats and he shoots me a merciless smirk. I run my hand over his bicep, a tingle already starting up between my legs. "There are way too many people in our house right now."

He bites my earlobe. "Agreed."

"Ahem." Celia clears her throat politely. "Gabe is starting to get a little cranky, so I'm going to take him and Mom back to the hotel."

I glance at the smiling and babbling baby on her hip. Then over her shoulder at our mother, who's scowling at her phone.

"Thanks for arranging everything, Celia," Anton says. "This was nice."

"You *could* have a second career in baby shower planning," I say as she leans in for an awkward hug around my belly.

"I'll think about that," she says quietly. "Though I might return to coaching after all." I tilt my head, but she turns away to grab her diaper bag. "Our flight leaves early in the morning, but give me a call sometime. I want to stay up to date on my niece."

By the time everyone else leaves, I'm so wiped out, I have to wave goodbye from the living room couch. Marisol made a hasty exit with a melting down Paloma, and Caprice took off when the last of my staff trickled out. Seth is the last to leave.

"So, we'll see you for dinner Sunday?" Anton says as he opens the front door. "I mean, I thought we could do like weekly family dinners. So it's a standing invite."

"Sure. I'm not about to turn down a free meal." Seth grins, then peeks over at me. "Congrats, Lyd. Great party."

"Thanks for coming," I say, kicking off my flats. "And for not hooking up with any of my employees."

Seth laughs. "Not to say I wasn't tempted . . . some of those groomers are cuties. But actually, I've got a date tonight."

Anton and I exchange a look.

"Like, with someone you've met?" I ask stupidly.

Seth actually looks a little shy. "You could say that."

"Well, bring her with you some Sunday," I say.

Anton walks him out, and Heartthrob comes to lay his head in my lap, looking just as exhausted as I feel. I rub the fuzzy tips of his ears, enjoying the silence until Anton comes back in and slumps next to me.

"At least there's so much food we won't have to eat out all week," he says.

"Good, cause I'm never moving again."

He pulls my feet into his lap and rubs them until I moan.

"Oh wow. If I wasn't so tired right now, I would kiss you."

"Here. I'll do it for you." He leans in, hovering close until his lips brush mine and my heart does a little flutter. I close my eyes and sigh. But when he pulls back, I grab his hand, looking straight into his eyes.

"I—I don't feel totally ready," I say, my voice coming out small.

"She's not coming tomorrow. We've got a little more time," he says gently. "But if it helps, I don't feel ready either."

I press my lips together and nod. As uncertain as I still feel about what lies ahead, I *know* now—I want this. And it does feel like we're doing it together.

"Some things are definitely about to change." Anton moves my hand and rests it against his chest, then mirrors the gesture, placing his own palm above my heart. "But what you and I have—that won't be one of them."

I go still, absorbing the warmth of his touch, grounding myself in the steady, regular beats of our hearts—until a firm kick to my ribcage makes me gasp.

"Ouch!"

Suppressing a smile, Anton moves his hand to my stomach. I guide him over to the side where she's making her presence known, and he chuckles, tapping my belly lightly in response to the little thumps. "Ten more weeks and it'll be my turn to hold her."

"I'd be okay with eight or nine."

He laughs, then squeezes in behind me on the couch so he's snug against my body. "Guess I'll just have to hold you both till then."

Thank you for reading!
Get more of Lydia and Anton in Caprice's story:
LOVE IN TRAINING
The Unmatched Series, Book 3

LOOKING FOR MORE?

If you'd like a peek into Lydia and Anton's future, you'll receive *Forty Weeks*, the bonus epilogue for *Love Mismatched*—plus other exclusive content from Emilia Reed—when you sign up for my newsletter!

SIGN UP HERE:
www.emiliareed.com/newsletter

LOVE IN TRAINING

BOOK 3 IN THE UNMATCHED SERIES

The only thing worse than her dog... is the man trying to take him away.

Journalist Caprice Phipps is no stranger to heartbreak—two years ago, she lost the only man who ever mattered. Since then, she's been head down, chasing leads, too busy building her career to dwell on past regrets. But her coping skills hit a wall when she receives an unexpected gift from her lost love —his dog.

Dog trainer Drew Forbes can't understand why his brother left Rufus, a war dog that meant everything to him, to the woman who drove him to end his life. Cold-hearted Caprice has no business owning a chihuahua, let alone his brother's military-trained Belgian Malinois. But when Drew demands Caprice hand Rufus over, he's shocked by her unequivocal *no*.

Caprice hates dogs almost as much as she hates Drew Forbes, the man who turned his back on his brother. But when Rufus wreaks havoc on her life, jeopardizing the biggest story of her career, she finds herself crawling to Drew for help. And he's only too happy to prove his point. But working together unleashes feelings—about the past, and each other—that could change everything Caprice and Drew believe.

THANK YOU FOR READING!

If you enjoyed Lydia and Anton's story, please leave a review at the retailer where you purchased this book, or on your favorite book platform. Reviews help new readers discover my work.

I appreciate you!

ALSO BY EMILIA REED

THE UNMATCHED SERIES

Love Unmatched

Love Mismatched

Love In Training

Love Rematched (TBA)

Love Bombed (TBA)

BONUS CONTENT

FREE when you sign up for my newsletter:

www.emiliareed.com/newsletter

In The Making - series prequel

Forty Weeks - *Love Mismatched* bonus epilogue

ABOUT THE AUTHOR

Emilia Reed was raised in Upstate New York until she fell in love and fled its gray skies for the sunny Rocky Mountains. When she's not attempting to substitute couples therapy with romance novels, she spends her time obsessing over dogs and searching for the perfect coffee and ice cream pairing. Emilia lives in Colorado with her family.

You can find out what's new with Emilia Reed and sign up for free bonus content at emiliareed.com